Redemption

Other books by
Justice House Publishing

Accidental Love
BL Miller

The Deal
Maggie Ryan

Of Drag Kings and the Wheel of Fate
Susan Smith

Hurricane Watch
Melissa Good

Josie & Rebecca:
The Western Chronicles
BL Miller & Vada Foster

Lucifer Rising
Sharon Bowers

Redemption
Susanne Beck

Tropical Storm
Melissa Good

Redemption

by

Susanne M Beck

Justice House Publishing, Inc.
Tacoma, Washington, USA
www.justicehouse.com

Acknowledgements: One of the best parts of getting to see your name up in lights, as it were, is to get the chance to thank those who helped put you there. And so, my heartfelt gratitude and love goes out to the following people, in no particular order:

Michael Brooks (the greatest), Sheri Hardwick (forever a part of me), Candace Chellew (a better person living would be hard to find), Elizabeth Baldwin (a life-saver, power tool aficionado, rat murderer, and sparkly blonde all wrapped up in one package), Rachel Dickinson, Lisa "Sulli" Sullivan, Jinny Hawkins, Linda Lynch, Mom, Dad, Paul, Steph, Julia and Alex Beck, Mary D, a certain Lunatic, everyone at JHP for believing, and every single person who ever took the time to drop me a line to let me know how I was doing. And lastly, my dogs Kricket and Pudderbear whose constant cold, wet nudges for attention kept me from gathering moss at the computer. Thanks!

DEDICATION:

To Alex and Kelly Moore

"Mmmm. Beer." —*Homer Simpson*

Chapter 1

My name is Angel, and around here, I'm known as the woman who can get whatever you need. 'Here', actually, is the Rainwater Women's Correctional Facility, more commonly known as 'The Bog', because we're safely tucked away in a nice cedar forest hard by a cranberry bog. That's probably more than you wanted to know, but I promised myself when I started writing this that I'd try my best not to leave anything out and so now you know the name of our little community.

As you may have guessed by now, my name isn't really Angel either, but I'm gonna save us both a bunch of heartache and just stick to the name I'm known by here. Names are really important in the Bog. To get one means you've succeeded in mastering some metaphysical rite-of-passage where the rules and players aren't really known until after you've succeeded. One day, they're calling you by your real name and beating you up at every opportunity; the next, you're given some sort of status and the abuse seems to lessen. Oh, it never stops altogether, unless you're really lucky or really strong, but at least you can close your eyes at night reasonably sure that your body will be in pretty much the same working condition as it was before you went to sleep. And believe me, in a place like this, that's really important.

They say that I was given the name 'Angel' because of my innocent looks. And, looking in the mirror, I guess that's true enough, though I can tell you that the face looking back at me isn't the same one that came into the place five long years ago. Back then, my hair was really long and more red than blonde. My face was unlined and my figure could best be described,

I suppose, as awkward young adult. Now my hair is short and blonde, my face has lines added by the sun and worry as much as by simple aging, and my body has muscles that would make even an aerobics instructor jealous.

My time here has certainly changed me, and not all of it for the better. But I'd like to think that I've been able to retain at least some of that youthful innocence that came into this place with me—and believe me when I tell you that that is very hard to hold onto here. I've seen good women become heartless killers in the Bog. I've seen strong women end their own lives at the end of a belt. There but for the grace of God, I guess.

I suppose that if I'm to keep to total honesty here, I might as well tell you why I got locked up in the first place. About five years back, I was convicted of murder. Of my husband, to be precise. Now, most women in the Bog will tell you they're here on a bum rap. I'm not one of them. I killed my husband. Oh, I didn't mean to, but, as someone or other has been known to say, dead is dead.

My story is pretty much the same as any other's: just your basic small town girl desperate to get away, grabbing on the first coat-tail heading out of town. My ticket happened to be my high-school sweetheart; a sweet, if rather dull, boy who happened to land a job at some steel mill or other in Pittsburgh. He wanted company and I wanted out, so we eloped, found the first Justice of the Peace who would marry us without our parents' permission, and set up house in a run-down studio in Pittsburgh. If you could ignore the squadrons of cockroaches who shared our apartment with us, noisy neighbors and middle-of-the-night shootings, our first six months together playing house like a couple of bona fide adults was pretty smooth. I managed to land a job as a secretary and general Gal Friday at a local warehouse while my husband worked nights at the mill. We didn't get to see each other all that much, but at the time, I was just so relieved at getting out from beneath the oppressive shadow of small town life that I didn't have time to be lonely.

Then Peter, my husband, started coming in later and later from his shift. He told me he was putting in a lot of overtime so he could buy us some nicer things, and I believed him. Then whole days went by without hearing from him and I began to suspect things weren't going the way they should. Then he'd come home from these binges smelling of sex and cheap booze and I realized that I'd made a very big mistake. But like many young women, and maybe you are one of them, I was too ashamed to reach out to my folks for help. Besides, I've always been an optimist and strong in my convictions. I thought I could change him. Of course, I was wrong.

What I called trying to change my wayward husband's habits for the better, Peter called nagging. He'd come home drunk, I'd start in on him, and the fights would begin. They weren't bad at first, mostly yelling. Then he started becoming a really big man with his fists and I started getting to try out my budding storytelling abilities in explaining just how a cupboard door can manage to hit your face in the exact same spot three weeks in a row.

Now I know that there are plenty of you out there who are just shaking your heads and asking why I didn't just up and leave the bastard. I've asked myself that same question more times than I can count since coming to this place. All I can tell you, and myself, is that I don't have any good answers. I was young, and naïve, and scared. But most of all, I was trying to hang onto any thread that would tell me that I hadn't just flushed my life down the proverbial toilet.

One evening, Peter came home smelling like a really bad whorehouse and demanding 'husband's rights' to my body. When I refused, he threw me down on the bed and started shredding my clothes. I snapped. I'd taken to sleeping with a baseball bat at the side of my bed for a sense of protection from intruders. I never thought I'd need to use it against my own husband. But use it I did. God knows, I didn't mean to kill him, just to stun him long enough to get away. But when that wood came into my hand, well…I can't really explain it. It was like I knew exactly how to wield it as a weapon, and did. I can still remember the sound it made when it crashed down on his skull. It makes me physically sick to think of it to this day. He went limp and I pushed him off of me. He was dead before he hit the ground. At least that's what the coroner said at the trial, and I've got no reason to disbelieve him.

To say that I was completely devastated over what happened would be putting it mildly. At the time, though, it all seemed sort of surreal, like a really bad underground film. I had reached another crossroads in my life; a place where the most important decisions I've ever been faced with would have to be made. Should I run? We lived in a very bad neighborhood. Chances are, the police might have believed it was a simple burglary gone awry. Or should I stay and face up to the fact that I'd just taken a human life?

Maturity is a funny thing. You never know how it's going to come into your life. Most people just go along gaining maturity drop by drop as they grow older. They don't know they've fully matured until they find themselves making the same remark to another that their parents made to them. It's a scary moment. For me, maturity just walked up behind me and tapped me on the shoulder. One moment, I was a sobbing young girl who had just killed her husband in self-defense. The next moment, I was a full-blown adult, with a telephone in my hand, ready to take full responsibility for my actions.

Maturity isn't always everything it's cracked up to be, however. It doesn't come with an instruction manual, and believe me, it should. When the police came to my home, I did the worst thing I could ever have done. I confessed.

Now remember, I grew up in a small town where the worst crime we ever heard came from old Mrs. Simpson getting another ticket for driving on the wrong side of the road. I was raised to believe that the policeman was your friend and you should always be honest with him. So, that's what I went with.

I was handcuffed and in the back of a squad car before the idiocy of my actions bloomed fully in my brain.

Still, I hung onto that naïve optimism for which I'm well known, even here, in a place as near to Hell as I ever hope to get. I mean, the evidence was clear, at least from my viewpoint. My clothes were ripped to shreds and I had bruises, old and new, littering my body bearing what I thought to be mute testimony to Peter's drunken actions.

I couldn't afford a lawyer, and was too mortified to call my parents, so they assigned me one. He was an older fellow who always sported a heavy growth of beard no matter how early in the day he came to see me. His suits were shiny, his shirts always stained, and he smelled of those red-striped mints people suck on to cover the scent of whiskey and cigarettes. He had a big mole on his right earlobe and whenever he would listen to me talk, he would rub at it constantly, as if trying, by sheer friction, to wear it away.

But still, I had faith in him and his big shiny briefcase and told him everything I could about the living Hell my life had become in the last six months. He always appeared distracted, as if listening to a sound that only he could hear. As I talked, he would scribble things down on his big yellow legal pad, using a mechanical pencil whose point invariably broke during the most important parts of my recitation. We would then spend the remaining time searching for another one. It got to be so bad that even the guards in the county jail where I was housed pending trial could barely cover their looks of sympathy when they'd bring him yet another pencil.

The days between my arrest and the trial dragged on interminably. Aside from talking to my lawyer, all I could do was sit in my tiny cell on my tiny cot and try to decipher the scribblings of the people who had been housed here before me. Jailhouse writings range from the profound to the sublime and if the day ever comes when I'm able to walk out of here as a free woman, I hope to write a thesis on them.

I won't go into the details of the trial. Suffice it to say that since I'm writing from within the hallowed halls of the Bog, the verdict didn't go quite as I'd hoped. My bruised body and torn clothes, which I had assumed would prove my case, were instead shown to be the marks of a valiant man's struggle against the rage of a jealous and deadly wife. My plea of self defense crumbled before my eyes and before I knew it, I was a felon, convicted of one count of second degree murder.

The part of me that was raised Catholic welcomed the verdict and subsequent sentence, seven years to life, as a justified penance for my sins. The rest of me grew red with rage. And believe me when I tell you, the color of rage *is* red. All bright and shining, like newly spilled blood, and impossible to think past once it has you trapped within its hungry grasp.

If red is the color of the enraged, the color of the despairing is green. Industrial green, as exemplified by the peeling, chipped paint adorning the interior of my newest home, Rainwater Women's Correctional Facility. It is the color of lost hopes and shattered dreams. It is the flat monochrome hue of the loss of innocence.

In the five years since I first entered the battered steel doors here, that color has become more of a blessing than a curse, but when I first set eyes upon it, I experienced this strange feeling of a huge ocean wave, green and silty and violent, drawing up and over me and bearing me down with it to rest, broken, at the bottom of its oceanic home. In a weird sort of way, that sensation was almost familiar, as if it had happened to me before in some unknown past life.

Now, normally I'm not the type of person who believes in karma and past lives and astral projection, but if, from somewhere down deep in my subconscious I can dredge up a comfort in drowning, I'm more than happy to go with it. That feeling kept me sane those first few months of my new incarceration.

As I look back on the four pages I've managed to write amidst the clanks and yells of a humid jailhouse night, I realize that I've gone off on an incredible tangent. This story's not meant to be about me, not really. But, since I'm a large part of this narrative, being your person in the know, so to speak, I'll just continue on this way in the hopes that you won't find it terribly inane and boring in the extreme.

As I said before I drove down this long side road, I'm known here as the person who can get it for you. Now I know that makes me sound like I'm some big woman on campus, and, in point of fact, it *does* give me some sort of pull with the guards and prisoners alike, but mostly it means that a lot of my fellow inmates, big ones who would otherwise like to see what interesting shapes they could twist my nose into, instead come to me with the tiniest shard of respect shining in their eyes. Now, despite the depravity of my crime, at heart I'm still Ms. Small-Town-America. What this means, in plain English, is that I only get what could be gotten by your average citizen, and that in a totally legal way.

So, if they don't carry your brand of cigarettes in the commissary, or if you're wanting to wrangle a conjugal visit with your old man, or any one of a hundred other small things, I'm the person you come to see. Because I don't really have much need for money in the pen, I only mark the price slightly above cost. A girl's gotta make a living somehow, and for me, this is as good as any. I've been able to develop a good rapport with the guards, and the prisoners who'd normally have fun preying on a woman like me give me a wide berth. So it works out quite well for me, as you can guess.

I suppose, to keep this narrative complete, I should backtrack a little, once again, and tell you a little about the hierarchical structure of this particular state prison. In the five years I've been here, I've seen two wardens grace the big office. The first, a woman by the name of Antonia Davis, was every writer's dream, if he or she were trying to think up a stereotypical warden for a revival of one of those horrid nineteen-fifties Women in Prison movies. Her blonde hair was always kept in the most severe of buns and her lips were always heavily glossed with a color red more common to fire engines and ladies of the evening than blushing passion. She wore her uniforms at least two sizes too small, as if to show us by the very size of her 'assets' how qualified she was to be the top sow in the pen. She was also known to have a voracious appetite, tending toward nubile young blondes fresh off the streets. As a member of that particular genus, I always found it a bit miraculous that I never came under her scrutiny. In this one thing, I consider myself well blessed, since her conquests never did fare well once she tired of them.

Antonia was the darling of the prison gangs, a subject which I shall delve into with a great deal more detail later in this missive. She curried their favor with a passion, and they, hers. Suffice it to say, for now, that when Antonia got over her latest convict du jour, she'd toss the leavings to her prison pets. What was left after they were through wasn't pretty.

The warden's downfall came when she let her hormones rule her mind and picked the wrong prisoner to love and leave.

You may remember, if you've been around town long enough, the story of one Missy Gaelen, a State Senator's daughter who was caught buying the wrong drug from the wrong dealer in a huge police sting. Not all of the mighty Senator Gaelen's money or prestige could get his daughter out of the trap of her own making, though he did manage to get her sentence reduced from five to ten down to two with one served. Nothing, however, could prevent her from being incarcerated in the Bog, and therefore coming under the appreciative and predatory stare of one Antonia Davis.

That Missy was a beauty there is no doubt. Tall and thin, she had a shock of white blonde hair tumbling in glorious waves down her back and deep green eyes that seemed to melt you even as they looked into the depths of your soul before finding you wanting and moving on. She was also so hooked on the eight-balls that consumed her existence that her beauty paled in comparison to her ravenous need.

Warden Davis hooked her talons into Missy right quick, discovering the quickest path to the young beauty's heart and trading drugs for sexual favors. At two months, the liaison lasted longer by far than any of Antonia's past conquests had, but in the end, she found her concubine wanting and tossed her into the tank with her pet sharks, daring them to do their worst. The repeated beatings and rough sex didn't do the young woman in. Rather, it was the abrupt loss of her drugs that cost her her life. She had turned up missing from the head count one evening, and by the next morning, was found in the laundry room, cold and stiff as the sheets which she had wrapped around her in an hallucinogenic nightmare of drug deprivation. The cause of death was easily discovered and Warden Antonia Davis, defiler of the innocent and guilty alike, went out in a blaze of glory, found at her desk with her service revolver, something she loved to use in her games of sexual power, gripped in a cold, dead fist.

As payment for not using his considerable influence in closing down the whole she-bang, Senator Gaelen was allowed to choose the next warden. And choose he did, bringing in a man who had as much experience in the administration of a prison system as I do in chicken farming. Which is to say none. What he *did* have, this man by the name of William Wesley Morrison, was the pastorship of the largest Pentecostal church in Pittsburgh and its surrounding environs.

William Morrison is a man who wears his religion, like a badge of office, on his sleeve. He is also the man who, through his gifts of oration, was able to get the Senator over that final hump and into the State House with a few votes to spare. Morrison had always expressed a fervent desire to 'minister' to a group of 'godless prisoners' and so, patronage being what it is in this country, his back was scratched quite nicely by the Senator from Pittsburgh as payment for services rendered.

The new broom swept through the Bog with a passion. Gone were the trappings of individuality so prized by the inmates. Bright orange jumpsuits, designed to stand out from the rest of society like the proverbial scarlet letter became the new uniform of the damned. Cells were turned out, personal items removed and replaced with crucifixes and bibles. A framed rendering of the Ten Commandments hung in each and every room in the prison, as if to make sure that we knew exactly which rules we were breaking. Cosmetics, jewelry, radios and televisions were confiscated. Mealtimes were preceded by prayers and on Sundays, chapel worship was mandatory no matter what God you did, or didn't, believe in.

Lily white he isn't, despite the most careful of appearances. William Morrison, almost immediately upon being instated in his high office, sunk his fingers into many of the prison pies and has, over the years if the rumors are to be believed, made himself a very rich man. Coveting his neighbor's goods apparently isn't a commandment Morrison feels the need to follow, and if the prison grapevine is any indication, he'll soon be coming to a rude awakening. This too will be delved into later in this story, and with much satisfaction, I might add.

Beneath the Warden come the guards, and unlike other prisons, our group is quite extraordinary. The Head Guard is a woman by the name of Sandra Pierce, and to the prisoners, she's a godsend. Tall and broad of body, with arms a bodybuilder would envy, her physical presence alone is enough to intimidate all but the most depraved inmate. Underneath it all, though, she carries a heart that is compassionate, caring and considerate. Her hazel eyes are always twinkling, as if laughing at a joke whose punch line only she knows. Her fellow guards follow her example well or risk expulsion or worse. But, cutbacks in the prison system being what they are, there simply aren't enough people who are willing to risk daily danger for the meager pay they're offered.

And so, when all is said and done, it's the prisoners who rule the roost.

Prison gangs are a fact of life in most facilities across the world, and the Bog is no exception. The gangs are separated along racial lines, with the African-Americans holding the top honors in terms of sheer size, followed closely by the whites, with the much smaller groups of Hispanics and Asians rounding out the top four.

Contrary to popular belief, not all prisoners are gang members. The top third of each gang is filled with predators, sexual and otherwise. Most of the rest are hero-worshippers and hangers-on who use the gangs to give them a sort of status that they otherwise would not have. The bottom rung is comprised of 'prey'. By this, I mean young women who haven't been able, for whatever reason, to find a niche in prison society and so are preyed upon daily by the other inmates. Many of these women turn to the gang for protection against this systemic abuse and so are swallowed up, never realizing that their protectors often turn out to be worse than their nightmares ever were. These hollow-eyed women, resembling nothing so much as World War II concentration camp victims, shuffle through prison life, merely existing day to day, subjected to the basest depravities their so called protectors see fit to heap upon them.

Young, innocent, naïve and on the verge of an all out suicidal depression, I was destined to become one of those women. Only a chance encounter with an extraordinary woman saved me from my fate. Though it was five years ago now, I remember the facts as if the scene had only played out earlier this morning.

I was running. Running as if my life depended on it, which in a way, I suppose it did. The remains of my breakfast tray were soggy on my cotton scrubs and my lungs were heaving with the need to draw a full breath. I had always been quick, but the heavy tread of my three pursuers told me I didn't have long to seek escape.

"We're gonna get you, bitch!"

"He-ee-ere, fishy, fishy, fishy!"

The taunting shouts echoed down the deserted hallways, making me want to burst my eardrums just to stop the vibrations from pounding in my panicked brain.

My jittering eyes spied a soft spill of light coming from a doorway just up ahead, and I made it my beacon, running toward it for all I was worth. The door was finally in sight and I plunged through it, tripping over a mop handle and skidding across the polished floor on my knees, still gasping for breath. "Please," I sobbed to the gray-haired figure seated behind the desk, "you've got to help me. They're gonna kill me."

The woman looked up from her reading and her face creased into a friendly smile. "What's wrong, child? You look as if you've seen a ghost."

"They're gonna kill me. Please, you've gotta help me. Please, I beg you. I'll do anything."

The sounds of running footsteps and heaving breaths came closer, then stopped right outside the door of my sanctuary. The largest of my pursuers, a women by the incongruous name of Mouse, stepped through the door, advancing on me with a predatory grin. "Gotcha now, fish."

The gray-haired woman stood up slowly from her desk, all evidence of her smile gone from her rounded cheeks. "Get out of here, Mouse. Your friends too, or you'll find out just what it's like to be hunted down."

The grin fell from Mouse's face. I almost smiled at the sudden look of fear I saw there. Still, she squared her shoulders and thrust her chin out defiantly. "You can't hurt me, old woman."

"No? Try me."

I could have sworn I saw my rescuer grow fangs. I blinked, then rubbed my eyes, finally dismissing the illusion as a trick of the light.

Mouse's deep voice showed a sudden hint of petulance. "She was ours first. We saw her. We got dibs."

I felt a thrill of fear work its way through my guts, wondering if I had just jumped from the frying pan and into the fire. I kept my eyes steadily upon the rotund form of the gray-haired woman.

"She's in my home now, Mouse. You'll do well to remember which boundaries you can and cannot cross. Now go, and take your friends with you."

After a long stare-down, Mouse finally capitulated, but not without a last parting shot at me. "You can't hide behind her skirts forever, little fish. One day you're gonna have to come outta hiding. And we'll be waiting." Flashing me an evil grin, she spun on her heel and collected her cronies with a jerk of her head.

I couldn't help the gasp of relief that expelled from between my lips and, upon hearing it, the friendly grin once again graced the face of my rescuer. Walking from her place behind her desk, she wrapped her black shawl more tightly about her shoulders, then reached down a soft hand to help pull me to my feet. I accepted the help gratefully. "Thank you," I said with all the heartfelt gratitude I had in me.

"Think nothing of it, child. I'm always happy to chase off those bullies." Adjusting her half glasses, she looked down at my food-spattered top. "What did you do that caused you to be wearing breakfast so early in the morning?"

I knew my cheeks flushed, I could feel the heat all the way down to my toes. "I . . .um . . .I guess I picked the wrong table to sit at this morning."

I had only been in the Bog for two weeks, and just four days out of the segregation unit that all new inmates are placed in upon first entering the prison. Since I had no friends to tell me the rules, I went down to breakfast with the rest and, after filling my tray with tasteless food, found an empty table tucked into a shadowed corner, figuring to both eat and observe quietly. Mouse and her friends had quickly changed my notion that anything in the Bog could ever be that easy.

My protector looked down at me with a knowing grin. "Happened to me a time or two. This place should come with an instruction manual." Her grin widened. "Maybe I'll write one. Sure to make me the darling of the new ones." Reaching out, she again took my hand in a gentle, warm clasp and led me over to a long, battle-scarred table, pulling out a wobbly seat and gently pushing me down into it. "Sit here and I'll get us some tea. Then we can talk like civilized adults. And believe you me, young one, that'll be a pleasant change."

As the older woman left, walking to a well hidden and highly illegal hot-plate, I took my first look around the room that was my haven. For the first time, I realized that I had somehow stumbled into the prison library. Three of the four walls in the small room were covered with floor-to-ceiling bookcases, which were crammed with all manner of reading material, most of which were dog-eared and tattered, with broken spines and missing covers. Taking in a deep breath, I let the comforting scent of printer's ink and musty paper enter my lungs, calming my racing heart. I'd always loved the library, even as a small girl. I used to spend most of my free time there when I was younger, caught up in fantasies no self-respecting small town girl would dare to have.

Returning to the table, her hands clasping steaming mugs of fragrant tea, the old woman set down the mugs, pulled out her own chair, and settled her corpulent frame down next to me. "What's your name, child?"

When I told her, a twinkle came into her dark eyes. "Here for killing your husband with a baseball bat, right?"

My eyes must have widened to the size of saucers. "Yes. How did you know?"

"Nothing's kept a secret for long in here, child. You'll learn soon enough that the prison grapevine is one of the most accurate sources of information in the Bog. Much better than the paper." She smiled again, placing a hand on top of my own. "We're kindred spirits then. I buried four of my own husbands and was working on a fifth before they caught me."

I let out a gasp, beyond horrified that five men would take to abusing such a sweet old lady. She looked to me like someone who should be sitting in a rocking chair in a big old home with a litter of happy grandchildren begging her for just one more story, their faces and hands smeared with homemade cookie crumbs. My second lesson came quickly that day. Looks can be deceiving.

The woman's smile turned hard. "I'm afraid I wasn't quite as bold about it as you were. Arsenic was my weapon of choice. Not quite so quick, but satisfyingly effective nevertheless."

The look of horror must have shown on my face, because the woman lost her smile. Her eyes took on a calculating look. "Don't get any notions in your head that you're *better than me, child. I've heard the stories that you didn't mean to kill your beau. Just because I did doesn't make you any better than me. We're both stuck here for the duration, isn't that so?"*

In a weird sort of way, the woman's words made sense and, after a moment, I let my revulsion drain from me, turning a weak smile to my benefactor before lifting my mug to sip my tea. Halfway to my lips, my hand paused, trembling.

The woman threw back her head and laughed, long and loud. "Don't worry, love. I'm not out to add you to my tally." Reaching up, she used a corner of her woolen shawl to dab at her tearing eyes. "Besides, you're much easier on the eyes than any of my husbands ever were."

And that's how I met the infamous Corinne Weaver, known as the Black Widow, a woman who married for money and killed for fun.

In her mid-sixties, Corinne had been behind bars for more than thirty years when we first met, making her both the oldest and longest incarcerated inmate in the Bog. She also had the distinction of being the first prisoner transferred after the prison was changed to female from male back in the late forties. Corrine was a cool and calculating woman who never expressed regret or remorse for her crimes. Indeed, she was known to say, and often at that, that if she had the chance, she'd do it all over again. She enjoyed killing and the money it earned her.

But she could also be gentle, considerate, kind and extremely loyal. Though she would cheerfully admit that reformation was a lost cause on one such as her, she was a zealot when it came to the reforming of others. Most of the inmates in the Bog weren't murderers. Rather, they were young women who had made stupid mistakes with their lives. Their short sentences would either reform them or make them worse than they ever were. That was the inmate's choice. And Corrine made it her sacred duty to set out and find as many as she could to make sure they made the *right* choice.

Every day, the library would see at least two or three young women studying for their GED amidst the musty papers and the yelling inmates. There were even a few, like myself, who studied for college courses. Yes, as of this writing, Yours Truly is the proud owner of a Bachelor of Arts in American Literature and is only six credits shy of obtaining her MBA. Now, before you ask what possible use a killer like myself would have for an MBA, let me remind you of what I've said earlier. I'm an optimist. And one day, I'm going to get out of this place. Now, given that I've already lived off of the generosity of your tax dollars for five long years now, which would you rather have: me, an able-bodied, intelligent young female spending the rest of her life on state aid, or me, an able-bodied, intelligent young female contributing to your local economy? Thought as much.

Corinne was a favorite of the guards, always able to lend a willing ear when troubles with husbands, lovers, children or finances abounded. Though she had killed her own husbands, she was a firm believer in the power of love and was known to give sage advice where matters of the heart were concerned. Her advice actually saved a number of marriages. She was also a financial wizard, somehow managing to retain the fortune obtained from the murders of her husbands. That fortune grew from behind bars, making her one of the richest women in Pittsburgh, a thought that brought her wild glee over the years. To Corinne, it didn't matter that she couldn't spend her money. All that mattered was that she was playing the system and coming out ahead.

Though growing ever older and tending toward frailty despite her rather rotund stature, Corinne was considered an untouchable inmate. Her library was inviolate and all within were under her protection for as long as they stayed within the safety of those four walls. Aside from earning the respect of most of the prisoners and all of the guards, it was also said (and I have since, to my joy, confirmed this to be truth) that she had the full protection of a prison legend who, though she wasn't in the prison at the time, had her finger firmly on the pulse of inmate life. To touch Corinne was to die slowly and no one wanted to risk that.

Though I was somewhat under her protection, that blanket didn't extend far enough to cover me completely. What I'm absolutely sure of is that I got nowhere near the amount of abuse I was destined for, but even 'light' pummeling is no picnic, as I'm sure you've guessed.

It was the day after I had first met Corinne, and I was making my way back from a day spent in her pleasant company. I had even taken my lunch within the warm confines of the library. The tuna sandwich and tea she offered was the best meal I'd eaten in months and I licked every crumb and drank every drop offered, much to my new friend's amusement.

I had spent a long winter's day wrapped up in the wonderful world of <u>Wuthering Heights</u>, a book I'd never gotten to read in high school, and was thinking about what I'd read. That meant that I was missing what was going on around me and thus breaking another sacred prison rule: "Always be aware."

I made it back to my cell, oblivious of the knowing, sneering looks being cast my way by my fellow inmates. To my great surprise, the cell was empty. My cellmate, a young woman who had earned five years tax-free housing for using an iron bar to beat up a fellow streetwalker who had invaded her 'corner', was usually camped out on her bunk, her nose glued to the television we used to be able to keep. In the past four days, I'd been told far more about the plots of various soap operas than I had ever wanted to learn. Checking the ever-ticking clock above the head of my bunk, I noted that it was time for her favorite show, and spared a brief moment to wonder where she'd gotten off to. Not wanting to leave the fantasy world I'd created for myself in the library, I simply shrugged the mystery off and prepared to get into my bunk and take a brief nap before the trial of dinner.

A squeak of rubber on tile caused me to whirl around and my heart rose up into my throat as I saw Mouse and her two cronies standing just outside my cell, evil leers on their faces. Mouse and one of the women stepped inside, leaving the third to stand outside my cell and guard the hall.

I looked them both over carefully, slightly relieved to see their hands empty. My eyes darted around my cell in search for a weapon, but, of course, there was none to be found. Squaring my shoulders as best I could, I took in a deep breath and faced them, locking gazes with Mouse.

"Told ya we would getcha, fishie. Your little…friend…Corinne, doesn't come out of that cave of hers, ya know. That's why we call her the Bat." Mouse cocked her head, her grin widening. "Maybe that's what we should call you, huh? You know a lot about bats, doncha."

"What do you want?"

Mouse's eyes widened in mock surprise. "Want? What do I want?" Turning, she poked her partner in the ribs. "Hey, Shorty, she wants to know what we want."

Shorty, who fit her name perfectly, simply laughed, displaying a mouth missing a few teeth.

Mouse took a threatening step toward me, her large hands fisted and held at waist level. "Well, blondie, I guess what I want is my pound of flesh. Ya see, you broke the rules the other morning. And when you break the rules, ya gotta pay the price." Shaking her broad shoulders, Mouse tried to look sorrowful, but failed miserably, the evil glint in her green eyes giving her away. "Wish it could be different, what with you being such a cute little fish and all, but…."

Before I even had the chance to steel myself, Mouse launched a hard fist into my gut, forcing the breath from my lungs in a horrible wheeze. The tuna fish sandwich and tea threatened to make a less than graceful return to the outside world and I swallowed hard against the bile rising in my throat as my eyes quickly blinked back tears of pain.

As I doubled over, my arms crossed over my belly, another fist blasted into my nose, causing me to see stars. Blood flew as my head snapped back, the pain agonizing in my head. My knees rebelled the abuse, turning to water on me, but my fall to the ground was halted by Shorty, who caught me under the armpits while kneeing me in the kidney.

I must have screamed, though I don't really remember. All I can clearly recall is being pushed forward into yet another rock hard fist which glanced off my right cheek-bone.

This time, I was allowed to fall, and fall I did, in an ungainly heap on the ground, using my arms to protect my head as best I could. The two fell into me with kicks and punches, none of which I really remember.

The next sound I can clearly remember is another fist on flesh, but this time, the flesh wasn't mine. Next came the noise of a softly cleared throat and with that, my captors backed off, straightening and breathing heavily from their depraved exercises.

My eyes were swollen almost shut and my vision trebled with tears, but I managed to pry them open enough to see a shortish woman wish long dark hair and a very muscular build. She had a grin on her face and her massive forearm was clamped hard over the throat of the third member of my beating party. "Hello, Mouse. How's tricks?"

Mouse rubbed the back of her hand against her nose. It came away bloody, but it was **my** blood that marred her freckled skin. "This ain't none of your business," she said, but her voice sounded scared.

"'Course it is," the dark woman remarked in a conversational tone. "You were beating up on a friend of Corinne's, and you know that's against the rules, Mouse."

"Fuck the rules! We seen her first! That makes this fish ours!"

The woman nodded, easing up some on the third woman's throat when gasping was heard. "She would have been yours, Mouse, if you'd have been just a little faster. Fact is, though, she found the library, and that makes her safe from you and your gang." Releasing her grip on the third woman's throat, she twisted the woman's arm around her back and pulled, forcing her up onto her toes. "Tell ya what, Mousie. I'll give this to you as a freebie. You got your pound of flesh, we'll call it even, ok? I won't even break your friend's arm here, alright?"

The third woman gasped again against the increased pressure on her arm. "C'mon, Mouse. Let's just call it quits, ok? Please?"

After a long moment, Mouse nodded, wiping her nose again and stepping out of my cell, giving the dark woman a wide berth. "Fine. But you ain't heard the last of us for this." Mouse turned to me, her eyes hard and glittering. "You either, fish. You won't know how, or when, but we'll be back." Grabbing her two compatriots, Mouse ran off.

Grinning darkly and wiping her hands off on the fabric of her scrubs, the woman walked into the cell, helping me to stand back up on my feet. Trying hard not to sob, I doubled over again, clutching my belly as spasms of pain shot through me. My nose was laying a bloody trail on the tiled floor and my head and kidneys were aching like rotted teeth.

My rescuer pulled the cover off my bunk and tore a strip from the threadbare sheet beneath. Dousing it in cold water from the sink, she tilted my head back and pressed the cool cloth against my nose. Then she grabbed my hand and put it over the cloth. "Keep your head back and the pressure on. The bleeding should stop in a few minutes."

"Sounds like you've been through this before," I groaned.

"A few times, yeah." She gave my battered body a cursory once over before placing a gentle hand on my shoulder. "Listen, I don't think you're busted up too bad. Much as I'd like to stick around and make sure, I just can't. It wouldn't do you any good. You need to build up your own rep in this place and that means that you have to take your licks like the rest of us. My friends and I will try to make sure things don't go too badly for you, but you need to learn to stand up for yourself, alright?" Her tone was gentle, her eyes kind. "We can't do that for you, and until you do, things like this will be an everyday occurrence."

Her words made perfect sense and I nodded, wincing in pain.

The woman smiled. "Great. I knew you were a scrapper. Listen, as soon as you get that bleeding stopped, come down to dinner, alright? I know you can't be too hungry, but it'll do Mouse and her groupies a lot of good to see you're not so easily scared off. I'll be down there and I'll point out a safe table for you to sit at, ok?"

I nodded again. "Thank you for helping me."

Smiling rakishly, the dark woman sketched a bow. "My pleasure."
As she turned to leave, I called out. "Wait! Please! What's your name?"
The rakish grin came again. "They call me Pony."

Though I didn't know it then, I had just met my first Amazon.

In the months and years to come, I would learn a great deal about this mythic gang. It was something of a secret society, comprised of the best of the best and carrying out the sacred duty of inmate protection. The Amazons were around to make sure the other gangs didn't get too much control over the prison population, endangering both inmates and guards. If a certain gang leader needed to be knocked down a few pegs without an all-out riot starting, the Amazons took the job. If a new fish like myself happened to luck into befriending a friend of the Amazons, we were protected, to some extent.

What made the Amazons so respected, and feared, is that they didn't try to control the other gangs or inmates. But they made sure *everyone* followed the rules. Much like my new friend Corinne, they were dangerous and ruthless, but they could also be kind and considerate, lending help to those in need. One thing was known about them as sure as the sun rises in the east. You didn't cross the Amazons.

Anyway, the next morning, I came into the library sporting two impressive shiners and a new attitude about my incarceration in the Bog. Corinne looked at me with a knowing grin and sent me, posthaste, outside to begin my lessons in self-defense.

The exercise yard is a study in segregation. It is bordered on all four sides by a fourteen-foot-high fence topped off by razor wire that loops in great silver-spiked coils along the boundaries. Guard towers, their mirrored windows reflecting the activity in the yard with benign introspection, stand sentinel over each of the four corners.

Within the fence lie the outdoor facilities for the inmate population. A softball diamond with a weedy outfield takes up almost half of the grounds. Closer to the main building, a basketball court, complete with cracked concrete and high backboards sporting rusting hoops without nets, comes next. Hard by the prison proper lies the large cement square that comprises the free weight area. Weight benches, their vinyl padding cracked and stained by the elements, sit, rarely empty of human companionship. Huge stacks of iron weights, collars, plates and bars, their shining finish long since flaked away, lay waiting for an eager hand to lift, push or press. A large, cinder-filled heavy bag hangs down on a thick chain from an overhang on the main building, its off-white canvas long stained by hundreds of angry fists.

The whites usually hold court in the softball field, while the blacks use the basketball court as their gathering arena. The Hispanics and Asians grab up what little room is left over for their own devices. The free weight area is the one place in all the prison, inside and out, where all the groups come together, if not in peace, then at least with a sense of mutual understanding. It's considered a serious breach of prison etiquette to show aggression in an area where weapons are free for the taking and displayed so prominently. And, of course, the Amazons hold dominion over the area, making sure the tenuous peace is held and doling out punishments to those stupid enough to break the rules.

During the weekdays, each cell block is let out into the yard for one hour to exercise, talk, make deals or do whatever else women kept together by forced circumstances are wont to do. My cellblock is designated with the letter "E" and so, for the past five years, the time between eleven and noon has always been associated with the outdoors.

I can still remember the first time I went outside, the smell of snow in the winter air, the dull pain in my belly and back from the beating I'd taken the night before, and the insistent throbbing of my nose to the beat of my heart with every step I took.

It seemed as if everyone in the entire yard, prisoner and guard alike, was staring at me and laughing. In truth, probably no one paid me that much attention, but as I stood, frozen like a deer in a hunter's sight, the relative safety of the warm brick of the main prison at my back, it seemed as if the whole world was having fun at my expense.

I could hear the sound of rubber meeting concrete as it mixed with the sounds of yelling coming from the basketball court. The solid 'crack' of a well-hit ball filtered through my senses and I looked up, my eyes following the graceful arc of a softball, jealous of its freedom to soar while I stood, hurting, land-bound, and locked up. The closer sounds of grunting came to me as sweat-stained women pitted their strength against unyielding metal, and the noises of steel on steel added to the cacophony of sounds flitting through my throbbing head.

Taking several deep breaths and trying to shore up the tattered remains of my spirit, I finally pushed myself away from the safety of the building behind me, walking with no clear destination in mind. My feet unconsciously led me toward the center of the free weight area and when I looked up, I spied, with a profound sense of relief, my rescuer of the evening before. She stood behind a low, horizontal bench, laughing and shouting encouragement as her friend strained and struggled to press what looked to me to be an impossible amount of weight over her chest. A taller woman, thin and sporting a mass of golden curls falling in ringlets around her head, got an evil glint in her eye and reached down to tickle the exposed, muscular belly of the reclining woman. With a shout, the weight lifter pressed the bar the remaining distance, set it on the hooks above her head, and shot to her feet, grabbing the blonde in a headlock. Grinning wildly, Pony separated the two laughing combatants, earning play slaps to her own muscled body.

My feet stopped of their own volition and as I stared at the scene before me, one of joyful camaraderie, it hit me, for the first time, exactly where I was and what I had given up. Tears of self-pity blurred my vision as I stared at the three laughing friends, my soul jealous for the friendly touch of another human being or even a smile free of cool appraisal or cold calculation.

Before my ill-fated marriage, I'd never been without friends. Outgoing and gregarious, there wasn't a person I met who I couldn't come to enjoy as, at the very least, an acquaintance. I had always surrounded myself with people and, to be honest about it, enjoyed being the center of attention.

Now I was a bit of plankton floating around in a vast ocean and surrounded by ravenous sharks. It probably showed in my rainbow-hued face because Pony chose that moment to look up from her tussle, pinning me with a glance, then smiling slightly and beckoning me over. It's hard to describe the feeling of utter relief that coursed through me at that simple gesture, but my feet resumed their pace with a step much less plodding than earlier and I even managed a return smile of my own.

"Hey, kid," Pony grunted when I came closer. "Wow. Nice face."

"Yeah. The freshly pummeled look is all the rage these days."

Poor though it was, it was the first joke I'd managed to crack in months, and I felt much better for it. The others laughed at my attempt, then grew serious as I turned back to Pony. "I…um…want to thank you…again…for your help yesterday." I could feel a blush rising as I studied the ground at my feet, feeling awkwardly adolescent for some reason. Taking another deep breath, I forced my eyes back upward to take in the faintly amused, but caring, gaze of my benefactor. "And I…um…remember what you said to me last night. I want to learn how to protect myself."

A friendly grin split Pony's face. "Yeah? That's great! Though now probably isn't the best time to learn."

"But why not?"

Pony gestured toward my aching body. "Gotta wait till you heal up a little first."

"What if I can't afford to wait? What if they're just waiting around to finish the job?" That thought caused last night to be a sleepless one.

"Don't worry about that. They'll stay away. For a little while at least."

"How can you be so sure?"

Pony's smile turned smug. "I have my ways."

I gulped. "Yeah," I returned weakly, "I guess you do."

"Anyway, let me introduce you to my friends. This," she said, motioning toward the dark haired weight-lifter, "is Sonny. And the blonde here is Critter."

I nodded solemnly at them both, trying hard not to laugh at the name the blonde woman had been given. She must have noticed the look in my eye, because her friendly smile turned to a scowl and she gave a mock punch to my shoulder. Playful or not, that hurt and I rubbed yet another sore place on my body, resolving to watch even my thoughts from now on. "Man," I mumbled half under my breath, "critters are tough."

"You got that right, kiddo." The sting of the words was softened by the reemergence of Critter's smile, which turned her face from somber to beautiful. I was drawn to it, as I was to the feeling of vague familiarity that came over me suddenly, seeing that smile.

I was just about to ask if we had met before when I noticed that the area around me had gone completely silent. Even the late autumn birds had stopped their chatter from the trees on the other side of the fence. My three new friends suddenly turned away from me, their bodies stiffening in an attitude of respect.

From between their closely pressed bodies, I could see a woman striding, almost regally, toward us. She appeared to be only slightly taller than myself (and I should tell you, if I haven't already, that I'm a bit vertically-challenged), with long hair so dark it was almost black and dark, intense eyes. Her beautiful face was almost expressionless, yet she seemed to exude power and confidence in equal measures. I found myself actively trying not to bow as she stopped before my little group, her effect on me was that strong.

As if reading my thoughts, Critter did bow, sort of, inclining her head in a show of respect. "Good afternoon, Montana."

"Good afternoon, Critter. Ladies." Looking past them, the woman set her eyes on me. I could almost feel her gaze crawling busily inside my skull, rooting out all my secrets and cataloguing them for future use. "And you are?"

She must have taken my voice with her, because, for the life of me, I couldn't answer, so trapped was I in the dark of her eyes.

Seeing my predicament, Pony once again came to my rescue, introducing me to the imposing woman. Montana smiled and nodded, finally releasing me from her stare. "You're the one Pony rescued from the Mousketeers, then?"

Swallowing frantically and clearing my throat, I finally managed to find my voice. "Yes, Ma'am. That'd be me."

Montana smiled at me then, though it was no more than the slight uplifting of one corner of her full lips, accompanied by a raised eyebrow. "Much as I'd love to hear more of the story behind that, I'm afraid I need these three for something. If you'll excuse us?"

Normally, I would have felt a sting at being dismissed so easily, but something in the woman's eyes made the request almost an honor to receive, and so I nodded and turned from the group. My retreat was halted by a gentle hand on my arm and when I looked back up, Pony was smiling down at me. "Give your body a couple of days to rest up. You should be good to go by this weekend. Meet us down here on Saturday around noon and we'll start on your training, alright?"

I could feel my smile threatening to engulf my whole face. "I'll be here! Thank you!"

That rakish grin popped back out on Pony's handsome face. "Not a problem. See you around, kid."

"Bye, Pony."

My walk back into the stale confines of my prison home felt as if I were striding on air.

The next six months of my incarceration managed to pass more smoothly than I ever could have hoped. Between the friendship of Corinne and the long-range protection and training from the Amazons (though it would be a few more months before I knew that this gang actually existed. Yes, I told you I was naïve.) I felt, if not happy, at least the beginnings of an acceptance for my particular lot in life.

Knowing of my interest in books of all kinds, Corinne immediately put me to work cataloguing her vast assortment of reading materials into some kind of coherent system. I was also appointed her chief scribe and soon developed blisters on my fingers from pounding out notes begging various governmental and non-profit agencies for books or the funds to procure more. More often than not, rejection notices filled our mail slot, but there were times of happy surprise, like when the ACLU donated seven cartons of used and new books as well as a five-hundred-dollar check to purchase more.

In addition to my own college studies, which Corinne insisted I pursue, I was also pressed into service as a teacher-at-large, doing my best to help several young women in their quest for educational advancement. Most of the women who came to see me weren't hardened criminals by any stretch of the imagination. Prison life scared many of these women straight, and they begged me to help them do whatever it took to be able to get a better life once outside these cold walls.

I must admit that it gave me a great deal of satisfaction to be able to help these women make something better of their lives.

It was during this heady time that I 'earned' the name Angel as well as the reputation as the woman who could get it for you. The Amazons had taken to giving me small jobs to do, which usually involved asking the guards for some inmate favor or other. Because I was young, innocent-looking, and unfailingly polite, my requests were granted more often than they were refused. I was soon able to set up my own contacts, both inside and outside the prison walls and before I knew it, other prisoners were coming to me asking for favors. By dealing with everyone fairly and granting as many requests as I could, my reputation grew and my status within the prison rose.

They say that pride goeth before a fall, and that was certainly true in my case.

Breathing a huge and heartfelt sigh of relief, I snapped off the final light, allowing the library to go dark and silent around me. I soaked in the feeling of peace with a hungry soul, taking in the comforting smell of printer's ink and binder's glue with a sense of satisfaction over another day ended without bruises or bloodshed.

The day had been a particularly trying one. I had offered to teach English as a Second Language to three young Mexican women whose knowledge of our language was sparse, to say the least. Because my knowledge of Spanish wasn't much better, our time together started off bad and only got worse as the day turned to night.

To say I wasn't looking forward to the next day's class would be putting it mildly and so I left the library, my head already filled with dread over another twelve hours of fruitless work. Arriving back at my cell, I decided to take a shower, figuring that perhaps the shock of cold, stinging water might force a plan into my head. In so doing, I managed to break yet another unwritten prison rule. Never shower alone.

To be perfectly honest, that thought did cross my mind, but to my shame, I dismissed it with a shrug and light laugh. My workouts with the Amazons had been inspiring and I'd taken to them like a fish to water after an initial brief bout of awkwardness. My body, after an hour a day and three on weekends for the past six months, was lean and tight with hard muscles beginning to emerge from the softness of my skin. I was quite proud of the work I'd done on it and felt much more capable of defending myself against all comers.

As I've already said, pride is a spiteful master. Just when you think you have a handle on it, it turns around and bites you on the ass.

If you've ever watched a prison movie, you probably already know what the inside of a prison shower looks like, being the site of so much action it seems, but in case you need to be reminded, I'll tell you.

The shower room in the Rainwater Women's Correctional Facility is a green tiled number that smells of mildew and sharply scented disinfectant. It's one large square without dividers or privacy of any type. Twenty showerheads, ten to each side, jut out nakedly from the wall. The knob beneath each head dispenses just two temperatures. Cold and colder. The water pressure is sometimes set to 'sandblasting' and sometimes, 'gentle rain'. It's always a bit of a gamble as to which you'll be blessed with. The floor is solid cement with a large drain in the middle and is always slimy. Shower shoes are always recommended attire.

Anyway, back to my story.

Shower time was usually closely regulated, but I'd managed to get on the good side of the guards and could pretty much shower whenever I pleased. This was the first time I went so close to 'lights out', but I figured myself safe enough, since most of the others would be busy wrapping up their business before turning in for the night.

With a nod to one of the guards who sat behind thick plexi-glass in the observation station, I took the short hallway and followed my nose to the shower room. By this time, our uniforms had been switched to those atrocious bright orange jumpsuits and I had a fresh one under my arm, with my shower shoes in my other hand.

Snapping the naked fluorescents on, I listened to the steady drip-drip of the faucets while I disrobed, tossing my dirty uniform into the laundry chute and grabbing a stiff and scratchy towel from the pile outside the showers. Slipping into my shoes, I walked into the shower proper, selecting the third nozzle from the end and, taking a deep breath, hit the button.

*Icy cold water shot out full blast, drenching me in seconds and sending a spray of fine, stinging needles to pierce the closed pores of my skin. We weren't allowed shampoo or conditioner, so the slimy bar of off white soap would have to do. Humming softly to myself, and let me warn you right now that I am **not** a singer, I proceeded to lather up as best I could, musing idly that my nipples were so hard, I could probably etch my name into the ceramic tiles with them and smirking at the thought.*

So wrapped up in idle thoughts and off key singing was I that I never heard the snickering coming from behind and to the left of me. I lathered up my hands and proceeded to start on my hair, at that time still long and thick, when soap made its stinging way into my eyes, causing me to drop the soap and reach blindly for the towel I'd dropped beside me.

My motion was arrested by the feel of thick hands on my hips and a pair of muscled thighs pressed tight to my bare ass, grinding into me wantonly. I tried to straighten up, but another pair of legs trapped my head between them, forcing my body to bow tautly.

The water shut off abruptly and evil laughter came to ears muffled by wet cloth. "Hello again, little fish. Tell me, do your little buddies get to play with you like this? You like 'em ta give it to ya up the ass, do ya?"

I tried to struggle, only to have the legs around my head clench tighter, crushing against my skull.

"Yeah, I thought so. Those freaks probably like it when you struggle." The body moved away from me slightly, though the hands remained tight on my hips. "Let her up, Shorty."

The pressure on my skull loosened and I shot up quickly, rubbing at my stinging eyes and whirling on my tormentor.

Mouse took a short step back and laughed. "Well, well, well. The little Angel has horns, huh? That'll just make this more fun."

"What do you want from me?"

"Same thing I've always wanted, fish. You. You're getting too big for your britches and ya need someone ta knock you down a few pegs. Your friends are always around to protect you." Mouse took an exaggerated look around the room. "Don't see 'em anywhere now, though." Her grin turned into a leer. Thrusting out a hand behind her, the woman grunted as a long length of wood, a mop handle by the look of it, was slapped solidly in her palm. "Let's see how pretty you can scream for Mouse, ok?" Looking past me, she set eyes on the woman still standing behind me. "Hold her steady, Shorty."

Hard hands clamped down on my shoulders, freezing me to the spot as I blinked my stinging eyes, trying to clear my vision enough to watch as Mouse took a few practice swings with her stick. "Here it comes, little fishie."

From the corner of my eye, I saw the tip of the stick start toward me as Mouse planted her feet on the wet concrete and swung. I tried to dodge out of the way, but Shorty held me fast and the wood cracked against my unprotected side, grazing my hip bone.

Clenching my teeth against a scream, I felt my knees buckle as my right leg went numb. Shorty held me up, tight against her body, and laughed as Mouse drew back for another swing. The stick went low, cracking solidly against the outside of my right knee, welting the skin and totally numbing my leg. I listed drunkenly, almost managing to get away from Shorty's slippery hold before she clamped down hard on me once again.

The room echoed with their laughter and my heavy breathing and something in me snapped. It was like that night in my apartment all over again, and the redness of rage washed over my vision once again. The mop handle came at me again, but this time I was ready. I caught it in my right hand and pulled hard, managing to grab it away from Mouse.

Like the bat before it, the weapon felt perfect in my hands. I found myself twirling it experimentally, getting the heft of the handle even as my body jerked away from

Shorty's grasp. My leg threatened to give out, but I willed myself to stand straight and steady, narrowing my eyes to mere slits as I stared down my tormentors.

"Think it's fun beating up on defenseless women, do ya?" I taunted, twirling my weapon again and enjoying the looks of uncertainty that were crossing the women's faces. "Well, this time, you miserable sack of shit, you picked the wrong girl!" Grabbing the handle firmly in my hands, I swung for all I was worth, listening to the satisfying crack as it landed hard against Mouse's arm, right above the elbow. Drawing back, I pivoted and swung again, catching Shorty behind the legs and neatly sweeping her off her feet. She landed with a splat onto the puddle-filled floor and rolled away quickly, her eyes wide and rolling.

I had no idea how I knew these moves, but I went with the feeling, enjoying my body's reactions and the adrenaline surge that accompanied them. Mouse was howling in pain, cradling her arm and screaming incoherently at me. I stood patiently, working some feeling back into my leg as I did so, and waiting to see what would happen next.

The third woman took advantage of my stillness to rush into the fray. I walloped her in the abdomen as she came at me, and when she doubled over, I finished her off with an upswing to the face, watching as teeth and blood fell from her face in a ghastly torrent.

With a bellow of rage, Mouse came at me again. I drove her back with a hit directly on her injured arm, but she continued to come at me, her eyes filled with hatred and rage. Raising my staff, I aimed higher, levering a blow at her unprotected skull.

A strong sense of déjà vu flashed though me and, suddenly sickened, I pulled the blow at the last moment, glancing the handle off her meaty shoulder and dropping my weapon in horror.

Still bellowing, she crashed full into me, taking out my already weak leg and bearing me to the floor with her. I immediately curled up into a fetal ball, legs tucked tight to my chest and my arms clamped hard around my head.

Jumping off of me, she grabbed the handle and brought it down on my back time after time after time until all I could feel was the sting and welt of the falling wood as my body rocked to the rhythm of her blows.

How long the beating went on I'll never know, because my body gave up the fight and I passed out, falling quickly into a place that knew no pain.

To this day, almost five years later, I believe the only thing that saved my life that night was the fact that I'd chosen such a late hour to go into the showers. The lights out head count is taken with the utmost seriousness in the Bog and the warning buzzer must have rung during my beating because when I woke up, I was alone, save for a broken and bloodied mop handle and the third woman's broken teeth sharing space with me.

When I came to full consciousness, my body was a flaming ball of exquisite agony, pulsing with a life of its own that mirrored the beating of my heart. My back and ass were on fire and I wondered idly if my spine had been damaged. Trying out an experimental move, I screamed out in agony as my muscles sent warning flares up and down my nerve endings. Doubling over, I retched weakly between my splayed arms, screaming as that action further jolted my already overloaded senses. "Oh God," I cried out softly into the emptiness of my seeming tomb. "Please help me. Somebody, please help me."

Only the dripping of the showers answered my plea.

I knew that the only person to get me out of this situation was me. Despite my agony, I shuddered at the thought of being discovered, huddled, bloody and shivering, the next morning. "Ok, Angel. This is your chance to show how tough you are."

I'd always been a big one for mental pep talks, and if there ever was a time one was needed, it was now. Breathing as deeply as I dared, I managed to drag myself up on my hands and knees, swaying violently as spots of pretty colored lights swam in my vision, threatening to engulf me and take me under with them once again. I spared a long moment considering exactly that option, before dismissing it out of hand. "Get a move on, woman. Don't let them beat you. You can do this. You have to do this, right? Right. So let's just get up and get moving."

The spirit was more than willing, but the flesh was beyond weak. Getting to my feet was not an option, so I resigned myself to a slow crawl across the slimy shower floor, fighting against the seductive pull of unconsciousness with every inch of progress I managed to make.

After what seemed like an hour, but was in reality no more than five or ten minutes, I managed to make it out of the shower proper and into the changing room. Just as standing was impossible, so too was clothing myself. Shaking my head and telling myself that only the guards would be around to see me in my helpless nakedness, I set off for the hallway using that same slow crawl and willing myself to stay alert and fully conscious.

I made it to the hallway and was slumped down, panting through the pain, when I heard the sound of running feet heading toward the hallway. I knew instinctively what had happened. I'd missed the head count and was being searched for. Luckily, I had spoken briefly to the guard as I went to the showers, and so I slid back against my haunches and waited for them to find me.

The sounds of running footsteps came closer and the light in the hallway dimmed as a large body filled the entrance. "Angel!" a voice cried out, spying my huddled form. The figure broke into a run once again, skidding to a stop bare inches from me. "What happened? Who did this to you??" Forcing my eyes open, I craned my stiff neck to look up into the concerned eyes of Sandra Pierce, who was pulling graveyard shift that month.

"Help me," I whispered, biting my cheeks against the sobs that were threatening to overcome my resolve. The relief at having been found left me feeling weak and nauseous, fully conscious of my pain for the first time since just after I'd awakened.

"Who did this to you?" she demanded once again, squatting in front of me and running tender hands down my lacerated and bruised back. She yanked them away quickly when I yelped, her voice sorrowful and tender. "Oh, Angel."

"Please...." was all I could manage to get out. "Please...."

"Simmons!" she shouted over her shoulder. "Get down here with a stretcher and tell Kotter to call the doc!"

Pulling my strength from somewhere, I managed to grab her arm. "No! Please. Just...take me to my cell. Please."

"Angel, I can't! You're badly hurt. I'm taking you to the infirmary. The doc needs to look you over."

"No! Please!"

"Angel...."

"No. Sandra, please. I can't let them win. Take me to my cell. Please."

"Angel, you know I can't do that. You've been badly beaten and your back's a bloody mess. You might have permanent damage. You need to be checked out."

"Here then," I pleaded, fighting the darkness that hovered at the edges of my vision. "Can't let them win."

"Who did this, Angel? Was it Mouse and her crew? Tell me."

My strength gone, I slumped against her, letting the sobs finally come.

Though to this day I'm not sure how I managed it, I was able to talk Sandra into allowing the doc to examine me in the hallway to the shower room. After determining that no major damage was done, the head guard agreed to take me back to my cell. Though she had to carry me in her arms like a small child, I felt an absurd sense of triumph in the fact that I would spend the night in my own bed, in my own cell. I can remember falling into bed, still sobbing, praying that one day, a way would be found to give my abusers the justice they so richly deserved.

I've heard it said that sometimes, when prayers are made with a pure and hurting heart, someone listens and gives an answer. Mine certainly were.

☙ ☙ ☙ ☙

It's nighttime once again, and as the prison settles down for the evening, I look back over these pages I've managed to write and can't help but wonder what you must think of my naïvete in the face of so much obvious danger. I've also noticed that I've managed to, yet again, bring the story back around to me, though it was never my intention to write a tale about myself. However, I've also discovered that if the Muse points you in a certain direction, it's always best to just follow along so your words don't turn on you and make you fight and scrape for every inch gained.

In the preceding twenty or so pages, I've used two different pens to differentiate between things happening now and scenes from my checkered past. Since I've grown to absolutely detest this purple pen of mine, I'm going to trust that you have figured out my writing style by now and will be able to tell the difference without it.

☙ ☙ ☙ ☙

The morning after my altercation in the shower, I woke up wishing I hadn't. There wasn't a place on me that didn't throb and my body was doing a very good job convincing me to just throw in the towel and spend the day in bed trying to let the blissful fog of unconsciousness soothe away the pain.

Luckily, my brain had other ideas, most of which involved dragging my ass out of bed and being seen as one who wouldn't back down from a fight anymore. After a long internal debate, I decided to go with mind over matter and slowly pulled myself, like an arthritic old woman on a rainy winter morning, out of bed and onto my feet. I stood by the side of the bed, panting, swaying and willing down the terrible nausea that had decided to come out to play.

After making sure that I wouldn't lose consciousness with the least of my actions, I slowly began to prepare myself for the day. The rough cloth of my prison uniform rubbed the raw welts littering my back and I used the pain to steady and center my wavering resolve. Come what may, I knew that the only way I would be able to face myself was to start my day under my own power and wear my injuries as a badge of honor for a battle well fought and hard won.

Deciding to skip a breakfast I would, by all rights, be unable to keep within the confines of my stomach, I headed, at a slow walk, toward my sanctuary, the library. As I walked, I took in the glances tossed my way, some filled with barely veiled sympathy, some with hatred, and some with a new sort of respect. The prison grapevine was apparently in good working order.

There was also a sense of excitement that permeated the prison, as if a very important event were about to happen and everyone but me knew all about it. I couldn't help but wonder if it had anything to do with me, while at the same time praying fervently that it didn't.

Corinne met me before I even made it to the library door, catching me under the arm and leading me into the warm room with a hard sheen of respect shining in her eyes. Helping me over to one of the tables, she sat me down in a newly padded chair and bustled over to her hotplate, quickly returning with a mug of fragrant tea.

"Drink this down, Angel. It's got some stuff in it that'll help ease your pain."

I took the mug gratefully, bringing it to my lips and inhaling the steam with a sense of pleasure. It smelled of mint and lemon and something almost familiar, though I couldn't quite put my finger on it. I took a sip, groaning out my gratitude as the mellow taste soothed the rawness of my throat and warmed my insides. My stomach was apparently happy with the gift, for it remained steady and silent. "So, you heard, I guess."

Corinne smiled, her grin almost hard and predatory. "Sure did. Mouse's arm is in a cast and her little friend won't be talking clearly for quite awhile."

I winced. "I didn't mean to hit them that hard."

Reaching out, my friend put a gentle hand beneath my chin, tilting my head up. "Don't ever be sorry for defending yourself, Angel. They would have killed you last night if they could have. You managed to stop them, and put them out of commission for a long while to boot. Not bad for a night's work."

I winced again. "I'm not proud of what I did, Corinne."

"You should be."

"Well, I'm not." I ended the conversation by taking another sip from the mug and tilting my head back, my eyes drifting closed. The fact of the matter was that my actions scared me. It's one thing to know you're capable of defending yourself. It's quite another to realize that you have the strength, the skill, and even the will to kill another human being. I'd already done that once. I had no desire to ever do it again.

Corinne sat herself in the chair next to mine, placing a warm hand on my wrist. "I'll cancel your teaching session for today."

My eyes popped open and I fixed her with a stare. "I'd rather you didn't. I made a mistake by taking a shower alone. I paid for it. Those women don't need to suffer for my ignorance."

"They won't suffer, Angel. It'll only be for a day or two, until you're well enough to teach again."

Somehow I managed to straighten myself in my chair, leaning over just slightly to meet Corinne's concerned gaze with a steady one of my own. "Corinne, please. I need to do this. I appreciate that you care for me, but I don't want to be coddled, by you or anyone else."

After a long moment, Corinne threw back her head and laughed, her soft round belly jiggling in time to her mirth. "Well, well, well, our little Angel is all grown up."

I looked at her for a long moment, then let out a slow sigh. I even managed to chuckle a little. "Not really. For a minute there, I was worried that I'd offended you."

Corinne laughed again, shaking her head. Then she leaned over and engulfed my upper body in a hug that smelled of cinnamon and warm affection. "Don't you ever change on us, Angel. You're perfect, just the way you are."

"Thanks. I think." The words, spoken from the warm heart of a cold killer, warmed me right down to my toes. It was one of those unexplainable paradoxes of prison life, but one I accepted gratefully. Love, after all, is love, and you learn to take it where you find it and be grateful for the giving.

Corinne finally released me and sat back in her seat. Looking closely, I could see that same sense of barely repressed excitement hovering around her.

"Corinne, is something going on here that I don't know about?"

The smile that crossed my friend's face would have done the Mona Lisa proud. "Could be," she allowed.

"Are you gonna tell me what it is?"

Her grin widened. "Angel, sometimes it's good to experience certain things by yourself."

Shaking my head, I heaved a sigh of frustration.

"I think you'll like it. You'll see."

"Can you at least answer two questions?"

"Try me."

"Ok. Will this thing happen today?"

"If the prison grapevine is correct, yes."

"Alright. Does it have anything to do with me?"

Corinne's thin brows knit together in thought for a moment. Then her face cleared. "Perhaps not at first, no. But I have a feeling that one day, it will have *everything* to do with you."

I resisted the temptation to roll my eyes. "So, that's all you're gonna tell me, huh?"

My friend smirked. "Yep."

Any retort I could have made was cut off by the entrance of my two students, who walked in giggling and looking at me in a way I'd never seen before. Hero worship.

This time, I *did* roll my eyes.

Some three hours later, I found myself in a blissfully quiet library, taking a well-deserved break. The session had gone only minimally better than the day before and I was beginning to despair over ever getting the basic concepts of English across to my two willing students. Several Spanish-to-English translation dictionaries hadn't helped as much as they should have and my mind was too tired to think up something new.

Corinne sat behind her desk, her gray hair sparkling in the round, soft light of her desk lamp. The sound of her ancient fountain pen filled the air with its soothing melody and I allowed my whirling thoughts to calm. The tea had done immeasurable good and, all in all, I was feeling as well as could be expected, given my ordeal.

The comforting sounds of pen to paper combined with the ticking of a clock to put me into a light doze which was more healing than all the sleep I had gotten the night before. A different sound cut through my senses suddenly, causing me to bolt upright in my chair, my body groaning out its protest quite loudly. "What was that?"

Corinne kept silent, smiling that blasted enigmatic smile yet again.

The sound repeated, then became a chant as more voices added their strength to the harsh chorus. Then the noise of metal on metal wove through, keeping time to the voices. My eyes narrowed, trying to make out the words. I stiffened suddenly as I realized that the chant wasn't a group of words, but rather one word repeated continually.

"Fight! Fight! Fight!"

Turning to Corinne, I struggled to get up out of my chair, thoughts of retribution by proxy tumbling through my scattered thoughts. In my mind's eye, I could see Pony going up against Mouse and her gang with inmates standing around, cheering their favorites.

As she was often wont to do, Corinne appeared to read my mind and smiled a calming smile. "They're not fighting. Listen closer."

Try as I might, I could only hear the word "fight" being shouted over and over and over again. I looked back over at my friend. "Is this the surprise you were telling me about?"

"Most likely, yes."

"But it's not a fight."

"No."

"Then what is it?"

Turning her attention from me and then back to her letter, Corinne smirked. "Only one way to find out, Angel."

Still not trusting my friend completely, I nevertheless managed to lever my sore body up and out of my comfortable chair and stand on my own two feet once again. "This better be a damned good surprise," I muttered half under my breath.

"Oh, it will be," Corinne smugly told her paper.

Shooting her a withering glance, I gingerly made my way out of the library.

The shouting and banging became ever louder as I made my way to the prison's main square. If I haven't described it before, the Bog is made up of eight levels of cells that run around an open central square. Two sets of winding metal steps, one on either end of the square, wait patiently, their railings rubbed raw of paint from the press of hundreds of hands.

As I made my way down the long hallway that housed the library and stepped out into the square, my vision was filled with hundreds of orange-suited inmates yelling, jumping and chanting in unison, their faces bright with excitement and anticipation. They had split into two huge groups, leaving a narrow alley in the middle, looking much like a gauntlet of old. Even the stairs were crowded with inmates all looking toward the far entrance with expectant expressions.

My lack of height compromised my vision, and by this time, curiosity was killing me. Like the Red, or to be more accurate, Orange Sea, the inmates before me parted to admit a grinning Pony who gently herded me though the crowd and up onto the first riser of steps. Critter and Sonny were also in attendance, and both grinned at me and slapped me on the arms, gently, in congratulations for surviving the beating of the night before. I grinned back happily. "What's going on?" I shouted above the din.

Critter grinned. "You'll see!"

Settling back and crossing my arms over my chest, I resolved to wait it out. The sound of the chant finally came together in my ears and I realized that the women weren't yelling 'fight', but 'ice'. I turned back to Pony, confused. "Ice?"

My friend simply nodded and directed my attention back to the far end of the square and the barred door standing there. My attention managed to wander at the exact second the chanting stopped and the cheers began, swelling in intensity until I was sure my eardrums were going to burst with the force of the noise.

Returning my attention to the waiting door, my eyes caught a flash of bright orange surrounded by the dun brown of guard uniforms. One of the guards stepped forward and grabbed the keys hanging from his belt, using one to unlock the massive door and sliding it open.

An expectant hush settled over the prison as the guard stepped back, hand on the butt of his baton, which was hanging from a loop at his belt. With a nod to his companion, he started forward once again. As they stepped through the door, the prison exploded into a cacophony of sound. Plastering my hands over my ears, I watched the spectacle unfolding before me.

The two guards stepped through with almost military precision, obviously well prepared for trouble. Then, walking a perfect half step behind, arms and legs firmly manacled, came the center of everyone's attention.

I found myself riveted. The sounds around me seemed to fall away into silence, though my body continued to feel their vibrations. Standing at least half a head taller than the men surrounding her, a vision stepped into the prison proper, moving with a regal grace the likes of which I'd never seen. She seemed to command the room with the strength of her spirit, issuing a compelling summons I found myself unable to turn away from.

Her hair was black and shining, tumbling in violent waves down her back and brushing over shoulders so broad and perfect that they strained the orange jumpsuit that clung to her magnificent form like a lover. In that moment, I would have given anything to be that particular prison uniform.

Her face seemed carved of alabaster, a perfect rendering of some ancient goddess full of fire and fierceness, all slashing cheekbones and full red lips.

But her eyes. If I live to be a hundred, I'll never be able to describe the beauty of their perfection. Shining fierce and proud, they glowed the deepest blue of the hottest part of a candle's flame. Or, perhaps, the center of a perfect block of ice.

With that thought, I came to realize the meaning of her prison name, and it fit her like none other has before, or ever will.

Her stare burned hot and cold at the same time, taking in the whole room while dismissing us all.

Closer she came on long, muscled legs that carried her like a predatory beast. Her guards followed like a retinue of fawning advisors, keeping her adoring public at a safe distance, lest she lash out, chained limbs and all, killing with just a thought.

Her gaze was straight ahead until she mounted the first step. Then, ever so slowly, her head turned and I felt the heat of those cold eyes as they engulfed me, drowning me in a pool so deep and so pure that I couldn't help but go willingly to my death. Our gazes locked and I'm sure my face went white. An eternity passed in that brief second. Her soul called out and mine answered as visions spun out between us of past lives led and sacrifices made. All in the name of a perfect love that was never born and would never die.

The attention of the entire prison was upon us, but I had eyes only for her. She represented freedom in a way that even life outside the confines of this prison never could. I saw the blue of a perfect summer's day in her glance and the promise of safety, and a tattered soul, and a love so deep, offered up in one brief look, if only I could gather the courage to reach out and take it.

My body followed where my mind had already lead and, quite beyond my conscious will, my arm lifted, reaching out to confirm with solid, human contact that this was no mere dream but a living, breathing reality that stood before me.

A flash of brown entered the periphery of my vision and I felt my arm being gently shunted aside as a guard stepped back, shattering the moment. A smirk curved the soft, full lips of my enchantress. With the raise of an eyebrow and the barest ghost of a wink, she turned her attention from me and headed up the stairs to the segregation unit, leaving me more bereft than I can ever remember being.

The sound rushed back, as if from a vacuum, and my head spun from the intensity of the moment. Pony caught me as I sagged back against the railing, the strength suddenly gone from my legs. As the prisoner was led into her new cell, the crowd started to break up and Pony and Critter each took one of my arms, leading me back down the stairs and toward the library, Sonny keeping close behind.

I remember very little about that short trip. The best metaphor I can come up with now is to liken it to the touching of an electrified fence unawares, being galvanized by the current, and, if lucky, living to feel the afterimages as they tingle through your seared nerve endings.

So wrapped up in these strange new feelings was I that I didn't even notice when we finally entered the warm dimness of the library. My new friends escorted me to my chair and parked me there, then grinned down at my dazed expression before talking quietly with Corinne and leaving me to my thoughts once again.

The next thing I can truly remember is Corinne approaching me with a mug of her famous tea. She handed it to me and I gulped almost the entire thing down, unmindful of the intense heat burning at my tongue and palate.

The pain hit a split second later, and I slammed the mug down, fanning my face as my eyes watered. My friend had the good grace not to laugh at my foolishness, but I felt like a child nonetheless. I know I blushed from more than the heat of the tea, and the scarred table top suddenly became an interesting work of art, one requiring my full attention and study.

Corinne patiently waited me out and, finally gathering up the tattered remnants of my courage, I chanced to look up, internally wincing against the look of gentle mocking I was sure was in her eyes.

Instead, her gaze was calm and compassionate and I sunk into it with a feeling of relief. "Are you alright?" she asked in a gentle, quiet voice.

"I…I'm not sure. I think so." Looking at her, I struggled to put my feelings into words. "What happened?"

Corinne smiled. "Ice happened."

"Who *is* she?" That one question suddenly encompassed all of me. It was something I needed to know as badly as I needed air to breathe and food to eat.

In answer, my friend rose from her chair and went back to her desk. Opening one of the drawers, she withdrew a scrapbook and came back to the table, sliding it in front of me. "That should give you some of your answers."

Opening the book, I looked down at the first newspaper headline and some of my feelings of recognition clicked into place.

Even if you're not from this area, if you are old enough to have been able to read during the late nineteen sixties, you may remember the name Morgan Steele. At the time, she held the dubious honor of being the youngest female mass murderer in American history. By now, I'm sure someone has surpassed her record, but it was headline news for the time period.

Morgan was fifteen, and a child of the streets, when her best friend was murdered in a drug buy gone wrong. It's said that Morgan was out of town on other business at that time, but when she came back and found out what happened, she went berserk. Stealing a gun from a pawn shop, the teen stalked the people who had murdered her friend and, almost a month later, trapped them all in a warehouse. There were sixteen members of a street gang in that warehouse that night. Morgan killed them all. When her gun ran out of ammunition, she went after the survivors with a tire iron. And when that broke, the finished the last teen off with her feet and fists.

Responding to a 'disturbing the peace' call, police entered the warehouse just in time to see Morgan snap the neck of her final victim. Then, her rage not yet spent, she went after the two policemen who tried to apprehend her.

She was shot five times and spent almost two months in the hospital before recovering enough to stand trial.

The verdict was a foregone conclusion and only the sentence sparked interest. Because she was a juvenile, the death penalty, though perhaps warranted, was not an option. Most thought she would spend her time in a juvenile hall until she reached twenty-one and was released with a clean record. In a landmark decision, the judge passed a life sentence without possibility of parole, to be served in an adult penitentiary.

There was some public outcry over the decision, but for the most part, people seemed satisfied that justice had been properly served and Morgan was taken off to the Rainwater Women's Correctional Facility to serve out the rest of her natural life behind bars.

However, there were things going on behind the scenes and Morgan's case wasn't left to lie in some newspaper morgue collecting dust. High-powered attorneys stepped forward and, during the next five years, managed to take the case all the way to the United States Supreme Court, which declared that Morgan's sentence was unconstitutional. Four months later, on her twenty-first birthday, Morgan Steele was released from prison, a free woman.

After my eyes scanned the last article, I closed the scrapbook and slid it back across the table to Corinne. "She was just a child when she came here. What happened to turn her into the person who would receive a welcome like the one I just saw?"

Corinne smiled sadly. "I think something happened to her while she was in the hospital recovering from her wounds. The person I met wasn't the same one who murdered all those teens in cold blood. She was quiet, respectful. She just wanted to do her time as smoothly as possible. She didn't want trouble." My friend caressed the leather cover of the scrapbook idly as her eyes took on a far away look. "Trouble managed to find her, though. In the late sixties, the gangs ruled this prison, even more so than they do today. Racism was a big issue and there were racial riots almost every week. Beatings. Stabbings. Fires. You name it. The guards were quitting faster than they could hire new ones. The governor even threatened to send in the National Guard to restore order."

Corinne sighed. "It got to the point where you either had to choose sides or risk being murdered even by your own 'people'. It was hell."

When my friend looked up, there was a twinkle in her eyes. "Ice was never known as a person who did things conventionally. Rather than join a gang, she started her own. The Amazons."

"Amazons? Who are they? Aside from being a group of mythical women warriors, I mean." "You should know, Angel. Three of the top members are your close friends."

"Who?"

"Pony. Critter. Sonny."

I was shocked. In all my association with them, I had had no idea that my friends were gang members. "You're kidding me."

"Nope. They're members of the Amazons."

Intrigued, I leaned closer to Corinne. "And what do these Amazons stand for?"

Corinne shrugged. "Whatever they want to stand for. They are *the* gang in this prison."

"But...but that doesn't make any sense! They all seem so nice!"

"They *are* nice, Angel. They can also be totally ruthless. It all depends on where you're standing." She caressed the book again. "Let me try and explain it to you. Like I've already said, the gangs were destroying this prison. No one knew what to do to stop it. Ice, who by this time had developed a reputation as the penitentiary's best fighter, approached some other women who were also known for their fighting ability, intelligence and loyalty. These women banded together to form the Amazons, a new gang, the best of the best, and dedicated to bringing the prison back under control. It took them several months, but when it was all over, the gangs had been pushed back. The Amazons became a sort of inmate peacekeeping force. They help people who need it and punish those who need that too. They make sure no one gang is overtly stronger than the others, and they help to protect the truly oppressed."

"And she did all this when she was *fifteen*?"

Corinne's grin turned smug. "Yup."

"Wow." Looking at the fond smile on my friend's face, I was moved to question further. "If you don't mind my asking, Corinne, what's your interest in all this?"

"Oh, that's simple enough. Even though I was an old lady without value as a fighter, I still had some influence in this prison. The whites wanted that influence and the blacks wanted to destroy it. It was the one thing they banded together in. One night, members of both gangs came with molotov cocktails, threatening to burn me and my library down if I didn't choose." Her eyes took on that peculiar hard shine that I had noticed from time to time before. "Ice came out of nowhere and took them all on by herself. The gangs lost eight people that night. One person's still in the hospital. In a coma."

I gasped out, horrified. "And the rest?"

"Oh, they all recovered. Eventually." Corinne sneered. "I was never bothered again. I think part of me fell in love with her that night: my dark avenger. What she did, it was...beautiful." She turned back to look at me, her eyes full of love for the woman known as Ice. "She's kept an eye out for me ever since. Even when she wasn't in prison, she made sure I was safe. The library has been allowed to exist, and grow, in peace and I've been allowed to do the same. Thanks to her."

"That's amazing."

"Yes, she is."

"So, do you know why she's back in?"

"It's not very clear. From what I've been able to gather, when she got out last time, she was approached by some very important people."

"Who?"

"Difficult to say, but I've heard that they're the type who wear dark suits and sport very Italian sounding surnames."

"The Mob!?"

"So I've heard. Somehow, they managed to get her to join up with them. I have to admit that I was pretty shocked. I felt sure she would go straight after her time here. But she didn't."

"So what happened?"

"My contacts tell me she was able to go quite far in the organization, despite the fact that she has absolutely no Italian blood in her whatsoever. Apparently she was some sort of gun for hire, on contract with these fellows. Quite good at her job too, as if you couldn't guess that already."

I listened to Corinne, shaking my head at her story. The mystery of why this young woman, who was given a miraculous second chance, would choose to go back to crime was one I really wanted to solve.

"From what I've heard, she was sent to take out a witness who was testifying at an upcoming extortion trial. The strange thing is, the witness was apparently testifying for the *defense*. That doesn't make much sense. Unless, of course, there's someone high up in one of the Families who wants this Boss behind bars for some reason. Something happened and she got caught. Word is that she was set up, big time."

"Do you think she did it?"

"I don't know. I don't think so. It's just not her style. The Ice I know doesn't take out witnesses, no matter which side they're testifying for."

"Well, it seems like the Ice you knew changed a lot once she left prison."

"True. But still, something just doesn't add up. I really became suspicious when I heard that she was stuck with a court appointed defense attorney. The Mob usually helps its own in these situations. Even when you screw up, they're usually behind you all the way."

I felt my own smile spread across my face. "Well, then. It looks like we've got our own mystery to solve. Colombo, watch out. Angel's on the case."

My mirth was halted by a hard hand on my wrist. "Angel," Corinne said seriously, "tread lightly. Ice is a very private woman and if you pry without her consent, you're going to end up on the receiving end of a whole barrel full of trouble, no matter *who* your friends are. Above all else, you need to remember that she is a very, *very* dangerous woman."

Swallowing hard, I remembered the icy eyes that had met my own only an hour ago, and nodded. "I understand."

Smiling again, Corinne gently squeezed my hand. "Ice can be the best friend you'd ever hope to have, Angel. She can also be your worst enemy. Like I said, tread lightly around her. Give her a chance to feel you out, to get to know you. She doesn't trust anyone, not completely. But if she thinks you're worth it, and I *know* you are, things will come. Good things, I think."

"When I was younger, I used to have a sort of talent for seeing things. Things that weren't really there." My friend's seamed face creased further in a grin. "Now, I suppose in most parts of the world, that would be called insanity. The good part was that those things often turned out to be true."

"You could see the future?"

"Some. Or the past. I wasn't always sure. It got confusing, sometimes." She laughed lightly. "Good thing was, I was born in Louisiana, were that sort of thing is pretty much accepted as a gift, rather than a curse. In the right circles, of course. It faded as I got older, but I still get flashes now and then. And I got a most definite flash the morning you ran into my library, covered with breakfast. It was something I saw in Ice that first day as well."

I looked up at her, sure my disbelief was showing clearly on my face. "Corinne, forgive me for saying so, but I find it hard to believe that Ice stumbled in here after being pursued by a bunch of crazed inmates. Especially wearing her breakfast on her shirt."

My friend laughed again, a light, musical sound that filled the library pleasingly. "No. I'm talking about what I saw in her eyes. Ice is an old soul. Ancient, in fact. I couldn't even begin to guess how far back she goes. Even when she first got here as a young girl, her eyes were ancient, as if they'd seen more of the world than any mortal had a right to. It was...disconcerting at first. I got used to it after awhile." She turned her gaze to me, appraising. "I see the same thing in your eyes, Angel. A wisdom that belies your innocence." Her grin deepened, and I swore for the second time that I could see the faintest glimpse of fangs in her mouth. "That, of course, only makes you all the more appealing."

A frightening tingle went down my spine and my skin humped up in gooseflesh. I suddenly felt very uncomfortable in Corinne's presence, seeing her for the first time as the woman she really was, an unrepentant murderer. The walls started to close in on me and I'll freely admit to the start of pure panic.

Seeing my state, Corinne broke the lock of our gazes, reaching down and smoothing the flesh of my arms. "Don't be afraid, Angel. I'm not here to hurt you." Her laugh, when it came, was almost bitter. "I'm nothing but an old woman, after all. Who's seen much too much of life."

Suddenly I felt very much ashamed of my reaction. Turning my hands, I gripped Corinne's arms tightly. "You're much more than an old woman to me, Corinne. You're my friend." I'm sure I was blushing by this time. "I'm sorry I reacted the way I did. It's just...all this talk about seeing things that aren't there and ancient souls...I'm just a small-town Catholic, after all. We're not supposed to believe in those things."

Corinne's expression gentled, changing her back into the lovable old grandmother I'd come to know. "It's alright, Angel. I've been here so long that I sometimes forget just how frightening this place can be." She shrugged. "It's home to me now, but I need to realize that most don't feel that way." Releasing herself from my grasp, she pushed her chair away from the table and stood. "Anyway, just remember what I said. Keep your eyes and ears open, stay gentle and unassuming around Ice, and you'll do just fine."

"Thanks, Corinne."

"No problem, child. No problem at all."

The next couple of weeks went by quickly. There'd been a breakthrough with my Mexican students and teaching them had turned from a chore to a pleasure. They took everything I gave them and practically begged me for more.

Money and used books started coming into the library in regular shipments and Corinne and I kept ourselves very busy cataloguing them and sending out thank you letters to our contributors. More and more people were coming to visit the library, for a variety of reasons, making Corinne a very happy woman. She continually bustled about, preparing her famous tea and sharing stories with the other inmates. There was almost always a class going on in one corner as well, making the library, for the first time, a crowded, friendly place to be.

Ice had been released into the general population after just two days in segregation and the prison, though the excitement had settled down somewhat from her initial arrival, still remained on its best behavior. Montana, who had been the head of the Amazons during Ice's absence, handed over her mantle of authority gladly and would sometimes come into the library, something she hadn't had time to do before, to chat or read. Though still quite intimidated by the somber, beautiful woman, I got to know her a bit better during these quiet times and found her to be a kind, considerate, intelligent woman very passionate in her beliefs.

She told me that she had once headed a Women's Separatist community in Montana, hence her prison nickname. When the Equal Rights Amendment came up for ratification, she headed up an all-out campaign to get it placed within the Constitution. That campaign eventually led to charges of blackmail and extortion, and she was convicted of those crimes in Pittsburgh. She'd been in The Bog for seven years, an abnormally long sentence for her crime, and hoped to be released soon. The women's community still existed and she missed her home terribly. I enjoyed listening to her stories of an entire community that existed without the presence of men.

My little side business started to really take off after the shower incident and I was busier than I'd ever been in my life. Despite the fact that I was locked behind high walls, I started to actually enjoy my life for the first time in a long while.

Taking Corinne's advice to heart, I stayed far away from Ice. As the days passed, my memories of our first encounter began to fade slightly and I chalked most of the bizarre feelings up to some sort of post-traumatic mental lapse combined with whatever special herbs were in Corinne's magic tea. Strange stories of past lives and old souls gradually took up space in some far, darkened corner of my mind, to be taken out and examined only in the deep quiet of a prison night.

As late spring passed into early summer, I ventured outside the dim cave of the library one fine day. The feeling of warm sun on my skin was pure bliss and I sank down into a small patch of soft grass with a feeling of pleasure. Relaxing my body and turning my face up to the sun, I let my eyes drift closed and listened to the sounds of insects and birds as they wove their natural song around the sounds of weights being pressed and balls being hit. The sweet smell of new life perfumed the air around me and I took in deep breaths of it, humming with pleasure.

As I'm sure you've noticed often happens with me, I was so wrapped up in the pleasure of the moment that I didn't notice that things had changed around me. My first clue came when part of my fuzzy brain suddenly noticed the absence of human sound in the yard. Then, feeling a very warm presence behind me, I whirled, managing to get to my knees and bring my hands up in a defensive posture as I did so. Breathing heavily, I managed to look up, then up again, till I met the fierce blue eyes of Ice, who was smirking down at me, apparently quite pleased with herself for catching me unawares.

After a moment, she squatted that long body of hers down in front of me, plucking a blade of grass and twirling it idly between her beautiful, tapering fingers. Then, casually, she met my eyes again, capturing me totally within her icy blue regard. "I hear you're the woman who can get things."

If I hadn't been trapped before, the sound of her low, resonant, melodious voice rolling through my senses did the trick. I'm afraid I blinked at her stupidly for a moment, trying to wrap my totally befuddled mind around her words. "What?"

As opening lines went, that one had to rank at the very bottom and my brain received a mental high kick for that particular piece of literary brilliance.

Ice smiled then, an oddly endearing and achingly familiar little cockeyed grin that sped my heart right up. "Was I wrong about that?"

"Uh…no. Not at all." Now if I could only figure out what she wasn't wrong about, I'd be ahead of the game. An old axiom of my mother's came into my brain: '*When in doubt, always try honesty.*' I gave a mental shrug, figuring at this point, it was better than nothing. "What were we talking about again?"

An ebony brow lifted as she regarded me more closely. "Is something wrong?"

"No! No. Nothing's wrong. Nothing at all. I…ah…just didn't hear you the first time." *Brilliant, Angel. Just brilliant.* "Could you…um…repeat your question? Please?"

A long arm tossed the blade of grass away and Ice clasped her hands between her spread legs. "I asked if I was wrong in assuming you were the person who could get things."

Oh! "Oh! No. You weren't wrong at all. About that, I mean." Taking in a deep breath, I tried again. "What I *mean* is that I *am* the woman who can get…things. For people."

To this day, I can still remember praying harder than I'd ever prayed in my entire life. I prayed that a huge riot would break out in the yard, or that a sudden rogue tornado would touch down suddenly, sweeping me away from this Oz I'd suddenly found myself in. Even an earthquake would do in a pinch, just so long as I was close to the fissure and could throw myself into the breach. The vivid flash of falling into a pool of bubbling lava went through my mind, shutting that particular fantasy down but quick.

Ice looked down at me with a look of almost infinite patience and a faint sparkle of amusement shining in those magnificent eyes.

I swallowed. Hard. "Is there…something I can get for you?" *Finally! My first coherent sentence of the day. And none too soon either,* my shrunken ego was more than happy to point out.

Ice appeared to consider the question, as if as surprised as I was that I'd actually managed to get it out. She met my gaze directly. "Do you know anything about Bonsai?"

Well, it was fun while it lasted. "Um…unless you're talking about the oath those Kamikaze pilots used to shout out before crashing into the Pacific, then I'm afraid I don't."

The dark head nodded. "Not many people do," she allowed. "Bonsai is…a sort of art." Her wonderful hands fanned out, describing her words. "You start with a tree. A small one. And you prune and shape and train it until it becomes like a vision you see in your mind."

"It sounds beautiful."

"I suppose."

Clearly, speaking of beauty made her uncomfortable. My mind was busy making mental notes. "So…you want me to get you, what. A tree?"

My tone must have sounded dubious, because she spoke up quickly to correct me. "No. I'm having some of mine sent over. I've already cleared it with Sandra Pierce. What I need is something called a bonsai rake."

"A rake?"

"Yes."

"How big a rake?"

"It's about ten inches long and has a three-pronged metal piece at one end. It sort of looks like one of those cultivating tools you would use for gardening to break up the soil. Only thinner. And the prongs are smaller."

Looking away for a moment, I tried to picture what she was describing in my mind without the distraction of her nearness clouding my thoughts. "I think you should know," I said after a moment, "I don't get anything that might possibly be used as a weapon. That's a line I won't cross."

Her eyes narrowed for a moment and I'll freely admit to a fine thrill of fear shooting down my back at the look. Then she smiled that cocky half-grin again and I breathed out a silent sigh of relief. "I assure you, I have no intention of using it as a weapon. It's a tool, nothing more."

"But still…." I knew I was taking a big risk, questioning her like this, but like I said, there was a line I wouldn't cross. For anyone.

"Tell you what. Why don't you take some time and think about it. I'll give you the money and the catalogue number and if you decide to go ahead and purchase it for me, great. If not, you can keep the money. No questions asked, no harm done."

"But…."

She held up her hand, silencing my protestations. "And if you *do* decide to buy it, you can take a look at it when it comes in. If it looks like something I'd use as a weapon, then you can keep it, or throw it away. Again, no questions asked, no harm done. Sound fair?"

"But…."

The hand she held up came down, approaching me, palm out. "Deal?"

We locked eyes again. Her gaze was direct and unassuming and I fell into it once again. That strange sense of drowning overwhelmed me and I felt my hand reach out to grasp hers. The touch of her warm palm to mine galvanized me and brought that image of touching an electrified fence blazing from that dark corner of my mind where it had managed to lay dormant until that moment.

Though I don't really remember, I must have stiffened, because she released me after a perfunctory handclasp and looked down at me curiously. "Are you alright?"

Several moments passed as I knelt there, looking stupidly at the money she'd cleverly pressed into my palm. Licking my lips, I desperately cast about for something to say. If there was anything I was definitely *not*, it was 'alright'. Such a mundane adjective didn't even come close to describing what I was feeling. Still… "Yes. I'm just fine."

After a final, appraising look, she smiled faintly again, then stood, smoothing the wrinkles out of her jumpsuit with her palms. "Good. Thanks for your time." With a final nod of her head, she turned and left, striding that long-limbed, cocky walk of hers over toward the free weight area.

My eyes followed her every step while I tried to find the most dignified way of gathering my jaw up off the grass at my knees.

Pony looked at me from behind Ice, giving me her rakish grin and winking at my obvious discomfiture. Then she laughed as Ice pushed her out of the way and commandeered the chest press bench, lifting an ungodly amount of weight with fluid ease.

My eyeballs joined my jaw on the ground as I watched her impressive chest and arms flex and relax against the weight of the iron she was lifting.

I was caught in a definite quandary. Those were my friends over there as well. Surely they wouldn't object if I were to join them. The problem was, however, how to make it from where I was to where I wanted to be without managing to lose the last shred of dignity I had managed to hang onto.

To give myself some time, I decided that a full body appraisal was in order. *One head, complete with befuddled brain and wide eyes. Check. Shoulders: sagging but still there. Chest: one heart beating three times its normal rate but in otherwise good condition. Arms: weak but present. Hips: let's just not go there right now. Legs: definitely the weak point of this assessment.*

Placing my hands firmly on the grass and absorbing some of the solid, sure strength of the earth through my flesh, I pushed myself up onto my feet, wildly pleased that my body seemed to bearing up well under its own weight. *Alright. We've got standing down pretty good here. Now, let's try out that walking thing, shall we?*

One step turned into two, which turned into three, and before I knew it, I was making steady progress toward the weightlifting area where a large crowd had gathered to cheer the object of my attention on in what looked to be a prison record amount of weight to be lifted. As more inmates gathered around, blocking my sight of the event, I once again cursed my parents for tossing me into the shallow end of the gene pool.

A huge cheer rang out and though I couldn't see anything, I imagined Ice had just managed to break whatever record she was trying for. As I stared at the inmates, trying to find a way through the sea of orange, something strange hit me. Whereas before, the exercise yard had always been rigidly segregated along racial boundaries, women from every culture were gathered around Ice, cheering her on. There was no sign of the tensions that usually permeated such gatherings. The yard was united in a common cause, to cheer a fellow inmate to victory. And somehow, by doing nothing more than pitting herself against several pieces of unyielding metal, this intense woman had managed to bring a harmony that was otherwise absent in the day to day running of the home we all shared.

A loud bell, signaling the end of the exercise period, freed me from my musings. With a sad sigh, I broke off my stroll toward the cheering crowd and made my escape back into the prison.

As I walked into the library, Corinne was there, as always, to greet me. The enigmatic smile creased her lips once again as she gestured, with her pen, toward one of the tables where a large book lay, its cover shining in the dim lighting like a beacon. Drawn toward it, my curiosity on full alert, I glanced at the shining cover, then back at my friend, my jaw once again becoming unhinged. "How did you know?"

She smirked, well pleased with herself. "I have my ways, Angel."

Shaking my head, I looked back down at the book waiting smugly for me on the table. My fingertips traced the title, my mind spinning with a sense of the macabre: *The Art of Bonsai.*

Chapter 2

The next morning dawned gray and dreary and, as it was a Saturday, I elected to spend most of it camped out in my bunk exploring the wonderful world of bonsai. Reading of its history gave me valuable new insight into the woman known as Ice and I was drawn up into it, passing many hours in pleasant solitude as life continued on around me.

By mid afternoon, I had finished the book and as my body was beginning to get a bit stiff and sore from lying against the scratchy sheets, I decided to go down to take a shower, secure in the belief that I wouldn't be molested.

The prison was rather quiet for a rainy Saturday afternoon and, as I walked past the cavernous laundry room on my way to the showers, I heard a soft, almost whimpering sound, followed by harsh whispering and the sound of flesh beating against flesh. Dropping my clean uniform to the tiled floor, I stepped around the corner, ready for action.

With the incapacitation of Mouse, the leadership of the white gang had been taken over by a huge mountain of a woman who went by the name of Derby. So named because she once was a queen of the roller derby, the woman was, not to put too fine a point on it, immense. Her face had the look of lumpy bread dough and her nose was so mashed that I wondered how she ever breathed through it. She didn't smile often, which was a blessing, because most of her front teeth were either missing entirely, or had blackened stumps to mark what could have been. Standing close to six feet tall (and, in the prison, only Ice was taller) she weighed in at least two fifty, easy. Most of that looked to be that hard, solid kind of fat you see in the pictures of hard working peasant women that decorate National Geographic from time to time. I knew from experience that she was as strong as an ox and twice as mean.

As I slipped between two industrial washers, taking care not to be heard or seen just yet, I peeked around the corner at the scene before me. A young woman, no older than myself, knelt on the floor, terrified. A piece of duct tape had been plastered over her mouth and her arms had been bound behind her back with what looked to be a still-wet bedsheet. Her jumpsuit had been rent at the neck and pulled back over her shoulders, exposing her heaving breasts. Her face was bloody from multiple blows and her eyes were beginning to blacken and swell. My mind flashed back to the time that I was in the exact same position and, again, I snapped as I watched Derby's coarse, blunt hands reach down to cruelly twist the young woman's nipples, earning another whimper. The gang leader's three companions, none of whom I recognized on sight, snickered and elbowed one another.

After a quick and fruitless visual search told me I'd have to go into this with no weapons but my wits, I stepped from my hiding place, body tensed and ready. "That's enough, Derby. Let her go." My voice echoed in the cavernous room, bouncing back at me from all angles.

Slowly turning her head, Derby's thick, rubbery lips split into a sneer as she spied me. "Well, well, well. If it isn't the Amazons' little fuck toy. How ya doin, fishie?"

"Let her go, Derby." Keeping alert, I shifted position, determined not to let myself be backed into a corner.

The other three women looked to their leader for direction.

"You just mind your own business, fish, or I'll forget that Mouse asked me to leave you for her to deal with."

"I'm asking you one more time, Derby. Let the girl go."

She sneered again. "Fuck you."

As the woman turned back to her prey, I took the opportunity presented and made a running leap, jumping on her broad back and latching a strong arm around her throat. Slightly unbalanced, she staggered back a step, but before I could reinforce my choke hold, the other three came at me from three different directions.

It was like being hit by a semi. Derby's knees collapsed from the pounding, and I went down with her, hitting the floor hard but refusing to release my now shaky hold. Brutal hands grabbed at me, but I used the newly developed strength in my legs to kick them away, listening with no small satisfaction as they grunted out their pain.

Reaching up, Derby wrapped a massive paw around my own hand and jerked it away from her neck, almost breaking my wrist in the process. Bellowing, she flung me away and I landed, slightly stunned, against one of the dryers. Ignoring the pain, I rolled to my feet quickly, my body still ready and balancing lightly on the balls of my feet as the Amazons had taught me.

"You little bitch," the giant said as she rubbed the rawness at her neck. "Fuck Mouse. I'm gonna kill you myself!"

She rushed at me, arms wide open as if meaning to give me a hug. Huge she might have been, but I was agile, and quick. As she lumbered at me, I simply ducked under one massive arm, spinning quickly and almost breaking into laughter as her momentum carried her into the dryer I had landed against just a moment before.

The air became blue with her curses as she turned around, holding her massive gut with one arm. "You're dead, fish. Do you hear me? Dead!"

"You'll have to catch me before you can kill me, tubby."

Sometimes my mouth has a mind of its own, and this was certainly one of those times. Derby's face turned a shade of red I'd never seen before and veins sprung like garden hoses from the thickness of her neck.

With a roar that shook the foundations of the room, she came at me again. As I dodged away for a second time, I spared a brief moment to wonder where the other three had gotten themselves off to. As she blundered past me, I looked around, finally seeing the other three gang members sprawled, unconscious, on the floor. Puzzled, I frowned, knowing that my kicks could not have possibly done so much damage.

My moment of inattention was about to cost me dearly. Recovering her wits, Derby had managed to come at me again and was, at that very second, cocking back a fist that looked to be roughly the size of a canned ham.

I froze, desperately trying to figure out which way to move to avoid being blown across the room. *Right? Left? Up? Down? What?*

It's truly amazing how fast your thoughts tumble through your head at a time like that. I still hadn't reached a clear decision when I saw the fist start forward, my face clearly in its sights.

I steeled myself for the coming blow while my mind still tried to talk my body into picking *some* direction in which to move. Finally, I decided left and was just starting to dodge in that direction when a long arm snaked into my field of vision, stopping the fist absolutely stone cold dead just inches from my face. The sound of the impact was amazing, ringing like a rifle shot into the room and rebounding back to me in echoes.

Derby actually whimpered as the tanned hand closed itself around her fist. I could almost hear the sounds of small bones breaking as her face turned from red to white in the beat of a heart.

A low, comforting and absolutely wonderful voice sounded to my left. "Why don't ya try picking on someone your own size, Derby?"

Though caught totally within the grip of another, Derby's false, bullying bravado showed no sign of shutting down. "I ain't afraid of you, Ice."

"No? You should be." Without releasing her grip, Ice reached out with her other hand and gently pushed me in the direction of the still bound young woman. "Keep an eye on her while I take care of this one, will ya?"

I nodded, stunned by the full smile she gave me, then walked over to where the wide-eyed woman still knelt. "It's gonna be alright now. You're going to be ok." Still crooning gently to her, I stripped away her bonds, taking special care with the tape plastered cruelly across her face. Finally free, sobs overcame her and she collapsed against me, grabbing at the fabric of my uniform as if to an anchor. Enfolding her in my arms, I gently rocked her as my eyes drifted back over to the center of the action, drawn, as always, to Ice.

After being assured by my calm presence that the young woman was as well as could be expected, Ice released Derby's hand and stepped back, putting her hands on her hips and appraising her panting opponent. "We can do this one of two ways, Derby. You can leave well enough alone and walk out of here with the broken hand I just gave you, *or* you can be an idiot and come at me, in which case you'll go out of here on a stretcher. Which is it gonna be?"

Shaking out her swelling hand, Derby stared daggers of hatred at Ice, who looked back, cool and calm as her namesake. "You think you're so damn tough, Ice. Well, you ain't." Trying the bull-rush maneuver once again, she lumbered at Ice. Instead of dodging, though, Ice met the huge onrushing body with a knee in the gut, doubling Derby over. A slashing elbow to the back of her skull, and the gang leader went down like a sack of over-ripe apples, howling as her face met the cold stone floor.

I couldn't resist. "Oooooh. Wrong choice."

Ice grinned fiercely at me, clearly enjoying herself as she danced out of the way of the falling body.

Actually *gobbling* in rage, Derby pushed herself up to her hands and knees, shaking her head and spraying fans of blood over the floor. Her face looked as if it had battled with a chainsaw and lost. Scrabbling back up to her feet, she came at Ice once again, her dripping blood staining her jumpsuit to a sickly rust color.

Ice met her with a high kick to the head, and then, in an absolutely incredible move, switched legs, straightening the behemoth's body with another high kick to the other side. As Derby pinwheeled her arms, trying to maintain her balance, Ice launched a truly spectacular, right-from-the-hip side kick that caused the gang leader to actually leave her feet and fly halfway across the room.

She landed hard against one of the washers, her back bending almost double over its edge. The back of her skull smashed against the top with a huge, gonging clatter. Her legs gave out and she slid down the washer, landing on the floor in a bleeding heap.

"Had enough yet, Derby? Cause there's plenty more where that came from." Ice smiled a smile that I can only describe as purely erotic. And I should know, because when I saw it, all the hormones in my body immediately sat up and did the mambo. "And it's all for you."

Though I have no idea where her strength was coming from, Derby managed, by slow inches, to get herself back to her feet and she stood there, tottering, looking as if one stiff wind would blow her back to the floor again. "You'll *never* beat me, bitch," she mumbled, half dazed.

I looked up at Ice, curious as to what she would do. Clearly, Derby wasn't a threat to anyone anymore. The woman half stumbled toward her taller opponent, dragging one leg awkwardly behind her while wiping the blood from her nose with the back of her hand.

Ice stood calm and still, watching everything with that intensely piercing gaze that reminded me of an inquisitive bird of prey looking at a potential meal.

The distance between them closed, Derby drew back her fist, moving as if underwater. At the last second, her eyes rolled back in her head and she collapsed into Ice's strong arms.

Smirking, Ice bore her weight easily.

At that very moment, as if by fortuitous circumstance, two guards strode into the laundry room, their batons out and ready. "Let her go, Ice," the taller one, Phyllis, said.

Shrugging, Ice did as she was told and Derby's limp body once again crumpled to the floor.

"Now back away from her. Slowly."

Keeping her hands open and away from her body, Ice did as requested, taking two long, careful steps away from the downed prisoner.

Phyllis stepped over to the slumped form of Derby as her partner, Nancy, kept a wary eye on Ice. Squatting down, she pushed the heavy body over then brought her hand back. It was covered with blood. She turned wide eyes up to Ice. "Jesus Christ. What happened?"

Ice shrugged again. "She tripped."

"Bullshit. Tell me the truth, Ice."

I was about to speak up, when Derby came back to struggling consciousness. Phyllis dodged the flailing fists as she struggled to push the inmate's huge shoulders back against the rough concrete floor. "Stay still, Derby!"

"Fuck that! I'm gonna kill that fucking bitch! Let me go!"

"Derby, I'm warning you, stay still!"

Nancy jumped in to help her partner and between the two of them, they barely managed to subdue the raging woman. Finally they were able to calm her and Nancy grabbed a fresh sheet from atop one of the dryers and pressed it down over Derby's flattened nose. "Now, what in the *hell* happened here?" Phyllis asked again.

"What? Fuck, woman, are you *blind*?" Derby bellowed, her voice muffled with blood and a sheet. "Fucking bitch beat the shit outta me here! Fuckin' dirty fighter."

"I'm not blind, Derby. I'm asking what happened."

Derby's eyes darted around quickly, her obviously laboring mind trying to come up with some sort of excuse. Ice waited patiently, the faint smirk still present on her beautiful face. God, the woman wasn't even *breathing* hard.

"Me and my buddies came in here 'cause we heard a noise," the huge woman finally said. "We found that bitch beatin on the little fish over there."

It was obvious the two guards hadn't noticed us before, because Nancy uttered an "oh shit" and bustled over, gently taking the young woman from my grasp and grabbing yet another sheet to dab away the blood on her face.

"Derby," I started, only to be stopped by a truly chilling glare from Ice. I looked back at her, confused, but kept my peace. The meaning of her look was clear. *Shut up.*

"We tried ta stop her, and she took us all out. Even hit me when I was down. Fucking dirty fighter."

I bit my cheeks against the need to say something.

Phyllis looked up. "Is that true, Ice?"

Ice shrugged.

Phyllis was a good guard and she obviously didn't believe Derby's story. But without any conflicting evidence, she couldn't do anything about it. "Damn it, Ice, say something! You know you'll end up in the hole if you don't."

Ice remained silent, immovable.

"Yeah, the hole. That's where that bitch belongs. Look at that little fish! She was gonna rape her if we hadn't come in!"

That did it. Freezing glare or no, I was not going to stand by and let Derby continue to spew her lies while Ice did nothing to defend herself. My arms free of my injured burden, I shot to my feet, fire in my own eyes.

"Angel…." The warning tone in Ice's voice was unmistakable, but I was having none of it.

"No, Ice. I'm sorry, but no." I turned pleading eyes on the guard. "Phyllis, you know me. You know I don't lie. I was on my way to the shower when I heard this woman whimpering. I walked in to find Derby and her three friends beating up on her. They'd tied her up and gagged her! I tried to stop them when Ice came in. She gave Derby the chance to leave, fair and square. Derby chose to fight."

"That's a fucking *lie*!" Derby roared, once again struggling to get away from Phyllis. "You fucking piece of shit lying bitch!"

Phyllis straddled Derby's immense body while looking over at Ice. "Is what Angel's saying the truth?"

Damn the woman to all seven levels of hell, she still wouldn't answer!

"Angel?"

"It's true, Phyllis. All of it. I swear. Ice didn't start the fight. She finished it."

Finally, Phyllis looked over to the young woman whose beating had started all this. "Laura, who's telling the truth, hon? Just tell us and we'll make sure they're punished."

Derby twisted her head to glare at the young woman, who caught the look and cowered against Nancy's protective form. "You better answer right, fish, or I'll fucking kill you."

Laura stifled a sob of fear.

"C'mon, hon. Just tell us. No one here will hurt you anymore. I promise."

After a long moment, Laura held out a trembling hand. "Sh...she did it."

"Who? Ice or Derby? Tell us, hon. Please."

"D—Derby. She....she was....was gonna r—rape me!" Laura broke down into sobs once again and Nancy cradled her shaking form gently.

"Alright, Derby. You've just earned yourself a nice long stretch in the hole."

"Fuck her! You're gonna believe that fucking fish? She's lying! They're *all* lying! They all just want to protect Ice, goddammit!"

Phyllis allowed Derby to struggle to her feet, then grabbed her arm and twisted it, high and tight, against her back. "The only liar here is you, Derby. Let's go." She looked over her shoulder. "Take her over to the infirmary and meet me back in the office." Then she looked over at me. "And you two, get outta here before the warden hears what happened."

Breathing out a sigh of relief, I nodded. Phyllis smiled slightly, then half shoved, half dragged the growling Derby out of the laundry room, followed closely by Nancy, who gently guided Laura down the hall toward the infirmary.

The coldness in the room was suddenly very palpable and I searched around for something to say. "Thanks for your help," I finally commented softly.

Ice turned her deadly cold eyes toward me, her face completely devoid of expression. "I can take care of myself, Angel." Her voice was as cold as the bottom of a new grave. Without another word, she spun and stalked from the room, leaving me to my utter confusion. The three still unconscious members of Derby's gang weren't any help either. With a small shrug, I turned and left the room.

So, this is what a broken heart feels like.

Now, before you go crazy on me and ask where a thought like that could possibly have come from, let me go on record as saying that I had no idea either, at the time. All I knew is that I had done something to displease the woman who I was rapidly coming to see as some type of knight in shining armor. And it hurt. Badly.

What I didn't know is why she had reacted so badly to what I had done. After all, I had stopped her from being branded a rapist, which, even in a women's prison, is something that ranks right on the low rung with child abuse and molestation. While I didn't expect gushing praise, I surely didn't anticipate the coldness I received.

All thoughts of a shower gone in the excitement and its aftermath, I wandered aimlessly, wondering what to do. Part of me wanted to talk to Corinne in the hopes she could tell me what I did wrong. But most of me just wanted to crawl back into my bunk and forget that the day had even happened.

That part won out.

I crawled back into my bunk and laid out on my back, crossing my arms behind my head and staring sightlessly at the ceiling. My mind kept replaying Ice's last words to me, trying to find a secret meaning that I had obviously missed. "She can take care of herself, she says," I mumbled to the silent plaster. "Well, of *course* she can. She managed to take out a woman the size of Texas without even breaking a sweat!"

My mind chose that moment to insert a scene depicting the fight in all its glorious detail. My hormones happily applauded as I shifted on the bed. Being attracted to a woman wasn't something I really considered before. But, then again, there was never a woman in my life who looked, sounded and smelled like Ice. Still, it didn't bother me too much. Small town girl or not, I had an open mind and knew how to use it. Usually.

My thoughts rode the morbid train right around to the beginning again. What did I do to earn such coldness? What was so wrong about speaking out to defend the innocent? If I hadn't spoken up, Derby would have gone free and Ice would have been thrown in isolation for something she didn't do. What unspeakable harm had I done?

Groaning, I flopped my weary body over onto my side, just in time to see the golden curls of Critter as she peeked into my cell. "Mind if I come in?" she asked with a friendly smile on her face.

Returning the smile, I struggled to sit up. "Sure! Come on in."

Nodding, Critter entered and sprawled out on my roommate's vacant bunk. "Heard what happened."

I let out a slow breath. "Did Ice send you?"

"Nope. Corinne did. Figured you might need someone to talk to."

I shook my head. "How does that woman *know* so much?"

My friend grinned. "One of the eternal mysteries of the Bog."

"So…are you here to yell at me?"

"Nope. I'm just here to listen. And help if I can."

I sagged against the lumpy mattress, looking down at my hands. "I sure could use some."

"I figured as much."

Looking up, I met Critter's dark, compassionate eyes. "Why was what I did so wrong? I was only trying to make sure justice was done."

"Justice has its own way of being served in prison, Angel. The one rule that stands above all the others is that you never rat out a fellow inmate. Even if they do something that to you is unspeakable."

"But…."

Critter held up one hand. "Angel, why didn't you tell Sandra it was Mouse and her gang who beat you up in the shower?"

Closing my mouth, I sat back and thought about her question for a moment. "Well….I guess it's because I figured that I'd hurt them enough."

"Exactly. Prison justice. From what I heard, Ice pretty much wiped the floor with Derby today."

That brought an involuntary smile to my lips. "Yeah. She did."

"Do you think Derby got a pretty good payback for what she did to the new girl?"

"Well, sure! But Ice didn't deserve to be put in isolation for something she didn't do! And I couldn't just stand by and let the guards, and everyone else, think that Ice was a rapist!"

"I know, Angel. I know. It's hard just to stand back and do nothing. But sometimes you have to. Especially in here. Most of the people in this prison know Ice. They know what she's capable of, and what lines she won't cross. They know she wouldn't stoop to rape. Hell, Angel, half the women in here would give their eyeteeth just to spend one night with her! She has no need to take what would be given freely."

I sighed, considering that thought. "I suppose you're right."

Smiling, Critter got up from the bed and sat down beside me, slinging a friendly arm around my shoulder. "Course I am." Reaching out, she gently cupped my chin, bringing my gaze up to meet hers. "Angel, you know this stuff already. You made a mistake. But it was an admirable one that came from a good heart. This place has all too few of those. Ice was upset, but she knows why you did what you did. Things'll work out. You'll see."

A horrifying thought came into my head. "But what if Laura gets into even more trouble? If I hadn't opened my big mouth, she wouldn't have been forced to tell the guards who hurt her! Oh God!"

"Shhh. It's ok, Angel. We're keeping a close watch on her. Nothing'll happen. I promise."

"But…."

"Trust me, Angel. Trust Ice. Nothing will happen. She'll be safe. In a way, you did her a great favor. Not everyone comes under the protection of the Amazons. Because of you, she is now. No worries, alright?"

Sighing, I looked down at my hands, which were twisted in my lap. "Sorry. I guess I just made more work for you."

To my great surprise, Critter threw back her head and laughed. "Oh, Angel. You're a treasure, you know that? An absolute treasure." Giving me a final hug, she rose from the bed and playfully cuffed me on the shoulder. "Take it easy, my friend."

Meeting her eyes, I couldn't help but return her smile. "You too, Critter."

"I'll take it any way I can get it." With a grin and a final wave, my friend left me to my thoughts, which were much lighter for her visit.

The next day was, of course, Sunday, and after taking my aborted shower of the day before and spending an hour in forced prayer to a God I wasn't sure I believed in anymore, I made my way down to the sanctuary of the library.

Some time during my tossing and turning the night before, I'd decided to go ahead and purchase Ice's bonsai rake for her. After seeing the woman fight first hand, I was sure she couldn't do any more damage with a gardening tool than she could do with her fists and feet. The images of the fight pervaded my dreams all night, causing me to wake up in a sweat more than once, and let me tell you, the sweat *wasn't* one of fear.

Before my shower, I'd managed to connect with one of my contacts on the outside who was just on his way to church himself. The deal was done quickly and with a minimum amount of fuss and I was assured that, if everything went well, I should see my new acquisition within the week.

Walking into the library, I immediately headed for my favorite chair at my favorite table and sat down, stretching my still sleepy body and rolling my neck to get the kinks out.

Corinne greeted me with a smile from her place behind her desk. "How are you doing?"

"Better, thanks. And thank you for sending Critter up to see me. She really helped."

My friend's face dimpled. "Don't mention it."

We sat for a few moments in companionable silence, the ever-present ticking of the clock and the scratching of her pen on paper the only sounds around us. Most Sundays saw the library empty, but since Corinne considered it her home, it was open all the time, customers or no.

I looked down at the table, my fingers tracing over some of the deeply carved graffiti, trying to put into words the flow of my thoughts. Finally deciding to grab the bull by the horns, so to speak, I looked over at my companion's gray head as it bobbed slightly with her pen strokes. "Corinne, can I ask you something personal?"

Her eyes were warm and kind as they met mine. "Of course, Angel. What's on your mind?"

"Do you…um…." My fingers investigated another piece of inmate art-work. "Do you find women…attractive?" I looked up to gauge the expression on her face from the corner of my eye, suddenly feeling very shy in her presence.

Placing her pen down on the desk, Corinne clasped her hands, appearing to give the question serious consideration. "Well, yes, I suppose I do. Not all of them, mind you. That Derby gives me a bit of a pain in my guts, but some…yes."

I nodded. "And…well…have you ever *been* attracted to one? A woman, I mean. I mean, I know you were married and all, but…."

Her seamed face creased into a grin as she appeared to read my thoughts perfectly. "Indeed I have, Angel. Quite a few, as a matter of fact. Still am, if the truth be told."

The way she looked at me made me blush and turn away slightly. Perhaps this wasn't such a good idea after all.

Seeing my discomfiture, she once again dropped that slightly predatory stare that she'd been known to grace me with from time to time. "You have to remember, Angel, that I'm quite a bit older than you are. Things were different when I was growing up."

"How so?"

"People weren't so…open…with their sexuality as they are now. If you happened to be attracted to someone of the same gender, you kept it well hidden, or risk a huge scandal. If word got out, you could be whisked away to an insane asylum or even jail and no one wanted to risk that. Plus, my parents had quite a bit of status in the community where I grew up. Our family name and the reputation that went with it meant everything to them."

"So, you never acted on your attractions?"

The grin became predatory once again. "I never said that."

"Oh." My eyes dropped back down to the table.

I heard the faint scrape of a chair against the floor and, a second later, felt Corinne's warm presence next to me as she took a seat at my table. "As I've said, things were much different when I was a young girl, and my family had status in my community. A marriage was arranged for me, and it was expected that I'd accept that as my lot in life. And I did, for awhile. I had no skills other than those of a wife and a hostess, and no money of my own with which to start a different life."

She paused, and when I looked up, I could see a faint smile on her face and a far away look in her eyes. "Then the war happened and Todd, my husband at the time, was drafted to serve his country. Suddenly, my little corner of the world was bereft of men and I found myself surrounded by luscious femininity." Her smile widened, though her eyes were still very far away. "Ah, what a blissful time that was. It was like tasting chocolate for the first time, or being under the influence of an addictive drug. Once I had it, I wanted more." Her pale cheeks took on a faint flush. "I'm afraid I went a bit overboard."

I was totally drawn into her story, my own questions totally forgotten. "What happened?"

"Todd returned from London and I'm afraid he caught wind of my little indiscretions. Now, when he went off to war, he was a placid, dull man. Easily manipulated. But he returned a greedy, power-hungry tyrant. He agreed to keep quiet on the subject if I would give him hush money. I tried that for awhile, but I'm afraid my parents became a bit suspicious. I had never asked for money before, and now it seemed that just about every week Todd would demand something more. Having no skills of my own with which to earn it, they were the only ones I could turn to. I'm afraid my excuses became somewhat repetitive."

"What did you do?"

"Well, Todd hadn't been so chaste himself while in London. It seems he dipped his wick into some dirty wax and managed to come home with a good case of syphilis." Her smile turned wicked. "At the time, some of the physicians still treated that particular disease with arsenic."

My mind quickly put two and two together, came up with the requisite 'four', and forced me to look at my friend with wide eyes.

"Exactly. The treatment for my husband's dirty little illness gave me the perfect means to extricate myself from his machinations. I made up a story about rats in the attic and he even went down to the store to buy me more of the stuff! Soon I was introducing it into his food, just small doses at first, of course. He'd never been very keen on taking his medicine, but I told him that I wouldn't allow him into the marital bed until he'd become completely cured. Todd wanted an heir above all, so when I suggested doubling up on his medication, he complied without complaint. It was glorious."

Shaking her head, she laughed softly to herself. "And when the stomach pains started, I played the dutiful little wife and made sure to be seen weeping over my agony-ridden husband. I worked quickly then, stuffing all the arsenic down him I could. He died two days later. Such a grieving and bereft widow this world has never seen, if I do say so myself. His death was attributed to a case of the gastric flu that was going around at the time, complicated, of course, by his syphilis. Naturally, that little bit of information was kept quite hush-hush and nary another word was mentioned. I was left with a tidy sum of money and a grand old house. And a maid who was young and beautiful. If there is such a thing as perfection in life, I had achieved it."

"So, what happened?" I'm sure I must have sounded like a persistent little child, begging for a bed-time story, but I couldn't help myself. I was utterly fascinated by her tale.

"The money ran out quite quickly, I'm afraid. As did the maid. So, being a poor widow in the prime of her life with some social status to boot, I moved away to a town close by and found myself another husband. This time, I was lucky enough to find a rich, older gentleman who already had some long standing stomach problems. He wanted to be married quickly, and I was happy to oblige him. I quickly set myself up as the doting, long-suffering wife. I accompanied him on his myriad of journeys to this doctor or that, always taking care to be seen and to be concerned. He was quite a hypochondriac, though in those days, it was known as eccentric. And you know what they say about the boy who cried wolf."

"He got eaten in the end."

Corinne flashed me that hard, triumphant smile of hers. "Exactly."

I shuddered at the expression but managed to keep my voice steady. "Why did you have to kill him, though? Did he abuse you?"

"Oh no. Randolph was quite a nice man when he wasn't complaining about his various aches and pains. We got along quite well, as a matter of fact."

"Then why?"

"Because I had discovered an elemental truth about myself during my time with my first husband."

"And what was that?"

"I enjoyed killing. I enjoyed the power it gave me, and I enjoyed the benefits I obtained. I had no need for a man in my life, except for the money they would leave me at their deaths. It was clean. It was simple. And it was fun."

I shuddered again, but Corinne didn't seem to notice. "And so you just…killed them. With no remorse."

"Precisely."

"Just like snuffing out a candle?"

"Very good analogy, Angel. That's exactly what it was like. There were no bad emotions behind the act. Though I must admit that I enjoyed watching them suffer and call out to me as if I were some malignant angel of mercy who could grant them eternal peace. I imagine that's what the old gods of death felt like when they snuffed out a life. Powerful. Happy. In complete control."

Swallowing against the dryness in my throat, I broke the lock of our gazes, once again looking down at the scarred table-top as if it would provide the answers I sought. Hard as I tried, I couldn't seem to wrap my mind around the concept of joy in murder. It was as alien a thought to me as there could ever be. I thought back to my own time of depression and profound remorse that followed the killing of my husband. And that was done in self defense! The thought of killing him because I simply wanted to tore at my guts like a razor.

And yet here was a woman who I'd come to care for and regard almost like a mother figure, sitting calmly next to me discussing her enjoyment of killing as if she were reporting the weather. I felt a cold, dead space grow inside me and my body drew in on itself as I wrapped my arms around my shoulders, elbows tight to my chest.

Corinne's expression became sad as she looked at me. "And now I've upset you, sweet Angel. That wasn't my intention, I assure you."

"I know that Corinne," I returned, my voice soft and introspective. "It's just that…It all seems so hard to believe, as if I'm having a dream and just waiting for something to come along and wake me up. I guess it wouldn't be so strange if I didn't feel so close to you, but I do. I've come to care for you a great deal, Corinne, and when you tell me things like this about yourself, well, it scares me. It almost makes me feel that that caring is for a person I don't even know, or maybe for a person who isn't even there. And that's frightening for me."

"And for that I apologize deeply, Angel. Though you've known who I was since the day you met me, I suppose that anyone can choose to overlook parts of someone they don't wish to see. It seems to be part of the human condition. As if in ignoring it, it will simply go away." When she looked again at me, her gaze was calm and direct, showing me through eye contact alone everything she was, and could be. "Angel, I do care for you. Very much. You've been a ray of light in this dark and dreary place. But if you can't look me in the eye without experiencing fear or revulsion, then I think it's best if we end this here and now and spare us both later heartache."

As I gazed at my friend, I thought long and hard over the things she had said. And I knew she had spoken the truth. Corinne had never tried to come across as someone she wasn't. She'd never hidden her deeds, nor made light of them. She spoke about her past with honesty and never tried to sugar-coat it for the benefit of my friendship. I realized that, in the time I had known her, she had always been a murderer, yet I had gotten to both know and care about her despite that fact, or maybe even, if I were to be totally honest with myself, because of it. And I also realized that without her presence, my life would be lacking something that I didn't want to give up.

"I don't want that, Corinne. I don't want to lose you as a friend because of my shallow thinking. You're an important person in my life and if you can forgive my fear and ignorance, I'd like to continue our relationship."

My friend smiled, obviously relieved. "I'd like that very much as well, Angel." With a happy grin, she slumped back into her chair. "Now, before we got off on this torturous tangent of ours, we were speaking about attraction to women, were we not?"

Her direct gaze made me blush once again and I nodded.

"Well, then. I'm assuming that you're asking me because there's a chance you might be attracted to someone right here in our happy little home?"

My blush deepened as I nodded again.

"Let's see. Who could it be? Perhaps our fair Critter? I've seen the way she looks at you."

Her eyes twinkled mischievously as mine widened. *Critter?* "No. No, Critter's a very attractive woman, but she's just a friend."

"Hmmm." Obviously having fun at my expense, Corinne pretended to ponder the question. "Pony, perhaps? Or Sonny? No? Is it Montana then? Now there's an intense, striking woman. Ah, if I were only a few years younger."

"No. None of them."

Her eyes went round with false innocence. "Then who, dear Angel? You forget, I'm an old woman. My mind isn't as sharp as it once was. These guessing games go right past me, I'm afraid."

I took a deep breath. And then another. "It's Ice," I mumbled to the tabletop.

"Who? Speak up, dear. My hearing's not what it used to be either."

If there were ever a moment in my life where I would have truly enjoyed killing someone, it would have been right then. Corinne's gaze was sharp and mirthful, allowing me no quarter. "It's Ice," I repeated, more succinctly this time.

Her grin was triumphant. "Ahhhh. So tall, dark and deadly has managed to mesmerize my sweet little Angel, has she?"

"Corinne...." I was surprised the sprinklers hadn't been set off, my face got so hot.

"Oh come now, Angel. You think I haven't noticed those cute little puppy-dog eyes you get every time you catch sight of her? I may be old, but I'm not blind."

"Corinne, please." If there had been an electric chair handy, I would have gladly strapped myself in and used a broom handle to pull the lever. *Is it possible to die of embarrassment?*

"Oh alright," my friend said, sounding a bit petulant. "You're just so much fun to tease, Angel. Your face gets the most delightful shade of red. Almost a rose color. It's quite beautiful."

"Corinne!"

"Alright, alright. I'll stop. For now."

A breath of thanks rushed out of my lungs. "Please," I managed to choke out.

"This attraction you have for Ice, does it bother you?"

"No. Yes. God, I don't know!" Propping my elbows on the table, I slumped my still heated face into my hands.

"Alright, let's go through this logically. Do you have a problem with the fact that she's a woman?"

"No. Not exactly. I mean, I'll admit it's a little strange since I've never been attracted to a woman before, unless you count my first grade teacher Mrs. Price."

"I think we can be safe in leaving her out of this for the moment."

"I think you're right. It's not the attraction itself that bothers me so much. It's the *intensity* of it. I've never felt something like this before. In *anything*. I know you've talked about the connection between us before and part of me wants to believe you but…." I sighed, unable yet again to voice my thoughts. "This is just so beyond my experience I'm having trouble knowing what to do with my feelings."

"Have you ever thought of talking with Ice about them?"

I looked up at her, stunned. My mouth opened and closed a few times but I couldn't get the words out.

"Cat got your tongue?" Corinne was positively smug.

"Are you *crazy*?"

"Some would say so, yes."

"I mean about this! Have you forgotten that I only talked to the woman for the first time the day before yesterday?"

"And your point would be?"

Still stunned, all I could do was shake my head. "You have got to be kidding me, Corinne. Please tell me you're kidding me."

"I was quite serious, actually."

"Great. That's just great. What do you suggest, Corinne? You think I should just waltz into Ice's cell, pin her to the bed and say 'Hey, Ice, I just wanted you to know that, even though we've said a grand total of five words to one another, I think I'm in love with you. And if it's not love, it's some intense kind of lust. Will you please kiss me'?"

My friend shrugged. "Why not? Works for me."

For the first time in my life, I actually growled with frustration. Collapsing against the table, Corinne started laughing so hard I was actually worried that she'd give herself a stroke.

As I sat there scowling and feeling rather petulant myself, my friend finally managed to bring herself under some sort of control. Isolated chuckles still escaped her as she dabbed at her tear-streaked face with a corner of her shawl. "Oh Angel, sweet, beautiful, wonderful Angel. How I ever survived thirty years in this depraved pit without your presence I'll never know."

"I'm not laughing over here, Corinne," I muttered, giving her my best impression of a displeased look.

"I know, Angel. And I apologize for my outburst. It's just that you forget about the beauty of innocence in a place like this. Its freshness brings a joy to my heart. Forgive me for expressing that joy through laughter. It's not something I did much of before you came into my life."

Suddenly, I felt very much like a heel. "Corinne, I'm sorry. This is just all so confusing for me. My dreams as a little girl didn't include serving time for murder or having an intense attraction to a fellow inmate, woman *or* man. I'm starting to feel out of control all over again, and I don't like that."

"Oh Angel, I know what you're going through, believe me. Just remember, though, you've only had a day or two to figure out what's going on with you in regards to Ice. Getting a handle on those kinds of feelings will take time, and if there's one thing we have in abundance here in the Bog, it's time." She laid a gentle hand on my wrist and I absorbed the warmth of her skin gratefully. "My suggestion to you is to just sit back, relax, drink some tea, and let the world go on without you for awhile."

Despite myself, I cracked a smile. "Is tea your answer for everything?"

"Pretty much, yes. Would you like some?"

"Sounds like the best offer I've had all day."

Brown eyes twinkled as they looked back at me from over one of Corinne's shoulders. "I could make you a better one."

"Don't start."

My day managed to end much better than it started and for that, I was happy.

The end of that week found me, as always, in the library, my thoughts on one subject in particular calmer if not more ordered. I'd only seen Ice to nod to in the hallways. Her eyes, when they met mine, were guarded, but no longer cold. I guessed that meant she'd forgiven me for my faux pas.

I had just put the finishing touches on an open book exam for one of my college courses when Phyllis stepped into the room bearing a small package and a smile for all of us, particularly Corinne. Since our discussion the week before, I'd taken the time to study the interaction between the two and noticed small things that I'd never had cause to see before. Though fraternization between inmates and guards was strictly forbidden, it looked like there was more going on between them than met the eye.

The tall guard headed over to my area as I closed my composition book, perching a hip on the corner of the table and looking down at me with warm eyes. "How's it going, Angel?"

"Not bad. Just finished up the last of my courses for the semester."

"How'd you do?"

"Well, since it was open book, I think I got an A."

She grinned. "Tough life."

Returning the smile, I pushed the tablet and pen away from me. "How's Laura?"

The young woman had remained in the infirmary most of the week, suffering from a skull fracture and a mild concussion from Derby's beating.

She'd just been released the day before and had been taken directly to the segregation unit for her own protection. I couldn't help but continue to feel guilty about that since, in her own way, she was as isolated as Derby was down in the hole.

"She's doin' alright. She kinda likes the seg unit. Makes her feel safer. I think we'll keep her there for a little while longer. Derby and Mouse are out of the picture for awhile, but there are others who'll try and finish what they started."

Some of my guilt must have shown on my face because she placed a hand on my shoulder, squeezing it slightly. "Don't feel bad for speaking out, Angel. Justice was served. That's a good thing."

"It's not such a good thing if it makes her even more of a target than before, Phyllis."

"Angel, I might not want it this way, but the sad fact of life, hon, is that kids like Laura are always going to be targets no matter what they do. She's little more than a kid who made a stupid mistake. God knows this isn't the place for her, but what can we do? We just do our jobs and protect her, and the rest of the inmates, the best we can."

"Forgive me for saying so, Phyllis, but from where I'm standing, it doesn't look like you're doing a very good job at all. If Ice hadn't walked in when she did, there quite probably could have been two of us beaten half to death instead of just Laura."

Shifting slightly, Phyllis curled her hand around the edge of the table, her knuckles whitening over the tan of her flesh. "It hurts to hear you say that, Angel, even though I know it's true. The economy being what it is, people are paying more attention to gas prices than to prison expenses. The pay just isn't high enough to entice anyone to come into this line of work. And the ones they *do* manage to entice usually don't stay very long." She smiled. "The working conditions aren't always exactly pleasant."

"I realize that, Phyllis, and I'm not blaming you, personally. It's just that I think that most of the outside world sees us as a bunch of depraved monsters getting our just desserts. Not everyone in here is like that, though. And, underneath it all, we're still human beings."

"I agree," the guard replied. "I just don't know what we can do to change things. I'm not happy about young girls getting beaten bloody either."

"I know." Leaning back in my chair, I laced my fingers behind my head. "Maybe I'll figure something out. After all," I glanced over to Corinne, "I've got a lotta time on my hands."

"I have faith in you, Angel," Phyllis replied, laughing. "Speaking of time, I need to get back to work." She held out the package she'd walked in with. "This came for you this morning. I rescued it before they could tear it to shreds."

Reaching out, I took the package, surprised to note that the wrapping was smooth and unbroken. As I'm sure you're aware, the rule in prison is to thoroughly search all incoming and outgoing packages for contraband. That's one of the reasons I never considered purchasing weapons for any of my customers, since I'd be the one sent to solitary and believe me, that's a place you most definitely want to avoid at all costs.

I looked up at her, curious. She just smiled and patted my shoulder. "When I looked at the return address, I knew who it was for," she said, as if that explained everything.

And perhaps, in a way, it did.

The package had come from the J & R Garden Supply Store and looked to be the bonsai rake I'd ordered the week before. My contact had come through for me once again. "Thanks," I said, for more than the package.

"No problem." Squeezing my shoulder once more, Phyllis levered herself off the table and turned to Corinne. "See you later?"

My friend dimpled. "Sounds good."

"'Till then."

As the guard sauntered out, I turned to stare at Corinne, a smug grin on my own lips. "Corinne," I mock-chided, "are you going to get that poor guard in trouble with your lascivious nature?"

She turned her own smirk back at me. "I never kiss and tell, Angel."

"You should. Peter was a bit…dull. I could use a few pointers."

Her smile turned into a leer. "I'd be happy to show you."

I made a show of rolling my eyes. "We're not going to start that again, are we? Besides, what would Phyllis think?"

"She'd think I was damned lucky," my friend growled.

Pushing myself away from the table, I stood, idly twirling the long, thin package in my hands. Walking over to Corinne's desk, I placed it in front of her. "Would you be sure Ice gets this?"

"I'm no postman. Give it to her yourself."

"No…I don't think that would be a good idea. Really. Maybe I'll get one of the Amazons to…."

"Angel, you're going to have to face her sometime, you know."

I sighed. "I know. But it's only been a week. For all I know, she'll take one look at me and send me flying out of her cell with one of those kicks of hers. I'll be laid up for weeks! Who'll help you with the library?"

My friend eyed me. "Don't make up excuses to cover your cowardice, Angel. This deal is between the two of you. No one else. Just go up there and give her the package. It's not like she's gonna bite you." The leer returned. "Unless you want her to."

"Corinne!"

She flapped her arm at me. "Just deliver your package and leave me be. I've got a date to get ready for."

Sighing, I retrieved the box. "This never gets any easier, does it."

"Nope. That's what makes it so much fun. Now shoo."

With a last pleading glance, and seeing no help would be found, I spun on my heel and made my way out of my sanctuary.

The mind is an amazing creature, especially in its morbid tendency to spew out thoughts best locked away deep in the cavern of the subconscious. As I walked down the long, dim hallway leading from the library to the prison proper, I could almost see in front of me a black-garbed priest softly chanting the Lord's Prayer as guards kept pace beside me.

The box in my hands became chains on my wrists and my heart sped up as my mouth became dry as dust. I imagined a cold gust of winter air that swept across my body and my skin responded as the hair lifted from my arms in stiff spikes. Just as I was beginning to wonder why my imaginary companions had morphed into the garb of Roman centurions, the hallway opened out into the prison's main square, leaving me slack jawed and blinking with its sudden brightness.

"Angel," I whispered to myself, "you've got to start getting out more. I think that library's starting to have a bad influence on you."

A few strange looks were cast my way by passing inmates and I firmly pushed the spectral visions from my mind, resolutely stalking toward the near stairwell as if I hadn't a care in the world.

Ice's cell was on the eighth floor and as I mounted the steps, quickly climbing, I wondered how she and the other inmates could stand to climb so much just to get to their rooms. My time with the Amazons had put me into pretty good shape by then, though, so the trek wasn't as bad as it might have been months earlier.

Still, a ball of cold lead seemed to have taken up residence in my stomach, growing larger and heavier each step I climbed so that by the time I had reached the top, I wasn't sure if I could take another step.

As I stood on the final landing, trying to regain both my strength and my will, I looked around and was thankful that most of the block seemed to be free of human habitation. Calming my breathing and centering my thoughts, I gave myself one of my patented pep-talks. "Alright, Angel, let's get moving. Nothing to it, right? Just go in there, give her the package and leave. It's not as if she's gonna ask you in for tea, right? She'll probably just grunt at you and send you on your way. No big deal, right?"

Right.

So why was my heart trip-hammering in my chest? Why was my skull pounding fit to burst and my guts twisting inside me like a roll of barbed wire? "Oh God. I think I'm gonna be sick."

A passing inmate, one of the few up and around on level eight, paused next to me, looking at me with concern. "Are you alright?"

I managed a weak smile. "Oh yeah. Never better." As she continued to look at me strangely, I frantically searched for something to say. "I'm…um…lost, I think. Can you tell me which cell is Ice's?"

The inmate's puzzled look turned into a smile. "Yeah, sure." Half turning her body, she pointed down the catwalk bordering the cells. "Last one to the left down there, in the corner. H-324."

"Thanks!"

"Hey, no problem! See ya around." I didn't miss the speculative glance I got from my new acquaintance, and for whatever reason, it made my heart lighter. *Ha! Take that, Ice! I don't need to be scared of you. There are plenty of other fish in the sea.*

Ok, so it was a bad analogy.

Heading down the catwalk with a lighter step, I glanced curiously into the cells I was passing. The eighth floor, for the most part, housed the most dangerous criminals in the Bog. Because of this, the prison authorities thought it best to give them single rooms. These rooms were the same size as the regular cells, but instead of a second bunk, a long stainless steel table ran along one wall.

Unlike the rest of the prison population, the warden's edict banning items of a personal nature didn't appear to extend to the worst of the worst. I wasn't sure why this was exactly, but figured that a happy murderer was a safe murderer and so left my thoughts at that, lest I start becoming perturbed at the unfair irony of the worst getting the best.

At long last, I was standing outside of Ice's cell, my body pressed up against the cool, pebbled cement of the wall. *Maybe she's not in!* my mind shouted. *Yeah, right. You're not that lucky.*

It's absolutely amazing how your body can ignore a firm directive from your mind. Of course, at the time, my mind was shouting conflicting orders at it, but still, it was more stubborn than a mule, confused or not.

Suddenly a deep, sensuous voice broke into my thoughts. "Ya might as well come in, Angel. I can hear you breathing out there."

Flushing with embarrassment and not a little shock, I pushed myself away from the wall and walked toward the open door of Ice's cell, pausing just outside and staring in.

Ice was lounging on her bunk, her back pressed up against the far wall as the rest of her long, strong body lay in peaceful repose, one leg cocked at the knee, the other fully extended. A thick paperback lay face down against her lower abdomen, its spine creased from many readings. The glare of the overhead fluorescents made catching the title all but impossible, not that I didn't try.

After a moment, I held up my encumbered hand. "I…um…your package came in today. Corinne suggested I come up here and drop it off."

Smiling slightly, showing no more than the barest quirk of her full lips, Ice shifted on the bed, then placed her feet on the floor, standing with the fluid grace that haunted my dreams. I was mesmerized. Again.

Watching as she came toward me, I licked my lips, still holding out my arm and willing my hand not to tremble as the heat of her body wrapped itself around mine, caressing my skin. Reaching out a long arm, she took the box from my hand, looking down at the untouched wrapping, then back up at me, one eyebrow raised to her hairline.

"What?"

"Oh, nothing. Just surprised it isn't opened."

"Oh. Well, I trust you."

The eyebrow went higher.

I smiled weakly. "Besides, I've seen you fight."

Her little half smile came out again and I resisted shaking my head against the feelings that simple expression engendered in me. Her fierce eyes softened as they regarded me and, from deep within my heart, I felt the tug of whatever connection we seemed to possess. "Thanks," she said, her voice soft, her hand hefting the package and tossing it lightly.

"No problem."

How long we stood there, looking at one another in perfect silence, I'll never know. As with our first meeting, whole centuries seemed to fall away with the weight of each breath. It was like looking at an old and cherished photo album that you forgot even existed and getting warm and happy from the memories. At the same time, it was much more, this connection. And much less. It had about it a simplicity so fundamental and a complexity so profound that my mind just decided to give up the ghost and simply 'be'.

Though I didn't want to break the moment, some part of me eventually came to the decision that this wasn't the best of ideas, and so I broke the lock of our gazes, my eyes touring the room, looking for some safe space to land my gaze.

As if by providence, my eyes landed on the metal table that ran the length of one wall of Ice's cell. Its chill, shining finish was covered with a beautiful silk cloth, done up in purples, yellows, blues and reds of varying hues and emblazoned with what looked to be Chinese characters. Or they could have been Japanese. My Asian isn't all that great, truth be known.

On the cloth, side by side, sat four bonsai trees looking like visions of a world far from here. The love and care that had gone into their shaping was obvious and, quite beyond my conscious will, my body was drawn to what my eyes were seeing. I barely felt the shifting presence as Ice stepped back to allow me into the cell.

Striding over to the table as if gliding on currents of warm summer air, I stopped at the boundary and simply stared, completely taken in by the vision before me. The four small trees bore the distinct stamp of proud individuality, yet when seen as a unit, they seemed to tell a story, the meaning of which darted teasingly around in my brain, tossing out hints which I failed to catch.

Looking at them was like seeing into someone else's soul, all violent beauty, gentle caring and turbulent emotions fighting for space within the fragile shell of a living being. The deep profundity of hidden meanings niggled at me, stirring my curiosity, but rather than give into them, I chose to look upon the stark simplicity of the works before me. I imagined feeling warm sunlight on my face as it shone, dappled, through the leaves of a forested glen. The feeling of ultimate freedom and tender peace filtered down to me with the light, cocooning me in its gossamer web. It was like looking through a window and seeing an unending vista filled with warmth, peace and love. "Beautiful," I breathed.

Looking at art affected me that way and, in all honesty, still does. I hope to never lose that part of myself that sees joy and wonder in the most simple of things.

The soft sound of a throat being cleared broke me from my rapture and I turned to see Ice, looking faintly embarrassed and staring down at the box in her hands. "Thanks," she mumbled.

The look on her face made her fully human for the first time to me and I couldn't help the feeling of surprised giddiness that went flowing through my heart and body. Laughter threatened to bubble up, but I remembered who I was with and tamped down on it, reining in control over my sometimes flighty emotions. "They really are beautiful," I replied softly. "Spiritual, almost. But primal too. A wonderful paradox."

When her eyes met mine, I saw the embarrassment had brought with it a bit of defensiveness. "Angel, they're *trees*."

"Lying won't help your case any," I replied, figuring that gentle teasing might do the trick. "They're more than just trees and the work you've put into them proves my point quite nicely, don't you think?"

She scowled at me, but didn't refute my words. Inside, I pumped a triumphant fist.

"Come on, Ice. People must tell you that a hundred times a day! These are magnificent."

"Actually, no," she countered, getting a little of her confidence back. "Aside from the guards, you're the first person I've ever allowed into my cell."

Oh shit. I reached my hand up to scratch at the back of my neck, something I did often when I needed to think quickly and the answers just weren't coming. "I'm…sorry… I…didn't mean…It's just that…they were so beautiful and I…."

She smiled, slightly, one that reached her eyes and made them soft and warm. "It's alright. I know you didn't mean any harm."

My relief was palpable. "Thank you."

"No problem."

For lack of anything better to do, I let my gaze wander again. On the wall above the bonsai was a large map that looked to be from National Geographic. It sported the title "Rise and Fall of the Roman Empire". With little icons of battle plans and weaponry, it seemed incongruous, sitting as it was above a scene of such absolute tranquility. As I looked around further, I noticed smaller maps scattered about on the green-painted walls, each showing the territory of a once powerful empire which was, eventually, crushed to dust beneath the boot-heels of a stronger army.

"Interesting hobby," I remarked, more to hear myself speak than anything else. "Is there a message behind these?"

"World domination."

I whirled back to face her, catching the slightly sarcastic grin that made its way across her beautiful face. "Very funny."

Her eyebrow went up again. "What makes you think I'm joking?"

I stared at her for a moment, then shook my head. Something told me there was more truth to those words than I wanted to hear.

The small space around us, and the energy with which we were filling it, became too intense suddenly. I'm afraid I took the coward's way out. "Well, I guess I should go now. I hope you enjoy your rake."

"I'm sure I will. And thank you."

I couldn't help it. I had to smile. "You're very welcome. Anytime. If you ever need anything else, just remember who can get it for you."

"I'll keep that in mind."

"You do that. Well, I guess I'll see you around?" Intense as the situation was, part of me, a big part, was absolutely loathe to leave.

At her nod, I grinned again and walked to the barred door of the cell. Just at the threshold, I paused and turned back. "Ice?"

"Yes?"

"I just wanted to say that I'm sorry. About what happened last week. My words put you in a bad position and I want you to know that I never meant to do that."

"It's already forgotten."

"Thanks!" I paused, desperately trying to think of something to say, but my words, it seemed, had been all used up. "Well, goodbye, Ice."

"Goodbye, Angel."

As I stepped from the cell, not looking back, I felt a distinct sense of loss. But the knowledge that she had both forgiven me for my indiscretion and allowed me into a place where no one else had ever gone warmed me like a blanket on a cold winter morning. I carried that feeling within me and savored it at odd moments.

It was a good day.

Chapter 3

The next several weeks plodded on in their usual interminable fashion. As before, I spent most of my time in the library, cataloguing, writing, teaching and chatting with Corinne and the others who also made this place their home. I continued my daily workouts with the Amazons and sometimes, if I was lucky, Ice would join us for a bit.

When that happened, invariably what seemed like half of the prison would gather around, watching her athletic form go through its paces while badgering and begging her for the finer points of some of her varied fighting techniques. Some questions she just ignored, while others she would answer with a demonstration, using one or another of the Amazons as a sparring partner.

Like the others, I watched her every move and when I wasn't drooling over the perfection of her body, I was taking furious mental notes, learning everything I could from a woman who was, in my estimation, one of the greatest fighters ever. Not that I'd ever had cause to see many up close and personal, mind you. But, as you can no doubt tell by reading this far into my tale, when it comes to Ice, I can be quite biased.

One such morning found me out in the yard, my bare foot red and stinging from repeated kicks to the canvas heavy bag that continued to mock me with its smug complacency. My lesson today was round kicks and Pony, as always, was a patient teacher. She'd started off easy, marking a spot on the dirty canvas with a piece of cinder and asking me to kick at it repeatedly with my right leg, demanding that I hit the exact same spot with each blow. After I had managed to hit the mark flawlessly for what felt like three or four thousand repetitions, she moved the mark higher, then higher again until my body was completely laid out and I was forced to stand up on my toes just to launch the kick. The tendons in my groin bellowed out their protests quite stridently.

After missing the mark for the tenth time in a row, I stopped, panting lightly and putting my hands on my hips. "I can't do it, Pony. I'm just not tall enough."

Suddenly, the radiating heat of another body slid itself against my back as hands moved to displace my own from my hips. Long, tanned fingers took their place, splaying slightly against my abdomen. "Sure ya are," came the low, sultry voice in my ear, its tenor, combined with the supple strength of the body behind me, sending entirely different signals to the tendons, as well as other areas, in my groin.

The voice came at me again, caressing my senses as the warmth of strong flesh leached itself through the resilient fabric of my jumpsuit. "You're just not in the right position."

As you might have already guessed, at that point in time, I could think of no other position in the world that could have possibly been more right than the one I was in.

Strong hips thrust lightly against my backside, angling my pelvis so that my right side was slightly closer to the hanging bag. "It's all in the position-ing, Angel. Feel my body as I make the kick."

Melding us seamlessly together, Ice launched a light round kick to the topmost part of the heavy-bag. Even with a teasing shot, the chain rattled out its protest as the bag swayed as if blown by a violent wind. The feeling of Ice's body uncoiling against me as she released the blow was indescribable.

"Feel that?"

"Oh yes."

"Ready to give it a try?"

"Uh…maybe once more?" Yes, I could play stupid with the best of them, alright.

Her hands tightened around my hips as a long leg slashed into my vision, rocketing into the bag and, it seemed, managing to sway the entire building with its strength. The metal links holding the bag to the eaves groaned again as if they seriously considered snapping in a shower of rust just to protest the abuse they were receiving. "Better?"

"Oh yes, much better, thanks. I'm almost sure I've got it down now."

"Almost?" From the tone of the voice in my ear, I knew my game had been discovered and I tensed slightly, waiting for the inevitable.

After a second or two with nothing happening, I relaxed. "Yes, almost. Once more should do the trick."

"Are you sure?" Ice's tone was rich with suppressed mirth.

"Positive. Just one more time. That's all I need."

"Alright. Once more and then you're on your own."

"Check."

Once again, her hands tightened against me and I leaned back into the strength of her body as the muscles clenched, then loosened, their motion caressing my back with sensual abandon. Her long, thick, soft hair fanned across my shoulder and slid against my cheek, filling my nostrils with its wonderful fragrance. My eyes slipped closed and I imagine I had the goofiest grin of pure bliss stamped across my face.

Unfortunately, in my pleasure-filled haze, I had forgotten about the difference in our heights. When my eyes opened again, I caught the twinkle of perfect sapphires as they gazed back at me in amusement. "Ya can't learn much with your eyes closed, Angel."

"Were they closed?"

A faint smirk was all the answer I needed.

"Oh. Well…I was…feeling the kick. With my body. Like you told me. Right?"

"Feeling the kick."

"Right. With my body. Just like you said."

"And what did it feel like?"

Involuntarily, my eyes closed again. "Heavenly."

A burst of laughter told me that my comment had been uttered aloud. I felt the blush begin at my toes and spread at a record pace throughout the rest of my body. I made a weak try to escape the situation but Ice merely tightened her arms, pinning me to her body. "Don't worry about Pony. She's just taken one too many hits to the head."

"Hey!" my friend shouted in mock outrage, tears still rolling down her cheeks.

"Just ignore her," Ice said as she released her grip on my hips and stepped back away from me. It took all my effort not to step back with her, but one long look at Pony's still red face convinced me to stay where I was.

"Alright, Angel," Ice said from her place behind me, "try it now. Remember, it's all in the positioning of your body. Visualize the kick and then go for it."

Visualize the kick, she says. The only thing I can visualize right now are her arms around me again. Alright, Angel. Enough of that. You've got a job to do, so just go on and do it.

Taking a few deep breaths to calm my racing heart, I ran through the kick once more in my mind, visualized my foot hitting that high black mark, then let loose, twisting on my foot and shooting my leg out and up.

I grinned as I heard the satisfying *smack* of flesh against canvas and felt the bag give with the force of my kick. Pony, who was holding the bag to steady it for me, flew away, almost colliding with a weight bench.

"Yes!" I crowed.

Pony turned wide eyes to me. "Where in the *world* did that come from?"

With a triumphant smirk of my own, I narrowed my eyes at my astounded friend. "Let's just say I needed the right motivation."

A soft snort sounded behind me and I whirled in time to see Ice quickly cover her mouth with her fingers as her eyes shot skyward in an expression of devilish innocence. When her fingers came away again, her usual no nonsense expression was settled firmly over her features. "Alright, you did it once. Good. Now keep practicing until you can hit that same spot repeatedly without missing."

I groaned.

She narrowed her eyes at me, then her expression cleared. "Angel, look. This stuff isn't easy, but if you want the tools needed to defend yourself against some of these idiots, you've got to practice." She smiled slightly. "Besides, you're a natural. You've got a good, strong, compact body with a low center of gravity."

"You mean I'm short."

"No. I mean you've got a good, strong, compact body with a low center of gravity. Makes you hard to hit. Plus, you're quick. If you try one of those high kicks at an opponent, say Derby's size, you'll surprise the hell outta her."

I nodded. "Surprise is good. Surprise is great, as a matter of fact. I just...."

"What?"

I sighed, feeling my shoulders slump slightly. "I just wish I didn't have to learn all this. Don't get me wrong, I know I have to learn to defend myself. I just wish I could learn without having to hurt anyone else, that's all."

Ice stepped close once again, reaching out and laying both hands on my shoulders. Her gaze was deep and direct and utterly serious. "Angel, in a place like this, sometimes you don't have a choice."

As she stood looking at me, the silence drawing out between us, I could tell she could feel the strength of my convictions because her eyes changed color with her thoughts. After a moment, she stepped away and turned toward Pony. "Come at me."

Pony blinked. Then a slow, pleased grin spread across her face. "Alright." She rolled her neck in slow circles, loosening the tendons, then jerked her head sharply left, then right. The resulting sounds of vertebrae realigning themselves made me faintly nauseous.

Then, with a shout, she threw herself at Ice, her hands, feet, arms and legs a wild blur of motion. It reminded me of nothing so much as one of those horridly dubbed Japanese 'kung fu' films that my father used to watch in lieu of going to church on Sunday mornings. I can remember being too sick to go to church a few times and snuggling on the couch with my father, trying hard not to laugh at the seemingly outlandish fight sequences lest my absorbed parent chase me from the room and back into my boring old bed.

Watching some of those same moves in person, however, gave me an entirely new respect for the techniques I'd only laughed about in the past. Wild though they seemed, each strike was furiously controlled, aimed at one specific part of the body, and determined to do as much damage with as little effort as possible.

Pony was truly a sight to behold with her slashing limbs and wild, almost feral smile.

Ice was a different beast altogether. Her eyes half lidded and almost bored, she blocked each and every blow with seemingly lazy ease, turning Pony's blows away and bleeding their strength while doing nothing to counterattack. The muscles of her body were loose and relaxed, her breathing even and steady.

I watched with absorbed fascination as I noticed that none of the slashing blows came anywhere near hitting her, though it was obvious that Pony was doing her level best to connect. Rather than become frustrated, however, Pony simply changed combinations and angles, coming in high, then low, then low again, trying to confuse her opponent.

Ice wasn't buying into the rapidly shifting tactics, content to maintain her 'lion lazing in the sun' pose as she used her long arms and legs to continue to shunt the blows coming at her from all directions.

The mock battle began to draw spectators from all corners of the yard, but I was adamant on maintaining my position at the head of the crowd, using my 'good, strong, compact body' and my 'low center of gravity' effectively. Ice watched me from the corner of her eye, grinning slightly as she saw me stubbornly battling the crushing press of the crowd at my back and sides.

Pulling out another weapon in her arsenal, Pony twisted her body, then launched a truly spectacular spinning back kick at Ice's midsection. Her reaction faster than a striking cobra, Ice neatly caught Pony's outstretched foot, turning the ankle outward just to the point of snapping.

Pony yelped, then slapped her thigh with her open hand, calling 'mercy' with the action.

After another second, Ice released Pony's foot and grinned as the other woman hopped backwards, cursing and rubbing her ankle. "You know that move never works on me, Pony. Why do ya keep on trying it?"

Planting her aching foot on the ground, Pony put her hands on her hips and scowled. "Because it works on everyone else, and one day, Ice…."

Ice snorted. "Dream on." Then she turned to me, eyebrow raised in silent question.

I nodded. "That was good."

"Alright, Pony. Get Montana and Critter to work with her. Half an hour of Aikido, half an hour of blocks. Hour and a half of each on Saturdays."

Pony nodded her dark head, her hair wet with the sweat of exertion. "You got it."

The warning bell sounded, ending the exercise period and I turned to Ice, smiling. "Thank you."

Nodding at me in acknowledgement, she turned and slapped Pony on the shoulder before stalking off toward the building, her boots kicking up tiny puffs of dust as she walked.

Pony came up to me, with her cocky grin and sweating form, and flung a casual arm around my shoulders, bulling us both through the dispersing crowd and back toward the prison that was our home.

"That was fantastic, Pony. How long did it take you to learn all those moves?"

She shrugged. "I've always been into karate and other forms of martial arts. Got my black belt when I was fifteen or so. When Ice was here before, she really helped me out a lot. Still can't beat her though."

"Do you think you ever will?"

"Nah. She's way beyond anything that's out there." She grinned again, that wild, free grin that sparkled her dark eyes. "Sure is fun to try though." Releasing me as we stepped into the building, she turned. "Heading back to the library?"

"Yeah. You?"

"Down to grab a shower. Tell Corinne I said hello, alright?"

"Will do. Thanks again, Pony."

With a rakish grin and an imaginary tip of a hat, she turned from me and was gone, her orange-clad form swallowed up by the long, dank halls of the prison.

I too continued down the hall a few more yards, then made a left into the library, catching a flash of orange as another inmate entered ahead of me. And found myself almost plowing right into the broad back of Ice as she stood just within the entrance to the room. Excusing myself hastily, I stepped away, watching as a huge smile crossed Corinne's face. "As I live and breathe. The great Morgan Steele has actually graced my library with her presence!" Standing, my friend grasped beneath her left breast in mock pain. "Take me now, Lord! I've finally lived to see it all!"

Smiling slightly, Ice shook her head and walked over to the desk, meeting Corinne half way and enveloping her in a massive hug.

I could feel my face go tight in shocked reaction as I watched the scene play out before me. In the time I'd known her, though not long, to be sure, I'd never *ever* seen Ice be so physically affectionate with anyone. In a way, it was akin to watching a statue come to life and grab an unsuspecting passerby. I was stunned.

Stepping away from the hug, Corinne held Ice at arm's length, looking her up and down. "My God. I thought growth spurts were supposed to stop at eighteen! You're even taller than when I saw you last!"

Ice rolled her eyes. "Corinne, I saw you last week."

"Yes, I do seem to remember someone grunting at me as I passed by in the hallway. Was that you? And here I thought we'd obtained a penitentiary pig."

"Corinne...."

Slapping Ice lightly on the arm, Corinne backed away, grinning unrepentantly. "So, what brings you into my evil web? Come to talk to an old, and I'm not getting any younger by the way, friend? Or was it something else?"

"Well, actually, I was wondering if that book I'd ordered had come in yet."

Corinne tapped her chin, her eyes twinkling. "Book. Book. Ah yes. The Gulag Archipelago, wasn't it?"

"*You* read Solzhenitsyn?" I blurted out before I could ram my foot down my throat.

Ice did a slow turn, facing me with narrowed eyes. "Something wrong with that?"

"No! No, not at all! I was just...um...he's one of my favorite writers."

As she continued to stare at me, I turned my eyes pleadingly to Corinne.

"Don't mind Angel. She's just a literary snob. Doesn't think the rest of us common folk could tell the difference between Dostoevski and Doonesbury."

"Corinne!"

Smirking, Ice turned back to Corinne, hands on her hips. "So, is it in yet?"

"Something I've asked my husbands many a time, my dear, though the answer in this case would be no."

"Alright, then. Would you please send someone to tell me when it *does* come in?"

"Ah, ah, ah, dear Ice. Not so fast. You're in my domain now, where I rule as Sovereign. Now sit down at that table over there, relax, and drink some tea or else!"

"Or else *what?*"

"Never you mind 'or else what', Ice. The tea's ready and waiting to be drunk. Get that cute little butt of yours over to that table and sit down."

There are times when I could cheerfully yank my tongue from my throat, and this was definitely such a time. A laugh erupted before I could stop it, earning me another icy-eyed glare from my intimidating companion. I winced, expecting some form of retribution, only to relax when none was immediately forthcoming.

Ice turned back to Corinne and the air became thick and heated with the intensity of their stare-down. After a long moment of utter silence, Ice threw up her hands and turned on her heel. "Fine." Stalking over to the table, she pulled out a chair, turned it, and sat down, straddling the back.

Corinne grinned triumphantly, though her eyes still held that teasing sparkle. "Good Lord, Ice, you were doing 'petulant' when you were fifteen! I would have thought that would have been one of the things you'd have grown out of by now."

"Just pour the damn tea, Corinne, or I'll show you some other things I haven't grown out of."

Tipping me a wink, Corinne turned and busied herself at the teapot, humming gleefully. A few moments later, she returned, bearing two steaming mugs, one of which she set before Ice, and the other slid home in the space beside the tall woman. "Such a bully," she murmured, patting Ice affectionately on the shoulder. Then she turned to me, hands on hips. "Well, what are you waiting for? The Second Coming? Get on over here, Angel, and stop acting like you're watching two dogs going at it in the front yard."

Blushing and properly chastised, I slowly walked over to the other side of the table. Slouching gingerly into my seat to avoid any more scathing commentary, I meekly took the offered mug and sipped down the hot tea, my eyes studiously avoiding the other two women.

"She takes to teasing almost as bad as you do," she stage-whispered to Ice.

"I wonder why," Ice remarked drolly. "You should have that tongue of yours declared a lethal weapon and confiscated as contraband."

Corinne smirked. "Then what would all my lady-friends think?"

A fine spray of hot tea spewed forth from my lips at Corinne's remark, managing to douse part of the table and part of, to my utter mortification, Ice. As Ice jumped from her chair, batting at the hot droplets clinging to her skin, Corinne collapsed against the table, howling with laughter.

I rose from my chair quickly, trying to help clean her arm, when Ice batted my hands away. "Please," I begged, "let me help you."

"No. No, you've done enough. Just sit back down."

Corinne laughed harder, slapping her hand down on the table, which caused the mugs to jitter violently, tea splashing over their sides and adding to the mess already there.

Ice walked over to the hidden hotplate and grabbed one of Corinne's neatly pressed linen handkerchiefs, dabbing the scalding liquid from her skin and uniform. All of our heads turned sharply toward the door as a badly out of breath Critter came to a sliding halt, just inside the library. "Ice," she panted, grasping her heaving chest, "you gotta come quick. Psycho broke out and she's got a shiv at some guard's neck. She's asking for you."

"Shit." Throwing the rag down on the table next to the teapot, Ice bolted from the room, Critter hard on her heels.

Corinne and I exchanged a look before I too jumped to my feet and ran out the door, trying hard to keep Critter's bobbing curls in sight.

🐾   🐾   🐾   🐾

As I look over these notes I've written, it occurs to me that you, the reader, are probably wondering exactly who Psycho is and why she needed to speak to Ice. As your faithful chronicler, it is my sworn duty to keep you informed, and so I shall.

The first thing you should know is that, although her prison nickname was 'Psycho', no one ever, *ever* called her that to her face. Her birth name was Cassandra Smythson, and that was the name she went by in the Bog.

The second thing you should know is that Cassandra was dangerously insane. A battery of psychiatrists performed a battery of tests to prove it. She was floridly psychotic but had many moments of perfect lucidity. She was also obsessive/compulsive, and one of her obsessions was Ice.

Cassandra had been in the Bog since she was eighteen, making her a resident for six years as of the time of the events I shall soon be recounting. When she was eighteen, and a senior in high school, Cassandra had come home after a night of drinking and drugging, to find her mother waiting for her. Words were exchanged and Cassandra went into the kitchen, pulled out a butcher knife, and proceeded to stab her mother thirty-seven times. The coroner stated that, based on the level of blood loss, fully ninety percent of the wounds were inflicted post-mortem. Then she went through the house and killed her two younger brothers as well as her sister, who was three.

After spending the night in the house with the dead bodies of her entire family, she went into school and killed three fellow classmates. She was working on her teacher when the captain of the football team rushed in and managed to subdue her, though not until he had suffered numerous cuts of his own in addition to a concussion and the loss of his previously capped front teeth.

It's no lie to say that it was obvious to everyone that Cassandra Smythson was totally crazy. The police knew it, the judge knew it, the psychiatrists proved it, and the public knew it. The best thing anyone could have possibly done for all concerned was to put her into a nice, safe, secure mental institution and throw away the key.

That, of course, wasn't to be. Juries being what they are sometimes, Cassandra was found competent to stand trial, and did so. Her guilt was a foregone conclusion, though a lot of credit should go to her team of lawyers. They did the best they could and put on a very strong case that pointed almost every finger imaginable toward her insanity.

The jury didn't buy into it and found her guilty of seven counts of first-degree murder. The judge should have taken the tiger by the tail and sentenced her to life in a facility for the criminally insane. Instead, in a show of infinite 'wisdom', he decided to take the jury's recommendation, and so Cassandra Smythson joined the 'lifer's club' at the Bog.

After a full month in the segregation unit, Cassandra was released into the general population. Two days later, she murdered an inmate, luring her into the laundry room (here's a hint from yours truly: if you ever find yourself in prison, stay *away* from the laundry room. Lots of bad things happen there) and stuffing her into an industrial-strength drier, setting the temperature on 'high' and leaning against the door for close to an hour, laughing and singing to cover the sound of the inmate's weakening screams.

After this little fiasco, the Division of Prisons demanded that she be placed in an insane asylum. The judge would hear nothing of the plea, issuing a counter demand, backed by a judicial order, to keep her locked up in the Bog.

The Warden decided to place Cassandra in the only secure place in the prison, the segregation unit, where she was to be locked into her cell twenty three hours a day, to be let out only for a shower and a brief walk around the yard, fully manacled and under strict supervision.

While this arrangement was infinitely better for the safety of the other inmates, it did nothing for their sense of peace. When deep into her psychosis, Cassandra would throw herself into the bars of her cell, screaming at the top of her lungs for hours without rest.

For obvious reasons, the time new inmates spent in segregation was cut from one to two weeks to two to five days. And still, most of the new ones would come out of their time in the unit white faced and shaking, needing nothing so much as a nice, long, quiet rest in their new cells.

After six months, or so I'm told, Cassandra began to calm down and her screaming outbursts didn't occur so frequently. Many of the guards felt that she was finally becoming accustomed to her new home. They soon found out the truth.

Many penitentiaries have stories of inmates who are well known for keeping, taming and loving pets of the animal variety. Alcatraz had its Birdman. The Bog had Cassandra.

It seems that an industrious gray rat found its way into both Cassandra's cell and her heart. Now, rats are very intelligent creatures who are easily trained to respond to the sound of their names being called by their owners. This particular rat, whom Cassandra named 'Heracles', was a fine representative of his species. In seemingly no time at all, the insane inmate had him doing little tricks for her, which in turn kept her subdued and quiet.

Cassandra's favorite trick was to wait until a new inmate had settled in for the night and was sound asleep in an adjacent cell. Then she would release Heracles, who would scamper through the bars and into the new one's cell, climb up the stiffly starched and threadbare sheets, and nose around until his twitching whiskers found bare flesh. Then he would stand there, doing his best impersonation of an innocent rat, while the inmate would scramble away, screaming as if all the demons of hell were at her heels.

Cassandra would throw her platinum blonde head back and laugh, an insane cackle that seemed to cut through your soul like the butcher knife she'd wielded with such devastating results.

Obviously, this behavior resulted in regular trips by the guards into Cassandra's cell, trying to take her prized pet from her. And, of course, the insane woman would go into a fit of fury until the guards just threw up their hands in capitulation and let her keep Heracles, with the admonition that she never do it again. It never worked.

No one knows exactly why Cassandra's other obsession was Ice. The two never talked, but when Cassandra would be led around the exercise yard like a dog on a leash, her deep brown eyes would remain pinned to Ice's long form for the duration, her face totally expressionless.

So concludes my exposition on the woman known as Psycho. Now, back to the story.

    ♪   ♪   ♪   ♪

I finally caught up to Critter just as she reached the second floor landing where the segregation unit was housed. All I could see before me was a press of brown-clad bodies standing stiffly, their night-sticks at the ready. Ice had just parted the crowd, stepping to Sandra Pierce's side as I ran forward, and the guards closed ranks behind her, blocking my view once again.

Grabbing my hand, Critter led me around to the side of the crowd and from there, I could peek over the head of one of the shorter guards by standing on my toes and lifting my head as high as it would go. A stiff neck and aching calves were but a small price to pay to assuage my curiosity.

Cassandra was standing just outside the barred steel door that led into the segregation unit. She had one of the newer guards, a thin, sour-faced woman named Carla, in a headlock and had a steel shiv placed on the woman's pronounced jugular. When Ice stepped through the crowd, Cassandra's face split with a coy grin. "Well, hello there, my dear Ice. So glad you could join my little party." Her sing-song voice was high-pitched like that of a young girl and her brown eyes were dark with insane glee.

"What do you want, Cassandra," Ice stated bluntly.

The other woman's head cocked to the side as her grin widened. "Isn't that so like you, Ice. No time for chit chat. Always busy." She tightened her grip on the guard's neck, who gasped wheezingly. "What do I want. What *do* I want? Well, let's see. I'd like world peace. A cure for cancer." Her grin turned malicious. "And to stick my little tool deep into this little piggy's neck and feel my hands turn hot with her blood." She winked. "Does that answer your question, pretty?"

"Cassandra…."

"Oh please, Ice. Must you be so formal? Just call me Psycho. All my friends do." Her leer returned as she ran her eyes brazenly over Ice's orange-clad form. "And I consider you one of my…closest…friends."

Ice turned to Sandra. "What happened?"

Cassandra cut in before the guard had a chance to speak. "Oh yes, Sandra, do tell our dear Ice what happened. And don't leave out any of the details. While she listens to the whole sad story, I'll just play pincushion with my sweet little piggy here. You'd like that, wouldn't you piggy? Can you squeal for me? Squeal nicely for your Auntie Psycho?"

The captive guard uttered a sound best classified as a cross between a scream and a squeal, aided as she was by the sharp jab of Cassandra's shiv into the tender flesh of her neck.

"Oh, *very* good, little piggy. I just might have to keep you around to play with for a while. Would you like that?"

"Cassandra, please."

The blonde woman sighed. "Oh alright, Ice. You know, you really should learn to be less serious about things. You're so much more beautiful when you smile." She released her tense grip on the guard just slightly, laughing as her shiv came away with a droplet of blood. Sticking the pointed end of it into her mouth, her eyes rolled back in her head as she licked the blood from the weapon, making the action an erotic display.

Sandra turned her gaze to Ice. "The Warden got another complaint from one of the newbies. He sent Carla in to get rid of Heracles."

Ice's eyes narrowed in anger. "Damn it, Sandra. That was just stupid."

The guard lifted her hands in a placating gesture. "I know, I know. And Carla broke the rules by not asking me first." She shot a glare to the captive guard who returned it with frightened eyes.

"Where's Heracles now?"

Sandra gestured. "Still in her cell. She grabbed the guard before Carla could make it inside. We've been standing here ever since."

"And what a *wonderful* stand-off it is too, wouldn't you agree, Ice? All these big bad guards against li'l ol' me. Whatever shall I do?" Grinning evilly once again, Cassandra pricked Carla's neck once again, laughing as blood welled up in the tiny puncture. The guard screamed again.

"Alright, Cassandra, that's enough!" Ice demanded. "You've made your point. Now let her go."

Cassandra moued her lips. "No can do, I'm afraid. No, this little pig needs to be taught a lesson. The only reason I asked you here, Ice, is that I know, of all the other little rodents in this festering boil they call a jail, you're the one who would most enjoy the sight of a good kill."

"Cassandra, please. You've already scared whatever little sense she might have had right out of her. Killing her will accomplish nothing."

"Perhaps not," Cassandra agreed. Then she grinned once again. "But it'll make me feel good. And I do *so* enjoy feeling good." The insane woman turned her gaze to the side a moment, then looked back at Ice, her eyes blazing with new purpose. "Tell you what. I'll give up this little pig of mine if you agree to take her place, Ice. Does that sound good? Think about it. You…me…together. Doesn't the thought of it make your blood run *hot?*"

Sandra stepped forward. "Forget it, Cassandra."

The inmate brought up her shiv again. "Stay out of this, head sow, or there'll be one less pig in the pen."

Grabbing Sandra back by the sleeve of her uniform, Ice stared down at the head guard. "Let me do this, Sandra. It's the only way this is gonna end."

"Listen to her, Sandra!" Cassandra crowed. "Ice has a fine mind trapped within that beautiful skull of hers."

"Ice, I can't let you do this. It's totally against procedure."

"*Fuck* procedure! Your procedure went right out the window the minute your guard went into Cassandra's cell alone."

"Ice…."

"Sandra, listen. This is the only way to resolve things. I'll be alright."

"Oh, she'll be *very* alright," Cassandra supplied.

"Ice, I can't."

"Then I'm not giving you a choice. You'll have to stop me, and I don't think you wanna do that." Ice's eyes grew cold and flinty. Sandra looked down after a moment. "Alright, Cassandra, we'll do it your way. Send the guard over here and I'll come to you."

"Sorry, Ice. I run the show here, in case you hadn't noticed. I'm the one with all the cards, after all. No, you come to me first. *Then* I release the little piggy."

"Alright, fine." Before anyone could think to stop her, Ice strode toward Cassandra, who tightened her hold around Carla's neck. Holding up her empty hands, Ice allowed the other woman to grab her by the arm while releasing her tight grip on Carla. Bringing her leg up, Cassandra kicked the guard back to the others, then twisted Ice's arm up behind her, putting the shiv to the taller woman's elegant neck. "Oh, Ice," she said in a throaty voice, "this is *so* much better. To think of all the nights I've *dreamed* of this. You in my arms, my knife at your beautiful throat. I'm getting chills just thinking about it. And now I have you."

Ice stayed as calm and collected as her nickname, her demeanor giving nothing away. "Alright, Cassandra, ya got me. What now?" The blonde's eyes became unfocused with thought. "Now? Well ya know? I hadn't really thought about that. I suppose I could kill you like the sweet little sacrificial lamb you are, but then I'd never see you again and that would be a pity." She rested her chin on Ice's broad shoulder, apparently deep in thought with what few working brain cells she still managed to possess. Then a smile lit up her face and she straightened behind my friend. "Got it. I'll let you go, my beauty, if you, in return, will fulfill two…small…conditions for me."

Ice's raven brow hiked upward to hide behind her bangs. "And those would be?"

"First you must promise to speak to that disgusting little warden on my behalf. Convince him that my sweet little Heracles is here to stay if he wants peace in his jail. Would you do that for me, Ice?"

"No promises, Cassandra, but I can try."

"That's all I ask. I know how…persuasive…you can be…when you set your mind to it."

"And the other condition?"

"Kiss me."

The other brow joined the first. "What?"

"Kiss me. Right here. Right now. Declare your passion for me in front of God and guards." Her grin became hard at Ice's surprised hesitation. "Answer me quickly, Ice, or you'll be trying to breathe through the hole I'm going to put in your neck."

"Alright," Ice drawled in a deadly soft voice, a totally feral smile putting its stamp across her features.

"Oh goody!" Cassandra chirped, pulling the shiv away as she turned Ice to face her. Turning her head to the side, she looked up into Ice's stormy eyes, her expression one of well-feigned innocence. "Will you lead or shall I?"

Smirking, Ice lowered her dark head, by slow degrees, the raven fan of her hair all but eclipsing Cassandra's fair features. I stared on, gape-jawed with shock and, if I'm to be totally truthful here, more than a bit envious, even with the current conditions.

The kiss was raw, hard, almost exactly how I pictured a kiss from Ice to be. As her mouth covered the soft, full lips of Cassandra, the blonde woman's eyes rolled back in her head as her eyelids fluttered, then closed completely. A deep moan sounded forth from her throat, clearly audible to everyone looking on.

A tan, long fingered hand threaded itself through the fall of Cassandra's hair, pulling them closer together as Ice deepened the kiss, seeming to devour the smaller woman's mouth with her own. Several of the guards shifted position. I shifted position, suddenly aware how intensely hot it had gotten in the prison. A hand clapped my shoulder, and when I turned my head, Critter was grinning and shaking her head. "Whoo hoo," she mouthed.

I nodded back, fervently, while another part of me sat back in shock at my supposed enjoyment of such a deadly situation.

Ice moved her other arm slowly from its place behind her back, trailing sensual fingers up Cassandra's thin, but beautiful, body. The moans increased in intensity, causing more shifting by the watching guards. Up those beautiful fingers went, playing over a firm, flat abdomen, trailing over full, firm breasts, across a jutting collarbone and down the nearest arm.

Even from where I was standing, I could see the gooseflesh that followed Ice's touch. I'm afraid I shivered at the sight, my own skin prickling in empathetic reaction as I imagined those fingers trailing over my own skin.

Then, with a swiftness that brought me out of my erotic haze, Ice's thumb jabbed at the nerves in Cassandra's wrist, causing the smaller woman to drop her shiv. With smooth economy, Ice brought Cassandra's arm behind her back, breaking the kiss and stepping behind the blonde woman as she did so.

Cassandra blinked in dazed confusion, her free hand coming up to finger suddenly chilled lips.

The troupe of guards rushed in then, bulling Cassandra down to the ground and quickly slipping handcuffs onto her slim wrists. One of the guards grabbed the shiv, tucking it away safely as Sandra pulled the blonde up by one arm. "Anyone call the State Hospital?" the lead guard called out.

"Yeah, Sandra. They're on their way."

"Good. I hope they manage to keep her locked up for more than twenty four hours, like last time." She turned a relieved look to Ice. "Even though you nearly cost me my job, Ice, thanks. You saved at least one life here. I owe you."

"No problem."

"You gonna talk to the Warden?"

Ice nodded, straightening her uniform. "Yeah. I made a promise. I'm gonna keep it."

Sandra returned the nod. "Good luck."

"Thanks."

The head guard grunted, tugging the bound inmate along. "C'mon, Cassandra. Let's go see your nice, new padded cell, shall we?"

"Eat dirt, pig," Cassandra replied, pursing her lips and spitting at the guard's face. "Goodbye for now, my dear Ice! Don't forget to write! I'll miss you!"

Shaking her head and dusting herself off again, Ice headed in the direction of Critter and myself, a totally disgusted look on her face.

"That was one for the books, Ice," Critter said, grinning.

"Yeah, whatever."

"Good luck with the warden," I supplied.

"For all the good it'll do." Turning on her heel, she strode down the stairs and off toward the separate building that housed the warden's quarters. Our eyes followed her as she went.

"I'm gonna have to add that particular 'kiss 'em senseless and then disarm 'em' move to my repertoire," my friend commented softly. "I'll be the happiest fighter in the Bog."

"Yeah, if you don't try and use it against Derby."

"Well *that* image just ruined my lunch! Thanks a lot, Angel." She elbowed me in the side. "And here I thought you were my friend."

Laughing and clapping Critter on the back, I turned and left the scene, the images of the kiss playing in a continuous loop through my head, despite my best efforts to stop them.

An hour later, Ice came back into the main prison, her expression stony, her eyes cold and furious. The inmates she passed on her trek, myself among them, ducked quickly out of her way, lest that piercing glance be cast our way. As she stalked up the stairs on her way to her cell, I couldn't help but wonder just what went on inside the warden's office.

Though I wasn't to find out what happened between Ice and the warden until some time later, something good *did* come of the meeting. Heracles got to stay.

There was a celebration in the Bog that evening.

✎ ✎ ✎ ✎

Nights are very long and very dark when you're an inmate. Time passes in eons instead of seconds. Your cell is freezing in the winter, when the storms come down from Canada, entrenching the old stone prison in a block of unblemished ice. In the summer, it becomes a sauna. If you listen hard enough, you can almost hear the heat as it insidiously radiates its way through the permeable concrete blocks, bathing you in its sticky essence.

As you lay in your narrow bunk at night, counting the lumps in your mattress and hoping you aren't sharing your sleeping space with creatures of the animal or insect variety, you can't help but hear the mournful sound of the wind as it whistles through the gables or the ghostly knocking noises that sound as the plumbing settles in for the night. Sounds of snoring, shouts and solitary pleasures filter through the bars of your cell on silent currents.

Your mind becomes your enemy during long prison nights when the lights have been shut off, turning your world into a darkness full of wanton killers. If you close your eyes to the darkness, you might imagine yourself in some faraway fantasy land with freedom as your most cherished possession. But, in darkness or light, the living reality of your condition exists in the form of a cold barred door not five feet away, standing silent sentinel over your dreams.

The memory of the kiss was with me that hot summer night. As I tossed and turned against my sweat-damp sheets, fruitlessly trying to get it out of my mind, darkness and silence conspired to taunt me, giving my thoughts no other direction in which to turn.

Over and over I saw Ice's sleek, dark head lower, her full lips encompassing those of a waiting Cassandra. I could almost see their tongues sliding against one another as they dueled in a sensual battle for supremacy.

I wondered again what it felt like to be Cassandra Smythson in that minute. How did it feel to be turned from predator to prey by the power of a kiss? How did it feel to be pressed up against the heat of that strong, perfect body? What was it like to feel those long, tapering fingers draw their way up your body, leaving trails of sensation in their wake?

When my hands started to roam in the direction of my thoughts, my mind made a firm decision to cease and desist. Taking matters into my own hands was something I hadn't done since I entered the Bog and if I was very lucky, that record would remain unblemished.

Blowing out a sigh of frustration, I turned over on my side, punched my pancake-flat pillow a few times and tried to get past the visions in my head.

Sleep, when it finally came, was anything but restful.

As the last warm days of summer gave way to the cool chill of fall, the colorful autumn leaves signaled my anniversary. One year behind bars. I was no longer the young girl who had first entered the building, trembling and crying so hard that every figure I passed seemed to glow with shimmering radiance as they taunted me and hollered names at me I had never heard shouted in quite that context before.

No, I was a year older, a year wiser. The Bog was still a very frightening place, but in that time, it had managed to become, in a fit of morbid perversity, a home to me and many of its inmates, family. I never really understood the phrase 'Institutional man' until the first morning I woke up after a sound sleep without one memory of a terror-filled dream of incessant claustrophobia and total loss of freedom. Somewhere along the line in that year past, I had stopped looking at each morning as one step closer to eventual freedom and started looking forward to the adventure it would bring.

That doesn't mean that I didn't long for freedom, because I did, and still do. I ached for it the way one would ache for a drop of water in the desert. I yearned for it. Hungered for it. But I no longer obsessed over it. That, in its own way, was a very liberating feeling for me.

Without doubt, my friends aided me in this transformation. Corinne helped every day, being at turns scathing and grandmotherly. The Amazons helped, teaching me to be the best kind of fighter, the one who defends the weak, while at the same time lending me their friendship and support unconditionally. And Ice helped. The mystery of her kept my mind occupied during times when it might otherwise have dumped me into a vat of depression too deep to crawl away from.

In the days after the incident with Psycho and Heracles, Ice had remained very distant and withdrawn, spending most of her time in her cell, staring at nothing and talking to no one. But gradually, with the speed of an iceberg melting in an Antarctic winter, she began to come out of her self-imposed prison, letting us in again. Or at least as 'in' as anyone ever was allowed to go.

Much to the surprise and delight of Corinne, she would sometimes make the trek into the library where she would sit, sip tea, and listen as we talked, occasionally adding commentary when she felt it was warranted. Wordy she was not, but, as I came to find out, Ice possessed a keen intellect; a razor sharp mind that, had circumstances been different, would have caused her to come out at the top of whatever profession she chose. That made her situation all the more heart-breaking for me.

Sometimes we would sit beside one another at one of the tables, talking about our common interests. Solzhenitzyn invariably came up as a topic for conversation and debate. She would speak with a quiet intensity about his message of the true freedom one gained from oppression, be it the body, as in Cancer Ward, or the entire being, as in Day in the Life of Ivan Denisovich or The Gulag Archipelago. Her arguments were always well worded, well thought out, and shone forth with the true belief in his vision, a vision that she shared under much the same circumstances as the writer himself.

There were other times when I would sit, sipping my ever-present tea, and listen to the interplay between Ice and Corinne. Though they spent most of their time batting keenly edged barbs back and forth, there was a strong undercurrent of deep affection between the two. I'd be lying if I said I wasn't even slightly jealous over the relationship those two women shared. Ok, I was *a lot* jealous. At least at first. As close as I'd gotten to Corinne, there was a line I couldn't cross. A line I didn't even know existed until I saw her interact with Ice.

Conversely, I was jealous at the seeming ease with which Corinne seemed to bulldoze down those walls around Ice's heart. I had known Ice for almost six full months and had yet to scratch the surface of the most intense person I'll ever have the privilege to know. I wanted so badly to sink myself deep within her, to get a sense of that person I had seen in her eyes the day we first met. I knew it was there, waiting for me to take it. I just didn't know how.

Still, the passing days saw us drawing closer, if only by mere inches, and I contented myself with waiting, watching and listening, secure in the knowledge that I would one day find the magic needed to look into the window of her soul. After all, didn't a person have to peel back the tough skin of an orange to get to the succulent fruit beneath?

The coming of fall also brought with it an increase in tensions among the inmates. It was as if, knowing that the coming winter would force them to be in one another's intimate presence for the next several months, they were staking out claims on prime territory early, so as to avoid the rush.

This was especially prevalent in the yard, where many petty skirmishes over the least of imagined transgressions turned to all out bloody wars among the gangs. The Amazons had been very busy trying to keep the peace over the last week or so and, to my dismay, I hadn't seen very much of any of them, Ice included.

On one particular day, I decided to venture out into the yard. Early fall had been cool and rainy, keeping me inside most of the time. The lack of fresh air had been making me feel restless and edgy and the thought of four or five months more of the same caused Corinne quite pointedly to suggest that I either go outside for awhile or stay away from her library until I could force myself into a better mood.

Taking her not so subtle advice, I decided to take a walk outside. It was a Saturday, the one day when there were no outside restrictions, and so when I stepped out into the cool, but sunny, fall air, I couldn't help but notice that most of the prison seemed to want an open sky over their heads. The yard was crowded with prisoners and, near the basketball courts, the two largest gangs seemed to be getting ready for yet another tussle.

After recovering from her injuries, Derby managed to regain control of the white gang, wresting the leadership from Mouse. It appeared that surviving a beating from Ice gave her more status with her cronies than Mouse's surviving a beating from me.

Shaking my head and smiling a bit, I moved toward the weight area where Ice was standing, nonchalantly curling a fifty pound dumbbell as if she were lifting a feather pillow and spotting Critter who was gamely trying to bench press ninety pounds over her head.

As I walked, I allowed my eyes once again to drift back toward the two gangs who were massing like thunderclouds toward the center of the yard. The other gang's leader, a woman who went by the prison name of Trey, was currently standing nose to nose with Derby. I'd always liked Trey. She was a tall woman with dark skin and dark eyes and a wide, infectious smile. She had, at one time, been the shining hope of the Lady Vols basketball team and still retained that athletic physique. She'd come down to the library occasionally to pick up some books that would help her complete her Physical Therapy degree and we always got along well enough. I found her to be soft-spoken and intelligent and was really surprised when I found out that she was a gang leader. Since that time, of course, I've grown to understand gangs and gang leaders and have come to the realization that not everyone is a Derby or Mouse.

I finally joined my friends in the free weight area, coming to stand beside Sonny, who was doing some bicep curls of her own, albeit with much less weight than Ice was using. The entire group seemed casual and unconcerned about the potential gang fight. "Hi, Sonny. Looks like a storm's brewing over there."

Grinning a greeting at me, Sonny looked over to the growing groups of women. "Nah. They're just having a pushy fight."

"A what?"

"A pushy fight. You know. Derby pushes Trey. Trey pushes Derby. They trade insults on whose mother is the bigger whore." She shrugged. "Shit like that."

"And that doesn't concern you?" Looking back over my shoulder, I estimated that at least a hundred women from either side had joined in and the crowd was continuing to grow.

"Nope. Everything's cool right now. If it gets worse, we'll step in."

The sound of a heavy weight hitting the cracked concrete interrupted whatever more I might have had to say and I looked up, catching an orange streak flashing out of the corner of my eye as Ice blew by me. "Let me guess. It just got worse."

Sonny winked, dropped her own dumbbell and shot to her feet, grinning wildly. "Yup."

Turning fully toward the group, I watched as my friends jumped into the developing fray, led by Ice who leapt between the two gang leaders, one long leg lashing out strongly. My eyes followed the arcing path of a shiv as it flew through the air, tumbling end over end and flashing brightly as the sun winked off its metal finish. Critter was on the weapon in a flash, scooping it up and slipping it inside her jumpsuit.

Ice interposed her long body between the two lead combatants, grabbing Derby by the front of her jumpsuit and pulling the huge woman up onto her toes. Pony and Sonny each grabbed one of Trey's arms, holding her back. "You know the rules, Derby," my friend said in a low, even voice. "No weapons."

Derby was red-faced with anger. "Fuck off, Ice. This ain't your fight. You got no business interfering."

"When you pull a weapon, it becomes my business. You want those guards up in the towers to spray this place with bullets?"

"I don't give a flying fuck. Just as long as I get what I want."

"And you can get what you want without the shiv. I don't give a shit if you beat one another to death, but no weapons. Got me?"

At Ice's statement, I looked up, noticing that indeed the guards in the two towers nearest the altercation were standing on the catwalk, their rifles aimed and ready. I felt a little shiver of fear race down my back at the thought of a high-powered weapon being aimed at me or at my friends. I hoped Ice would be able to settle the dispute peacefully.

Looking around, I noticed the hard smiles on the faces of the inmate onlookers. Off in a corner, a woman was taking bets. It sickened me but I struggled not to let that sense of disgust show. It was like being present at an execution.

After a long moment of tense silence, Derby finally nodded and Ice let her go and stepped away. She turned her head toward Trey, nodding to the Amazons to let the other woman go, which they promptly did. "What about you, Trey? Have any weapons?"

Trey snorted. "Me? You think I need a knife to beat this two-bit wannabe honky piece of trash?"

Roaring, Derby lunged at Trey, to be stopped by Ice's firm hand against her chest.

"Answer my question, Trey."

"No. I don't have any weapons." She tipped a wink in Ice's direction. "But you're more than welcome to search me if you like."

At Ice's nod, Sonny and Pony patted down the taller inmate. "She's clean, Ice."

Ice smiled slightly. "Alright then. Have fun."

With a regal elegance all her own, the leader of the Amazons strode forth from the circle of inmates, the smirk on her face faintly pronounced. The prisoners closed ranks again as the Amazons followed Ice out of the crowd.

"So, what now?" I asked as my friends walked over to me. Behind them, the two gangs had resumed their tense stand-off.

Ice shrugged. "Guess they'll pound the shit outta one another and be done with it."

"What are they fighting over?"

Sonny stepped into the conversation. "Use of the basketball court. Derby wants it for her gang and Trey isn't willing to give it up peacefully."

"All this for a basketball court?"

Sonny shrugged. "It's territory. That's important to people like them. Law of the jungle."

I looked over at Ice, who wasn't inclined to disagree with Sonny's blunt assessment. "Well that's about the most ridiculous thing I've ever heard. They're willing to risk getting killed for a *sport*?"

"That's about the size of it," Critter replied.

In front of me, the voices had risen once again as Trey and Derby began to shove one another back into their respective groups. I could feel my own anger build up inside me. "This is just idiotic! I can't believe grown adults would stoop to something this…this…juvenile!"

"We're talking about hardened criminals here, Angel," Critter supplied. "Not exactly an Einstein in the bunch, ya know."

"Yeah," Sonny jumped in. "Besides, it's not as if this shit doesn't go on in the outside world. Whole empires have been overthrown for lesser reasons."

"That's ridiculous. We're not talking about the acquisition of land here."

"That's exactly what we're talking about," Ice interjected softly. "Trey's gang has the basketball court. Derby's gang wants it. It's that simple."

"And you don't see any problem with that," I replied, disbelief evident in my tone.

Ice shrugged. "As long as they stay outta my way and don't endanger anyone else, nope."

"Well I do." Giving them all a last baleful glare, I spun on my heel and started walking toward the huge crowd, determination in my every step.

As if surprised to see me with such an expression on my face, and I'm quite sure most of them were, what with me being Little Miss Innocent and all, the crowd parted and I slipped through the throng of onlookers without difficulty, managing to make it up to the very front. I stood there, hands on hips, waiting to be noticed.

After a moment, Trey turned her head to meet my gaze, a small smile playing over her lips. "You better get outta here, Angel. You're gonna get hurt."

Derby took that moment to chime in in her own literary style. "Yeah, fishie. Wouldn't wanna get that cute snatch of yours all busted up now, would ya? Your Amazon buddies wouldn't be happy if they didn't have their little play-toy around to fuck anymore."

She made as if to grab me, then froze, looking over my shoulder. I didn't have to turn to guess who was behind me and I'm afraid my smile grew rather smug. "Can I ask you a question?" I directed my words to both parties.

Derby grunted.

"What in the *hell* are you doing here?"

"What the fuck does it look like we're doin', fish? Playin' checkers?"

"What it looks like is two three-year-olds squabbling over a plastic shovel in the sandbox. I'd like to think that you're both a little more mature than that."

Derby scowled, no doubt trying to wrap her lumbering mind around the visual I provided. "Shows how much you know," she finally mumbled.

"Then tell me, Derby. Because I really want to understand."

Clenching and unclenching her fists, the huge woman looked down at the ground, unable to say anything.

I turned to Trey, who was standing there smirking at me. "What about you, Trey? Can you tell me why you're doing this? I thought you were more intelligent than this."

The tall gang leader shrugged. "Intelligence doesn't have anything to do with it, Angel. It's a simple matter of space and possession. There isn't much in the pen you can call your own. This is ours. Someone comes along and wants to take it from us, we fight. Nothing more to it than that."

"You *do* realize that the guards could come out here and take it from you in a second, right?"

Trey smiled that dazzling grin of hers. "Course I realize that, Angel. We all realize that. But until the guards come and take it away from us, we'll fight to keep it. They have their space, we have ours. It keeps us happy. Well, for the most part, anyway."

I sighed and scratched my chin, trying to think of some logical argument that would sway her to my view of things. "Alright. How about if you guys trade up? Derby's gang takes the basketball court and Trey's gang takes the softball field. Would that work?"

"What the fuck are you, crazy?" Derby exploded. "Ain't no fucking way we're givin' up the field!"

"But I thought you wanted the basketball court."

"I *do* want the fuckin' basketball court, ya idiot! *And* want the field!"

"And what are you going to do if you get the basketball court?"

Derby squinted her eyes at me. "You mental in there or somethin'? We're gonna fuckin' play basketball on it!"

Taking a deep, cleansing breath, I slowly counted to ten, willing my frustration to drain away. "Alright then, how about this? It seems like you're willing to beat each other's brains in for a few square feet of broken concrete and rusty backboards, right?"

"Now ya get it, fish. Very good."

"Well, instead of fighting for it, why don't you play for it?"

"Play what? Fuckin' Twister?"

There are some moments in every person's life when they fantasize about seeing whether it really is possible to twist someone's head off. This was one of those moments.

Luckily, Trey took that moment to step in and save me from my second, and this one intentional, murder. "Basketball, Derby. She wants us to play basketball."

"Well no *shit*, Sherlock! That's what we're fightin' about, ain't it??"

Trey rolled her eyes. "Against each other, Derby. Am I right, Angel?"

I smiled in relief. "Exactly right, Trey. Five of your best against five of Derby's best in a 'winner-take-all' game. You win, you keep the court. They win, they get it. Make sense?"

Derby did her level best to imitate a large-mouth bass, and I must say, her effort was a good one. If I'd have had a pebble in my hand, I might have been tempted to play my own little basketball game. Forcing my evil thoughts down and away, I simply waited for Derby to fully process my idea.

Trey stepped to my rescue once again. "I think that sounds like a great idea, Angel."

"Thanks," I replied, grinning at her.

Nodding, she turned her attention to the still gaping Derby. "How 'bout you, white bread? You up for a little five-on-five?"

After a moment, the large woman nodded vehemently. "You got it, spade. I'll wipe up the court with your ass."

"Yeah, if you can even *see* the court past that inflated tire you call a belly, honkey. Your fat gut'll be bouncing more than the ball!"

I rolled my eyes, tensing up as the two behemoths started going at it again. This was definitely not what I had in mind when I started this little windmill tilting expedition. "Enough, you two. Save it for the game, alright?"

"Alright," Derby spat. "Fine. We get Ice."

That statement caused the courtyard to erupt. Derby's gang was shouting in frenzied appreciation while Trey's gang was protesting quite loudly.

"Forget it!" Ice's low timber was easily heard above the din of the crowd. The inmates went silent. "It's your game. You play it."

"At least referee, Ice!" someone shouted, to the agreement of the rest.

Ice held up her hands. "Oh no. No thanks. It was Angel's idea. Let her ref."

I spun on my heel, wide-eyed. "Are you joking? Look at me, Ice! I wouldn't last a second with these monoliths. You'd do much better." I tried out a smile. "Besides, you're much more intimidating than I am." As I met her eyes, my smile deepened. I just couldn't help myself. And if you ever had the chance to look into those perfect sapphires, you wouldn't either. I decided to go for broke when it looked like she wasn't going to waver. "Please?"

"C'mon, Ice!" another inmate shouted.

"Yeah, c'mon!"

Isolated pleas continued from the crowd until Ice finally relented. "Fine. Be here tomorrow at noon. Whoever wins gets the court for the next year and all my decisions are final. Got it?"

The courtyard erupted again, the inmates joining together in mutual excitement of the next day's contest. Chancing a look into the corner of the yard, hard by the fence, I saw the resident bookie had garnered some helpers and was doing a brisk business.

Shaking my head at the sheer unreality of it all, I graciously accepted words and pats of congratulations as I made my way from the center of the melee.

"Great job, Angel!" Critter shouted as she came over to me and slung an arm around my shoulders, hugging me briefly as we walked. "When they spring ya, you should apply for a job at the UN. Those bureaucratic idiots could use people like you!"

Blushing, I allowed Critter to lead me back to the free weight area, where Ice was lounging on one of the benches, watching me with a smile on her face.

I stopped before her. "I hope I didn't break any rules or anything."

The smile broadened, sucking me in. "No. Ya did alright."

My blush deepened, beyond pleased at the unexpected compliment. "Really?"

"Really. Great job of negotiating there."

"Thanks. And thank you for watching my back. And agreeing to referee. I really appreciate that."

"No problem. Ya owe me one."

My mother was always fond of telling me that when someone opened a door, you'd best go through it before it slammed in your face. "You name the time, Ice, and I'll name the place."

The other Amazons went absolutely silent at my bold comment. From the corner of my eye, I could see incredulous expressions on every face save one. Ice narrowed her eyes at me in an expression that became extremely predatory and caused my mouth to instantly dry. "You've got yourself a deal, Angel," she said, the low, soft, smoky voice caressing the vowels and consonants of my name like a lover.

Oh boy.

❧   ❧   ❧   ❧

That evening, I stood in my cell, shoulders slumped, head down, sweat-streaked, covered with printer's ink and dust, and totally exhausted. We'd finally received the shipment of textbooks we'd been begging for for months. When we opened the boxes, it was apparent that they had been sitting in some warehouse or other since, perhaps, World War II. Maybe even earlier than that. The dust on the boxes and books was thick enough to cut with a knife and was that greasy kind that just makes you shudder when your hands sink into it. My sinuses were stuffed so full of it that I remember being surprised that when the inevitable sneezing fit came along, I didn't shoot my head clear off my neck.

To say I was miserable would be putting it mildly, but it was late and I wasn't about to chance another encounter in the showers no matter how good at defending myself I'd become. Though Derby and her cronies seemed to be pleased with the arrangement I'd managed to work out, the woman's mercurial mood swings made her too dangerous a fate to be tempted a second time.

Resolving to bear my misery stoically until morning, I turned down my bed, wincing at the thought of laying my grimy body down on the still-pristine sheets. In the Bog, you get clean sheets once every two weeks, come hell or high water. And since I was already in hell, and a rescuing flood didn't appear to be on the horizon, I didn't appear to have much choice in the matter.

Just as I was stripping off the last of my jumpsuit, Critter and Sonny showed up outside my cell wearing identical grins. Those expressions quickly turned to amused smirks when they caught sight of my dishevelment. They entered the cell, threw my grimy uniform up over my chest, grabbed my arms and quick-marched me down to the showers, promising to stand guard outside the door to protect me from any unwelcome surprises.

Once I realized my eventual destination, my struggles ceased quite quickly.

It was disconcerting being in the shower alone again and my mind didn't help, insisting on showing me flashbacks in vivid detail of my previous encounter with Mouse and her crew. Though the rational part of me knew I was as safe as could be expected, the cautious young woman in me still checked every shadow in every corner to make sure I was well and truly alone.

Satisfied with my assessment, I peeled off the rest of my clothing, grabbed a clean towel and padded into the dank shower room, listening as the dripping faucets laid out a counterpoint to my soft footsteps. I added a melody line, humming quietly to myself to keep the demons at bay as I walked over to a gleaming showerhead and prepared to be assaulted by the frigid spray.

"Damn, that's cold!"

My flesh humped right up in swift agreement and I had to force myself back under the stinging spray, rubbing my hands furiously over my grimy face to restore circulation as much as to remove the dirt and dust that had accumulated on my face.

Grabbing the slimy cake of soap, I hurriedly got right down to it, once again cursing the hard mineral water for the pitiful attempt at lather I was able to work up.

After I scrubbed my skin to the point of rawness, I set to work on my hair, wincing as I worked my fingers through the wet tangles, resolving to myself once again to just get the whole mess chopped off and be done with it.

Despite the temperature of the water, I found myself relaxing as my body became clean once again. A final rinse and I turned off the shower, grabbing my towel and drying myself off briskly, still humming.

As I turned from the wall, my towel gathered up to my chest, I froze. There, standing no more than five feet away, hands on hips and an unreadable expression on her face, was Ice.

Shock poured through my body with the speed of a freight and I felt my muscles tense up again, as my hands gripped the towel spasmodically. "Jesus, Ice! You scared me! Where did you come from?"

My silent watcher merely raised an eyebrow and smirked, her eyes drilling into mine. I stared back, thoroughly disconcerted. "Is...there something you wanted from me?" I asked finally.

Her gaze dropped down to my feet, then did a slow crawl up the rest of my body till she looked into my eyes once again. "The time is now, Angel. Is this the place you had in mind?"

I looked around the empty shower for a moment, trying to figure out exactly what she was referring to. When it hit me, suddenly, I whipped my head back to face her, sure that all the blood had drained from my face. "What—?"

As she closed the distance between us in one easy stride, I could feel the almost unholy heat as it radiated from her body through the thick fabric of her jumpsuit. Still looking at me through those piercing, hard-cut gems, she reached up casually, grasping the front of my towel and drawing it easily away from my body.

My brain must have short-circuited because the messages it was sending to the rest of my body were indecipherable. I stood there, gaping up at her, as she reached out that same hand and tilted my chin upwards.

"Is this what you wanted?" she murmured as she brought her head down slowly, still pinning me with her bright gaze.

The first touch of her lips on mine brought out feelings I'll never be able to fully articulate. It was like dying. It was like being born. Like drowning. Like flying. Like unsullied innocence and primal want. It was raw and tender. Achingly familiar, though I'd never felt anything like it before.

Contradictions? You bet. But they didn't stop my body from completely melting into hers as she deepened the kiss and slowly moved forward until my back was pressed tight against the tiled wall of the shower, which produced within me another set of contradictions. The tiled wall was cold and damp against my back while the front of my body was pinned to a great wave of living heat. The clean scent of her was almost overwhelming, as was the silken texture of her thick hair as it brushed lightly against my cheek and neck, to fall against my shoulder and linger there in a soft caress of the finest silk.

I'm sure I moaned, but she swallowed it up as the very tip of her tongue danced across my lips, seeking out an invitation which I willingly granted.

As my lips parted, she engulfed me, pressing ever harder against my trembling body as she explored my mouth with probing sweeps of her tongue, mapping, it seemed, every inch within. When my knees threatened all-out rebellion, she smoothly insinuated her own leg between them, bearing my body up against the length of her thigh.

I *know* I cried out then; as a part of me that had become molten slid along solid muscle.

Breaking off the kiss, she slid her hands between the wall and my body, her palms and fingers cupping themselves against my backside as she looked down into my eyes. "You're very beautiful, you know." Her voice was husky with some unnamed emotion, though by the look on her face, I guessed it to be desire.

I tried to return her compliment in kind, for she was *incredibly* beautiful, but my ability to speak must have fled with my senses because it was no-where to be found. Instead, I nodded, hoping to get across to her the intensity of my feelings without benefit of words.

The kiss had left me reeling. My only anchor to reality seemed to be the rock-steady leg seated between my thighs and the hot hands beginning a slow caress against my back.

"So innocent. Pure," she continued in an almost-whisper as she brought her lips down upon mine again.

This time, I returned the kiss, reaching up to tangle my fingers in her hair, pulling us closer together and inhaling great lungfuls of her scent as it mixed with the arousal in my own. She growled, deep in her throat. Sharp teeth nipped at my lips and I felt them start to swell, tingling as they pulsed with the beat of my heart. Not wanting to be left out of the picture, my hips picked up the rhythm of our dance, guided by the hands on my back.

I could feel the big muscle in her thigh clench and relax beneath me, pressing into me smoothly before withdrawing, then pressing again, relent-lessly. Her large hands kept me steady and the feelings continued to increase in intensity until it was all I could do to lay my head back against the chill wall and let my body take over completely, which it did willingly and without complaint.

Ice followed me, lowering her head still further and attaching lips, tongue and teeth to my neck, nipping, suckling and tonguing as my head whipped back and forth like a sunflower in a windstorm. I could feel the hard ten-dons in my neck stand out as my jaw clenched hard against the pleasure soaring through my body.

Her hands seemed to be everywhere on my body; measuring the breadth of my shoulders, running up and down my clenched and straining arms, cupping my breasts and molding them to her palms, trailing down the outsides of my spread thighs and back up, grasping my waist and aiding in my ever-quickening rhythm.

Colors spiraled in kaleidoscopic patterns behind my tightly clenched eyelids and I know I must have begged her not to stop because I could feel her chuckles against the skin of my neck. I bit on my own lips hard enough to draw blood, and it was that taste that followed me down as my body became one tiny, brilliantly shining point of light in that eternal half-second before detonation.

As she leaned in slightly closer, the slight brush of coarse fabric against my painfully erect and wanting nipples was all the catalyst I needed.

I know she felt it coming, because she released from my neck, buried her face into my shoulder and grabbed my hips, thrusting her thigh up against me smoothly. I trembled and shook as a great braying sob burst from my captive lungs.

"Don't be frightened," she whispered into my ear. "Let it out. Let it come."

My body released, pulling in energy, it seemed, from the world around me and sending it back out in torrents of sensation and light, thundering through my body like a herd of untamed horses stampeding across acres of fertile land. I could feel the sting of tears in my eyes as I furiously chewed the inside of my cheeks to keep from screaming out. My body wasn't under my own control anymore and the feeling, quite frankly, scared the hell out of me.

Finally spent, I collapsed into her all-encompassing embrace, my tears falling on the fabric of her uniform and glittering like tiny diamonds in the muted lighting. "I'm sorry," I whispered, still sobbing and not knowing quite why.

"Shhh," she crooned, her voice low and comforting in my ear. She took us both to the floor, cradling my body like a mother would her child and rocking me with my head tucked under her chin.

After what seemed like an eternity, my crying tapered off and she pulled away slightly, once again lifting my chin with gentle fingers. "You alright?"

Meeting her glance briefly, I lowered my eyes, blushing. "Yes. I…don't know what came over me."

"Sometimes it hits people that way," she said, smiling slightly.

"Don't look a gift horse in the mouth, right?"

"Something like that, yeah." After placing a tiny kiss to the crown of my head, she rose, bearing me up with her and setting me on my feet. Then she reached down, picked up my towel and handed it to me, helping me wrap it around my body.

Then she stepped back and looked at me, her eyes so warm and full of caring that I felt my eyes begin to water once again. "Ice, I…."

"Shhh," she whispered again, reaching out a finger and laying it across my lips. "Thank you, Angel."

With another crooked smile, she turned on her heel and was gone from my sight.

A half hour later, I was standing in my cell, looking at my face through the wavery lines of a cheap prison mirror bolted securely to one wall. The picture I saw was identical to the one that stared back at me an hour earlier, though much cleaner, to be sure.

Why, then, did I feel that a stranger was looking back at me?

I remembered the stories I used to hear in the girls' room at school, about the first time you went 'all the way' with a boy and how much different you were supposed to feel the next morning. Fitting my mother's definition of the sexual behaviors of a 'proper' young woman to a T, I'd waited until my marriage bed to see if that old adage bore fruit. But, aside from some slight soreness between my legs, I didn't feel any different than any other morning. The loss of my virginity didn't usher forth any blinding wisdom or staid maturity. It just…happened.

I'll admit to a bit of disappointment, but soon chalked the whole thing up to another of the seemingly unending 'old wives' tales' taught to almost every young girl during her formative years.

Apparently, I was wrong. Whatever had happened between Ice and myself in the showers had changed me in some fundamental way that I couldn't quite put my finger on. The change eluded me the way a word will dance tauntingly on the tip of your tongue, refusing even the most desperate pleas to come forward and announce itself.

One of the worst parts was that I couldn't tell exactly how I was feeling about the whole thing. Good? Bad? I didn't know and that frustrated me. On the one hand, I was happy, gloriously so, that my midnight fantasies had finally come to fruition. On the other, I felt a curious sense of emptiness deep within me, as if I'd been shown the glimpse of a wonderful future full of possibilities, only to have it snatched from my grasp at the last second.

Perhaps it was the casualness of the entire encounter, at least from Ice's perspective. Living life between high walls and steel bars hadn't robbed me of that mushy romantic side. Many things shone through in my dreams, but being pressed up against the shower wall by a fully clothed Ice wasn't one of them. At least for a first time, anyway.

But I knew, too, that Ice had enjoyed herself. At least on some level. I could tell by the way the taste of her kisses changed. By the way she breathed and moved over me. By the way her heart thundered against my chest.

And she was tender, beyond all doubt. Incredibly tender. Especially in the way she held and soothed me at the very end.

Why, then, when I was strong enough to once again stand on my own, did she leave? What went through her mind at that moment? Was I just another assignation? Another seduction in a long line of them? The rumors of her sexual appetite were as great as those of her fighting prowess. Everyone, it seemed, had a story to tell. And if even one quarter of the stories were true, she had slept her way through the entire Bog, twice. And that was before she was let out the first time.

Obviously, I was intelligent enough to realize that the vast majority of rumors came from deluded thinkers with serious wish-fulfillment issues. But I also knew that within every legend lies a kernel of truth. If I ever wanted to learn the real story behind the myth, I suspected that I would have to quickly become very adept at separating the wheat from the chaff.

All these feelings accompanied me, laying on my shoulders like the world upon Atlas, as I slid between the cool sheets of my prison bunk. The shifting, mournful wind matched my turbulent thoughts perfectly and it was a long time before sleep finally claimed me that night.

When the morning brought with it no inspiration, divine or otherwise, I decided to give in to my demanding stomach and head down to breakfast. Arriving earlier than I normally would have, I was faintly surprised to see the cafeteria filled almost to capacity. I might have imagined it, but the noise level seemed to dim appreciably as I stepped into the muggy room, only to rise once again by the time I'd grabbed my tray, waiting in line behind the others for my serving of thick gruel that tasted like nothing so much as library paste.

After grabbing the bowl thrust at me and picking up a mug of horridly strong coffee, I looked around to see if anyone I knew occupied the tables. When only strangers' faces stared back at me, I quietly made my way over to one of the corner tables and sat down, determined to enjoy what passed for breakfast in peaceful solitude.

As my senses got used to the crowded din of the cafeteria and began to settle in on little snippets of conversation, the gruel turned to a hard leaden ball in my stomach. Turning my head slightly as I lowered my spoon, I set my gaze upon four women who were sitting at the edges of their worn, metal seats, their heads bowed conspiratorially together. "Yeah," one said in a voice full of brazen mirth, "the perfect little Angel got her wings clipped but good last night."

"Ice bags another one!"

The group slapped hands as they laughed and elbowed one another.

"I heard she squealed like a pig," said the third.

"No, it was more like a bitch in heat!" The fourth lifted her head and let out a screaming yowl to demonstrate her point.

Other heads turned and laughter began to roll through the group seeming to pound upon the concrete walls like some maleficent wave.

Dropping my spoon, I stood up so quickly that I sent my chair flying back to clatter against the far wall. At the sound, heads turned my way and the laughter died off quickly.

Caught halfway between crying and screaming, I settled for stalking out of the cafeteria with as many tattered shreds of my dignity as I could possibly preserve. Which wasn't much.

I know I must have looked like Satan come to earth as I marched out of the cafeteria and toward the stairs. Inmates took one look at me and gave me wide berth. The expressions on their faces would have caused me to laugh had I been in the mood for it.

Instead, I ignored them, taking the stairs two and three at a time, my breath coming short and fast through my nose. As I reached the top floor, I strode down the long corridor, the paint-chipped bars of Ice's cell growing larger with each step I took. Gone was the trepidation I'd felt in my last trip to this particular inmate's home. I was an angry woman on a mission of retribution.

I strode through the open door to her cell, then, not breaking step, stalked over to where she sat on her bunk, her back up against the wall, her long legs splayed, feet firm to the floor. I stopped in between her knees, staring down at her, hands on my hips, knowing my eyes were flashing messages which I hoped were well and easily read.

She looked up at me, her expression calm and serene as an unblemished lake, waiting.

I took in a breath. Then another to calm my temper enough so that I could speak coherently. Her calm attitude only made my anger burn hotter. "God *damn* it Ice! Isn't it bad enough that you fuck me and leave me standing there like some two dollar whore? Did you have to go and brag to your god damn friends about it too?!" Now I'm not usually much for swearing, thinking the words trite and very overused, but there's a time for everything and, for me, the time for swearing was then.

Though the expression on her face didn't change, oh, her eyes…. The vibrant blue leached out of them, leaving a glittering silver behind. It was like looking down into the twin barrels of a shotgun and I found myself actively fighting back a strong current of almost primal fear. "Finish what you came here to say, Angel," she purred, her voice deathly soft and smooth as satin.

"Finish…." I trailed off, disbelieving. "You don't get it, do you?! They're *laughing* at me down there, Ice! It's nothing but a *joke* to them! Well, it's *not* a joke to me!" I threw my hands up in the air, keeping myself from breaking down by the greatest force of will. "My god, Ice, I thought we were friends. I thought I meant more to you than…than…than just another notch on your goddamned bedpost."

She stood so quickly that I didn't realize what had happened until I felt her long body pinned up against mine. "That's enough, Angel," she said in that same quiet voice.

"No, Ice, it *isn't* enough! It isn't *nearly* enough!"

"Yes it is." Pushing me away slightly, she turned and headed for the door to her cell.

"Wait! Where are you going?"

For a long moment, it looked as if she wasn't going to answer me. Then she turned, slowly, that glittering steel still very present in her eyes. "Alright," she drawled, smiling a smile so cold it chilled me to my very marrow. "I'm going to pay Sonny and Critter a little visit. We'll see how well they can spread stories with their tongues ripped out of their mouths."

As she turned once again, I reached out, stopping just short of touching her arm. "No, wait. Don't do that. They wouldn't spread stories about me. They're my friends."

Back came those eyes again, though this time I swore I could see a small seed of hurt in them before the emotionless mask settled back down over her face seamlessly. The corner of her mouth turned up in a smirk. "I see. Your…friends…wouldn't spread tales out of school, but I would, is that it?"

I stood there, hundreds of conflicting feelings shooting through me at her soft, uninflected words. The anger drained from my body, leaving me off balance and uncertain.

She closed the distance between us and looked down into my face, sharp gaze assessing. Was that disappointment I saw? "Tell me Angel," she said in a completely emotionless tone, as if she were talking about nothing more important than the sports scores, "if your opinion of me is so low, why did you let me fuck you last night, hmmm?"

With that, she turned away and stepped to her bed, reclining lazily on the mattress and dismissing me completely. I stood there, rooted to the floor, my mouth opening and closing, fruitlessly trying to form words to thoughts that weren't even complete. "Ice, I…."

She held up her hand, not looking at me. "No, Angel, it's alright. I think we've said pretty much everything that needs to be said. You don't have to worry about the stories; they'll be stopped. You have my word on that. As for the rest…." She twisted her wrist, as if throwing something away to the wind.

As I stood there, staring at her like a cross between a spanked child and a spurned lover, my mind sifted through a myriad of things I wanted to say. I bit at my lip, a bad habit of mine, and winced at the soreness still present from the evening before. Taking a deep breath, I decided to go for broke. "Can I ask you a question, Ice? Can you at least tell me why?"

"Why what," she muttered, staring down at her hands.

"Why you did what you did. Last night, I mean. Why you came to me in the showers. Why you made…." My voice trailed off, together with my thoughts. What *did* we do last night? Make love? Have sex? What? That I didn't know was the most frustrating part for me. Looking down at Ice and trying to read her emotions through the carefully blank tableau of her face was something akin to being blind and entering the Philadelphia Art Museum. Not very enlightening, to say the least.

It was by the barest of margins that I resisted stomping petulantly on the floor. "Damn it, Ice. Say something! Anything!"

The eyes that finally met mine were cold and hollow. "What do you want me to say, Angel?"

"Tell me why! That's all I'm asking here!"

Her broad shoulders shrugged slightly. "You made an offer. I took you up on it. Simple as that."

If you are incredibly lucky, there will be very few times in you life that you will ever feel what I did when those softly spoken words seeped into my ears. I could almost feel my heart close in upon itself as it shrank from their meaning, cowering. Tears came again, but I held them back with steely determination.

"Why are you looking so surprised? It's what you expected to hear, isn't it? A cold blooded murderer takes an innocent young girl as a trophy then brags about it to her friends?" She shrugged again. "Happens all the time here. If it wasn't me, it would've been somebody else."

That did it. The damn broke and my anger rushed forth, controlling my emotions once again. "You cold-blooded, heard-hearted, evil son of a *bitch*!"

I felt my hand go up, though to this day, I have no idea what I was planning to do with it. It was caught in a grip of iron and I suddenly found myself, once again, face to face with Ice. She smiled coldly down at me. "I wouldn't do that if I were you, or ya just might find out how true those words really are."

Tugging hard, I was surprised when my hand came easily free. Still, I met her gaze dead on, vowing not to show any fear. I was with a predator and I knew it. If she smelled fear on me, the situation could turn from bad to worse in a heartbeat.

Refusing to even give her the satisfaction of seeing me rub my tingling wrist, I stood my ground, staring up at her, almost daring her to show me her worst. When she didn't, my racing heart started to calm and my anger along with it.

As I looked at her, her face seemed to change, as faces often will when you stare at them long enough. I began to imagine I could see past that carefully cultivated fierceness and into the woman beneath; a woman who had held me so tenderly in the shower the night before, rocking and soothing me with a gentleness this present persona belied; a woman who could create such a marvelous sense of freedom with just a few hand-held tools and a few stunted trees; a woman who would unhesitatingly thrash the living daylights out of an inmate twice her weight for laying on an innocent girl. Most of all, though, I imagined I could see a woman with whom I felt a profound connection that not even the heat of our anger could dissipate.

"I don't believe you, you know," I finally managed to say in what surprised me by turning out to be a normal tone of voice.

"About what?"

"About what you said. That it was a game, that I was a trophy. You may have said those words, but I don't think you meant them at all."

Raising one eyebrow, she continued to stare down at me, her face still completely expressionless.

"You're hiding something."

"Oh? What am I hiding?"

"Your feelings."

The eyebrow arched higher as a faint smirk played across her face. "I'm a murderer, Angel. An assassin for hire. I lost anything that even resembles feelings a long time ago. Don't waste your time looking for something that isn't there."

I allowed my own smirk to curve my lips. "Oh, it's there alright. You just have to know where to look."

"And you know where to look."

"No, not yet. Not completely. But I will." Taking a big risk, I brought up my hand again, one finger extended, and poked Ice in the chest. "Beneath that oh-so-cold exterior lies a living, beating, *feeling* heart, Morgan Steele. And I'm gonna find it. I've got nothing but time on my hands, and believe you me, I *will* find it." Grinning triumphantly, I turned on my heel, prepared to make my dramatic exit.

I was a step away from the door when the barely whispered words met my ears. "I hope you do, Angel."

Lacking the courage to turn back and catch the expression on her face, I continued out of the cell and into the hallway, a woman whose mission had been changed irrevocably.

✒ ✒ ✒ ✒

Sunday dawned cold and with a drizzle that was just a degree or two short of being sleet. Apparently, though, I was the only person in the prison surprised when the much anticipated basketball game managed to go off without a hitch.

That's not to say it was smooth sailing. It appeared that the game of 'inmate basketball' was quite a different animal than any I'd seen before, and believe me when I tell you that, being from the midwest, I'd seen enough of 'normal' basketball to last me several lifetimes. The rules seemed to be nonexistent and the object appeared to me to be 'stuff the ball through the net while injuring as many opponents as it was possible to without becoming a victim yourself'. There were several instances when I began to doubt my wisdom in assuming that this would be a peaceful way to settle the differences between the two gangs.

For her part, Ice appeared to be having fun. Her job seemed to be to keep the fights from becoming too bloody and interrupting the flow, if it could be called that, of the game. Rain glittered in her thick, black hair and every so often she would shake it out, sending a fan of fine mist out over the yard.

Our eyes would meet occasionally and, for those brief moments, nothing else seemed to matter to me. Her small grin warmed me inside and the rain, as well as the roar of the crowd and players, seemed to fade away to nothing. Then, invariably, another fight would break out and her attention would be called back to the game and I would feel the cold and damp all over again.

When it was over, Trey's team easily maintained possession of the court for the next year. The score might have been closer, and the game more interesting, if Derby had put some of her more athletically inclined people in to play. Since her overblown ego didn't allow that, it was, quite simply, a rout. Trey, who by herself managed to score more points than Derby's entire team combined, was paraded around the court on the shoulders of her teammates, grinning wildly and proclaiming her dominance to all who would listen.

It was with a feeling of great relief when I finally pulled my protesting body up off the rain-slicked tarp that Critter had managed to put down and escaped back inside the warmth and quiet of the prison walls. All in all, I was quite pleased with myself. My plan, for better or worse, had worked and peace, or what passed for it in the Bog, reigned for one afternoon at least. Ice wasn't mad at me and our connection seemed as strong as ever, despite the wounding words of the day before.

It was another good day.

Chapter 4

The last warm day of the year dawned sunny and clear as if Mother Nature was snickering behind her hand, giving us a last glimpse of a summer we wouldn't see for another half year or more. Ducking outside at the earliest opportunity, I strode onto the nearly empty field and sat cross-legged in grass that still managed to maintain some measure of its vibrant color despite several hard frosts that had ravaged it.

Closing my eyes and tilting my face toward the sun, I imagined that if I could just listen hard enough, I'd be able to smell the fresh cut grass and hear the sounds of summers past; the laughter of children, the splashing of water and the almost monotonous drone of a baseball announcer coming through the tinny speakers of an old transistor radio. The images playing behind my closed eyes warmed me inside and I felt a smile break across my face as I was swept up in my fantasy world. The cold walls of my prison home were far away as I sat there, determined to enjoy this fleeting glimpse of both summer and freedom for as long as I could.

My training had caused me to become more aware of the world around me, even while deep in my musings, and so I almost immediately caught the subtle current of change in the air around me. With a sense of disappointment, I lowered my head and opened my eyes to find Ice lowering herself to sit, also cross-legged, on the ground some feet from me. Her hands snaked across the carpeting of grass, plucking one thin stalk and twirling it between her fingers as she looked around the yard for a bit before turning her head to meet my interested gaze. Her lips curved into a gentle grin that lit up the vibrant pools of her eyes and softened the harsh planes of her face. "Morning, Angel."

The sound of her slightly husky voice warmed me more than the sun and my memories put together and I couldn't help but return her smile. "Morning, Ice."

Nodding her dark head at me, she broke the lock of our gazes, seeming inclined to allow the comfortable silence to stretch out between us as she continued to casually scan the yard.

I, however, wasn't one to pass up even the slimmest chance to get beneath that armored exterior. My mind whirled, tossing out and discarding several opening gambits. Finally, I decided on the old tried and true direct route.

"Can I ask you a question, Ice?" I winced as the words slipped past my lips. They always seemed to be the first ones out when I talked to her and some part of me wondered if she'd ever get tired of hearing them so often repeated.

She turned to me slowly, a small smile playing across her lips. "What's on your mind, Angel?"

"Well, I was wondering about your trees. I don't know if I'm breaking some code of conduct, but I've been thinking about them a lot. They're each individuals, but when I look at them as a group, they seem to tell a story. I was wondering if, maybe, you could tell me what that story was."

She looked away again, scanning the fat clouds strolling across the sky for so long that I was sure she wasn't going to answer me. When she turned back, her face was less open, but her eyes weren't completely shuttered and that gave me some hope. "I call them the Four Freedoms," she said in a voice soft as the wind rustling through the grass.

"The Four Freedoms?" I asked, careful to keep my tone neutral. There were times, especially ones like this, when Ice reminded me of a skittish colt, all fire and nervous energy. One wrong word and I knew she'd bolt. I sensed I was going to get to the bottom of something very important here and so I did my best to keep things as calm and peaceful as I could.

Nodding, she tossed the blade of grass into the wind before picking another and looking down at it. She took a deep breath, as if contemplating whether or not to go further, then tossed the second stalk away and interlaced her fingers. "The one on the very left, the small one that's kinda wild? That's the Freedom of Innocence. The one next to it, the big one, is the Freedom of Power. The next is the Freedom of Love, and the last is the Freedom of Wisdom."

As I sat there, pondering her words, I tried desperately to think of what to say next. Knowingly or not, she had just given me a huge insight into the workings of her soul and I wanted to dig ever deeper to bring out the person who could see freedom in concepts like innocence and love.

But I also knew that if I gave in to my urgings and pushed too hard into the rich subtext, I'd soon find myself alone. Backing off a bit, I decided to attack the general overriding concept rather than look too hard at the specifics.

"Do you think about freedom a lot?" While it sounded like a stupid question, there was a method to my madness.

She shrugged. "Not too much anymore. I'd rather not waste my time thinking about things that can never be." There was a deep sadness in her eyes and I sensed, with a sinking heart, that she was talking about far more than simple freedom from this prison we called home.

"You'll get out someday, Ice. Your sentence carries a chance of parole, doesn't it?"

Smiling sadly, she nodded after a moment. "A slim chance, yes. But it'll never happen."

"Why not?"

"I'm a murderer, Angel. Simple as that. I was convicted of killing a government witness." She shrugged again, then shook her head, laughing mirthlessly. "Not something the parole boards like to hear when they're looking at your release papers."

And with that statement, I realized I'd blundered into yet another hidden landmine. In all the time I'd known her, I'd never asked whether she had indeed committed the crime for which she was convicted. She'd never volunteered the information and as far as I knew, only Ice herself knew where the real truth lay.

I felt, in that moment, how I imagined a novice firewalker must feel. Afraid to go forward and risk getting burned; afraid to step back and risk losing face.

Faced with those choices, I picked the third. To do nothing. Leaning back slightly and letting my arms bear the weight of my upper body, I looked up at the robin's egg blue sky as I felt the gradual ebb of edgy tension from the body close to mine. I smiled internally, knowing I'd made the right decision. The comfortable silence stretched out between us and, for once, I wasn't inclined to break it.

After several long, peaceful moments, Ice softly cleared her throat. I could feel the heat of her eyes upon me, but I continued to look up at the sky, waiting for her to share whatever was on her mind. "How about you?" she said finally. "Do you think about being free again?"

Smiling, I turned to face her. "Not as much as I used to, but yes, almost every day."

"What do you think about?"

"Mmm." My smile widened, unbidden. "A walk in the park at dusk. Eating an ice-cream cone. A nice, long, hot bath." Trite, but true. All of it. Especially the bath part. It had always been one of my favorite things to do, especially on a cold winter's evening. "But when I really feel like the walls are closing in on me, I remember this place I used to go to in the summers when I was a young girl."

Ice nodded at me to continue, her eyes bright and interested.

"My father had a friend who owned a cabin on some property in Canada. It was a wonderful place, all glass and wood, with a huge porch that ran along the front, a loft upstairs where most of the bedrooms were, and a fireplace so big my father could fit inside without bending over." Shifting slightly, I stretched my legs out, running them back and forth over the nubbly grass. "It sat in the middle of a huge pine forest, about fifty yards up from a beautiful lake. The path from the house to the water was covered in a carpet of pine needles and if you tried to make the walk with bare feet, you'd wind up covered in sap."

I felt a warm tingle begin inside me as the pleasant weight of my memories settled in. "There was a short green dock by the shore where my dad's friend kept his speedboat tied. It wasn't a very big one, but it was fun to go out in. I can remember sitting on the dock, feeling the sun on my shoulders as I looked over the lake at the colorful sailboats that raced almost every day. They reminded me of butterflies in a meadow and I remember envying the passengers their freedom. My father had something against girls learning to sail, but he couldn't stop me from watching. They were so beautiful."

I shifted a little, plucking at the grass with my fingers, not really seeing it. "There were a couple of kids my age there and I remember us racing out to another dock which sat out in the middle of the lake. Well, it wasn't really the middle, but it seemed that far when I was young. All I knew was that the water was over my head and that scared me, at first. But once I learned to swim, it was fun to go out there and dive off the dock. My friends used to go underneath, where there was an air pocket." I found myself laughing at the memory. "Not me though. Never was brave enough."

Some more grass came loose under the relentless assault of my fingers. "We'd go up there for a month every summer. We never had a television, but my dad would bring his radio. At night, after dinner, he'd build a big fire in the fireplace and sit listening to baseball while my mom did her jigsaw puzzles. I'd sit there, listening to the crackle of the fire, and read. Then, when it got late, I'd go upstairs and fall asleep to the sounds of crickets, bullfrogs and the wind whistling through the pine trees."

I hugged my arms tight around my knees, awash in the memories. "Those were the happiest times of my life." I sighed. "My father bought the cabin and land from his friend when I was thirteen. The cabin burned down the next year. But one day, when I walk out of here, I'm gonna go back up there and rebuild that cabin from the ground up with my bare hands and spend the rest of my life there, free and at peace."

When I turned my gaze back to my silent listener, I found her eyes so full of utter longing that it made my heart stop just looking at her expression. I felt my hand go out to her, felt her own capture it and cradle it tenderly as a sad half-smile crooked the corner of her mouth. "It sounds…like a good place to dream about."

I smiled. "It is. It's a wonderful place. I can share it with you, if you'll let me."

Compressing her lips, she gently let go of my hand, then drew her knees up to her chest, wrapping her long arms around them. "No, that's alright. It's your dream. Something that belongs to you and only you. Something this place and these people can't take away from you. You keep it."

I sidled closer until we were almost touching. "I'd like to share it with you, Ice. The only thing better than having it all to myself is being able to share it with someone. With…you."

Catching the odd expression on her face, I allowed my grin to broaden. "C'mon, it'll be fun! Just close your eyes and imagine you're in the middle of a forest, surrounded by trees. Feel the warm wind brush against your skin. Smell the pine all around you." I took in a deep, bracing breath. "Isn't it wonderful?"

"It's crazy."

I laughed. "Of course it is! That's what makes it so much fun! C'mon, Ice, let your hair down a little. Just close your eyes and think about what I told you. Think about the warm sun on your face."

After rolling her eyes at me, she lowered her chin onto her knees and closed her eyes. Taking a chance, I closed the last of the distance between our bodies, then reached up a hand to lay gently against her broad back. The muscles I felt were pronounced and tense and I couldn't resist rubbing them gently in a smooth, circular motion. She began to relax just the slightest bit. "That's it. Can you hear the birds chirping? The water lapping gently against the wooden dock?"

There were several long moments of silence interrupted only by our breathing. "Well? Can you?"

Faintly amused eyes opened and met mine. "Nope."

This time I rolled my eyes. "That's just 'cause you're not trying hard enough. Let me help you." Pursing my lips, I proceeded to deliver my rendition of "water gently lapping against a wooden dock," followed close behind by chirping birds.

I felt her muscles clench under my hand a split second before a deep, rumbling laugh burst up from her chest. It was one of the most joyous sounds I'd ever heard and, within seconds, I was joining her, tears of mirth streaming down my cheeks as I realized just how horrible I must have sounded.

When my laughter finally tapered off, I wiped my arm over my watering eyes, brushing away my tears as I looked into Ice's radiant face. "God, you're beautiful." The words came out before I could edit them, but this time, I didn't want to take them back. She *was* beautiful, and I wanted her to know that.

Both of our expressions turned serious and I felt more than saw her head incline toward mine. I could feel myself moving at the same time, my lips suddenly aching to meet hers.

I could feel her warm breath tickle the fine hairs of my face as the incredible heat of her body radiated against mine. We were a hairsbreadth apart, my eyes already closing in anticipation, when the sound of a softly cleared throat startled me out of my bliss.

Before I could even fully open my eyes, Ice's arm shot up, grabbed a handful of jumpsuit and yanked a startled Critter's upper body down so that her face was just inches from ours. "The prison better be burning down," she growled, "or you're gonna find out how well you can walk with two broken legs."

"I…just thought you needed to know…that Psycho's loose again," Critter wheezed, her face turning an interesting ashen color.

"Great," Ice muttered, letting go of Critter's uniform and jumping to her feet. Reaching down, she grasped my hand and hauled me up as well. "Thanks for the dream, Angel," she said, laying a quick hand against my cheek before turning and running back into the prison.

Turning, I looked over at Critter, who was rubbing her throat and coughing. "Are you ok?"

She cleared her throat again, then nodded. "Yeah, I'm alright. I should know better than to interrupt her."

"What's going on with Psycho this time?"

Critter shrugged as she straightened her uniform. We both broke out into a trot as we headed back into the building. "She's got another knife to the throat of some newbie."

"Newbie? I didn't think we had anyone come in in the last month."

"Neither did I. I heard she was brought in last night after everyone was asleep. Real hush-hush."

Coming to the top of the stairs, we were confronted with an almost exact duplicate of the scene a month before when Psycho had captured the prison guard. The guards were standing around in a tense knot, their batons out and clutched in tight, knuckle-whitening grips. The prisoners stood behind them, the shorter women up on their toes trying to get a glimpse of the unfolding drama.

As before, Critter led me around to a more open space off to the side where I could look into the circle of tense women. Psycho had what looked to be a butcher knife, though how she managed to get a hold of one of those I have no idea, to the neck of a striking woman. The woman looked to be in her late forties, with long, black hair shot through with strands of the finest silver. Her skin was olive-hued and her eyes dark and shining. She had a regal, old-world elegance that even her current circumstances did nothing to diminish.

At the front of the pack stood Sandra and Ice, who was gesturing wildly with her arms, more demonstrative than I'd yet seen her, even when fighting. My ears strained to pick out her low toned words among the excited chatter of the other inmates.

"Alright, Cassandra, you've made your point. Now drop the knife."

"No can do, my dear Ice. This little fishie has to die. I'm sorry if that upsets you, my love, but some things just can't be helped."

The woman's eyes widened as the sharp edge bit cruelly into her neck. "Morgan, please!"

Cassandra yanked the woman's dark hair back, baring her neck even further. "I told you already, you miserable piece of dung, her name is 'Ice'! Use it!"

"I'm sorry!" the woman cried out. "Please stop hurting me!"

Cassandra bared her teeth in a malicious grin. "Oh no, my pretty. I haven't even *begun* to hurt you."

"Drop the knife, Cassandra!" Sandra shouted, raising her baton.

Turning toward the head guard, Psycho's grin broadened. "I'm sorry, Sandra, did you say something? I'm afraid I couldn't hear you with this poor dear fishie moaning in my ear. Would you care to repeat yourself?"

"I *said* drop the knife!"

"That's what I thought you said." She shrugged. "Sorry." Closing her eyes, she slowly drew the knife across the captive woman's throat, drawing a shallow cut from which thin trickles of blood streamed. "Ahhhh, nothing like the smell of fresh, hot blood, is there."

"Cassandra!"

The blonde turned her gaze to Ice, mouing her lips in a coquettish pout. "Oh come now, Ice. You above all others should know just how good it feels to draw your blade against the tender flesh of an innocent victim." She giggled girlishly. "Just the thought of it gives me shivers. How about you?"

"Cassandra, please. I'm asking you to drop the knife."

"Oooooo. Begging! I *like* that in a woman! Try getting on your knees next time though, Ice. It enhances the effect."

From my vantage point, I was able to see Ice's expression as her eyes darted intently between Cassandra, her knife, and the terrified woman in Cassandra's deadly grasp. It was quite obvious that Ice knew the captive. I turned to Critter, a question in my eyes. She shrugged and shook her head.

As I turned back to the action, Sandra took a small step forward, her empty hands upraised in a gesture of placation. "At least tell us why you're doing this, Cassandra. I want to help you if I can."

"You can't help me, you pitiful excuse for a cop wannabe. I'm crazy, remember? Nuts. Crackers. Off the deep end without a net. I'm Psycho!"

"Please, Cassandra," the head guard tried again. "Just tell us why."

After a moment, she nodded, relaxing her grip just the slightest bit on her captive. "Alright. That's a fair question, I suppose. Why don't you tell them…what was your name again?"

The woman choked.

"Her name is Josephina," Ice said, her voice firm and deadly serious.

Cassandra smiled brightly. "That's right, Josephina! How stupid of me to forget such a beautiful name. Josephina, tell our admirers here just why you're in such an uncomfortable position."

"I…I don't know!"

"Of course you do, my darling. Speak up loudly so everyone can hear you, dear. Mustn't let the people in the back miss your words of wisdom, you know."

Josephina remained silent and Cassandra shook her like a rag doll, her brows knit low over her eyes in a fierce scowl. "Mustn't keep our public waiting, dear Josephina. Now spill it."

"We…we were talking," Josephina gasped out, "this…morning. In our cells. And…and I mentioned that I was a friend of Ice."

"You *liar*!" Screaming in rage, Cassandra tightened her grip around the older woman's neck, bringing the knife up against her chin once again. "Ice *has* no friends except *me*! *I'm* the one that she loves, do you understand me?! *I'm* the one that she thinks about at night when she runs her hands down that exquisite body of hers! Me! *Only* me! Do you hear me, you sniveling piece of trash?! Do you?"

Josephina screamed hoarsely as Sandra and Ice took identical, purposeful steps forward. Cassandra's head jerked up and she dragged the terrified woman back a step, waving the knife in front of her. "Back! Get *back* before I cut her pretty little head off! And you know I'll do it, too."

Both women halted their forward progress, still several feet from Cassandra and her knife. I wondered if Ice would try for a disarming blow, but for some reason, my friend seemed hesitant, as if unsure of herself. It was a strange thing to see and I had to fight down a sudden sense of dark foreboding, watching her.

Cassandra's left foot slipped slightly in a spot of wetness on the prison floor. The knife bit deeply into the juncture of Josephina's neck and shoulder, causing the older woman to scream as a gout of blood streamed forth. The blonde chuckled as the blood flowed. "That's gonna leave a stain," she remarked conversationally, reaching up to run her fingers through the blood, then reaching still higher to wipe her wet fingertips across her captive's cheek.

"Morgan, please," Josephina moaned.

The slap of Cassandra's palm against Josephina's cheek echoed through the prison like a rifle shot. Spinning the older woman around toward her, Psycho brought her face down so close their lips were almost toughing. Her eyes were wide with rage. "I *told* you, you bitch! Her name is *Ice*!"

Raising her free hand, Cassandra backhanded Josephina then raised her knife, its cruel edge glittering in the harsh fluorescents.

Things seemed to flow in slow motion from that point. Again, Ice and Sandra stepped forward simultaneously. With one hand, Ice pushed the guard away, while grabbing at the descending knife with the other. Sandra was thrown back into the crowd of guards while Ice, Cassandra and Josephina became locked in a deadly embrace.

Ice had at least five inches and fifty pounds on her skinny opponent, but Cassandra had the strength of an insane rage backing her up. The battle for control of the knife quickly became a stalemate, with Ice's hand locked around Psycho's wrist while Cassandra was trying desperately to plunge the knife into any bit of warm flesh she could.

The two women grinned fiercely at one another, obviously getting some sort of perverse enjoyment out of their dance of death. The thought chilled me inside as I attempted to reconcile this Ice with the one I'd shared my dreams with just moments ago. It wasn't an easy match, I have to tell you.

I turned once again to Critter, who was watching the scene with fascination. "Why don't they do something?" I asked, gesturing to the guards who were, like my friend, motionless as they watched the battle taking place just scant feet in front of them.

Critter looked down at me and shrugged again. "I dunno. Maybe they're trying to figure out what to do?"

"This is ridiculous," I commented, turning my attention back to the action. Cassandra's arm was shaking visibly with her attempt to plunge the knife downward against the implacable strength of Ice's sure grasp. Her eyes fluttered closed for a moment and then a truly evil smile spread over her features. A slight nudge with her free arm was all it took to send Josephina stumbling over into Ice, who reflexively caught the sobbing woman, also with her free arm.

That minute distraction was all Cassandra needed as she twisted her wrist sharply, breaking free of Ice's hold. The knife glittered again, then continued its aborted plunge downward. There was a loud scream, and when the weapon again appeared, it was coated with blood.

"NO!" I screamed, beyond sure that Ice had been the recipient of the deadly thrust. I started forward, only to be pulled back by Critter's strong hold on me.

Cassandra threw back her head and laughed, a truly terrifying sound. As she stepped away, Josephina slumped into Ice's arms, blood pouring from the wound in her chest. The look of shock on Ice's face was intense as she looked from Cassandra's cackling form down to the bloody woman in her arms. She bore Josephina gently to the ground, a small moan coming from deep in her chest, as the guards chose that moment to attack.

"Oh *yes*!" Cassandra purred. "I just *love* pig roasts, don't you? C'mon, piggies. Who's first to die today?" She swung her knife back and forth in viscous sweeps. The guards jumped back, uncertain, and Cassandra laughed again. "Come on, where's that bravery you pat each other on the back for having, hmm? It only hurts a little! Just ask my little friend here!" Her screaming mirth filled the prison.

Another guard ran to assist Ice, who slammed an elbow into her gut, sending her back over to her fellows. With one large hand covering the blood-drenched wound, Ice used the other to tenderly brush back the sweat-soaked hair from Josephina's brow. "Just hang on," she murmured. "Help's on the way. Just hang on."

"That's right, Josephina," Cassandra yelled, still swinging her knife to keep the guards at bay, "listen to our dear Ice. Hang on, won't you? I wouldn't want you to miss even one *second* of your glorious death."

I looked on in absolute horror as Ice brought down her other hand to join the first in its futile attempt to staunch the flow of blood draining from Josephina's wound. Blood pumped from between her fingers in a red river, continuing unabated even after my friend had put almost all her strength into the pressure hold.

The wounded woman was still conscious, though barely, her face a doughy white. She and Ice were carrying on a murmured conversation that was too soft for me to hear. My heart clenched at the look of grief on Ice's normally stoic features. Who *was* this woman that she could etch those deep lines across the tableau of my companion's beautiful face?

Ice's dark head slowly lowered. Her head turned as if to listen to barely whispered words. From where I was standing, I could see Josephina's striking features go slack as her body relaxed beneath Ice's large form.

"Noooo!"

The mournful howl echoed through the cavernous building, seeming to gather strength as it rebounded off cement walls and steel doors, filling the space around us all with a haunting melody of loss.

The wail cut off abruptly as Ice slowly rose, looking down at her blood covered hands as if they belonged to someone else entirely. I caught just the faintest glimpse of her expression as her head raised in the direction of Cassandra and I swear my heart stopped dead in my chest. *She's going to kill her. My God, she's going to murder Psycho with her bare hands!*

One step forward and Ice obliterated Cassandra's wrist with a kick, sending the butcher knife spinning through the air to land against the far wall with such force that the blade snapped from the hilt with the ease of a twig being broken. Continuing her forward momentum, she reached her bloody hands out and wrapped them around Cassandra's neck, bearing the still laughing woman off her feet and pinning her up against the barred door that protected the entrance to the segregation unit.

The back of Cassandra's skull hit the metal bars with a resounding clang as her own arms came up, feebly attempting to loosen my friend's strangle hold. The grin was still firmly in place on her face, though her skin had begun to turn a ruddy color.

Sandra jumped forward quickly. "No, Ice! Let her go! Let us take care of her!" The last of her plea was lost in a gust of breath as Ice's foot connected with her chest, sending her flying back through the air to land against some of her fellow guards who were bowled back like tenpins trying to catch her hurtling body.

"Stay back!" Ice screamed. "I'm gonna give this bitch exactly what she deserves!"

"Ice, no!" Sandra ran forward again, more cautiously this time. "Ice, please. Think about what you're doing. Don't do this. Please!"

"Get *back*! Don't come any closer, Sandra. I don't wanna hurt you too."

"Don't do this, Ice!"

As I struggled against Critter's tight hold, I could see Ice's knuckles whiten as she squeezed her hands ever tighter around Cassandra's thin neck. Her captive's face was slowly turning from ruddy to ashen, her eyes wide and staring. Still she smiled as if death were a friend she was beckoning closer with each heaving try for breath.

A murmur started through the heretofore silent crowd and when I looked around, my eyes set upon the figure of the warden, making his first ever appearance within the prison proper. He wore a black suit over a blindingly white shirt, a large golden cross pinned garishly to his left lapel. Bulling his way to the front of the crowd, he took in the scene, hands on his hips. His face was red as old brick and a temple vein throbbed prominently. "What's going on here? Guards! Separate those two women now!"

Sandra turned to look at him, an expression of frustration plainly evident on her face. "We're trying, sir. It's not as easy as it looks."

"It doesn't look like you're trying at all, Ms. Pierce. Now do your job and separate these women or I'll find someone who will!"

The head guard turned back to the scene, twirling her baton. "Please, Ice! I can't give you any more chances here! Think about what you're doing! Please, I'm begging you. Let her go! Please!"

"Separate them *now*, Ms. Pierce!"

"Ice! Let her *go*! I don't want to hurt you!"

"*Now*, Ms. Pierce! Do it *now*!" The warden looked around at the other guards. "All of you! *Now*!"

"Ice! This is it! Last chance! Please!"

When Ice gave no signs of having heard, Sandra let out a huge sigh of defeat, turned slightly to the rest of the guards, and nodded. "Try not to hurt her."

As Sandra stepped forward, prepared to lead the charge, the warden grabbed her by her baton and pulled her up short. "Now see here, Ms. Pierce. I don't care if you have to break every bone in that murderer's body. Just do your job, do you hear me?"

When Sandra opened her mouth to begin a counter-argument, I saw my chance and took it. Lifting up my foot, I slammed it down hard on top of Critter's instep, and when the pain made her loosen her hold on me, I bolted, using every ounce of defensive training the Amazons had taught me to rush through the restraining crowd and into the center of the action.

The warden and Sandra made a last ditch effort to catch me, but I used a whirling chop-block I had been perfecting and slipped through their defenses like oil through water, inordinately proud of myself. I skidded to a stop just feet from Ice. From this distance, I could easily see that we were just about out of time. Cassandra's lips were blue and her eyes were wide and bulging from the pressure on her neck. That damn, smirking smile was still on her face and I wanted, at that moment, to do nothing more than to reach up and slap it off.

"Ice, it's Angel," I began, using my voice like a hypnotist would use a pocket-watch, trying to calm the unfettered beast my friend had become. "Don't do this. Please. Killing her won't bring your friend back no matter how much you wish it would. You know that. Please don't make things worse."

"Get out of here Angel." Ice's voice was guttural, raw with rage and grief.

"Sorry, Ice, but I'm not going anywhere. You don't want to do this. Please, just let her go."

"Oh, you're wrong, Angel. I very much wanna do this." Her muscles tensing, Ice lifted Cassandra higher, slamming her body once again against the steel bars, which rattled, protesting. Her grip loosened for a brief instant, allowing Cassandra to gasp in a breath. The blonde woman tried to say something but it was lost as her air supply was once again choked off. I couldn't believe how she'd managed to last this long against Ice's rage-fueled strength.

I could hear the guards shifting behind me and knew I didn't have much time. "Ice, remember what we just talked about. About dreams. About how no one can take them away from you. Don't do this, Ice. Don't let her take your dreams away from you."

I kept my voice smooth and steady, my cadence deliberate. I could see my words were having some effect by the minute lessening of tension in her broad shoulders. Taking a huge gamble, I reached up and put my hand on her back, rubbing gently as I'd done just a short time earlier in the yard. "That's it, Ice. Let her go. It's alright. It'll be alright. Just let her go."

The warden's screamed command to attack was drowned out by the huge gasp of breath from Cassandra as Ice's hands loosened their deadly grip around her neck.

Hands slashing almost too quickly for the eye to follow, Ice caught Cassandra's slumping body and tossed her the length of the corridor, where she landed in a heap against the far wall. Turning quickly, Ice shoved me behind her long frame as the guards began a concerted rush toward us, the warden, baton in hand, in the lead. Reaching out, Ice caught the baton and hauled the warden up to her, their bodies just inches apart.

The other guards came to abrupt halts as they watched the new scene unfold.

"Don't touch me." Ice enunciated her words clearly from between clenched and bared teeth.

The warden's eyes went wide as his face became distinctly pale. Curious, I watched from my safe vantage point behind Ice. "You're going to the hole for a month for this infraction, Ms. Steele. Release me or I'll make it two."

"Touch me, Warden Morrison, and I'll send you to a hole of your very own. Permanently."

"Are you threatening me, Ms. Steele?"

"No, Warden Morrison. I'm just giving you the facts."

Setting himself, Morrison yanked his baton hard, the smirk on his face freezing when the weapon didn't budge in the slightest. Though the situation was immanently explosive, I found myself having to hide my own smirk behind Ice's back.

"Call off the dogs, Warden, and I'll turn myself over to Sandra peacefully. Do we have a deal?"

"What makes you think I make deals with murderers, Ms. Steele? Despite what you and others might think, I control the prison here, not you. I could have you beaten senseless in the blink of an eye."

Though I couldn't see it, I just knew that one of Ice's elegant brows had just made a dramatic elevation. "Try it." Her voice was a sultry purr and my flesh pricked in unconscious reaction to the seductive tone.

I could literally feel the energy both of them were giving off as their wills battled. Though I knew Ice could easily follow through on her threat without blinking an eye, I could also sense the coiled tension in her body as she fought down her primal instincts to fully disarm the man and be done with it.

After several long, tense moments, I could see the warden's shoulders sag as he took a slight step backwards, conceding the round. "Very well, Ms. Steele. No one will hurt you. But realize this. You have just made yourself one very large enemy. Your time won't go quite so lightly from here on out. And that, my dear, is not a threat. I'm just stating a fact."

Ice nodded slowly, then released the baton back to the warden. I could feel her muscles tense as if expecting a blow. I tensed as well, ready to jump in if needed. Not that I ever would be, mind you, but it felt good to know that I had the skills, in any case.

Sandra and another guard rushed forward, each taking one of Ice's arms and forestalling any retaliatory action the warden might have been wont to take. Two other guards grabbed Cassandra's unconscious body and dragged her down toward the stairs.

"Sixty days in isolation for each of them," Morrison ordered. "And Ms. Pierce, when you return, please come to my office. We need to seriously discuss your lack of…preparedness in these situations."

Sandra's shoulders slumped. "Yes, sir."

"Oh, and one more thing."

"Yes, sir?"

Morrison smirked, flinging a negligent hand toward Josephina's body. "Get someone to take out the trash, will you?"

The crowd dispersed as Ice and Cassandra were led away surrounded by guards. Standing there, I watched Ice, head held high and proud, as if surrounded again by a retinue instead of guards intent on making sure she didn't escape. The idea of two months in utter isolation and total darkness didn't seem to faze her one bit, and I shook my head at the wonder of it all. I also knew that I would miss her, badly.

Our interaction in the yard had given me a very good feeling about the direction our relationship was heading in and I very much wanted to continue down that path with her if only to see where it would eventually lead.

With a dejected sigh, I turned to find myself faced with Josephina's body lying, alone, on the floor, a pool of thickening blood surrounding her tattered jumpsuit. Her eyes were open; glassy and staring forever into eternity. Stepping around the pool of blood, I squatted down and closed her lids, sending out a silent prayer to whatever higher power might be listening.

Pushing her way through the final knot of prisoners, Critter limped her way over to where I knelt, waiting silently off to the side while I finished my prayer. When she sensed I was done, she reached down a hand to help me to my feet. I brushed off the knees of my jumpsuit, then flashed her a rueful smile. "Sorry about your foot."

She returned the grin, winking at me. "Not a problem. I'll have to remember that move."

"You should. You're the one who taught it to me."

"I was? I must be a better teacher than I thought." My friend looked quite pleased with herself. Then her face turned somber as she looked down at Josephina's body. "What a mess."

I nodded in agreement. "I wonder who she was. It's obvious she and Ice were friends at some point."

"Maybe Corinne would know?"

"Maybe. I just don't think I'm ready to face her, or anyone else, right now. I think I'm just gonna go back to my cell and think about things."

Critter nodded, clasping my shoulder. "You did good up there, Angel. I don't think anyone else would have been able to talk Ice down in the state she was in. You prevented a bloodbath. Great job."

The compliment should have pleased me, but it didn't. I'd seen much too much of the dark side of humanity this day. I needed a long time alone to process things before I could even begin to believe that what I'd done had been for the best. Still, I nodded, reaching up to squeeze my friend's hand as I did so. "Thanks, Critter."

"See you later, Angel."

I stood there for a long moment, watching Critter's golden curls disappear back down the stairs. Taking one last long look at Josephina, I turned and made my way back to my cell, just managing to get inside before I broke down.

It was a long time before sleep came to claim me.

❧   ❧   ❧   ❧

My sleep, when it came, was bathed in sweat-soaked dreams of violence and death. They ran pell-mell through my mind, as dreams often will, making little or no sense to the conscious mind, but spelling out easily deciphered messages to the unconscious will. For the first time in months, Peter featured prominently in them, though his killer was as often Ice and/or Cassandra as it was me. I relived his death over and over again, running through tight knots of laughing people, always getting there just a split-second too late and finding him, slumped and bleeding, in my arms. Always that accusing stare haunted me.

The last was by far the worst. It started out peacefully enough. Ice and I were sitting, unclothed, in the middle of the yard. Though I should have been uncomfortable at the exposure, I wasn't, for some reason. I felt completely safe. At peace, even, and I welcomed that feeling after the nightmares previous to it. She was facing away from me and I was stroking the velvet soft skin of her back, marveling at the texture of warm, pliant flesh over hard muscle and bone. The slight breeze brushed the scent of her into my nostrils and I breathed deep of it with a sigh of contentment.

I remember talking, though I don't remember the subject. Something unimportant and nonsensical to be sure, thought it seemed profound at the time. She sat, unmoving, accepting my touches and words, her raven hair falling in soft waves to lay against her full breasts. Shifting slightly, I could see the breeze flutter the dark tendrils, giving me the briefest of glimpses of what I suddenly needed to see more of. Putting my hand on her shoulder, I turned her upper body toward mine, my other hand already moving of it's own volition toward her chest to brush the hair away. It stopped, frozen, as I looked into her face to see death staring back at me. Her eyes had become Josephine's, then Peter's, then Cassandra's, before switching back to her own vivid blue. Her stare empty and hollow and dead, but accusing just the same. Blood dripped slowly from the corner of her mouth and when she opened it to speak, her flashing white teeth stained red with blood, I screamed.

I was still screaming when I awoke. The sound rebounded around me as I pushed myself up on my elbows, trying desperately to free myself from the constricting web of my sheets. The walls closed in on me like a living thing and my lungs, already heaving from my nightmare, strained to draw in air. My heart thundered in my throat, making it even more difficult to breathe. My hair stuck to my face and neck in sticky tendrils.

Awareness came upon me with insidious slowness as my breathing gradually started to ease and my heart once again took up its rightful place in my chest. A soft, scuffing sound outside my cell made me turn my head in the direction of the barred door as I pulled the now freed sheet up to my chin.

One of the night-shift guards looked in, her large form backlit by the banks of fluorescent lights as they were turned on row by row overhead. "Are you alright, Angel?" she asked, her voice concerned.

"Yeah. Yeah, I'm fine. Just a nightmare." Pushing the sweat-sticky hair from my face, I managed a shaky laugh. "Haven't had one of those in awhile. Guess I was due for one, huh?"

The woman's expression became sad. "Someone like you shouldn't have nightmares, Angel. You should be out living your life somewhere, doing good for people. You don't belong locked behind bars." Sighing, she shook her head. "This is one of the worst parts of my job: guarding an innocent woman."

"I'm not innocent, Peg. I killed my husband."

"You might have killed him, Angel, but you sure as hell didn't murder him. I read the reports. The man was raping you, for God's sake!"

"Raping me or not, I still killed him. The law demands I pay the penalty for that, and I am. But thank you for your concern. I mean that. It means a lot to me to know that people care."

I could see the faint sign of color on her face as she fiddled with the keys on her belt. "Anyway, you wanna get sprung? Almost time to start a new day."

I felt myself grin, unaccountably glad that the night was finally over. "Sounds wonderful."

A rattling of a key and the turning of a lock and another day began in the Bog.

After forcing down some breakfast, I made my way to the library. Corinne greeted me with a smile and gestured me over to my customary seat, where a pile of newspapers, some yellowed with age, awaited my perusal. At my questioning glance, she came to my table, tea mug in hand, and nodded toward the stack. "Heard about what happened yesterday," she began, setting the fragrant tea down on the table. "I wondered a bit about this Josephina myself since Ice never mentioned her to me. I did a little digging and came up with some interesting items. Have a look."

Sitting down, I sipped my tea, which was a definite step up from the sewer sludge they called coffee in the Bog. As I blinked the steam from my eyes, I picked up the top paper, which, by the date, was only a few days old, and shook it out. Halfway down the front page was a picture of a very familiar woman surrounded by dark clad lawyers and holding her hand up in front of her face to avoid the snapping cameras. The caption read: "*Wife of Mafia Don to be Transferred to Rainwater.*"

Scanning the columns of text, I learned that Josephina was also known as Mrs. Josephina Briacci, the wife of Salvatore Briacci, a noted underworld figure in Pittsburgh. It appeared that Mr. Briacci had gotten himself into a bit of trouble over some extortion, failure to pay back taxes, and conspiracy to commit murder charges and was indicted by the Commonwealth of Pennsylvania.

Reading further, I discovered that Josephina had refused to testify against her husband. While it's illegal to force a wife to testify against her husband, refusing to do so gets the prosecutors upset. The newspaper speculated, in an editorial in the same edition, that Josephina's charges, of accessory to conspiracy after the fact, were the State's little payback for her refusal to play ball with them.

Usually people bound over for trial spent their time like I did, in the county jail. That she was sent, under cover of darkness, to the State Prison to await trial was a definite mystery and one that I was determined to solve.

The other papers contained more information on Salvatore Briacci and his crime syndicate, but very little else on his wife. My tea was cold by the time I put down the last paper, now knowing more about the so-called Mafioso than I'd ever wanted to learn. Stretching, I looked back over at Corinne, who had gone back to her desk and was leafing through some book or other, her half-glasses settled low on her nose. "Well, that tells me a *little*, anyway."

Looking up, she smiled at me, eyes warm over the tops of her glasses. "Not nearly enough though."

"Not even close. What is her connection with Ice? You didn't see her out there, Corinne. She was absolutely devastated when Josephina died. It was almost like a member of her family had died or something." I couldn't help shivering as I remembered the mournful howl and Ice's murderous attack on Cassandra.

"Well, she certainly never talked to me about her, that's for sure," Corinne replied, sounding just the smallest bit put out. "I do have some ideas, though. For what they're worth."

I folded my hands over the stack of papers in front of me. "And they are?"

"Well, one of the things that I *do* know, as I've told you before, is that Ice was tied up in organized crime when she was released from the Bog last time. I've never heard her name mentioned in connection with this Salvatore Briacci, but her whole trial was very hush-hush, so we can't rule out that connection. Perhaps that's how they met?"

"Possibly, but you said that the Mafia backed off when she was indicted for murder. It doesn't make sense that they would treat each other so warmly if Ice was betrayed by her husband, does it?"

Corinne lifted her hand in an equivalent of a shrug. "Who knows with Ice? That woman's more close-lipped than a virgin wearing a chastity belt."

I choked for the second time on my cold tea. That was one thing about Corinne; the woman had more off-the-wall sayings than anyone I ever knew. You never knew what was going to come out of that prim and proper mouth next. Swallowing the dregs, I set the mug down on the table and worried the newsprint off the side of my hand with my thumb. "I wonder how she's doing."

"Ice? I imagine just fine. She managed to find herself in a bit of hot water from time to time when starting up the Amazons. The hole is almost like a second home to her." Corinne sat back in her chair, took off her glasses and smiled. "She always did prefer her own company to that of other humans anyway. Don't worry about her, little Angel. She'll do alright."

Nodding, I turned my attention to my hand, managing to pretty much smear newsprint everywhere in the process of trying to wipe it off.

"What about you?" my friend asked.

"What *about* me?"

"Well, I heard about what happened yesterday, obviously. It must have been difficult for you to witness that."

"Which part?" I snapped. "Where Cassandra murdered Josephina in cold blood or where Ice almost strangled Cassandra to death with her bare hands?"

Obviously startled, Corinne stared at me, open-mouthed and blinking.

I let out a long sigh, dropping my hands back down onto the table from where they had been enunciating my point. "I'm sorry, Corinne. You didn't deserve that."

My friend smiled once again. "That's alright, child. I was just startled because I've never heard you speak out quite so emphatically before."

"Well, you've never seen me witness a murder and an attempted murder within the space of a half hour before either. It was…tough." I rubbed at my forehead, trying to ward off an impending headache. "I didn't sleep well last night and I have a feeling those particular nightmares are gonna stick around for a long time to come."

"I imagine they might," she commiserated. "On a more pleasant subject, how are things going with Ice? Obviously they're on hold for the moment, but I managed to get a peek at the two of you out in the yard yesterday." Her smile was a sly one as she looked penetratingly at me, obviously in search of an answer. To her credit, she never did ask me about the truth to the rumors of what I termed, in my mind, the 'Shower Incident'. "The two of you looked rather…cozy."

Managing to keep the blush from showing on my face, I nodded, continuing to meet her direct gaze. "They're going. She's a tough nut to crack, but crack her I will. One way or another."

Corinne nodded, crossing her arms over her ample bosom. "If anyone on God's green earth can, my sweet little Angel, you'll be the one to do it."

I stared back at her, wishing I could be so confident and praying to that same God, as well as any others who would listen, to be given the chance to find out.

🗝   🗝   🗝   🗝

The next two months passed slowly and quickly at the same time. Winter had finally come, sinking its icy talons into us all, raising tempers and lowering spirits. During a time when the outside world was roasting chestnuts over an open fire, trimming trees and making snowmen, the residents of the Bog were trying to keep warm and stay alive. Since Ice's detention in isolation, tensions had risen in the prison. Montana had finally been given parole two weeks after the incident, leaving the Amazons effectively leaderless.

Critter was a good administrator, but she didn't have the overbearing sense of machismo that characterized both Montana and Ice. Pony and Sonny didn't want the job, preferring instead to remain in their roles as enforcers and the other Amazons, quite frankly, had neither the tenure nor the drive to lead such a diverse group of women in a common purpose.

Derby's gang, especially, began to test the waters, moving in like a shark among a school of weaker fish. So far my friends had been able to hold their own but it appeared that it would be a race to see if they could hold off Derby's advance long enough for Ice to be released from isolation.

The other gangs, emboldened by Derby's seeming successes, began to make their own voices heard, managing to set off several small riots which the guards and the Amazons were hard-pressed to quell. All in all, it was a difficult time for us all.

For my part, I continued to live my life as best I could, staying, for the most part, in the background of prison life. My side job as purveyor of things great and small picked up some during the holiday season, managing to keep me busy enough that my mind didn't constantly dwell on a certain woman spending two months of her life in darkness and solitude. My only saving grace was Corinne's repeated assurances that Ice felt quite at home in the hole and would be fine.

I, however, was not fine. I found that I missed her terribly. Even on days when we didn't speak, just knowing she was there made me feel safe and content in a way I hadn't at any time before, even when I was free. This seeming connection that we had was something that I'd come to rely on as a lifeline and while in a way that feeling of dependence was frightening in the extreme, when thought about in the right way it helped to keep me grounded and centered. It was like waking up to find something you never knew you'd lost and so was all the more precious for the having.

To keep myself busy when the days wanted to drag, I made it my duty to keep up Ice's cell. Though I wasn't an expert by any means, my reading up on Bonsai gave me the basic skills needed to at least keep the trees alive if nothing else.

The first few times I made the trek to her cell, I was careful to keep my hands and eyes to myself, tending only to the trees and nothing else. I was very loathe to intrude on her personal space, so fiercely protected and cherished by this very private woman.

One of the first things I noticed was that the bonsai rake, its acquisition starting things between the two of us, was looking ragged and worn. I hefted it, surprised at its small weight, rubbing my thumb along the smooth wood handle as I imagined Ice quietly tending her garden. The thought brought a smile to my face and I quietly began to hum as I worked with the trees, trying to keep them as healthy as I could. I promised myself I'd replace the worn rake with a new one as soon as I could.

My resolve to let sleeping dogs lie started to waver, however, the more I visited the cell. The temptation to look around was just too great and I found both my mind and eyes wandering as I tended to the Bonsai. My gaze strayed from the trees to the maps, which hadn't changed since I'd last visited Ice there, to the neat stack of books by the short bunk. One day, finally giving up all pretense of remaining uninterested, I walked over to the books as if drawn on a lure.

Tilting my head to look at the spines, I saw the complete works of Solzhenitsyn, which didn't surprise me. Beneath that was a book on Ancient Mythology which was laying atop hard cover texts for Chemical Engineering and Aeronautics respectively. I shook my head in wonderment as my eyes continued to travel down the titles. "Egg-head books," I whispered, disbelieving. "She reads egg-head books."

Unlike the collections of other inmates' I'd viewed, and knowing the library's check-out pattern by heart, I was slightly surprised to note that there were no torrid romance novels in the stack. 'Bodice-rippers', my mother liked to call them, her passion for the genre well known. My father often joked that she alone managed to keep the Harlequin people in business with her avid reading.

The biggest surprise, by far, was a copy of the entire Tao Te Ching, written in its original language. To me it was a masterful feat of intellect that she could even manage to read the thing, let alone understand and ponder it. But by the faint crease in its spine, the Tao appeared to be a book she went to often.

Squatting down carefully so as not to disturb the meticulous stack, I pulled the book from its resting place, glancing at the cryptography on the covers and running my finger over the spine. After a long moment, I opened the book, surprised when a small white square of paper slipped from beneath the cover and fluttered to the floor to land face down. Placing the book on the bed, I reached down and picked the square up, flipping it over but determined not to pry if it appeared to be something important.

My resolve lasted all of about two seconds.

What I had in my hand was a black and white photograph of three people and a dog. The man, tall and well built, was incredibly handsome. His dark hair slicked back, his chiseled face sported a pencil-thin "Clark Gable" type moustache. He wore a conservative dark suit, a bright shirt and narrow tie. Standing next to him, arm clasped under his, was an absolutely gorgeous woman. Tall and exotic, she wore her hair in a "Jackie Kennedy" flip with a small pill-box had set carefully atop it. She wore a light colored skirt-suit, white gloves and a matching purse clutched in one hand. Her free hand rested atop the shoulder of a young girl I recognized instantly as Ice. Dressed in what looked to be a plaid jumper, knee socks and patent leather shoes, her long hair tumbling over her shoulders, I could easily see the first blush of what was to become a great beauty in her fine features.

But what struck me the most, and in fact caused my heart to squeeze up in my chest, was the radiant smile on her face and the look of innocent, trusting happiness in those light-colored eyes. At that moment, I wished for nothing more in the world than for the ability to just step through that photograph, kneel down, and stare into the open and honest face of the young girl Ice had once been.

I didn't realize I was crying until a tear landed on the picture, causing the features of a huge, black shepherd to become magnified under the salty liquid. Ice had the dog's thick ruff caught in a fierce embrace and the camera had frozen the large pink tongue forever just inches from the young girl's face.

Sniffing back my tears and carefully wiping the precious photo on the sleeve of my jumpsuit, I stared it once again for a long, intense moment. Reaching out a trembling finger, I gently brushed the frozen bangs on Ice's head, smiling a little in reflex at the broad grin directed my way. "This part of you is in there, Ice. Somewhere. And I'll help you find it again. I promise."

✿   ✿   ✿   ✿

That evening, as I lay on my bunk, my mind was continually drawn back to the photograph and the sense of wistful happiness it invoked within me. Not only was the expression on Ice's young face something to ponder, so too was the obvious love her family had for her. It got me to thinking about my own family and my place in it.

As I read these latest lines, I realize that I haven't told you, the reader, very much about my own family, aside from some random sayings of my mother and the like. I suppose now is as good a time as any to rectify that situation.

I was what is known as a 'change-of-life' baby. My parents were staunch Catholics, and so had been trying very hard to have and raise a large family in keeping with the tenets of their church teachings. Every month they plotted and planned, keeping strictly to the laughable "rhythm method," and every month they failed.

When my mother's reproductive system finally decided to start giving up the ghost, what she thought to be menopause turned out, nine months later, to be me.

My father, who had always wanted a boy to carry on both his name and his legacy, was sorely disappointed when a howling daughter was presented to him instead. I've heard it said that in other families, fathers of this sort just pushed the tiny matter of gender aside and raised their daughter like a son.

Such was not the case with me.

Born to a family replete with old-world traditions, I was raised as primly as a proper girl could be. Frilly dresses cut carefully below the knee so as not to tempt the other toddlers milling about, white hose and patent leather shoes, ribbons and bows in my hair were my daily uniforms. Sewing and cooking and learning to be a proper woman were my lessons, my mother and her cronies, my teachers.

I hated every moment of it.

While the other children of the neighborhood were riding bikes, building tree-forts, having mock wars and playing kick-the-can, I was inside learning the finer points of baking muffins that would turn out airy and light every time. After time. After time.

Books were my only refuge from the world of boredom. I read voraciously, getting swept up in the fantasy worlds of Nancy Drew and the Bobbsey Twins, solving the mysteries of Encyclopedia Brown before he did, the list went on and on. Books were my island, my safe harbor in a world of confusion.

My father and I never bonded. When I wanted love and approval, I received remote coldness. I loved him desperately, and I know he loved me in his own way in return, but we were never close.

I know I broke their hearts when I eloped and shattered them beyond repair when I took Peter's life. Since his death, I've only seen my parents twice. Once was on the day of my conviction. I remember being shocked speechless over how old they'd gotten in such a short time. Or maybe they'd always been old and I was seeing them for the first time through the eyes of an adult. The last time was two years ago as of this writing, and it was just my mother I saw. She came to tell me that my father had passed away the previous month and that she was moving to Phoenix to live with her younger sister.

Though we met in the visitor's room with nothing between us but time and cool reserve, she never once touched me, nor truly looked me in the eye. When I told her I loved her, she didn't respond. I knew then that I was as dead to her as her husband was.

It should have broken my heart, but it didn't. I'd finally grown up enough to realize that sometimes the families you made were as important as the families you were born into. And that was enough for me.

Chapter 5

Three weeks later, I once again found myself in the library, though this time I was surrounded by Amazons. Bruised and battered Amazons, to be precise. The prison had exploded in a flurry of violent outbursts, each one larger and more destructive than the last. Pony had one arm in a sling, her fingers massively swollen and Sonny was sporting a truly spectacular shiner to go with her broken nose. Only Critter seemed to have gotten off relatively unscathed.

"Someone needs to talk to her," Pony said, wincing as she stretched. "We can't hold the line anymore and the guards can't either. The warden seems to be getting off on it, the idiot."

Several sets of eyes turned to Corinne, who held her hands up. "Don't look at me, ladies."

The eyes then turned to me, pleading. I shook my head slowly. "I don't think so, guys. She hasn't been out of her cell once since she got released. You all saw what she looked like, half dead and insane. I've tried twice already and almost gotten my head bitten off both times. Maybe someone else should try."

"C'mon, Angel. You talked her down after that fight with Cassandra. You're our only hope here. If Ice doesn't snap out of it soon, we're all gonna be in a world of hurt." Critter's dark eyes drilled into mine. "You know it's true, don't you? We need her. And we need you to get to her."

Breaking down under the weight of their gazes, I sighed, then nodded my assent. "Alright, but if I don't come back down in a few hours, remember that I don't want a viewing, will you?"

The sense of relief in the room was palpable and Critter gripped my hand as I rose to my feet. "You can do it, Angel. You're the best."

"Keep on saying that, Critter. Maybe one day I'll actually start believing it."

Turning on my heel, the weight of their hopes resting heavily on my shoulders, I left the safety of the library, once again a woman on a mission.

I eased my way up the stairs and down the catwalk, dreading what I would find. The day of Ice's release from isolation had been a horrendous one for me. Like a teenager awaiting her first date, I spent the day in nervous anticipation, fixing my hair and pressing the wrinkles out of my jumpsuit so many times that I earned regular teasing cracks about my habits from Corinne and some of the others.

When I finally saw her, late that afternoon, she was practically being held up in the steady grips of Sandra and another guard I didn't recognize. She was bone thin. Her uniform hung off her like a sack. Her skin was almost snow-white and her hair, once a luxurious mane, was brittle, snarled and lifeless. Her beautiful face sported a multitude of draining sores around her mouth and her eyes were totally bereft of any spark, any sign of the life within. They sat in deep hollows surrounded by circles of the darkest brown.

Almost moaning, I walked up to the trio, reaching out to touch this apparition that appeared in the guise of my friend. She actually *flinched* away and I cried out. Sandra sadly shook her head, gently pushing me away as they passed, heading for the stairs.

Horror-filled, I turned and rushed back to the library, laying into Corinne as soon as I saw her.

I'd been to Ice's cell twice since then, both times to be chased out by the snarling, half crazed animal Ice had become.

Since then, I'd made regular trips to both the guards' station and the infirmary demanding answers. None were provided me except the fact that Ice's time in isolation had not gone as expected. When I asked why she wasn't in the hospital where she surely belonged, I was ignored.

And here I was, trying yet again.

As I moved further down the catwalk, I was drawn on by the sound of soft humming. The tune was mournful but melodic and brought the sting of tears to my eyes. As I stepped up to the open cell door, I noticed Sandra sitting on the bed next to Ice, holding her hand and stroking her hair. On the floor beside the bed was a tray of half-eaten food and by the quality of the meal, I guessed that it hadn't come from the prison's kitchen.

Ice sat on the bed, her back against the wall, her head bowed and her free hand in her lap, repeatedly clenching it into a fist, then relaxing, only to clench again. Sandra's soft melody filled the air. Warm tears spilled out of my eyes and I brought my hand up to my mouth to mask the sounds of my crying.

The humming trailed off as Sandra's head lifted. When she saw me standing there, she smiled. "Angel! C'mon in! Ice, look. Angel's here." When Ice didn't respond, Sandra beckoned me closer. "Come, sit on the bed next to her. Take her other hand. Her nails are chewing the hell out of her palm."

Doing what she requested, I gingerly entered the rest of the way into the cell, then lowered myself onto the bunk. Reaching out, I grasped Ice's free hand and, as gently as I possibly could, uncurled the tight fist, threading my fingers through her much longer ones.

God, her hand was like ice! Where the heat of her had always burned a path right through to my soul, this coldness was frightening. I could feel small dots of blood where our hands met, the only points of warmth on our joined flesh. I looked as well as I could into her eyes, but there was no one looking back at me. Shuddering, I looked past my friend and into the compassionate eyes of the head guard. "How's she doing?"

"A little better. At least I got her to eat something this time. I'll be the first to admit that I'm not the world's greatest cook, but anything's better than the slop they feed us here."

Looking down at the tray, I could only nod in agreement. At least the items on the plate were readily identifiable, which was more than I could say about the prison's version of food.

"Anyway, I was just telling her about Diane when you came in."

"Diane?"

Sandra smiled. "My daughter. Ice saved her life. Didn't ya." When Ice didn't respond, the guard looked back over to me. "My husband was a police officer who was killed in the line of duty when Diane was six. Since I needed to keep working to keep a roof over our heads and meals on the table, I'd drop her off at my mother's before school and pick her up after I got off of work. It worked out ok for a little while, but my mother's old and a bit frail."

Sighing, she adjusted herself on the bed and gripped Ice's hand tighter. "As Diane got older, she fell in with a rougher crowd. Petty vandalism at first, then shoplifting, then drugs. My mother didn't say anything until it was almost too late. I'd come home so tired every evening that I didn't see the signs, though I should have." She sighed again. "Then she got involved with a gang and I got a call from the police station one day while I was at work. It seemed she'd been the lookout for a home burglary and she'd gotten caught with the rest of her cronies. It was the last straw. The police agreed to drop the charges, but I knew she needed some help. So I brought her here. It was the first time she'd ever seen the inside of a real prison. Ice volunteered to help. She took Diane into a small room off the visitor's room for about an hour. When my daughter came out, she looked a lot like Ice does now."

Sandra gently brushed the bangs away from Ice's head again, smiling tenderly at my friend. "Though neither one have ever talked about what happened in that room, Diane never went back to her old ways again." Her smile turned proud. "She's a sophomore at Stanford now, making straight A's."

"Sandra, that's wonderful!"

"Yeah, it is. And I owe it all to this woman here. When Diane heard that Ice'd been sent back to prison she was devastated. Kept saying that there should have been something she could have done to prevent it; to help Ice like Ice helped her."

"Not...her fault."

Both of our heads shot up at the hoarse, almost unrecognizable voice. "Ice?" Sandra asked, astounded. "Did you say something?"

"Not...her fault," Ice repeated, her eyes still hollow, her mouth working to form words. "My fault. Not her fault."

My tears, which had stopped falling during Sandra's story, resumed their course down my face. Overwhelmed, it was all I could do to pick up the chilled hand laying in mine and raise it to my lips, brushing the softest of kisses against Ice's knuckles. "Thank God you're back," I whispered through the veil of my tears.

Just then, the sound of a muffled explosion filtered through to us, followed by an inmate's piercing scream. Alarm bells sounded next, their klaxon call to arms echoing stridently through the entire building. Then, like a tsunami, came the ever increasing sound of triumphant inmates cheering.

With a muttered curse, Sandra, though hours off duty by this time, jumped from the bed and grabbed her baton. She ran out to the catwalk and looked down, then turned to us, the smallest touch of fear in her eyes. "It's a riot!" she yelled to be heard over the sounds of screaming and the alarm. Running back into the cell, she laid a quick hand on my shoulder. "Watch her. I'll bet my paycheck Derby's behind this and this is the first place she'll come."

"Well, well, well," came a harsh voice from behind us. "Looks like the butch little head guard has a brain after all, eh girls? Better pay up, butchie. It's a sure bet you won't be needin' the money after we're through with ya."

Sandra and I turned our heads to see Derby and five of her cronies standing outside Ice's cell door, all armed to the teeth. Derby had appropriated a guard's baton and was rhythmically slapping one end into her palm as she grinned ferally at us. "I always knew there was somethin' goin' on between you and the Ice Maiden, Sandra. I just didn't know you pulled sweet little Angel into it too." Her sparkling gaze turned to me. "Tell me, Angel, do ya like the taste of guard-snatch? Does she make you scream the way Ice does?" Throwing back her head, Derby howled to the ceiling while her friends grinned and slapped palms.

That did it. I rocketed up out of bed like my pants were in flames, only to be held back by Sandra. "No. Let me handle this. You just keep an eye on Ice, alright?"

Though I considered slipping out of her hold, I calmed my temper and nodded, finally. Grinning slightly, she squeezed my arm in a gesture very reminiscent of Ice. "Good girl."

"Yeah, you go ahead and listen to your Mistress there, little girl. Keep an eye on poor ol' Ice, will ya? I want her all nice and het up when I come to break her fuckin' neck."

With that, Derby hefted the baton above her head and stepped into the cell. Sandra spun quickly to meet the downward strike. The sound of wood hitting wood filled the room and the guard grunted from the stinging contact but refused to yield.

Mustering her strength, Sandra pushed Derby back outside the cell, then moved forward to block the entrance with her large, wide body. I sat back down on the bed, grasped Ice's still cold hand, and watched intently.

It felt very strange to be in the position of protecting the woman I'd grown to view as my own protector. At the same time, however, it felt very right, as if in some other time and in some other place, I had done exactly that. I wondered, briefly, why Sandra didn't just lock the door with us inside, but the next thrust from Derby's weapon drove that thought from my mind as Sandra was driven back a step. I looked quickly at Ice, trying to gauge her reaction to the fight, but found myself looking into the eyes of a woman lost once again.

Sandra managed to bull-rush Derby back outside of the cell again, holding her nightstick parallel against her body and taking on comers one and all. Reaching behind her like a relay-race runner, Derby received a shiv from one of her underlings and thrust it forward, trying to get past Sandra's defenses. Breathing heavily, Sandra managed to block every thrust but I could tell she was tiring, especially when the other gang members started poking the ends of their batons through the bars, jabbing at her.

Still, she held her position valiantly, using her baton strictly for defense while trying to evade as many of the blows as she could. Her hair became wet with sweat and I could see the blood from several tiny cuts begin to well up on her flailing hands and arms.

When Derby began to tire, one of her cronies stepped in, shiv in hand, and began a vicious attack on the larger guard, scoring several hits in rapid succession. I could easily see that Sandra's blocks were getting sloppier as the relentless pressure just kept coming in the form of armed, jeering inmates.

Coming together finally, the group gathered behind the lead inmate and pushed, en masse, forcing Sandra from her post at the door and following her into the cell, still swinging their clubs and knives with wanton fury. Sandra's legs weakened and she fell against me, her own club dropping from a suddenly nerveless hand.

I saw my chance and took it, scooping up the falling baton before it could touch the ground and powering up from the bed. Finding myself face to face with a leering Derby, I twirled the baton then brought it down hard on the hand that held the shiv. The solid, polished wood cracked down hard on her unprotected wrist and she dropped the knife as she howled and cradled her arm. Following through on the blow, I caught another inmate in the chest. Her wheezingly expelled breath blew back my hair and I kicked her out and away from me, managing to catch two other women with the one move.

As the remaining gang members formed a wary half-circle around me, I chanced a quick look down at Sandra, who'd managed to make it to her knees and was shaking her head to clear it. "Are you alright?"

"Yeah, I'm ok." She sounded woozy and her face was pale.

"Just stay close to Ice. I'll handle these idiots."

"Like hell you will, little girl," Derby snarled, grabbing another baton from one of her cohorts and coming at me with awkward left-handed blows. I deflected each crude thrust quite easily, turning her momentum back onto her and dancing out of the way when I could. I was quite conscious of the fact that I needed to keep Ice and Sandra at my back at all times and it was limiting what I could do.

Another woman swung a baton at me but I blocked it easily, the move-ment feeling more natural than it should have. Twirling quickly, I managed to catch another woman under the chin, snapping her head back and send-ing her into dreamland.

I heard the whistling of a club a split second before I felt the blow. Derby's baton came down hard at the juncture of my neck and shoulder, instantly rendering my arm useless and numb. My own weapon dropped and a kick to my side sent me into Sandra, who collapsed back against the bed with me in her arms.

Derby was on us both in an instant, pushing away the other assailants in her lust to be the one to finish us off. Her good hand curled into a fist and she drew it back like a catapult, grinning fiercely at me as she did so. "This is gonna feel *so* good, fishie."

Trying to sit up behind me, Sandra inadvertently pinned my arms to my side. All I could do to avoid being punched in the face was to duck my head and hope Sandra had the same idea.

She didn't.

As Derby's fist pistoned forward, I ducked left and immediately heard the crunching impact of knuckles breaking a nose. It had become a sound I was well acquainted with during my time in the Bog. As Sandra moaned out her pain, I drew my knees up to my chest then launched them toward Derby's ponderous gut.

Unfortunately for me, it was just then that Derby's rarely used 'quick-gene' decided to kick in. She grabbed my ankles inches from her belly and, grinning evilly, yanked hard. I winced as my tailbone smacked down on the floor. Looking up, I stared at the sea of faces that surrounded me. They were all peering down at me with avid, malicious stares.

"Would ya look at this. Little Miss High-and-Mighty doesn't look all that special anymore, does she girls."

The other women snickered and elbowed one another.

"Hey Derby," one spoke up, "how's about givin' us a piece before ya do her?"

"Yeah, Derby!" others chimed in, "save some for us!"

There was no way I was going to take that lying down, as it were. Levering my upper body up on my arms, I used a sweet little twisting move that Montana had taught me before she was paroled, then used the momentum to jump to my feet. My own fists clenched solidly, I delivered a rapid one-two punch to Derby's belly, causing her to double over and gasp for breath. As she did so, I lifted my knee, wincing as it collided with her forehead, snapping her neck back.

Her cronies were on me in an instant and though I fought like a woman possessed, their sheer numbers overwhelmed me in a very few moments.

Standing straight again, Derby brought her large body within inches of mine, tilting my chin up with one meaty hand. "Ya know, I was gonna keep you around for a few laughs, blondie. But that little move just earned you a ticket to hell. Don't worry about not saying goodbye to your lover-girl though. She'll be meeting you down there shortly."

I should have been terrified. Any sane person would have. Instead, all I could feel was a bottomless well of icy cold rage that numbed the place where my heart should have been. Inhaling deeply through my nose, I gathered whatever moisture was left in my mouth and spat it at my tormentor, baring my teeth in a grin when it hit her right below one bulging eye. "Bite me."

Roaring incoherently, Derby squeezed my jaw so tightly I was sure I was going to crack under the pressure. With her free hand, she wiped the spittle from her cheek, then used her momentum from the gesture to back-hand me across the face. Letting my head roll with the blow, I turned back to her, allowing a dark grin to spread my lips. "Is that the best you got, Derby? And here I thought you were tough."

Don't ask me why I was taunting a raging bull, because, in all honesty, I have no idea myself. It was as if I knew I was going to die, right then, right there. And I didn't want to go out like a coward. Something primal and dark licked at my guts and the feeling terrified me. But in a way, it felt very right, as some things do from time to time. It was also exhilarating in a way that a very scary carnival ride is exhilarating.

I'd be lying, however, if I didn't admit to some deep, dark part of myself who was absolutely begging, groveling on her knees, for Ice or even Sandra to snap out of their respective stupors and get me out of the hole I'd just dug deeper for myself.

Derby's hand returned to my jaw, then trailed almost sensuously down the line of my neck. Her smile, though predatory, was almost sad. "I always did enjoy a good choking, fishie. That's how I killed three of my 'friends', ya know. It…does…something for me, if ya get what I'm sayin. It pissed me off when ya stopped ol' Ice over there from doin' Psycho that way. Really pissed me off. And I hate bein' pissed off, right girls?"

I didn't have to move my eyes to see the confirming, anticipatory nods of the women surrounding me.

"Right. So, I figure, since you took that away from me, I'll just have ta take it away from you." Her fingers clenched spasmodically around my neck, cutting off my air and blood supply in a heartbeat. A heartbeat that I could feel struggling to push blood through to my brain. Dark spots circled enticingly before my eyes, asking me to join their macabre dance.

"Ya know, it's amazing how good a neck feels under your fingers, fishie. All nice 'n warm. The life beatin' away, getting weaker and weaker the longer ya hold on. Your face gets this really cool red color, then purple and your lips turn blue. Your eyes kinda bug out and look all scared. Really gets me off."

The black roses of oxygen starvation bloomed in my vision and I found myself beginning to welcome their presence. I tried to lift my arms but found them pinned against my body by a strength I couldn't seem to break. Moving didn't seem to be all that important anymore.

As if from far away, I could feel Derby's free hand slowly trail down over the front of my body, stopping to cup, then squeeze, one of my breasts. The pain registered as a very faint, unimportant thing. Her lips were moving as she leered at me but the sound of her words was lost in the buzzing in my brain.

I remember trying to think of something, something that seemed very important. But my resolve was lost; fogged within the clarion call of sleep, of peace.

My eyes began to slip closed as I gave into the urgent summons. I felt myself falling and can remember thinking that death wasn't really all that bad after all. It was kind of peaceful, actually.

Until the air that rushed back into my heaving lungs was forced back out again by the weight of an impossibly heavy body that collapsed across my own.

I blinked quickly against a headache that screamed through me with the speed of blood rushing into my deprived brain. Then looked up into the eyes of my savior who at that moment looked like a demon spawned from the deepest pits of hell, her hair and eyes wild and rolling, her teeth bared in a primordial snarl.

Realizing I was still among the living, I began to struggle against the weight pinning me to the floor; a weight which was gone abruptly as my dark avenger reached down and pulled Derby from me, tossing her aside with no more effort than a blade of grass into the wind. She reached down once again and hauled me to my feet. Then, after looking at me with that penetrating gaze, turned and handed me off to Sandra, who had managed to regain consciousness.

"Watch her," Ice croaked out before turning to deal with the massing inmates. She became a being of fists and fury, punching inmate after inmate into painful unconsciousness and tossing them out of her cell to land slumped against the peeling green of the barred catwalk.

I looked on, safe within the nest of Sandra's strong arms as I struggled to recapture the breath I'd lost. Every time one of Ice's opponents would get near the long table holding her precious trees, I'd wince, but she always managed to brush them away before any damage could be done.

Bone thin and wan, she still possessed a strength that I'd never seen in anyone before. Inmates flew like dolls from the force of her blows, piling up outside the cell door in jumbled heaps. She moved with the speed of a shooting star, always deflecting a blow a split second before it was set to connect.

She was silent, this specter of death-made-woman; fulfilling her duties with calm, even breaths, yet full of passion's fury that blazed from her eyes like the god of retribution come down to earth.

Grabbing the last of the upstarts by the back of the collar and seat of her pants, Ice tossed the woman into the living pile she'd made, then followed, wiping her hands casually on her jumpsuit. Pulling away from Sandra, I rushed up behind Ice, still panting from my close brush with the beyond. From my place by her side, I could see Derby struggling to get out from under the pile of beaten women, her face flushed red from her frantic efforts.

Unthinking, I put my hand on Ice's back. She whirled, her eyes still mad with rage, and lifted her hand, ready to swing. We stood frozen through the lock of our gazes for several seconds. I watched, helplessly, waiting for some spark of sanity or humanity to darken those arctic eyes.

A noise off to our left and she blinked, then turned, pushing me carefully behind her. Her thin body was thrumming with energy and I felt as if I were standing next to a high-tension wire, the hair lifting on my arms and at the nape of my neck.

From behind her still-broad back I could see what looked to be an army of inmates running toward us. There was another sound to the right and, looking back, I saw the same army coming from the other side. "Oh shit."

The dark head turned fractionally, and I swore I could see the beginnings of a smile on her pale visage. "Just stay behind me at all times." Her voice was still hoarse and whispery from disuse, but to me, it was the most beautiful melody in the world.

"I'm there." After what had just happened between us, I'll never know what possessed me to put one hand on her hip, but I was glad I did, because she reached over and gave it a quick squeeze before releasing me.

Her arm shot out quickly and pushed the cell door closed, trapping Sandra safely inside, then backed us both against it. Though her head never moved, I could just guess that those eyes were tracking each group easily, determining strengths and weaknesses in the time it took me to silently admit how scared I was.

It was amazing how different my attitude toward death was since Ice had rejoined the land of the sane. It wasn't alright to die anymore and so the fear came back, clutching at me with its slimy fingers. Biting my lip, I forced it down, deep and far.

Sandwiched between steel bars and Ice's long body, I looked left and right in rapid succession. The inmates had slowed to a stop and seemed to be waiting for something. They'd strung out along the catwalk, ten to a side, all bearing weapons and looking like they knew how to use them. I counted several more batons, obviously stolen from the guards, some lengths of wood, a few thick chains from the auto shop, no doubt, and several crude shivs. The women in front of Ice, still jumbled in a pile of battered bodies, made no attempt to move. Even Derby seemed content to let things play out.

It was a very tense situation. Below us, I could hear the sounds of the riot continuing. Yells and screams filled the air, though sometime along the line, the alarms had stopped ringing. Ice turned her head again, her raspy voice pitched low. "Whatever happens, remember to guard the door. Sandra needs to be kept safe, alright?"

"Got it."

"Good."

The stand-off continued on for so long that finally Derby, from her place at the bottom of the pile, lifted her head. "Well? What the fuck are you guys waiting for, parole?! Get her!"

Hefting their weapons, the inmates started forward on either side of us, filling the catwalk with their threatening yells. Ice stood absolutely still, waiting for them to come at her. When they got in range, she grabbed each of the front-runners by the front of their jumpsuits and threw them together. The sound of bodies colliding was loud in the small space we shared. Then she separated them, tossing each back the way they'd come and succeeded in bowling down the women who were second and third in line.

The others scrambled over their fallen comrades and came at us hard. Ice turned left while I turned right. We moved at the same time as if connected through some sort of strange martial ballet where we two were the only ones who knew the moves and heard the music as we warded off our assailants. Weapons flew; bodies behind them by just a breath.

I ducked as the end of a thick chain came at my face, wincing as it clanged against the steel bars of Ice's cell. Jumping up quickly, I managed to grab the end as it was being drawn back and tugged hard, pleased with how easily it became mine. Wrapping both ends around my hands as Montana had taught me, I used it to block the thrusts of batons and shivs as they headed my way. As I raised my hands to block an overhead blow, a kick to my belly doubled me over briefly. A punch to the back of my neck drove me to my knees and left me seeing stars.

A hand to the back of my jumpsuit and I was back on my feet again, though one of my attackers had managed to grab the chain. She was a big woman, thick with muscle and sporting a white-blonde crewcut and several facial scars. Grinning at me through a mouthful of half-rotted teeth, she jerked her massive arms back, pulling the chain, and myself, along with her. Using the chain, she managed to turn me, then slammed back against the steel bars. I remember crying out as they cracked along my spine and the back of my skull and a sense of dizziness washed through me.

Her hands between mine, she pushed the chain up toward my neck, but I wasn't about to be choked half to death for a second time that day. Quickly twisting my hands to unwrap the ends, I let go of the chain and, during my attacker's start of surprise, grabbed in between *her* hands, my leverage preventing the weapon from being raised any higher against me. Then I kicked up in between her splayed legs, and let me assure anyone who thinks women aren't vulnerable to that particular move that they most definitely are.

Dropping the chain into my hands once again, she howled, her own hands going down to cup against her groin. I pushed her backward, toppling her into the woman coming up behind. Then I spun just in time to see Derby reach for one of Ice's legs as it came down from a beautifully delivered high kick.

I yelled out a warning, but it was too late. Ice lost her balance, dropping to one knee. The crowd of women erupted en masse, jumping on top of my fallen friend. Derby made her way up finally from the bottom of the pile and added her bulk to the pile of flying fists and feet.

Dropping my chain, I bolted to the pile, trying my best to drag the women out of the way but having little success at it, ducking blows as I was.

The mound of inmates seemed to freeze for a moment, then explode outward, bodies flying pell-mell against the catwalk railing, against the bars of the cells, and down each side of the catwalk. Ice stood tall from within the center of the pack, a dark Venus rising from the waves. Derby lunged again, her hands wrapping around Ice's neck. My friend's head drew back as a dark grin bloomed over her face. Lightening quick, she shot her head forward, cracking it against Derby's skull.

Derby's hands dropped away as her arm pinwheeled, trying to keep her balance as she landed high against the catwalk rail. Her backward momentum carried her over the low rail and she screamed. Ice's arm shot out and managed to grab Derby by the arm of her jumpsuit as she plummeted over the edge. Somehow, against all odds, the fabric held and the large inmate swayed, screaming and kicking her legs frantically, eight stories above the hard prison floor.

"Hang on and stop kicking, Derby, and I'll pull you up!" Ice shouted to be heard over the other woman's screaming.

Derby's free hand moved slowly up, fingers splaying before clamping convulsively on Ice's arm. Around and below us, all sounds of activity stopped as every woman in the Bog focused on the drama unfolding high above their heads.

Bracing herself with her free hand, Ice began to slowly pull Derby's large body up toward the railing. A foot or so from the top, she stopped suddenly as the sound of fabric tearing reached our ears. Derby kicked frantically again as the seam at her shoulder suddenly started to tear loose from its moorings.

"Stop struggling or I'll drop you, Derby!"

"Fuck that!" the terrified woman screamed. "If I'm goin', you're comin' with me, bitch!"

So saying, Derby began to jig her body left and right like a bass on a hook. Ice's back bowed completely as she was smashed against the short rail. Shouting out, I ran over and grabbed her tightly around the waist to keep her from going over.

"God damn it, Derby, stop fighting it!"

"Fuck you, Ice!" She jerked her body harder, twisting this way and that, trying to unseat Ice from her perch against the rail, her hatred for my friend more important to her than her own life.

Setting her legs, Ice tried pulling upward again. I helped to steady her as much as I could, tightening my grasp around her narrow waist and interlacing my fingers together. The others watched us, open-mouthed and wide-eyed. Her progress was slow and steady but effective as she managed, by slow inches, to pull Derby's twisting body upward once again toward the safety of the rail.

With a final ripping tear, the resilient fabric of Derby's jumpsuit gave up the ghost, leaving Ice with just a handful of sleeve. Luckily, however, the gang leader was close enough that her now freed arm was able to grasp onto the lowest rung of the barred railing.

Ice tugged upward again, still attached by Derby's grip on her arm. Her motion was halted abruptly as the other woman refused to let go of the railing. "I told you, bitch, you're goin' down."

Anchoring herself with her grip on the rung, Derby began to tug at Ice's arm once again, pulling it with all of her considerable strength. I could feel my friend's body go taut with the effort of remaining where she was.

"Oh no ya don't," Ice countered, using her knee to mash Derby's fingers against the railing. With a howling wail, the other woman released her grip on the rung. Ice tugged upward, hard and fast, and Derby, flailing out again, missed her grip and she twisted again, much harder this time.

I knew what was going to happen a split second before it did. I could see Derby's fingers loosen their grip on Ice's arm with the momentum of her motion and start to slide away. I know Ice saw it too because she made a desperate grab for the gang leader, missing by just the barest of margins.

With a scream of revenge denied, Derby plummeted to her death eight floors below. I turned my head and hid behind Ice's back as Derby fell the final few feet, not wanting to see her body splatter as it hit the ground. The sound of her hitting the flagstone floor echoed resoundingly through the now silent prison.

Ice slowly straightened, pushing herself away from the railing. Turning her head slowly, she pinned each one of us with a steely glare. "This riot is finished, understand? Put down your weapons and return to your cells or you'll have me to answer to."

Hoarse and broken though her voice was, it permeated every corner of the Bog and the inmates responded, dropping their weapons to the floor and turning away from one another to head back to their cells. The women on the catwalk with us did the same, their shoulders slumped and their heads hanging low like whipped dogs, which, in a way, was exactly what they were.

Ice's cell door creaked open and Sandra stepped out, walking over to the railing and looking down at the bloody scene below as her hand came up to lay against Ice's back. "Good try. I wanted to get out here and help, but those idiots had the door blocked."

"What happens now?" I asked.

Sandra turned her head to me, smiling in understanding. "Don't worry, Angel. Reports have a way of getting edited and misfiled around here. I'll figure out some tale that the warden'll believe." Turning back to Ice and giving her shoulder one last squeeze, she sighed and threaded her baton through the loop in her uniform belt. "Well, I guess I'd better get at it. This place is gonna be a bitch to clean up."

Ice turned with the guard. "Sandra…thanks. For everything."

Sandra smiled, her eyes warm and compassionate. "Think nothing of it, my friend. I can't even begin to pay you back for what you did for Diane. I was just glad I could help."

"When you speak to Diane again, tell her…tell her it wasn't her fault. Tell her…we all make mistakes."

"I will. Be well. Both of you." With a final smile and a wave, she turned from us to walk down the catwalk toward the stairs.

When Sandra's head disappeared beneath the level of the stairs, Ice turned her gaze to me. "Angel, I'm sorry about the way I treated you before. I wasn't myself."

I couldn't help but grin, guessing how hard apologies must be for her, warranted or not. "I'm just glad you're back, Ice." I threaded my arm around her waist once again and squeezed her to me. "I missed you, you know."

The very corner of her mouth twitched upward. "I know. I missed you too." Turning her head in the direction of her cell, she gestured with one hand. "Did you have anything to do with my trees still being alive?"

"Guilty as charged, so to speak. I couldn't stand the thought of such beauty wasting away." As I spoke, it hit me how much more meaning those casually used words held for me. Squeezing her once again for the sheer pleasure of it, I released her and backed away. "So…need any help cleaning up your cell?"

"Nah. I can take care of it later. I wanna go down and check out the library first."

An icy fist of dread clenched in my belly, drying my mouth from within. *The library! Corinne!* "Um…mind if I come down with you?"

"C'mon."

I barely kept myself from running as we started toward the stairs. I was suddenly sure that the library had been destroyed and my friends injured or even killed.

I cried out in horror as my fears seemed to be confirmed. As we ran down the final hallway, in the feeble light cast from the library's open door lay Sonny on her back, the crude handle of a shiv sticking obscenely from her upper abdomen. "Sonny!" I cried, running over to her and kneeling down. "What happened? Who did this to you?"

Barely conscious, my friend turned her head painfully toward the sound of her voice. Licking her lips, she tried to speak. "The library…attacked …Corinne…hurry…."

"Stay with her. I'll check it out." Ice ran past me and into the library. "Son of a bitch."

The quietly uttered expletive jerked my head up in alarm. I was torn between wanting to stay with Sonny and wanting to go into the library to see what had caused Ice's reaction. Sonny solved the problem for me, putting a hand on my shoulder and pushing me away weakly. "Go . . .help her. I'll...be alright."

"I should stay."

"No! Go...please. Help them. I've...managed to make it this long. Please." Helpless to resist the pleading in Sonny's dark eyes, I rose to my feet and turned toward the library. As I stepped inside, I couldn't contain my gasp of horror.

The room itself looked as if a tornado had hit it. Books and pieces of books lay scattered on the floor. Most of the tables and chairs, rickety to begin with, were now kindling. The bookcases we'd painstakingly crafted were overturned and shattered. Even Corinne's heavy desk was upended, her precious papers and texts littering the floor around it.

Next to the desk, Critter and Pony lay in a tangled heap, Critter bleeding heavily from a cut to her scalp. Ice stepped past me and squatted down next to the two, laying a gentle hand on Critter's shoulder and pulling her over to her back. "Critter. Critter, c'mon, wake up now."

Critter started and her eyelids fluttered open. I stepped over to the pair, squatting down next to my blonde friend. "Ice? You're...oh my God!" Critter tried to sit up but was restrained by Ice's grip on her shoulder.

"Relax. It's over. Who did this?"

Sinking her hand into her golden curls, Critter moaned in pain. "It was Derby's gang. We tried to fight 'em off but there were to many of them. They just kept coming. We couldn't stop them." Her eyes widened and she struggled against Ice again. "Pony! Where is she?"

"It's alright," Ice consoled her. "She's right here. Looks like she took a pretty big knock to the head too. I think she'll be alright, though."

Critter relaxed. "Thank God. My leg got trapped when they turned the desk over and she went at them. I saw her go down, then...nothing. I must have gotten clonked from behind."

I had to ask. "Critter, where's Corinne?" Looking around the destroyed room, I couldn't find my friend anywhere and it terrified me.

My friend turned her head, her dark eyes darting around the room. "She's...God, I don't know. Last time I saw her, she was holding off some of Derby's gang with her damned tea pot and then...I don't know."

Standing quickly, I walked past the overturned desk and over to the hidden little alcove that hid Corinne's hotplate and tea cozy. There, lying on a heap on the ground, her brass-coated teakettle battered and almost unrecognizable in one clenched fist, was Corinne. Her half-glasses had one lens shattered and lay askew on her nose and a magnificent shiner decorated one puffy eye. A small line of dried blood traced a path from one corner of her mouth.

Dropping to my knees, I reached out a trembling hand toward her neck, beyond gratified to find her skin warm and dry, her pulse beating strong and sure in her throat. "Oh, thank God," I whispered. "Corinne. Corinne, it's Angel. Time to wake up now, my friend. Corinne, come on, wake up!"

In response to my urgent summons, Corinne moaned, then fluttered her eyelids. Then, in a burst of quickness and strength that belied her advanced years, she brought up the battered teakettle and almost succeeded in knocking me senseless with it.

Ducking out of the way, I grasped her swinging arm gently but firmly. "Corinne, it's Angel. You're safe now. Just relax, alright?"

After a long moment, she slowly opened her eyes, blinking them rapidly as they watered in protest. A slow smile blossomed on her face. "I must be in heaven."

I couldn't help the laugh of relief that spilled from my lungs. "No, you're still in the Bog."

"Same difference, my Angel." She lifted her free hand to cup my cheek as awareness slowly came back to her eyes. The grin disappeared, setting her mouth in a hard line as she began to struggle against my restraining hand. "Oh, God, my poor library. That Derby is going to pay for this."

"It's alright, Corinne. Derby's dead. The riot's over."

She looked up at me, eyes wide with shock. "Dead?"

I nodded and she followed my gaze over to where Ice knelt tending our wounded friends.

"Ice?" She looked back to me. "You did it. Bless you, Angel."

"I had a little help," I replied, gently aiding her to a sitting position. "Derby and some of her friends decided to finish Ice off while Sandra and I were up there. She wound up taking a high dive off the eighth floor catwalk." I winced. "It wasn't pretty. Ice tried to save her but Derby was an idiot."

"I hope she felt every second of it."

I bit back words of reproof as Corinne released her teapot and eased the glasses from her bruised and battered face. We both startled as the sounds of sirens filtered through the thick library walls. "Are you alright for a moment?" I asked her. "I need to get back to Sonny. She was stabbed."

"Will she be alright?"

"I'm not sure. She told me to go on ahead and check in on you guys. You'll know more as soon as I do."

"Go to her, Angel. And thank you."

"No problem." Jumping back to my feet, I brushed past Ice, Critter and a still unconscious Pony, then stepped out of the library. Sonny was still awake and aware by the time I made my way back out to her. "It sounds like help's on the way," I told her. "You just hang on, alright? I'll get someone back here."

"Everyone else...okay?"

"Yes, just a few bumps and bruises. Corinne's a mean one with that teakettle. She could teach us a few tricks, I think."

The choked sound of Sonny's breathless laughter followed me down the hall as I went off in search of help. As I stepped into the prison proper, I could see the floor and walls bathed in the red and blue lights of emergency vehicles. At least a dozen blue-clothed police officers were milling around the guard room where Sandra and some of the others were talking with them. Every so often the air would erupt in static as one officer or another would speak into his walkie-talkie.

After another moment, one of the officers raised a hand to the open door and paramedics and ambulance crews rushed inside bearing stretchers and emergency medical equipment nestled in bright orange boxes.

I hustled up to the nearest team, a group of three long-haired and bearded men in pale blue jumpsuits, and stopped in front of them. "Please, my friend's been stabbed. We need your help."

The men looked at me, then over at the knot of police officers still clustered around the guard room. Seeing what was happening, a harried looking Sandra stepped away from the group and waved the men on. "Go ahead and do as she asks. Hurry."

Nodding, the men followed me back into the narrow hallway, stopping just in front of Sonny's splayed body. Despite their rough appearances, the men were gentle with my friend, checking her over carefully and stabilizing her for the trip to the hospital nearby. I held her hand on the trip from the ground to the stretcher, then placed a kiss to her sweat-soaked bangs before they wheeled her off back down the hallway and out of my sight.

One tech was left behind and he looked at me questioningly.

"There are more injured in the library. Could you follow me?"

"Sure lady." Lifting his medical kit, the young man followed me into the destruction of the library. "Holy shit," he breathed, taking in the scene. "What the hell happened here?"

Ice rose up from her place next to Pony and Critter, pinning him with her steely gaze. "We have two more injured down here."

"Uh…yeah…right. Ok." Hustling over quickly, he knelt down beside the two women and set his kit down. He turned his attentions first to Critter, checking her scalp wound and shining his small penlight into her eyes. "This cut'll need a couple stitches, but you seem ok otherwise. Any nausea or anything?"

"Nothing except for a headache."

"Alright. If you wanna go back to the main room, one of my partners'll get you into the ambulance."

"That's alright. I'd rather not, if it's all the same to you."

"But lady, you need stitches!"

"I know, but I can get them at the infirmary. The doc'll be here in the morning."

"You could bleed to death before then!"

Critter grinned, but her eyes were hard. "I'll be fine. Trust me. Just look after Pony here."

A brief moment later, the tech looked away from the determination in Critter's eyes and turned his attention to Pony. He looked her over quickly and professionally, humming quietly to himself as he did so. When he looked back up, his expression was grim. "She's gonna need to get to the hospital as quickly as possible. I'm not sure, but there's a chance she's bleeding into her brain. Does anyone know how long she's been unconscious?"

"Ten minutes, maybe more," Corinne said, coming over to join us. "It's difficult to tell. We were all knocked out."

"I'll go commandeer a stretcher," Ice said quietly, then left the room.

"Wow. She always that intense?"

"Yes," the three of us answered in unison.

Grinning wryly and shaking his head, the young man turned back to his patient, preparing her for her journey to the hospital. The sound of rattling steel was heard shortly, coming steadily closer. Two men in hospital whites blew through the doorway pushing a stretcher. Ice followed behind at a more leisurely pace, a self-satisfied smirk painting her lips.

I rose to join her as the two men crowded around Pony. "You sure lit a fire under them."

"Mmm."

"I don't want to know how, do I."

"Probably not."

"Didn't think so."

A moment later, they bustled past us with Pony's unconscious form strapped securely to the stretcher and covered with a sheet to her chin. I sent out a swift, silent prayer for her recovery as she became lost to my sight.

Turning back to view the library, I let out a sad sigh. All the work we'd put into it gone in a flurry of violence without cause. A part of me wondered why I'd ever thought something like this couldn't happen. This *was* a prison, after all.

Then I had a laugh startled out of me when Corinne retrieved her mashed kettle and shook it, glaring into its now tarnished finish. The words were out of my mouth before I could stop them. "Corinne, in the library, with a teakettle. Who'd have thought it?"

I ducked as said kettle winged its way past my head and suffered the outraged groans of my companions. My mood lightened. Trashed though it was, the library was still there. My companions, though injured, were alive. And Ice was back.

In a place where hope and happiness were supposed to be foreign concepts, I felt filled with them both in the aftermath of one of the worst days I'd ever been through.

Chapter 6

The New Year came and went with a marked absence of fanfare. The prison was slowly getting over the effects of the riot. Three inmates, including Derby, and one guard had been killed. Forty-seven had been injured, seven severely enough to require prolonged hospital stays.

Sonny and Pony were two of those seven, but lucky for us all, they came through their brushes with death with flying colors. Their scars became badges of courage; their bravery garnered new respect among the other inmates. They were seen as heroes in a world which had none.

In a move that surprised no one, it seemed, but me, Ice formally inducted me into the ranks of her Amazons. It wasn't much, as inductions went; more along the lines of her saying, "You're a good fighter. You wanna be an Amazon?" And me replying, "Sure, I'd love to." And her saying, "Alright, you're an Amazon."

My friends welcomed me warmly into their ranks and I acquired a new job, one of protection of the weak. It felt good.

In the next couple months, we also were able to rebuild the library into something even bigger and better than before. The fact that Ice pressed into service those women who'd wrecked it in the first place was a huge help. Not surprisingly, these women were excellent workers who bore up well, if shakily, under Corinne's constant criticism and did their best to right the wrongs they'd perpetrated upon her precious home. The new teakettle I'd gotten for her was always nearby if any of them needed a reminder. Which, of course, they didn't. Their still-healing bruises were reminder enough.

Like the sea at low tide, the gangs themselves settled back into a state of quietude. Under Ice's expert guidance, another, more prudent leader was installed to head the white gang. The leaders of the four gangs met together, with Ice as mediator, and hammered out some hard and fast boundaries and rules to go along with them. After many days of debate, a peace treaty of sorts was brought into being, with the Amazons, as always, appointed overseers.

The passage of time also allowed Ice and myself to begin coming closer together once again; a closeness that was interrupted by Cassandra's bloody assault and Ice's subsequent hellish isolation. Though at the time she never said a word about her time in the hole, Ice did gradually open up to me enough to tell me who Josephine was and what the older woman had meant to her.

Salvatore Briacci had followed Ice's case from the moment the police shot her down in the old abandoned warehouse. Perhaps it was because Ice reminded Briacci of his only child, a daughter name Lucia. Lucia was killed in an airplane crash when she was just fifteen years old and both Briaccis had mourned her death every day since the accident. Ice told me that even at ten or more years later, her room was still set up as if just waiting for the young girl to walk back in and resume her life once again. The same magazines, getting further out of date with each passing year, sat upon the same vanity. The same hairbrush, replete with fine raven hairs caught in the thick bristles, waited patiently beside them.

Ice said that Briacci listened aghast to the news that she was to be incarcerated, at fifteen, in an adult prison for the rest of her life. On the day of sentencing, he sent his own lawyers out to investigate and challenge the case; a challenge that made its way up to the State Supreme Court, where the ruling was finally reversed. Because of Briacci's persistence and money, Ice was released on her twenty-first birthday.

While in prison, she knew nothing about her hidden benefactor, nor did anyone else in the jail. On the day of Ice's release, Briacci himself showed up in the back of a stretch limousine, bearing flowers, good wishes, and an offer she couldn't refuse. Being penniless, homeless, and without significant educational skills to make it easily in the outside world, she accepted.

At first, she said, Briacci and his wife treated her like a long lost daughter, lavishing her with expensive gifts and bountiful attention. At twenty-one, however, after six years in prison, she was streetwise and cock-sure and spent every day waiting for the other shoe to drop.

Despite her cool reserve, however, she felt drawn to Josephina, Salvatore's quiet, elegant wife. She was the first person who ever took the time to reach beyond the brash, armored exterior and into the sensitive soul of the young woman beneath the mask. Josephina encouraged Ice, whom of course she called Morgan, to study for her GED, correctly spying a fine mind behind the icy eyes. When Ice passed the tests with ease, the older woman encouraged her to take college courses, which she did, even receiving an academic scholarship for her efforts.

From what Ice told me, Josephina was typical of the wives of the Mafia members she'd come to know. Purposefully naïve to her husband's other life, she turned a blind eye to everything that wasn't above board. Briacci himself also took great pains to keep his two lives separate and treated his wife as one might a precious object beyond price. The two were very obviously in love with one another, she said.

With Josephina's further and loving encouragement, Ice tried to make a life for herself in a legal trade. But her past preceded her, stonewalling most every attempt she made to better herself and her circumstances. She readily admitted to me that she could, and should, have simply moved to another part of the country where no one had ever heard the name Morgan Steele. The Briaccis weren't holding her against her will.

But the love and support she received from Josephina filled a huge hole in her life; a hole that was dug on the day her parents died in a car accident, leaving her an orphan. The hole was widened and deepened upon the death of her best friend, whom she'd known since childhood and who was the last link to a past she could never relive. Though a full grown and powerful adult, Ice was in many ways still that young girl craving love and acceptance of a family.

The choice was an easy one, she said. After a year of trying and failing to obtain gainful employment in a town that spurned her name, she simply walked into Salvatore's offices and offered her services.

And that was an offer *he* couldn't refuse.

I remember her telling me the story of the first time she handled a gun. Shortly after she had had her 'talk' with Salvatore, he'd taken her to his exclusive Hunt-and-Gun club where he showed her off like a proud father. Then he'd taken her back to the outdoor shooting range where several of his cronies were standing in the stalls, shooting at man-sized targets with rifles, shotguns, pistols and all other manner of projectile weaponry.

The sound of shooting was loud in her ears but she disdained the use of thick ear protectors. Upon seeing their leader with this young, beautiful stranger, the men had gathered quickly around, distributing pats to Ice's head, though she was taller than the lot of them.

She told me that they hid their laughs quite well when Salvatore told them he was teaching her to use a gun. Apparently, the Mafia is very much an 'old boys' network where women, for the most part, are seen as fragile and peaceful doe-eyed creatures needing the protection of strong men. She was given a pistol along with explicit instructions in its use.

When she indicated she was ready, she was led to a stall of her own, with a bevy of middle-aged Mafia cronies watching her every move. When her first shot went errant, the wave of tittering, 'I told you so' laughter was cut off quickly by a look from Salvatore. After the next five shots were fired in rapid succession, the entire range was so silent Ice said you could have heard an ant crawl across the finely cut grass. Each shot had hit the target dead center.

After that, Ice told me, Salvatore Briacci knew he had the makings of a first-class assassin on his hands. And that's exactly what he molded her into.

At first he sent her out with partners. The hits were simple and direct and caused her conscience, a tenuous beast even at the best of times, no remorse. Then she started going out on her own and the jobs became more demanding and difficult. And high profile, as well.

To this day, she's never gone further than that on this subject, but I'd venture to guess that some of the more popular unsolved murders in this town may have their source in her; especially if the victim was a well-known Mafia member.

Like Salvatore, Ice went to great lengths to keep her 'other' life hidden from Josephina's warm gaze. Briacci set out to find her gainful employment in one of his many legal business ventures. As a private citizen, he was best known for his string of new and used car lots and that's where he sought to fit her in.

Direct and penetrating by nature, she would have made an abysmal car salesman, but when Briacci showed her to the auto-body shop, they both knew she'd found her calling. I've heard it said, and with no small amount of envy, that Ice can make a car walk and talk. Extremely talented with her hands, she is a mechanical genius. It wasn't long before she was developing a client base of her own beyond the Mafia cronies and hangers-on that her benefactor so graciously supplied the up and coming young mechanic.

Again, I asked her what seemed to me to be the obvious question: why, if she had found legal employment, did she continue to work in another capacity for Briacci? She closed up some and told me the answer was complicated and to leave it at that. I suspect one of the reasons might have been some sort of debt she felt she owed him for getting her out of prison and taking her into his home and family. Though it pains me to say so, I think another reason was that she enjoyed the feeling of power being a hired gun brought to her. The same kind of power over life and death that Corinne so often talked about.

That insidious craving for the power of life over another remains, even after five years of living among women who feed on it like caviar, a thing as foreign to me as any other. And I pray every day to whatever higher power is out there to grant that it will always remain that way.

As if realizing, for the first time during our conversations on the subject, exactly how much she'd opened up to me, Ice shut down completely for a time, refusing to discuss anything more of a personal nature. Though

I ached to push further inside her slowly opening shell, I knew to respect her boundaries and so resolved to wait for her to make the next move, if, indeed, one should ever come.

❧ ❧ ❧ ❧

At long last, the deep bone chill of winter gave way to spring's gentle warmth. The bright sun, birdsong, and return of green life to the land was a welcome change after winter's brown, desolate and empty harshness. Inmates streamed out into the yard by the dozens, their skin winter-pale, pleased at last to have no roof over their heads save the sky, if even only for a short while.

One the first warm day, at the very toll of eleven o'clock, I strode out with the rest of them, blissful with the happiness only spring can bring. New life was everywhere I looked and it settled something deep in me that had been missing since the first hard frost had blanketed the earth several months before.

I walked into the fresh, tender grass, feeling the dew soak through the hem of my jumpsuit and grinning at nothing. My new status as an Amazon gave me the freedom to go where I pleased in the yard, and, believe me, I used that privilege for all it was worth. Skirting around the basketball court, which was definitely worse for wear after the brutal winter we'd suffered, I walked the newly limed foul line of the softball field, watching the women warm up.

Some of the inmates were taking batting practice while infielders and outfielders peppered one another with scorching tosses of the shiny white softballs. A pop fly headed out my way and, without thinking about it, I reached out and snagged it from the air, enjoying the looks of surprise when I threw it back to the catcher on the fly.

Softball was a sport that I both dearly loved and was very good at. It was also the only thing in my life, prior to my elopement, that I was able to gather enough courage to stand my ground on. Despite my mother's thinly veiled disappointment and my father's snide comments, I tried out for and won a starting position on the Varsity team in my sophomore year of High School. I played shortstop, and don't think I haven't heard every single joke there is about being the perfect height for the position, because, believe me, I have. A dozen times over, at the very least.

In answer to the congenial summonses, I was drawn into the inmates' game and took up my accustomed position, pounding the webbing of the grubby mitt I'd been given. Crouching low, my muscles feeling limber and loose despite the winter's confinement, I swept the hair from my eyes and began to heckle the batter, giddy with the feeling of being five years younger and a lifetime more free.

The coordination and skills came back quickly and I lost myself in the game, scooping up grounders, tagging out runners and batting the living hell out of the ball like a woman possessed. I was dirty from sliding and sweaty from running and generally feeling just fine.

It was the top of the sixth and my team was leading by a comfortable margin. The batter was arguing with the umpire over some disputed call and I found my attention wandering. Looking over toward the prison, I watched as the door opened and several of my friends filed out, followed by Ice. There was a rare smile on her face and though it wasn't directed at me, I felt myself smile in response. She'd gained back all the weight she'd lost while in isolation and while still pale, her normal olive skin tone had returned to her face, making her look vibrant and healthy. An errant gust of wind lifted her hair from her shoulders and blew it back from her face, exposing its angled planes in all their glory.

No doubt about it. I was smitten.

So much so that I almost had free orthodontia courtesy of a blistering line-drive headed right for my face. In total reflex, I brought my glove up and neatly snared the screaming missile, thereby ending the game.

I soon found myself buried under a mound of cheering teammates, suffering congratulatory pats on every exposed part of my body and grinning like a fool, I'm sure. I was finally rescued from the pile, pulled to my feet and brushed off by a solicitous first-baseman who smiled shyly at me as she brushed the last bit of dust from my shoulder.

Warning bells went off in my head and I toned down my smile, flattered at her shy interest, but wanting only one person to look at me that way. I increased the distance between us smoothly on the pretext of straightening my sleeves. "Thanks."

The young woman's smile broadened. "Oh, hey! No problem! You did great, by the way. What an arm."

"Thanks. You did pretty well yourself."

She shrugged self-depreciatingly. "Eh, I was kinda rusty, but I'll get better once I have the time to work the kinks out and get back into the groove. Say, you wanna practice together sometimes?"

Uh oh. I could feel my smile become a little forced but hoped she couldn't detect it. "Um…yeah. Sure. Why not?"

"Cool! That'd be great! My name's Digger, by the way."

I grasped her extended hand, pumped once, then released it again. "Nice to meet you, Digger. I'm Angel."

Her smile went goofy. "Yeah," she said, drawing the word out. "I know. I've seen you in the library and with the Amazons and stuff. You guys are so cool."

Oh boy. I mentally rolled my eyes but managed to keep a straight face. "Thanks."

"No, thank *you*. So…can I walk you back inside?"

I reached up to scratch the back of my neck, neurons firing at a rapid rate trying to come up with some graceful way to decline the advances of my newfound admirer. The rest of me was just laughing its fool head off. "I…um…appreciate the offer, Digger. Really. It's just that…um…I…." My eyes lit upon the answer. "…promised my friends over there that I'd meet up with them as soon as I was done here."

Her whole face lit up like a kid's on Christmas morning. "You're going to hang out with the Amazons? Wow! Maybe you could, like, introduce me to some of 'em?"

Wrong excuse, Angel. Declining was on the very tip of my tongue when I remembered a slightly younger version of myself being warmly welcomed among those women for the first time. Unlike me, though, Digger obviously already had friends in her gang. However….

I turned to her, smiling again. "Sure. C'mon."

"Alright!"

She followed along behind me like a newly trained puppy and I winced at the smug grins I was getting from my friends who, as always, had gathered in the free-weight area. As I entered the area, Pony sat up from her place on one of the benches and gave me a pat on the side. "Way to save the ol' puss, Angel."

I wrinkled my nose at her, my own version of a smirk. "Better than you, at any rate."

My friends all laughed as Digger stood open-mouthed, doubtless shocked at my seeming audacity to kid Pony about the skull fracture she'd received during the riot. Pony laughed with the rest of them, then mock-punched me in the gut before laying back down to push out another twenty reps on the chest press.

Stepping back, I pushed my new friend forward a little. "Everybody, this is Digger. Digger, these are the Amazons."

As Digger began her effusive greetings, I looked around, searching for and failing to find Ice anywhere within the group. Raising questioning eyebrows toward Critter, she nodded at me, gesturing with one arm toward some spot behind my left shoulder. Doing a slow turn, I saw Ice standing up against the nearest part of the fence, her body taut with tension and her hands gripping the chain link so tightly I could easily see her whitened knuckles even from this distance. I looked back at Critter again, who shrugged.

Squaring my shoulders, I completed my turn and began to walk toward the fence, eyeing the nonchalant tower guards as I went. Normally, of course, the guards get itchy when you walk too close to their precious fence but, at least so far, they seemed singularly uninterested and so I quickened my pace.

As my steps brought me closer to Ice and the fence, the corner of the prison slid out of my vision, giving me a clear view of the parking lot beyond. It was painfully obvious to me that Ice was watching with grim determination something happening in that parking lot and I very much wanted to know what was going on.

Standing slightly apart from my friend, I peered into the lot, spying the warden talking to a short, well-built man wearing a dark suit and sunglasses. One of the stranger's hands rested possessively on the hood of a shiny black Cadillac while his other gestured wildly in time with the movement of his lips. His dark hair gleamed in the bright sunlight whose rays bounced and twinkled off the layers of gold jewelry he was also sporting. He threw back his head in laughter after some comment of the warden's, and then stuck out his hand to be shaken, which it was. After another moment, he got into his expensive car and drove off. The warden returned to his office.

I could easily feel the tension radiating from the body of my friend as her head turned to follow the path of the Cadillac. A moment passed, and then another. Then she grasped the fence so hard I was sure the metal links were going to simply shatter under the force of her hands. She shook it once, violently, then turned and, without a word or a look in any direction save straight ahead, stalked back into the prison.

I barely restrained myself from running after her, remembering my promise to myself in the nick of time. With a sigh of dejection, I turned and walked back to the weight area, where my friends looked at me with expressions of concern on their faces. I shrugged my shoulders and shook my head just as the change of shift bell sounded, signaling us all back into the building.

Chapter 7

As I sat in my cell that evening, I thought about what had transpired during the day. Ice had disappeared, as was usual with her when she was upset, into her cell and was not seen for the rest of the day. Corinne and the others badgered me, asking me what I'd seen and why I thought Ice had reacted the way she did. I could tell that they didn't trust her seemingly tenuous hold on her sanity. But I did, and I refused to give them fodder for their grist mill. That she'd known the man speaking to the warden was obvious. Who he was and what his presence meant to her remained, however, no one's business but her own.

I'm afraid I got a bit cross with them all and, rather than subject them further to my fit of temper, retreated to my own cell, well realizing the irony of my actions. I'd gone through several roommates in slightly over a year and presently my cell was empty of any other human habitation, so I was free to mope in peace.

Though it was still relatively early in the evening, I decided to call it a night, thinking that perhaps sleep would provide me with the answers to my questions. I was in the process of turning my bed down when a soft sound just outside my cell caused me to stop and look over my shoulder curiously. Ice stood in the hallway, arms loose at her sides and a slightly chagrined look on her face. I smiled hesitantly.

"You busy?"

"No! No, I was just...." I gestured toward my half unmade bed.

"Wanna go for a walk?"

As I turned, my grin became full-out. "Sure. That'd be great."

Smiling, she bowed me out of the cell, then led the way back through the main part of the prison before going down one of the many hallways that branched off the main square. A left and then another left and we were heading into a section of the prison I'd never been in before.

One of the first things you learn when you're incarcerated is to not stick your nose into too many places because you can bet you won't like what you find. Or, often, what finds you. Following that particular philosophy like a bible, there were many places in the Bog still unknown to me.

Still, I felt little unease with the developing situation. I trusted Ice with my life, and I also had a pretty good idea where we were going.

Before I continue forward, it might be best to step back a moment and explain the employment system at the Bog. While in many prisons, inmates are expected to work for their room and board, it's different in the Bog. Those inmates who have a desire to work, for either the money or to make the time pass more quickly, do so. They are paid a flat wage of twenty-five cents an hour, which goes into their personal prison account. Those prisoners who don't feel like working aren't required to.

The work I do for Corinne in the library is done out of love and I won't accept any payment for it. My 'side' job, that of article-obtainer, more than pays for whatever frivolous items I might want. There are plenty of opportunities for work in our happy little home, ranging from laundry and cleanup to cooking and grounds-keeping. In the nineteen fifties, a large new wing was added to the main prison and housed the new workshops which were added to increase prison income. An auto shop, a sheet metal shop and a woodworking shop share space in the new wing and I'm told the profits from these slave-labor ventures are quite high.

Given her background, or at least that part which constituted legal income, it shouldn't be hard to guess where Ice went to pass the time by working. Sure enough, after we walked down the last hallway, the area opened up into a larger space with several doors all on the far side of the wall. Three guards patrolled the area and looked up inquiringly as we entered. They all waved and one walked over, smiling. "Puttin' in some overtime, Ice?" The others chuckled at her witticism.

"Something like that," Ice allowed, lifting her arms so the guard could pat her down.

"How 'bout you, Angel?" the guard asked me, reaching out her arms to pat me down as well. "Gonna build some new bookcases for your library?"

"Nah," I replied, trying not to giggle as the guard's professional hands patted over some very ticklish spots. "Just having a look around. I've never been to this part of the prison before."

The guard grinned and stepped back. "That's fine. Don't stay down there too long, though. Lock down is in a couple hours."

Ice nodded and the guard led us to one of the center doors along the wall, reaching down to unlock it with of the keys hanging from a huge ring on her belt. The door unlocked with a quiet click and she pushed it open, gesturing us inside.

As we stepped through the door, Ice reached off to the left, snapping on the large banks of fluorescent lights that were set into the high ceiling. As the door closed softly behind us, I took the chance to look around, blinking in the suddenly bright lighting. The room was huge, with six bays, complete with lifts and huge orange boxes of mechanics' tools. It smelled of grease and rubber and reminded me of the days when my father would take me along as he got the oil changed or the tires rotated.

She led us down a short set of concrete steps and onto the main floor of the room. Two state police cruisers in various states of disrepair sat quiescently in the bays. The other spaces were empty. We walked along the oil-stained concrete floor, our footfalls echoing through the cavernous room. There was another door, made of plain wood, which sat off to one side along the wall, and it was to this door that Ice took us. I assumed it was an office of some sort and so didn't give it much thought when she took the key from its hiding place on top of the jam and thrust it into the lock.

The door opened on silent hinges and Ice stepped through, leaving me to follow as she flipped on the lights of the new room. I could see immediately that my assumption about it being an office was way off the beam. This second room was a smaller version of the first, with two bays instead of six, but with all the rest of the equipment in place. Two cars sat in the bays, almost filling the room to capacity. One was an almost thoroughly dismantled Volkswagen Beetle and the other looked to be a Corvette which was obviously undergoing a new paint-job.

I looked over to Ice, a question in my eyes.

"Chop shop."

"Excuse me?"

"That's what this is called. A chop shop."

"And a chop shop is...."

"It's a place where stolen cars are either dismantled for parts or given new, untraceable, identities and resold."

I know the shock and disbelief showed on my face because she narrowed her eyes at me, smiling slightly. "Didn't think our dear friend the warden had it in him, huh?"

"I...I don't know what to think. This is unbelievable. You're sure he knows this is going on down here."

Her smile turned to a full blown smirk. "Who do you think set it up?"

"You're kidding!"

"'Fraid not."

I looked around again, hands on my hips. "How did *you* know it was here?"

"Ahhh. Now there's the story. C'mon."

Throwing my hands up in frustration, I turned and followed Ice out of the room, through the regular bays, up the stairs and out of the auto shop. I endured another quick pat-down from my grinning guard friend, then almost had to run to keep up with Ice's long strides as she made her way back down the myriad of twisting hallways and into the prison proper.

She hit the stairs running and kept on going. I followed right behind, slightly out of breath as we finally reached the top. Looking at Ice's retreating back I tried to guess whether she was running toward something, or away. Shrugging, I broke into a jog, entering the cell a moment after she did, putting my hands on my hips and staring down at her as she sprawled on her bunk, one arm behind her head and her eyes far away.

I tried. I really did. But as silent seconds turned into silent moments, I could feel my frustration level rising. "Well?" I asked finally, unable to bear the silence any longer.

At the sound of my voice, she blinked, as if startled that I was even in the room with her. She turned her head slowly to meet my gaze, her own expression thoughtful and sad. "Cassandra didn't kill Josephina."

Whatever I might have been expecting, that softly uttered statement certainly wasn't it. "Wha-at?"

Rolling up to a seated position, Ice tucked her long legs up, winding her arms around them and resting her chin on her upraised knees. "What I mean is…well…she killed her, obviously. But not for the reason she said."

"I don't think I'm following you here, Ice." My mind was desperately trying to forge some sort of logical connection between the illegal operation in the auto shop and the information Ice had just given me. I was failing miserably.

"Cassandra said that she killed Josephina because Josephina called me a friend. That's not true."

"How do you know that?"

"Because she told me."

"Who told you? Josephina?" I had the strangest feeling of sinking in quicksand and was casting about for a way to drag myself up from the mire.

"No. Cassandra. When we were in the hole."

"Ice, Cassandra's nuts. She's so obsessed with you she'd probably say anything to get you over wanting to kill her."

"I believe her."

"Can you tell me why?"

She smiled slightly. "Lots of reasons. One of which was confirmed for me this afternoon."

Ahhh. Now we're getting somewhere. "I was wondering about that."

The smile broadened. "I know." Shifting a little, she patted the area beside her and I took her up on the offer, lowering myself down onto the lumpy mattress and scooting back until I was against the cool concrete of the wall. A more comfortable silence stretched out between us and I forced myself to be content with just the sound of our breathing. When she finally turned to me, her gaze was direct, but shuttered. "Angel, why haven't you ever asked me if I did what I got put in here for?"

The quicksand was back and I suddenly found myself sunk up to my neck in the stuff. I could feel Ice's body tense up beside my own as she waited for an answer. "I…um…I guess because I figured that if you wanted me to know, you'd tell me. It's really none of my business."

She nodded at my answer, then turned her gaze back to the opposite wall where the Bonsai were flourishing in all their artistic glory. The silence stretched out once again, though not quite as comfortable as before. I could feel my own body begin to tense up. I think I may have held my breath, though I'm not positive.

Her voice, when it sounded, was barely above a whisper. "I'm guilty of killing a lot of people, Angel. But that man wasn't one of them."

I nodded, feeling indescribable relief wash through my body. "What happened?" I asked, praying that the door she was so tenuously holding open for me wouldn't suddenly slam shut in my face.

"It's a pretty long story," she replied, giving us both an easy out.

I didn't take her up on it. "Well, considering that I'm in here for at least six more years, I'm sure you can squeeze it in if you try."

That got a genuine smile out of her and I patted myself on the back. "Alright. I told you I was a hired gun for Briacci, but I didn't always take my orders directly from him. He has a bunch of underbosses and other lackeys that relay his orders for him. One of them is a guy named Nunzio Callestrano." She made a face. "Ugly guy with more hair on his knuckles than most guys have on their heads."

I couldn't help but laugh at the image and she lifted one shoulder in a shrug. "It's true. Anyway, Briacci and his wife were in Sicily for the funeral of one of his great Aunts when the word came down. Nunzio sent one of *his* lackeys over to tell me that they needed someone taken care of. This guy was supposedly really bad news; into things that even the Mafia didn't mess with, like kiddy porn. This guy told me that Callestrano told him that this man, whose name was Tony Selleti, was making a play for some of the dope houses that Briacci controlled. Like any other gang, the Family doesn't give up its territories without a fight and I was obviously being brought in to take care of the 'little problem' once and for all."

"So then what happened?"

"I always do my homework before making a hit," she continued matter-of-factly. "And this time was no exception. I cased the guy's home and his work to generally get a feel for him and, perhaps, get a feel for the place that I could take him out with a minimum amount of hassle."

Her words and the flat, emotionless tone of her voice sent chills through my body. I crossed my arms to try and hide the goosebumps that spread their way over my bare flesh. Her eyes told me that she'd seen through my little deception and I again held my breath, wondering if she'd continue.

Letting go a long breath, she settled her chin on her knees once again. "Let's just say that what I learned was at odds with what I was told."

"What do you mean?"

"Instead of being this wild-eyed kiddy porn dealer who raped babies for a living, I found a quiet, hard-working family man who bore no resemblance whatsoever with the man I'd been ordered to kill. Now, before you say anything, I know that most criminals of this type don't have stamp on their forehead, but I've learned to trust my instincts in these situations and my instincts were telling me that this was bad news." She shifted again. "During my time with Briacci, I'd learned the value of obtaining private contacts and they came in handy here. From a friend, I learned that the only truth I'd been told about this man was his name. The rest was a pack of lies wrapped up in pretty paper guaranteed to get my temper hot and tied up with a neat little bow. I also found out something very important."

"And that was?"

"That he was a government witness for a trial involving a rival Family."

Now the pieces, or at least some of them, were starting to fall into place. I nodded in what I hoped was an encouraging manner for her to continue.

"Many of us have lines we draw in the sand and this was one of my lines. I never killed innocents and I never killed witnesses, no matter *who* they were testifying against. Needless to say, I had a very large bone to pick with Salvatore Briacci for setting me up like this and I made a quick call to Sicily to let him know that. Unfortunately, he wasn't available when I called, so I left a message. Then I went back to Nunzio's lackey and told him 'no deal'. I went home, stowed my gun, and went to sleep, thinking that was the end of it." She snorted softly through her nose. "I should have known better."

The shuttered veil slid over her eyes again and I resisted the urge to put my hand on her arm in support.

"I woke up the next morning to the sound of a dozen police officers beating down my door. It seems that Tony Selleti had a little accident during the night and they had five witnesses ready to swear in court that I was seen walking down from his office, gun in hand and blood all over me." She laughed mirthlessly. "It's amazing what a little money in the right hands will cause a person to see, isn't it."

I nodded, understanding her perfectly. Though the witnesses in my trial weren't bribed, or at least not that I knew of, it's amazing what neighbors think they hear in the dead of night and from behind closed and locked doors. The mind is a very selective thing. I'd learned enough about that first hand. Add a little incentive to the pot and…well, it's said that every man has his price.

"Was it Salvatore?" I asked after a long moment of contemplative silence.

"I thought so, at first. I wracked my brain trying to think of something I'd done to make him want to set me up like that. I couldn't think of anything. I'd always been a good soldier, listening to his orders and obeying them without question. This was the first time I'd turned my back on a hit." Rolling her head against the concrete wall, she ran a hand through her hair, settling it somewhat. "What I couldn't figure out was why he would want me to take out a witness who could put a rival behind bars. It didn't make sense to me. At all. Briacci had always had trouble with this guy. I'd have thought he'd be happy that there was finally enough evidence to get him out of the picture without having to get his own hands dirty."

"You're right. That *doesn't* make any sense."

"Then I started having my suspicions, but by then, I was tried, convicted, sentenced, and on my way to the Bog."

"If you had suspicions, why didn't you fight it?"

She laughed again, though I could see, in the bright of the lights, the glitter of tears in her eyes. It was an astounding sight. "I didn't fight it because I belong where I am, Angel. I might not have killed Selleti, but I've killed so many more. I'm too dangerous to be left out on the streets."

"Ice…."

"No, Angel. It's true. I'm where I belong. Where I've always belonged." She wiped her eyes harshly with the back of her hand, obviously annoyed at the wetness she found there. "Anyway, after he heard, Briacci backed off from me totally. I wasn't too sure why, since even though I'd turned away from the hit, his objective got accomplished. Maybe he was just pissed that he'd had to use someone else to do what I should have done in the first place." She shrugged. "I dunno."

"I'll bet that hurt."

She looked at me for a long moment, then turned away, hiding her face with the fall of her hair. "Yeah. It did. What hurt worse was the fact that Josephina wouldn't talk to me either. It didn't matter to me what the rest of them thought, but I wanted…no, I *needed* her to believe my version of the events. I tried calling her a couple of times but there were always excuses about why she couldn't come to the phone. After awhile, I just gave up."

"Then why did she…."

"I'm getting to that. When I saw her that morning, I knew something wasn't right. Aside from Cassandra's knife at her throat, that is. Josephina may not have been a saint, but regardless of who her husband was, she was a good woman. There was no reason for her to be locked up here, unless someone else was behind it. And for her to be brought in in the middle of the night…." Her words trailed off as she shook her head.

"You've heard about Salvatore's troubles with the law," I ventured.

"Yes, but not until it was all over. Her refusal to testify against her husband was just like her and the prosecutors wanting to play hard-ball just added to the equation. And then she was killed and I wound up in the hole."

"With Cassandra."

"Exactly." Her smile was hard; devoid of any warmth. "She told me an interesting little story. It seems that the night Josephina was brought in to the Bog, the warden paid her a little visit. In exchange for him letting her keep Heracles, a deal which I'd already worked out with him, as you know, he had a little job for her to do."

"To kill Josephina," I breathed, my heart beginning to race.

"Exactly. He gave her a knife and left the door to her cell unlocked so she could carry out his orders. He only had one other condition."

"And that was?"

"That I had to be there to witness it. She told me he was very adamant about that."

"My God. Why?" Suddenly, the mystery of his presence in the jail on that day became very clear.

"Because Josephina was carrying a very important piece of information. And if I received that information, his whole little fiefdom here could come tumbling down around his ears."

"What was the information?"

"The name of the man who had killed Tony Selleti. Before she died, she managed to tell it to me. It was the lackey of Nunzio, the guy who had given me my orders in the first place. A man by the name of Joseph Cavallo. And the same man you saw outside today shaking hands with the warden."

The whole puzzle suddenly came together with blinding force. Our pious warden was up to his eyeballs in corruption that went far beyond some stolen car ring.

"What does this have to do with Cassandra, though?"

"Oh, it has everything to do with it," she replied, smiling ferally. "When Cassandra acted up the first time and I went to talk to him about Heracles, he made me a deal. The continued liveliness of her pet in exchange for my participation in a little business venture he was starting up."

"The chop shop."

"Right. I knew there was really no getting around it, so I agreed. I started having my suspicions back then when I thought I recognized some of the guys who were bringing in the hot cars. But I bided my time until it was too late. Cavallo's supplying Morrison with the cars and no doubt paying him a tidy sum of money to break them down or paint them up. The warden pockets the money, Cavallo gets new cars at cut rate prices, and everyone's happy."

"I'm still not sure exactly how Josephina's death plays into all this, though. Beyond the obvious, of course."

"It plays for a number of reasons. First, with her as a living witness to the actual events that took place on the night that Selleti died, I could get a new trial and stand a good chance of being acquitted. That would leave me wide open to expose the warden's little money making scheme and that would be the end of him. In addition, there are some higher-ups in the State Capitol who would very much not want to see that happen, given the fact that Morrison helped them get elected in the first place."

"That's very true." The prosecution's sudden desire to get tough with Josephina made much more sense now, given who signed their paychecks.

"Add to that the fact that if you put two and two together, you get a picture of one Joseph Cavallo working as a mole for the rival Family who had a vested interest in seeing Selleti go down permanently. It was the perfect set-up. Cavallo gets me to kill the witness against his real boss, the rival don. It didn't matter that I refused because he had it done anyway and put my name to it. Briacci never received my message so he had no choice but to believe the little weasel. Josephina also told me before she died that Salvatore had long suspected a plant in his own Family. Cavallo convinced him it was me to get the heat off himself. Josephina's dead, so the chances of my getting a new trial are nil. But, since I now know who the real killer is, and since I also know he's a plant, and further that he and Morrison are business partners, I just might have some leverage with our dear warden."

"What kind of leverage?"

"I'm not sure yet. Morrison made his biggest mistake when he made Josephina's death such a public spectacle. He should have had it done in private, or at least somewhere where I wouldn't be around to see it. But he got cocky. He took a big risk and he lost." Her teeth flashed again. "He just doesn't know it yet." Straightening slightly, she stretched, bringing her long arms up over her head and arching her back. The sound of her vertebrae crackling was loud in the quiet room. "But one thing's certain. Joseph Cavallo's days are numbered. I'm going to see to that *personally*."

I couldn't help the thrill of fear that skittered its way down my own spine and I kept myself from looking at her, knowing that the expression on her face would doubtless deepen that. This Ice wasn't a noble woman trying to make life better for the women she shared space with. This was a trained killer full of the fire of retribution and the cool cunning of a prowling cat.

When she spoke again, her voice was soft and contemplative. "There are probably many who say that Briacci's only getting what he deserves, and that Josephina, by extension, did too."

"No one deserves to die, Ice."

She turned to me, a wry smile lighting her eyes. "Remind me to argue with you about that one later."

I smiled back, backhanding her lightly on one arm. "Deal."

"They took me in when no one else would. They gave me food, shelter. Family. Just because I chose to move down a dark path doesn't make that gift any less precious to me. I owe them both a debt, and I *will* pay it."

As her eyes took on that faraway glint once again, I found myself studying her hand which was placed flat against the white sheet of the bed. It was a strong hand, tan and well-veined, with long tapering fingers that were graceful and deadly in the same breath. Like a curious child, I placed my own atop it, wondering at the softness and warmth beneath my palm even as I laughed inwardly at the size difference.

When I turned my head, I found her eyes upon me, totally awake, aware and in the moment. I knew this time my heart would not be denied what it was so patiently seeking. Our lips met with an infinite sweetness that all but wiped out the primal carnality of our first encounter.

The warm softness of her lips covering mine in gentle exploration melted me inside, all but fracturing who I thought I was and birthing a new woman to stand in her place. Warm and wet, our mouths moved together in a graceful dance of turning heads and deepening breaths. My hand traced a line up the long elegance of her neck, sinking my fingers into the thick fall of her hair as I felt the tip of her tongue trace the seam between my lips.

My mouth opened under the teasing gesture and I took her in willingly, moaning softly as she mapped out what she found within with deft, sure, sensual strokes. My head began to swim, though whether it was from lack of oxygen or overwhelming emotion I'll never know. I pulled away reluctantly, savoring the last taste of her as my head came forward to rest against one broad shoulder. "God…that was ….Wow."

Her arm threaded its way behind my back and I soon found myself caught up in a strong embrace. A gentle kiss was pressed into the crown of my head and I relaxed against her, enveloped in a cocoon of warmth and tenderness. I listened to the music of her heart as it beat steadily just beneath my ear as I waited for the tingling that engulfed me to subside. I felt the warmth of her cheek as it rested against the top of my head and my eyes slipped closed in contentment. It was a bit disconcerting that my husband would have to die so I could find my home, but the truth was laid out plain for me to see.

Her low voice burred into my ear. "I'm sorry, Angel."

I tried to pull away, but her strong grip prevented me from moving, so I laid my head back on her shoulder and sighed. "Sorry for what?"

A wry laugh rumbled. "For lots of things, I suppose. Shutting you out. Keeping you at a distance when all you offered was help. But mostly for taking something that is so precious on a dare."

It was the opening I'd been waiting for for months and the paths that suddenly appeared before me were many and varied. Humor seemed to work best with her and so that's what I tried first. "As I recall," I replied, adopting a dry-as-dust tone, "*I was the one who dared you.*"

The wry laugh came again, vibrating against my body where our flesh met and merged. "Perhaps. But I knew what I was doing. Knew what I wanted. And I'm used to getting what I want." She signed. "But this…this is something that should never be taken. Not even as a joke."

My heart crawled into my throat, forcing the words hiding there out into the open. "So you feel it too."

There was a long beat of silence as I felt her own throat work against my head. "Yes," came the whisper after what seemed an eternity. Another silence descended, longer than the first. "From the moment we met." She shifted, bearing my body up to settle more comfortably against her. "I tried to ignore it. Tried to shove it down deep where the rest of my feelings are buried. Obviously, it didn't work."

I was about to say something when the lights flickered, signaling lockdown in ten minutes. She squeezed me to her more tightly for a second, then her arms released and she moved away. I caught her hand and brushed a kiss on the back before placing it over my heart. "This isn't over, you know."

Her lips compressed, obviously trying to bite back a smile as one eyebrow rose over a cerulean eye. "It isn't, huh?"

"Not by a long shot." And with no hesitancy or fear, I moved closer, covering her mouth with my own, showing her in a kiss the passion that was hidden in my soul. Her hand slid down from its place on my chest, sliding over my left breast with a gentle touch.

Responding in kind, I touched for the first time in desire the breast of another woman. Soft and warm and pliant under my inquisitive fingers, I gasped into the kiss as I felt a responsive nipple brush against my palm. My thumb, of its own volition, gently brushed over the cloth that separated it from the warm flesh beneath and I felt her body shift closer to mine as a low moan whispered forth from her throat.

I was suddenly seized with a great need to feel the responsive flesh under my fingers and so I broke off the kiss, growling as I reached up for the zipper that held her jumpsuit closed. I managed to yank it down only halfway when the lights flickered once again and an anonymous voice crackled over the PA system, announcing lock-down in five minutes.

Dropping my fingers inches from their goal, my eyes found themselves glued to the magnificent scant inches of cleavage my efforts had provided. My mouth watered and the urge to bury my head amidst that tempting flesh to taste and smell was almost overwhelming in its intensity.

Shaking my head to fracture the vision, I looked up to find Ice looking back, the color of her eyes deepened to a stormy indigo that framed her dilated pupils like a corona around the sun. Her breathing was slightly labored and beads of sweat dotted her upper lip. God, but it was the most beautiful thing that I'd ever seen.

The sound of someone softly clearing their throat drifted through the pounding in my ears and I whirled around to see a blushing guard standing outside the entrance to Ice's cell. "Ladies," she said almost apologetically, "it's time for lock-down. You need to get back to your cell, Angel."

I turned back to Ice who was smiling that cockeyed grin at me. Believe me when I tell you that particular expression did *nothing* to damper my ardor.

"Angel...."

"Alright! Alright. God." I had to tell my muscles what to do and was gratified that my legs retained enough strength to bear my weight up and off the bed. It was a close call, really, but they managed to get the job done. "Remember what I said, Ice. This is not over."

Her grin grew a touch smug. "I'll remember," she replied softly. "'Night, Angel."

☙ ☙ ☙ ☙

But it *was* over. At least for the time being. True to her nature, Ice closed up once again, as if our evening together had bared too much of her innermost self to me. I won't say I wasn't disappointed, because I was. But I also tried my best to understand things from her point of view. Each delve into that battered soul gave me more insight into the woman that I was able to confess freely, if only to myself, I had fallen in love with.

But each baring of that soul came with a price to her and to myself. I suppose it's akin to a leaching out of toxins in the body. You always need a recovery period just to regain the balance you'd lost.

In the meantime, I kept myself busy with my library work, my teaching, and even managed to allow myself to get roped into playing on the so-called "Inmate All-Stars" softball team that was set to go up against the guards during the first week of summer.

My status as an Amazon allowed me to speak to people I wouldn't have dreamed of speaking with before. I listened to their concerns and questions and tried my best to help in any way I could. As I've said before, most of the Bog's inmates weren't hard-core lifers. Most were young women serving short sentences for stupid mistakes. Though I helped as much as I could with their continuing education scholastically, I wanted to do more to help prepare these women for their eventual lives outside these prison walls. With the help of the guards, several non-profit organizations and the local universities, I was able to set up various classes for the inmates. Classes such as "Anger Management", "Parenting", "Household Budgeting" and "Career

Paths" were, surprisingly, very well attended and it made me feel good to be able to have a positive effect on the lives of my fellow inmates, if only to do my best to make sure that once they left the Bog, they'd never return.

My second spring in the Bog also saw the first time I was able to intervene in a fight without assistance. And, in fact, I didn't even need to resort to violence.

I was on my way to the laundry room to pick up some clean uniforms (and if you've managed to stay with me this long, you'll no doubt remember my warning about prisons and laundry rooms) when I stepped into the outer antechamber and saw two inmates, both rather new themselves, standing over another prisoner who'd just gotten out of segregation. All three wore bruises of beatings past, the kneeling woman's fresher and more vivid against the pale tone of her flesh.

I came fully into the room, letting my presence be known by the force of my stride. The kneeling woman looked up at me with a plea in her eyes; the others, anger. "What's going on here?"

"I don't see as it's any of your business," one of the standing ones replied.

"How about if I say I'm making it my business. Does that help?"

The second woman released her grip on the front of her captive's jumpsuit and started toward me.

"I wouldn't if I were you. Those bruises can get a whole lot worse real fast."

Catching the tone in my voice, she trailed to a stop, looking at me questioningly, assessing.

"Well?"

She looked over her shoulder at her compatriot, who shrugged. Then she turned back to me and raised her hands in front of her chest. "Didn't mean nothin' by it."

"I see." I smiled. "Well then, I'm sure you won't mind letting this woman get what she came for and leave, right?"

"Sure," said the first after a moment. "No problem."

"Good." I nodded encouragingly to the kneeling woman, who nodded back and struggled to her feet, her eyes still wide with fright. A further nod from me and she turned and walked into the laundry proper, reappearing a moment later with a stack of clean jumpsuits. Taking one last look at us, she bolted for the door. I could see the second woman, the one who had aborted her advance on me, shooting daggers with her eyes in the direction of the door.

"You know," I continued conversationally, "it wouldn't be the wisest move to go after her once I'm gone. Do yourselves a favor and leave it alone. You'll both be a lot happier, believe me."

"Who *are* you?" the first asked.

I could feel my grin widen. "My name's Angel."

"Angel, huh?" said the second, appraising me once again. She was a medium-sized woman with lank brown hair which hung down over her eyes, which were currently squinting myopically at me.

"That's what they call me, yeah."

"You don't look so tough."

"Looks can be deceiving. You're welcome to try and find out, though I'd rather go about this in a more adult fashion."

The second woman walked over to her companion and I took the time to study them both carefully. "Looks like someone came down on the both of you pretty hard," I observed. When they both turned angry looks my way, I held up a hand. "It's alright. Happened to me too. More than once."

"Nothin' happened to us," the first protested. "We just got . . . clumsy."

Though I wanted to laugh, I managed to keep it inside. "Yeah, I've been known to have a sudden attack of 'clumsiness' myself a time or two. Hurts, doesn't it. Kinda makes you want to make others feel as 'clumsy' as you, huh?"

Now I had *both* of them squinting at me. "What in the *hell* are you talking about?" the second asked finally.

"I'm talking about beating up on someone because you've just gotten beaten up yourselves. I'm talking about how you think that'll make you feel better about what happened to you. But I'm here to tell you that it won't. The only thing that will even begin to make you feel better is to learn how to stand up to the people who hurt you. Not to become bullies yourselves. Because let me tell you something about bullies, ladies. There's always someone a whole lot bigger, a whole lot stronger and a *whole* lot meaner than you around."

"You?" the first asked, snorting in disbelief.

"I'll do for a start. But I'd really rather give you lessons on how to defend yourself rather than defend myself against you. Whadda ya say?"

They looked at one another, then back at me, obviously beyond knowing what to make of me. "Alright," they finally said, in unison.

My smile brightened. "Great! I'm out in the yard every day at eleven. A lot of my time is taken up by softball right now, but if I can't help, I've got a bunch of friends who will. Meet me out by the free-weight area tomorrow and I'll introduce you to them, alright?"

"The free-weight area? But that's where the Amazons hang out."

"Exactly."

"You're an Amazon?"

"Sure am." I'm afraid my smile grew a trifle smug, but, really, wouldn't yours? Their expressions were tinged with a new emotion: respect, and it made me proud to be who I was. "So, do we have a deal? No more beating up on anyone?"

"Uh…yeah. Deal."

"Great! See you both tomorrow then." Brushing by them, I continued on into the laundry and picked up the uniforms I'd originally come for. When I came back out, they were both still standing there, staring at me. Giving them a final wave and a bright grin, I left on my way.

The prison grapevine was in perfect working order, as I found out when I walked into the library later that afternoon. Half a dozen Amazons and one elderly librarian converged upon me in an orgy of congratulations and back-slapping. I looked around in disbelief as they applauded me for the success of my first 'solo'.

Raucous laughter and talk of 'busted cherries' accompanied the good natured teasing and had me blushing to the roots of my hair. Pony almost did me in when she pushed forward bearing a cupcake she'd scrounged from the commissary vending-machine, complete with lit candle. I was serenaded with "For She's a Jolly Good Amazon" and the wish I made when I blew out the candle is mine alone to know.

🗝   🗝   🗝   🗝

As the warmth of spring gave way to the heat and humidity of summer, Ice began to come out of her shell once again, as if drawn out by the steamy days and balmy nights. We'd often sit outside near dusk, after I'd been given leave by the guards, and just talk, generally about nothing. It was obvious that the wound of Josephina's death was still sore, but it appeared to be getting better, little by little.

Many times I found myself telling her little stories of me as a young girl. I hoped these would open her up enough to tell me some stories in kind, but that was a horse of a different color. Still, storytelling was something I'd enjoyed since I was young, even if I didn't usually have any audience but my hated dolls.

Most of my stories centered around our summer cabin in the Canadian wilderness. I told her about the time that my mother's parents had come to visit for a week and my grandfather had dumped all the dirty plastic eating utensils in the fire, stinking the house up for days. Or about the one and only time I'd gone fishing with my father.

My father didn't think it was a girl's place to fish, but lacking any other, more suitable, companionship one day, he grunted at me to join him in the small boat we kept tied to the dock. Fancying himself a master fisherman, he had a beautiful rod and reel and an expensive tackle-box with all sorts of fascinating lures, none of which I was able to touch lest they be tainted by girl-cooties or something. I was presented, with great pomp and circumstance, a simple bamboo rod with a length of wire and a small hook dangling from the end. I was also given a styrofoam cup of nightcrawlers and the admonition that I'd better not ask him to bait my hook for me. Apparently, my father's notions of femininity didn't extend to getting one's hands dirty impaling worms on pointy hooks.

He took us out to a tiny island in the middle of the lake, where he dropped anchor and fixed his rod and tackle. He cast out into the clear blue water as I was still trying to figure out the best way to bait my own hook without getting worm guts all over me. I imagined I could hear the poor creatures cry out as I stuck the sharp point through their tough flesh and watched the blood ooze out of the hole I'd created.

Swallowing back the bile, I completed my task, determined not to give my father yet another reason to be disappointed in me. The very second I swung my line out, I felt a sharp tug and pulled up on the pole to find a nice-sized perch struggling on my hook.

That's pretty much how the day went. Every time I dropped my hook, a fish seemed to latch itself onto it. My father, on the other hand, even with all his fancy equipment, managed to snare himself two bluegill and a perch too tiny to bother keeping.

To say that my father was in a bad mood two hours into the venture would be understating the fact. Without saying a word, he abruptly stowed his gear, pulled up anchor, and turned us back toward land.

That evening's fish dinner was the best I'd ever eaten though my father looked like he was choking down every bite.

I even managed to get a rare, full-throated laugh out of Ice when I told her the story of the week we had some friends of the family up to stay with us. It had been raining all day and my mother and her friend had placed their shoes by the stone fireplace to dry out. Apparently, a chipmunk had chosen the fireplace as its summer nesting place. Even more apparently, it found my mother's friend's shoes a perfect retreat from the drudgery of its rock home.

The next morning, my mother's friend slipped her foot into her shoe, then let out a scream loud enough to wake the dead. By the time I made it to the ground floor, my mom and her friend were screaming, had brooms in their hands, and were running around the house chasing after a tiny, terrified chipmunk who'd picked the wrong shoe to sleep in.

Ice was always a wonderful listener and seemed always keen on having me tell her of my childhood summers in our cabin by the lake. By the far-away look in her eyes, I think I'd finally managed to get her to at least try and visualize the place that brought me such a sense of peace and serenity.

She always seemed calmer and more open after listening to my tales; softer, somehow. Her pale eyes would take on a deeper, more vibrant hue and the sharp angles and planes of her face would smooth out some as she looked tenderly in my direction; that child I'd seen in the photograph not far under the surface of the woman grown. It was a part of her I so much wanted to know. But like a clear pool whose depths aren't fully known until you find yourself up to your neck in them, there would be layers upon layers of mystery and emotional armor I'd have to patiently pry my way through to get to the soul underneath.

There were other times that she'd come and watch me play softball, her eyes raking over the field and its players, that blasted enigmatic smile painting her lips. I learned quickly to force my attention onto the game or risk fat lips, black eyes, and the unmerciful razzing of my teammates. There were times when I could almost feel the heat of her gaze upon me and I had to actively resist shifting out of my stance to turn and meet that smoldering gaze with my own, knowing it would be my undoing if I did.

The kisses we'd shared in her cell woke an animal I hadn't even known was hidden inside me. My nights were filled with images both erotic and tender. My days weren't all that much better, truth be known. There were times I thought I'd explode from the pressure, the pieces of me left to flutter down in ribbons of frustration.

But, if there's one lesson I learned well in the Bog, it's that patience is a virtue. And when I put my mind to it, I can be truly virtuous. My name *is* Angel, after all.

Too, there were times when the smile on her face would gauge the lightness of her mood and I'd try to draw out her feelings and plans for the retribution she promised for the warden and her betrayer. Try as I might, I could never get any hints from her and knew well enough to back off or risk retribution of my own. Still, I couldn't help but worry about the drastic measures she might see fit to bring forth in her quest for what she considered to be justice, albeit of the most base sort.

In reality, there was nothing to keep her from going directly after Morrison. She was, after all, a lifer with no hope, at least in her own mind, of ever seeing freedom again. I think that thought must have been tempting in the extreme for her at times, especially on Sundays when we would all be forced to sit through three hours of his pious preachings, knowing all the while the vile creature which lay beneath the vestments. Why she didn't take that road, I have no idea. It doubtless would have been easy for her and, really, what more punishment could she possibly receive?

Another avenue I considered was the one that comes most easily to the mind of almost any prisoner, whether it be in the Bog or elsewhere. Escape. Talk to any ten inmates of any prison around the world and nine will admit to having thoughts of escape. And the tenth will be lying. It was the thing you talked about over meals and thought about when the darkness of the prison night came home to roost in your cell.

Almost every inmate could tell you at least a dozen ways to leave the Bog without benefit of parole. And, truth be known, some of these ways even stood a good chance of success. This was the Bog, after all, and not Alcatraz. Corinne, who was most in the know about such things, stated with authority that there were twenty one successful escapes from the Bog in the years since it had been turned into a women's prison. Of those, fifteen were eventually recaptured, two were killed outright and the remaining five were never heard from again.

The most popular and successful escape route, though horribly cliched, was the old 'slip out in the clean-laundry basket' maneuver. Two of the five inmates who weren't killed or recaptured chose this route for their dash to freedom. In 1966, however, the prison lost its State laundry contract and that closed off the laundry avenue for good.

Tunneling was out as a means for escape. The Bog is aptly named, as it sits on many acres of swamp land. Tunnels crumble and fall apart, filling with water almost as soon as they were dug. To date, again according to Corinne, twelve inmates have drowned attempting to tunnel out of the prison.

The award for the most idiotic escape attempt, and one which was very nearly successful despite its stupidity, goes to a woman named Slick. Unlike the Bog, she was *not* aptly named, for she was anything but. Slick worked in the auto shop and by all accounts, she was a good mechanic. She was also a crazed and dangerous killer who would stop at nothing for the chance to escape. One evening, as she was putting the finishing touches on a State Police cruiser, she decided to hide beneath the tarp covering the flooring of the back seat and leave the Bog in style. The guards rarely inspected the police cruisers, figuring the patrolmen who drove in them would be in the best position to know if anything was out of place in their own vehicles.

What Slick forgot, however, in her zealous, if not overly bright, planning was that the backseats of police cruisers don't have door-handles. Nor does the thick plexiglass shielding the front seats from the back allow for easy passage from one compartment to the other. When the officer who drove the car got back from his briefing at the station, he found, to his great and amused surprise, an escaped inmate all boxed up and awaiting her return trip to the Bog.

Guard dogs specially trained to sniff out the human scent and the advent of electronic garage door openers ended the chances of escape through the auto bays once and for all. Each car was inspected as if it were waiting at a border crossing and anything seen out of place was immediately attended to.

Corinne told me that in the ten years since that incident, there had never been a successful escape attempt. Some women still tried to climb over the fence or slip out with the visitors, but no one ever made it off the grounds.

Even if that hadn't been the case, I had my doubts that escape was something that Ice would ever seriously consider. She was the rare inmate who truly believed that she belonged where she was. And even if she was incarcerated for a murder she didn't commit, her sense of guilt over crimes she *had* gotten away with continued to weigh on her heavily. She believed justice had been well and truly served in her case and seemed content to stay where she felt she belonged.

But I also knew that however long it took, somehow, some way, Cavallo and Morrison would also have justice served to them on a platter no doubt stained red with blood. And that was what worried me.

Another worry, though one more annoying than frightening, was the continued intrusive presence of my own little shadow named Digger. It seemed that no matter where I was or when I was there, Digger was always somewhere in the near vicinity. To be honest, my routine of library, softball, library, meals, library, cell wasn't that difficult to figure out, but it was still disconcerting nonetheless.

I tried talking to her. I had Corinne try talking to her. I had the *Amazons* try talking to her. Nothing worked. She seemed to be one of those people who couldn't see the facts in front of their face. It got so bad at times that I seriously considered asking Ice to intimidate the ever loving hell out of her, but my more polite side kept that tucked down deep to be used only as a last resort.

Still, Digger *did* manage to have some use for me and so I put up with the constant frustration of having a living shadow and kept telling myself that at least she wasn't Psycho. Or so I hoped.

Digger was, not to put too fine a point on it, a neat freak. The inside of her cell was clean and sparse as a monk's and her uniforms were always just so: wrinkle-free with perfect creases. It often amused me how she would spend several minutes during a softball game brushing the resilient fabric after sliding into a base to avoid a tag.

As a cleanliness nut, she was a natural in the janitorial jobs so abundant in the Bog. Let's face it. It takes a rare woman to enjoy swamping out toilets for a living, but Digger did it with a smile. Other inmates had taken to calling her "June Cleaver" behind her back and it was the cause of much teasing in our own little corner of Hell.

Her tidy tendencies didn't escape the notice of our warden, who also seemed to ascribe to the notion that cleanliness was indeed next to godliness. When it came to pressed suits and swept floors, that is. The man's soul was as dirty as the bottom of a taxi.

In any event, never one to pass over an easily used and abused resource, the warden appointed Digger his personal housekeeper, which meant, of course, that she was in the perfect position to pick up and deliver juicy little tidbits that Morrison let slip during the course of his daily business. And believe me when I tell you that Digger was very good at her job. Suffice it to say, William Morrison had the cleanest brass doorknob in all prisondom. Of course, Digger kept it well polished with her ears and eyes, but he didn't need to know that.

✒   ✒   ✒   ✒

The morning of the first inaugural Inmate/Guard softball game dawned with the "three H's" in attendance. Hazy, hot and humid. The sky was a flat, monochrome gray and the air was thick enough to be cut through with one of Psycho's knives. At nine in the morning, the temperature was already eighty-two and climbing. I had decided, spur of the moment, to come out a couple hours early to get in some extra batting practice, knowing our pitchers would be out practicing as well.

As I stepped out into the sauna the yard had become with the rising of the sun, I silently thanked our team captain for lobbying for the uniform I now wore. Instead of the thick, heavy polyester of my prison jumpsuit, I had on a simple cotton T and loose-fitting cotton shorts. Sweat immediately beaded between my breasts and at my hairline. I had pulled my hair into a loose tail for the game and vowed once again to get it chopped off at the next opportunity.

A body brushed by my side and I almost soiled my new shorts as I whirled, hands up in a defensive posture. Digger jumped back, a chagrined smile on her face, her hands also raised. "Sorry, Angel. It's just me. Musta been thinking about the game, huh?"

I returned the smile, though weakly. "Uh, yeah, Digger. You just startled me." I fought hard to keep the annoyance from sounding in my voice. "What are you doing out here so early?"

"I figured you'd want to get in some last-minute practice, so here I am." Her grin widened as her eyes roamed over my body. "You look real nice, Angel."

I looked down at myself, seeing places where my sweat had glued the cotton to my skin in dark patches. There was already a 'V' forming between my breasts and I resisted the urge to cover myself up. "Thanks," I managed. "So do you."

In truth, I didn't think it was possible to get cotton so white and absolutely wrinkle-free, but somehow Digger managed it, as usual. Unlike me, her sweat didn't dare stain those pristine garments. I chuckled inwardly as I imagined her yelling at her pores, demanding they stay shut nice and tight for the duration.

"So," she said, fidgeting slightly to break the silence, "you ready to kick some guard ass?"

"Sure." Switching my mitt to the hand closest to Digger, I started across the grounds, taking the still air and the muggy, slightly swampy smell that hung on the mist surrounding us. Our pitchers were looking warmed up and ready and I stood just outside the foul line, watching and cheering them on for a moment.

Players from both teams began to drift onto the field, calling out to one another in shouted greetings and good natured ribbing and kicking up the dust to hang in the still, humid air. Another body came close, but instead of brushing by me, it moved forward until we were almost touching. Two strong hands settled onto my shoulders in a grip I recognized and a low, sultry voice sounded very close to my ear. "Give 'em hell, Angel." The hands gave my shoulders a brief squeeze before a head swung briefly around into my field of vision, depositing a soft kiss to my cheek. "For luck."

A subtle shifting and the figure was gone, leaving behind a wonderful scent and me, staring dazedly at nothing with a flush rapidly darkening my face and wondering why in the world I had thought the day could possibly be lousy.

"Was that Ice?" Digger said from beside me, her voice filled with hushed awe.

I blinked in annoyance, the spell Ice had woven over me temporarily broken. "Yeah, that's Ice."

"Wow. That is *so* cool! Hey! Do you think if I asked, she'd give me a kiss too?"

Before I knew it, I had whirled around to face her. "Don't even think about it."

Her look of surprise was so comical I had to bite back a bray of laughter. "Let's just go practice, alright?"

"Yeah. Sure. Anything you say, Angel."

✦ ✦ ✦ ✦

The game was fast and furious from the start. The guards had an excellent team with a pitcher who could thread a needle with a softball and set your bat on fire if it got in the way. Their batting was good too, as was their outfield, who had rifles for arms. Their only weakness was their infield and I set out to exploit that as best I could by peppering line-drives up the gap between short and second, a particular sweet spot of mine anyway.

Our strength *was* our infield. Though annoying, Digger was an outstanding first-baseman, well earning her nickname by digging out a few errant throws that might have gone on for extra bases had she missed them.

It was the top of the fifth and the score was tied at one apiece when I bobbled what should have been an easy double-play ball, then managed to get it stuck in the webbing of my glove, thus allowing *both* runners to advance. In a fit of frustration, I threw my glove down on the ground and stomped around, much like a child having a tantrum, which, I suppose, I was.

In the middle of my tirade, I felt a pair of eyes on me and I whirled, expletives still spewing like sewer water from my lips. The torrent ceased abruptly as my gaze locked with Ice's, allowing the calmness and confidence in her eyes wash over me like a soothing balm. I suddenly forgot why I had gotten so angry in the first place and felt a blush of embarrassment creep into my cheeks, heating my ears. Her eyebrow arched as a smile played across her lips. She gave me a brief nod before deliberately breaking the lock of our gazes as she looked toward the batter's box, studying the new guard who'd stepped up to the plate.

Bending down to pick up my glove, I murmured my apologies to my teammates and readied myself for the next play, bolstered beyond belief by the confidence one woman had in me. Taking a few deep breaths, I leaned forward in a crouch, my glove before me flexed and ready for anything.

When the blistering line drive came at me, I felt my glove raise in an almost unconscious reaction. It sunk quickly, but I managed to scoop it up on one hop and this time I didn't bobble it. Standing up quickly, I stuck my mitt out to tag the runner leaving second for one out, stepped on the bag for the second out, and threw the ball to Digger who caught it a split-second before the runner crossed the bag for a triple play.

You might have thought I'd won the World Series the way my teammates dog-piled on me, screaming their fool heads off. Even the guards applauded and shouted their congratulations. Once again, Digger came to my rescue, threading her way through the pile and pulling me to my feet. Though I welcomed her help, I gently resisted her attempts to brush me off, not wanting her hands on me any more than necessary and figuring I'd earned the dirt I wore.

The bottom of the same inning, we managed to get a jump on their pitcher, who was tiring. Digger doubled into the gap between left and center field to start us off. Trey, who had forgone gang loyalty to offer us her strong bat, smashed a towering hit almost to the fence in straight away center, but the outfielder had her played perfectly and caught the ball with ease. However, Digger tagged and advanced to third, beating the throw by a hair. The next woman got out on a short pop fly that barely cleared the infield and left Digger no room to run.

And so it was my turn. I suddenly felt that good kind of nervousness that you get deep in your gut when the game's riding on you and your teammates are cheering you on. I looked over at the woman I now considered my lucky talisman, and got a half-grin and a pumped fist for my efforts. Returning the grin, I stepped into the batter's box and dug in.

Everything telescoped around me. The crowd's shouting grew dim and far-away. My eyes were only for the opposing pitcher, who was giving me a feral smile of her own as she nonchalantly tossed the ball up and down in her hand.

My hands were sweaty on the bat's handle and I twisted my grip several times to solidify it. Then I took a few experimental swings and dug my toe further into the loamy dirt as I chanted the silent litany of "eyes steady, shoulders square, easy swing".

When the pitch finally came, it floated to me on an arc so lovely and graceful and perfect that I could have sworn it had "please knock the crap outta me, Angel" stitched into its hide. And so, of course, I obliged. The ball impacted my bat right at that perfect spot where the feeling in your hands and the sound of the contact lets you just *know* you did good.

It flew from my bat, just barely avoiding giving the pitcher a haircut, before again splitting the gap between short and second, then hitting a wet patch of outfield grass and just . . .dying. The short-stop, second baseman and centerfielder all converged on it, missing a three-way collision by the barest of inches. Digger floated home while I took second with ease before the ball finally made its way back to the pitcher, who tipped her cap at me before turning to deal with the next batter. I couldn't help the grin that spread its way across my face nor the turn of my head to meet the pale eyes of my silent supporter. Receiving another brisk nod and a quick wink for my efforts, I felt as though I were floating on air.

The pitcher dug down deep and struck out our last batter to end the inning, but I'd done my job, helping us to go up by one run. Now all we had to do is hold them for three more outs and the game would be ours.

Unfortunately, Sandra Pierce wasn't privy to that plan. Stepping up to the plate, she blasted a left-field home-run that went so high and so far that I think even now, seven years later, it's still floating somewhere in the stratosphere.

Phyllis stepped up to the plate next and, taking a page from Sandra's book, blasted a hit to left field. Trey had a bead on it, however, and showed us all just why the Lady Vols were so devastated when she left. In a leap the height of which I'd never seen a human produce before, she reached up and snagged the ball just as it was about to sail over the fence. While the rest of us looked on in open-mouthed awe, she casually tossed the ball in to the pitcher and straightened a non-existent crease on her uniform shirt.

Grinning and shaking my head, I returned my attention back to the game, secretly wondering in my heart of hearts why a woman who had taken the life of another deserved to feel so good. I shook off the feeling quickly before it ruined what this day had become, figuring that sometimes, things just *are* and it's best to leave it at that.

The next two outs were routine grounders that we had no trouble handling and then it was time to run off the field and hope for the best in the bottom of the last inning of the game.

It was also the bottom of our line-up, where our weakest batters were. All three were looking nervous as they realized the positions they were in. We all did our best to calm them down as the chanting and cheering of the crowd reached an almost deafening crescendo.

Our first batter stepped up and dug in. I could see her legs shaking from my spot behind the batter's cage and swallowed hard in empathy. The first pitch came, sinking fast into the dirt and she swung at it for strike one. The second one blew by her before she was fully into her stance for strike two. She pounded the head of the bat into the dirt in frustration, then settled again. The next pitch was perfect and she swung for the fences. It shot down the first-base line, skittering off the glove of the woman defending the bag and rolled onward, allowing her a stand-up double.

In the dugout, we all went crazy, seeing a possible light at the end of this particular tunnel. The next batter was a quick out, leaving our baserunner on second, but the next was a hard grounder that saw both women safe on their respective bases.

Flustered and tired, the pitcher then walked the bases loaded and our weakest batter stepped up to the plate. Three swings later, she stepped away from the plate, swinging her bat dejectedly and apologizing to us all as she stepped back into the dugout.

It was one of the situations every ballplayer, from Little League to the Majors, dreams of. Bases loaded, bottom of the last inning with the score tied and two outs. It's also the situation every player dreads.

Two quick pitches and she was in the hole, the rest of us right along with her. But she wasn't our lead-off batter for nothing, and so she simply squared her shoulders and waited patiently for the next pitch.

Three more pitches and the count was full. The yard went silent as we all, prisoners and guards alike, leaned forward for what promised to be the final pitch of the game. Even the birds went quiet, as if knowing the somewhat dubious importance of this event about to transpire but respecting it nonetheless.

Our batter stared at the pitcher. The pitcher stared back, not quite so cocky as before. She fiddled with the ball nervously before putting it behind her back and leaning forward to catch the signal from the catcher.

Every eye in the yard followed the ball as it rose up in a majestic arc through the hazy air. We watched as it hit the pinnacle of its trajectory and then began to give in to gravity's unbreakable summons. It finished its graceful ballet by landing cleanly in the catcher's glove. Our batter had never removed the bat from her shoulder.

All eyes then turned to the umpire, awaiting her fateful decision. Small eternities were born and crumbled to dust under the weight of her pregnant pause. Her jaw moved, forming words we all fought to hear.

"*Ball four!*"

Ok. So it wasn't the most exciting way to win a game, but it counted. The batter smugly dropped her bat in the dirt and trotted over to first base, bringing the runner on third home. When she crossed the plate, the yard erupted and a frenzy of cheers and we all piled on the hapless runner to get in on the action.

Forgetting for the moment that they were our keepers, the guards jumped into the crowd of bodies, laughing and shouting with the rest of us. For a moment, we weren't prisoners and guards forced by circumstances to co-inhabit a stinking pit in a far-away corner of nowhere. For that brief moment of time, the weight of our crimes broke under the exhilarating feeling of freedom. We were just two teams battling it out on a lazy summer's day. The prison, and our places in it, felt far away as we whooped and danced around like crazy idiots, hugging one another and slapping each others' backs and butts.

I chanced a look up at the red-brick building. It seemed smaller some-how. As if its very existence fed off the fright and guilt of the women it housed and when those emotions weren't there, it shrunk in upon itself like a flower that wilts from lack of sunlight.

I stuck my tongue out at the building, then turned as something smooth and cool was slipped into my hand. Looking down, I saw a bottle of spar-kling grape juice waiting for me and, grinning wildly, I shook it, then popped the plastic cork, spraying guards and teammates alike with the chilled, sticky liquid. Corks popped across the field and we laughed like children as we doused everyone within reach.

In the midst of the revelry, I took the time out to commit the scene and its feelings to memory, knowing that there'd someday be cause to draw it out like a treasured photo when the nights were long and freedom seemed ten lifetimes away.

When the celebration began to wind down, I looked back over the yard which was awash in orange, brown and white, looking for a hint of black hair and blue eyes; disappointed when I didn't find them. I indulged myself in a brief but harmless fantasy of receiving a more private congratulations, then snorted softly at my foolishness. Snapping out of my reverie when I felt a companionable arm slip over my shoulders, I looked up to see Sandra standing next to me, clinking my bottle of ersatz champagne against her own.

"Hell of a game, Angel. They should sign you up for the Majors with that triple play you turned."

"Ah, that was easy. I think that homerun you hit landed in Harrisburg somewhere."

She laughed, then knocked back a swig of her grape juice. "That felt good. Been a long time since I've had fun like this, though. Thanks."

"No. Thank *you*. For the first time in a couple years, those bars didn't seem quite so close."

There was a moment of companionable silence as we watched the in-mates and guards slowly walk back into the prison. "Where's Ice? Figured she'd be here to congratulate you personally."

I know my blush was evident as she regarded me with twinkling eyes. Then I snorted. "Who knows? She's probably off preventing another riot or delivering a baby or beating the snot out of someone. Or something."

Sandra threw back her head and laughed, squeezing my shoulders in a comradely hug. "That's our Ice." She released my shoulders and turned to face me fully, her expression suddenly serious. "Underneath all that bluff

and bravado, Ice is a good woman, Angel. I know you know that, but sometimes it's hard to remember when she closes herself up in that shell of hers.
She's made a lot of mistakes, but they don't change the person she is underneath." A sad smile bowed her lips as she reached out and laid a gentle hand
on my forearm. "You've been good for her, Angel. I really thought we'd lost
her after all that time in the hole, you know."

Swallowing hard, I nodded. "Yeah, I know. I thought so too. That
was…scary."

Returning my nod, Sandra squeezed my arm. "I don't know the whole
story behind it and I don't wanna know. But she was just…dead inside. But
when that idiot Derby got her mitts around your neck, you should have seen
the spark that came back into her eyes. God, it was a beautiful thing."

"Sorry I missed it," came my droll reply. "I think I was almost unconscious
at the time."

She laughed, then released my arm. "Ready to go back?"

"No, but that's where the showers are, so I suppose I have to. God, I'm
a mess."

"You and me both, kiddo. I've got grape juice in places the good Lord
didn't intend grapes to go."

I took one last long look around the yard, watching as the last few
stragglers made their way back into the building. Empty bottles littered the
base pads bearing mute testimony to the celebration just passed. I felt a bit
of melancholy steal through me and so I blinked the image away. "Sure.
Let's go."

* * * *

Though I intended to head directly to the showers to wash the grape-
juice, dirt and sweat from my suddenly tired and aching body, my plans took
a sudden detour when an inmate came to me, tears streaming down her
face, begging for my help. Her baby daughter had gotten sick and was rushed
to the hospital, but the baby's father, who was watching over her, wouldn't
give her any information and she was frantic.

I pulled her over to the guards' room and called in a favor, which was
the use of their phone. There were three pay phones situated throughout
the prison for inmate use, but I wasn't carrying around any spare change
and hospitals usually don't like to accept collect calls. But, as I've said, most
of our guards are a compassionate bunch, even if we *did* just kick their butts
in softball, and I was waved into the room with nary a murmur.

Half a dozen calls later and the problem was solved. The baby had been
taken to Pittsburgh Children's Hospital with febrile seizures and was released back to her father and grandparents after some Tylenol had taken
care of the problem.

After enduring her thanks for what seemed like hours, I was finally able to affect my escape to the showers, knowing that by now most of my teammates had probably gone on to the somewhat greener pastures of the mess hall and common room.

Shrugging my shoulders, I made my way down to the showers, happy to hear that at least one person was inside by the sound of the water. Quickly stripping out of my sticky clothes with a sigh of profound relief, I slipped into my flip-flops, grabbed a towel, and made my way into the shower proper.

And stopped, frozen, before I'd even gotten a foot into the room.

There, facing me, her hair slicked back and tumbling over her shoulders like freshly spilled ink, stood Ice. Her body glistened from the water pouring down from the showerhead and her neck arched back to wash the last bit of shampoo from her hair, thrusting her wet and shining breasts out toward me, the nipples hard and tight.

My mouth actually *watered* at the sight as the towel slithered from suddenly nerveless fingers to land in a heap at my feet.

She straightened back up, but her eyes were still closed, and I continued to take the opportunity to play voyeur as my own eyes feasted on the perfection of her body. From the way she wore her jumpsuit, from the way she carried herself with athletic grace, I would have expected all slashing angles, and to be truthful, there were. Her musculature was long and lean, like a hunting cat's, with long lines of ropy, veined muscles stretching across her shoulders and down her arms. Her legs were especially developed and I watched them flex and relax as she shifted under the spray of water.

But what intrigued me the most was the lush femininity also present within that same body. Though not especially large, her breasts were full and proud. Her hips flared out slightly from a well-tapered waist in very pleasing curves that drew in my eyes and held them for a timeless moment.

I swallowed hard, shocked with my body's response to another woman, even given what Ice and I had already shared. But it was as if this woman, this body, had been made just for me, given my own responses to it. It was as if someone or something had pulled the vision from the realms of my deepest subconscious, from a place so deep within me that I didn't even know it existed.

Regardless, my body was sending me some very definite and urgent signals and my feet followed along for the ride, moving me closer to the vision beneath the stinging water, my towel forgotten behind me.

Azure eyes opened and froze me once again, mere steps from my goal. She blinked once, freeing beaded water from her long lashes, then smiled slightly. "Like what you see?" Her voice was a sensual purr and the summons became all the more urgent.

"God yes," I replied, my hands aching to do—I didn't know what—but something.

"So do I." I could feel the heat of her gaze as it traveled a leisurely path over my own equally naked body. My arousal was building by the moment from a simple look. I didn't know if I'd possibly be able to live through what looked to be the final consummation of the feelings between us.

I took another step forward, only to be stopped by Ice's upraised palms. "This probably isn't the best place to be doing this."

The memories of that morning in the cafeteria flashed through my mind and I nodded, biting on my lip. "Um…yeah. I…I guess you're right."

She smiled crookedly, then stepped out from beneath the shower. "Why don't you get cleaned up. I'm sure we can find a more private place to…continue this discussion."

I nodded again and she slipped past me, allowing our bodies to brush against each other just slightly. The feeling of her water-slicked smooth skin sliding briefly against my own almost did me in as I felt the strength in my muscles begin to flee. I braced one hand against the tiled wall as the other fumbled with the knob. For the first time since I'd come to the Bog, the icy cold spray was a welcome relief.

Though the chill dampened my raging lust somewhat, my mind was free to wander. And wander it did, with the speed of a tornado. Anxiety, performance and otherwise, displaced hormones and my body trembled with it. I didn't remember being that nervous on my wedding night, and that was going some.

While I had my hopes, I realized truthfully that I had no idea where this all would lead. All I did know was that I had no desire to be another name-less, faceless assignation in some broom-closet somewhere. My feelings for Ice ran much deeper than that and I resolved that, burning body or no, if she didn't return them in at least some measure, I would suffer the consequences of lonely nights and a broken heart. Whatever else, I still had to live within the shell of my own body and look at myself in the mirror every morning.

My resolve thus fortified, I set about the task of removing the grime from my hair and body and did so in record time. As I turned off the water, I noticed that sometime during my mental perambulations, Ice had returned to place a fresh towel over a neighboring showerhead. Though it made me feel a bit uneasy that I hadn't heard her approach, I felt pleased that she had at least noticed and helped in this small way.

Drying off, I wrapped the towel around my body and stepped into the changing room to find Ice, fully dressed and sitting on one of the benches, her hands clasped loosely between her knees. She smiled at me, then turned her head prudently as I snagged a clean jumpsuit from the pile by the bench and dropped my towel to dress.

Once fully clothed, I realized I didn't have a comb to run through my hair and could have kicked myself. As if reading my mind, she handed me a black comb. "It's clean. I washed it when I brought over your towel."

I accepted it gratefully, wincing as I pulled the fine-toothed implement through my tangled hair. "I swear. One of these days, this is all coming off."

"It's very beautiful."

Suddenly, combing out the tangles didn't seem to be so much of a chore. "You really like it?" Yes, it was lame in the extreme, but I was fishing for conversation here.

"Yes. It reminds me of a sunset in Phoenix."

"You've been to Phoenix?" Two for two. I was doing better here than during the game.

"Yes, many times."

Finishing my task, I handed the comb back to her, then pressed my palms down the front of my uniform, feeling like a new bride.

"You ready?"

Oh, *that* particular question covered a whole myriad of bases, sticking for the moment to the softball analogy here. "Uh…yeah. Sure. I guess." How was *that* for a decisive answer?

If she read anything into my hesitancy, she didn't show it. Instead, she stood and beckoned me to follow her. "C'mon."

As we stepped out of the shower room, who should I almost run straight into, but my ever-present shadow, Digger. Her face lit up into a smile as she saw me. "Hey, Angel! I was looking all over for you. They're showing Wuthering Heights in the common room tonight and I remember you telling me you liked the book. You wanna go with me?"

"Oh…hi, Digger. I'd…um…love to go but I'm kind of busy right now." I gestured to the tall woman standing at my side.

"Oh. Ok. I understand. Next time then, alright?"

"Yeah. That sounds great."

"Well…see ya!" With a jaunty wave, she walked off.

I turned to see a very amused Ice smirking down at me, one eyebrow held aloft.

"What?"

"Next time?"

"Hey!" I said, poking her in the side. "You try living with a shadow every minute of every day who doesn't seem to know the meaning of the word 'no' and we'll see how *you* handle it."

"Thanks, but I'll pass. Let's go."

My assumption that we were heading for the stairs to Ice's cell was put to rest as she passed them by and instead continued into the long series of branching corridors that lead to the shops. Within moments, we were in the room with all the doors and getting patted down by the guards once again.

Satisfied that we weren't carrying any concealed weaponry, the guard let us into the auto shop. Not bothering to turn on the lights, Ice led us down to the 'chop-shop' door in the darkness and ushered me through, flipping on one set of those lights. I looked around as I stepped inside, noticing both bays were empty.

Ice walked over to a barren, battle-scarred desk sitting off to one side and settled her long frame down on it, patting the top for me to join her, which I did. My nervousness, which had subsided somewhat during the walk, came back with a vengeance and I resisted the urge to fidget with it. Silence bloomed between us suddenly, heavy and oppressive as a living thing.

"So," I said finally, just to break the tension, "that was some game, huh?"

"Yeah, it was. Nice triple-play, by the way."

"Thanks." My fingers found themselves wanting to drum on the desk-top. "How come you don't play?"

"Say again?"

"How come you don't play softball? I bet you're good."

Her soft laugh sounded beside me. "It's not really my game."

"Do you have one? A game, that is?"

"Hmmm. I like football." She shrugged. "Track and basketball too, I suppose. Martial arts."

"You're probably great at all of them."

The broad shoulders shrugged again. "I do alright."

More silence.

"Ice…."

"Angel…."

"You first."

"No, please. What were you going to say?"

I opened my mouth, then closed it, my words drying up. Sighing, I shifted on the desk until I faced her. *Alright, Angel. This is it. Whatever she says, whatever happens from here on out, at least you'll know. There's something to be said for that, isn't there?* I truly hoped so, because I was about to lay my heart out on the line. "Ice, I need to tell you something. Something very important to me and I hope, maybe important to you too."

Her eyes were steady as they met mine. "What is it, Angel?"

"I care for you. A lot. And sometime during the past week, I've finally been able to put a name to these feelings." I shifted again. "Now…I know that what I'm about to say might make you feel uncomfortable, but I need to tell you how I feel before we do anything further." I took a deep breath and stepped off the cliff, though without the bravery to look her in the eye as I made my confession. "Ice, I think…no, I *know* I'm in love with you. I'll understand if you don't feel the same, but I need you to know this. This place, this prison, is too small for things like this to go unmentioned."

The silence came back as I fingered the lines in my palms. Tears sprang into my eyes as I figured the answer and I wiped them away, willing myself not to crumble. A gentle hand displaced my own, cupping my cheek as a thumb dried the tears from my eyes. "Don't cry, Angel," Ice murmured from beside me. "I'm in love with you too."

I hitched in a breath. "I'm sorry I made you feel uncom—What? Could…would you mind repeating that please? I'm not sure I…."

"You heard me. I love you, Angel. I have for a very long time now. I told you as much in the cell, remember?"

"Well…yeah, but I didn't think we were talking about the same thing."

"We were." I chanced a look up and what I saw made my breath catch in my throat. Her eyes, usually so shuttered and cold, were open and warm and caring and sparkled with an adoration that I'd never seen in another person before. And it was for *me*.

Those damn tears stung at my eyes again, but this time it was for an entirely different reason. As I sat pondering the wisdom of having my tear-ducts surgically removed, Ice turned fully to face me and, cupping my face in both hands, laid gentle kisses to each of my eyelids, neatly solving the problem in a far more pleasant way.

"I love you," she whispered, placing a kiss on my forehead, then one to each cheek. "I love you," she whispered again as her lips met mine with gentle warmth. The kiss was almost reverent and stole my breath as she pulled away, tucking her chin and looking directly into my eyes. "I love you, Angel."

"Oh God," I exclaimed, half sobbing and half laughing in absolute relief as I fell into her body, my mind a whirling torrent of emotions, none of them nameable. Her arms wrapped tightly around me and I could hear the rapid beating of her heart through the fabric of her jumpsuit. *She's as scared as I am!*

Though perhaps not a revelation to you, that thought filled me with wonder, and a large kernel of happiness blossomed, banishing my nervousness to the farthest reaches of my soaring soul.

I felt a brief instant of panic as she shifted against me, but her embrace held tight as she came to stand before me, pressing another kiss on the crown of my head. Pulling away finally, she held me at arm's length, hands clasped on my shoulders. Her eyes were full of questions.

Reaching up slowly, I touched her cheek with trembling fingers. Speechless, I watched her eyes flutter closed as she leaned into the tentative caress. As if watching from very far away, I felt my hand cup her cheek more purposefully, then slide down to her jaw and back, beneath her ear, to curve around the base of her skull.

I bunched my arm slightly and she bowed to the pressure, moving smoothly under the summons of my hand. Our lips met and merged like satin on silk and my fingers tangled in her hair as my mouth opened under the tender assault of her lips and tongue. My free hand cupped around the taut curve of her waist and I pulled her body closer to mine, spreading my knees wider to accommodate her flaring hips and muscled thighs.

She rocked up against me, tight against the stretched and protesting fabric pulled taut between my legs. I whimpered out a need I couldn't even identify, let alone articulate. Her hands clenched my waist and pulled us closer still as our tongues entwined in a sweet duel.

Bereft of air, we pulled away at the same time and looked into one another's eyes as she continued to slowly rock against me. Her hand reached up and toyed with the pull to my zipper briefly before grasping it fully and slowly pulling it down to stop where my cleavage began. Reaching up again, she slid her fingers beneath the fabric at my shoulders, parting it further as she drew it, whispering, over my heated flesh.

Her hair, still damp from the shower, brushed against my lips as she lowered her head. I could feel the warm smoothness of her tongue as she tasted my collarbone, tracing a slick trail from my throat outwards to end with a light nip to my shoulder. The process was repeated on my right side as her fingers worked the zipper again, pulling it down until it reached the end.

My eyes closed and my head fell back as she lipped my pulsepoint before suckling at the hollow of my throat. My nostrils flared with the sweet scent of her hair. I leaned back, taking my weight on my hands, my hips responding to her continued slow rocking with thrusts of their own.

Her lips detached from my neck and I thought to open my eyes, but that fast became a faded memory as her warm, wet mouth closed itself over my breast, the gentle suction of her lips' caress sending molten fire through my veins. My heart fluttered in my chest, then pounded strongly, sending my blood in rapid spurts exactly where it needed to be, engorging me and making me full. I could smell the faint scent of my own arousal which only served to excite me even more.

My head fell back further, my wet hair tickling against my shoulder blades, my breath coming in rapid pants. Her tongue trailed a line between my breasts before latching onto the other, pulling in my nipple as her teeth grazed against it, teasing it into a wonderfully aching hardness.

I moaned out my need in some unintelligible language known only to lovers and she responded in kind, the vibration of her lips against my flesh fanning the flames my body had become.

Drawing away again, she smiled tenderly down at me as she sat me up and pulled the fabric of my jumpsuit off my arms altogether, leaving it to puddle around my waist in a fan of orange on the rickety wooden desk. Her eyes blazed a trail down my body once again and I felt the flames of my desire grow hotter beneath her liquid blue fire. "Your body is perfect," she purred, drawing a single fingertip down the centerline of my torso. "Soft.

Firm." She cupped one breast in her palm. "Warm." Then she leaned in again, capturing my lips in a soul-melting kiss. "Mmmm. Delicious."

As she began to straighten, I reached up and grabbed the tab of her zipper, determined not to be denied. It bunched, as zippers often do during the most urgent of times, and she laughed softly at my grunt of frustration. It was apparent that my grace, dignity and verbal skills were having a four-some with my nervousness somewhere because they certainly weren't readily available to me.

Releasing my grasp on the tab, she stepped back one step. Two. Then she squared her shoulders as she leveled me a challenging stare. Swallowing hard, I gave her my own rendition back, pleased when she acknowledged the expression with her eyes.

The sound of her zipper lowering was loud in the small confines of the room. Inch by slow inch she revealed more of her flesh to my heated gaze; taunting me, tempting me, teasing me beyond all rational thought.

Once her zipper reached the end of its long, solitary journey, her smile became a teasing smirk. Her hands came up and grasped the fabric at her breasts, parting it, then slipping the top down off her proud shoulders. The jumpsuit slipped to the floor in a whispering of fabric and when she stepped out of it, that magnificent body came within my hungry grasp.

I took in her firm breasts with their tight, peaked, rose-hued nipples and licked my lips as if inspecting a king's feast put before me. Leaning forward, I captured one in my mouth, savoring the taste and feel of her against my tongue and lips. My mind was shouting stridently, reminding me that I hadn't the faintest idea what I was doing, but I cheerfully told it to shut up as Ice moaned deep in her chest and threaded her fingers through my hair, clearly enjoying what I was offering her.

Her scent, musky and exotic as Eastern spices rose up to curl around me, making my head spin. Wanting more, I switched my attention to her other breast, taking in her murmurs of contentment with joyful ears. I might have been flying by the seat of my pants, but God, what a ride it was turning out to be.

I suckled like a hungry infant, jumping as a tentative bite caused her to surge into me, almost knocking both of us back across the desk. Deciding I very much liked that reaction, I nestled my teeth together once again, moving with her forward motion better this time.

After another moment, her hand tightened in my hair and she pulled me away from my feast. My moan of displeasure died on my lips as my gaze caught hers. Smokey and smoldering, her indigo eyes seared into me, touching me in places that fairly screamed out in primal want. My heart beat out a staccato tattoo in my chest. "Please," I whispered, though I had no idea what I was asking for. "Please."

Her hands began to map out my body once again in slow, teasing strokes of lightly callused fingertips. She trailed down my newly muscled abdomen and paused to play at my navel briefly, smiling as I squirmed.

Then her fingers went lower, slithering beneath the fabric to rest just above my pubic bone. Her eyes again asked a question.

"Yes. God, yes."

Smiling slightly, she slid further inside my uniform, giving me the briefest of gliding touches where my need was the greatest. My hips exploded off the desk and I thought I would release right then and there. Again her fingers stilled and she turned wide eyes to me. "So responsive." The low register of her voice tickled at my hearing as I tried to will myself back under control.

After another moment, she withdrew her hand and I swallowed back my reaction to the glistening wetness that coated her middle finger. The very tip of her tongue darted out as she tasted my readiness. Her eyes never leaving mine, she sucked her finger into her mouth in the most erotic gesture I think I have ever seen. "Perfect."

As she leaned in to kiss me again, I tasted myself for the first time and decided I liked it. Her hand was warm against my upper back and with gentle pressure, she lowered me down on the desktop, covering me with the weight and heat and scent of her body.

Her kiss was deep, lustful and ravishing. I took it and gave back in kind, squirming beneath her, feeling the scarred wood beneath me rub against my naked back. We locked together for what seemed a blissful eternity before she growled and pulled away again, trailing feathery kisses down the front of my body.

Her hands followed her lips, skimming lightly over my breasts and down my sides to pull the jumpsuit down over my hips and legs. She tapped me slightly and I lifted my lower body, feeling the fabric give way and free me from my cloth bonds. She planted a kiss to my pubic hair and as her mouth engulfed me fully, I climaxed, unable to hold back the tide anymore.

When the tremors ceased, I felt her mouth still holding me gently, her motion still and quiet. When I lifted my dazed head to see what was going on down there, I was suddenly filled by what I assumed to be her fingers hooking into me and rubbing against my inner walls in a most delightful way. My head fell back to the desk as her tongue began moving against me in time with her strokes. I could feel the peak within me rising again and this time I did nothing to try and hold it back. Within moments I released again, breaking off a chunk of the gently rotting wood I was laying on as my body convulsed against the pleasure I was receiving.

As I began to come down from this high she didn't stop. Instead, she increased the strength of her thrusts, adding a slight twisting movement that promised to drive me absolutely insane. I felt her teeth graze against me, sparking the third orgasm in what seemed to be as many minutes.

This time, however, when I finally stopped shaking, I tossed away the wood that had practically pulverized in my hand, then sunk my fingers into her thick hair, fending off her continued advances. "Please," I gasped, "no more. You're…gonna…kill me."

Her twinkling eyes met mine and for a moment, I really thought she was going to ignore my pleading. But then, to my great and utter relief, after delivering a final kiss, she pulled away, withdrawing her fingers gently at the same time. I couldn't believe how suddenly empty I felt.

As if reading my thoughts, she lifted me by the shoulders and cradled me against her, stroking my sweat-soaked hair and murmuring soft endearments that slipped just past the edge of my hearing and made me feel full once again.

Concentrating on steadying my breathing, I ran a hand down Ice's thigh, watching as her flesh humped up with the passage of my fingers. As my hand retraced its path back up that strong leg, I was surprised by the slick dampness coating the inside of her thigh. Tilting my head, I looked up at her. The gaze which met mine was steady but not coaxing. Looking back down, I blindly followed the trail upwards as she spread her legs wider, giving me freer access.

I couldn't believe the heat radiating from her; heat which almost scorched my hand as I moved in further, brushing against soft hair which tickled against my fingers. Finally I reached my goal as heated wetness coated the backs of my fingers in a lover's intimate embrace. I heard her take in a breath of air and release it as a moaning sigh. "Ice? I…um…I'm not sure what I'm doing here."

Her laugh sounded through her nose. "Believe me, Angel, you're doing just fine."

"But…I…um…."

"Relax. Here." Her larger hand came down and cupped over mine, pressing it against herself.

I gasped out at the slick, heated moisture waiting for me and moved my fingers through it, causing another surge in her body, accompanied by a moan. "Oh…perfect, Angel."

Moving again, I marveled at the softness under my fingers. I know I must have been driving her crazy with my fumblings, but I couldn't for the life of me stop. I was drawn in like a bee to honey of the sweetest kind.

I knew I'd pushed to her limits when she grasped my hand again, forcing it downward. "Angel. Now. Inside."

Following her terse, panted instructions to the letter, I gasped in wonder as her velvet walls hugged around my fingers in a hot caress as I became sheathed fully within her. I moved my fingers and she groaned, her hips thrusting back against my hand. I smiled. I could do this.

"Harder," she gasped, her fingers digging into my wrist so hard I began to lose circulation. Still, I struggled to comply, working my hand as best I could given the constriction. I felt her expand around me, then clamp down hard as her body began to buck and shudder, leaning against me heavily.

Using my other arm to bear us up, I continued at my task, grunting with the effort to prolong her pleasure. With a last, low, shuddering growl, she relaxed against me, breathing heavily through her mouth and nose. I made as if to withdraw, but she clamped down on my wrist again. "No. Stay. Please."

I nodded, panting with exertion and the incredible feelings that washed through me at what we had just accomplished. Shuddering tremors played across my fingers until finally all was quiet. She removed her hand from my arm and I withdrew slowly, taking care not to stretch the tender tissue clasping me so intimately.

We fell into an embrace, our bodies glued together with the sweat of our passion.

Chapter 8

It was all I could do not to start humming at odd moments the next morning as I dressed, ate, and made my way down to the library to begin another day in the Bog. The memories of the evening before played in a continuous loop behind my eyes and I'm sure I was probably glowing like some preternatural mist. Try as I might, I just couldn't manage to wipe the silly little grin off my lips, as the imp in me responded to the looks I was receiving with an internal *You just wish you knew what I'm smiling about, don't you.* I'm afraid I was quite insufferable that morning.

Corinne greeted me with a 'cat-ate-the-canary' grin of her own that set alarm bells jangling. Determined to play it cool and not give her any ammunition, I walked over to my desk and sat down as if I didn't have a care in the world. It wasn't really an act, given the fact that if she had pressed a gun to my head and told me to name a worry, I wouldn't have been able to think of a one.

Her smile faltered just slightly, then grew wide again as the tipped a wink at me, conceding the round. She peered at me over the tops of her glasses as she relaxed back in her chair, stretching her corpulent frame just slightly. "So…I hear congratulations are in order." Her smile turned sly, daring.

Play dumb, Angel. She's just fishing for information. Don't fall into her trap. "Thanks," I replied, smiling brightly, parrying her leer with feigned innocence. "It was fun."

"Mmmm. I'll just bet it was."

Oh, she's good ."It was," I agreed. "Very…exciting. Stimulating, even."

Her eyes widened infinitesimally before the smug expression slid back down over her complacent features. "I heard you were…quite good. With a very fluid stroke."

I narrowed my eyes. "Yes, well, I've been doing it since I was a young girl."

"A young girl, eh?"

"Oh yes. I have lots of experience, you know. Don't let these innocent looks fool you, Corinne."

"Lots of experience, you say?"

"Indeed. Just ask around. There are plenty of women here who'd be happy to prove my point."

We looked at one another for a long beat of silence before both breaking out in gales of laughter. I laughed so hard that tears ran down my face in buckets. It provided an excellent release of the sexual tension that had been building since I'd woken up that morning. Not quite how I *wanted* to release the tension, mind you, but it would do. For starters.

When we both managed to calm down, Corinne dragged herself out of her chair and came over to me, bearing the sheaf of newspapers I'd requested. Setting them down in front of me, she took the chair next to mine and lowered herself into it. "My apologies for teasing you, Angel. Though you certainly have learned to give as good as you get. It's just that you have this sort of glow about you this morning and I have the feeling it's from more than just winning a softball game."

I patted her hand as I looked into her solemn eyes. "Corinne, I don't think it's any surprise to you that I'm in love with Ice." At her nod, I continued. "Well, yesterday I found out that she feels the same way about me. So, if you see a glow about me, let's just say it's been well earned and leave it at that, ok?"

Her smile, this one almost one a proud parent might bestow a favored child, reappeared on her face and she nodded. "Fair enough, Angel. Fair enough." She gestured to the stack of newspapers lying before me. "So, what of these? I thought you'd already given them a good going over. What more do you hope to find?"

"I don't know, exactly. But there's got to be something here. Something I'm missing." A week earlier, Ice had given me permission to share the full story of Cavallo and his cohorts with Corinne and I did so without hesitation. I was bound and determined to see justice done against Morrison and Cavallo, and to see it served well before Ice had the chance to do anything damaging to herself and her soul. Corinne, with her wisdom and street-smarts, was a perfect compatriot in my quest.

I looked up at my friend. "Corinne, do you think I'm doing the right thing? I know Ice wants to handle this herself and I know I'm kinda prying here, but…" I sighed. "I just don't want to see her get hurt."

Corinne looked back at me, compassion in her eyes, knowing I was talking about far more than mere physical injuries. "A little digging won't hurt matters any, Angel. But if you get to the point where action's needed, you'd best speak with her first before doing anything. She doesn't take well to betrayals. Even if they're supposedly in her own best interest." She finished the last with a pointed look and I read the message clearly.

Taking in a deep breath, I let it out slowly, my eyes scanning over the newsprint that I'd already studied a dozen times over. Logic warred with my heart. My heart won. I eyed Corinne. "Looking can't hurt anything. I promise, if I find anything, I'll go to Ice with it, alright?"

My friend smiled. "It's not me you need to be promising that to, Angel."

Chagrinned, I nodded. "Yeah, I know. And I will. Take it to her, I mean. When I've found something worth mentioning. Until then…." Running a hand through my hair, I set out, once again, to try and read between the lines of the text, scanning every inch for a clue well hidden. "If I could only get a hold of the trial transcripts," I half-muttered, more to myself than anyone.

I didn't see the brief smile that crossed Corinne's lined face as she pushed herself away from the table and returned to her desk.

♪ ♪ ♪ ♪

With a strangled moan, I collapsed down on top of Ice, snuggling into her strong, sweaty frame as I tried to regain control of my breathing. Withdrawing her hands from their pleasurable task, she enfolded me in an embrace and pulled the sheet up to cover my naked body from any prying eyes that should happen to be about.

Making love in Ice's cell hadn't been my first choice, but when I'd come up there to visit with my new lover, one thing quickly led to another and soon any cares of being spied upon were swept away in the rising tide of our passion. I lay smiling on my human mattress, listening to the music of Ice's heart as it gradually slowed its frantic beating and feeling warm tingles that spread though my spent body in time to her tender stroking of my hair and upper back.

I had found a haven in this hell, or, more accurately, a Heaven. It was here, in the all-encompassing embrace of the woman I loved, surrounded by sure strength and the perfume of clean sweat and musky arousal. My very pores were open wide, drinking it in, fusing it to me in a primal mating of the senses. My eyes fluttered closed and I rested in a cocoon of love.

Sometime later, I woke up out of a wonderful dream and immediately flushed with embarrassment as the living reality of my situation filtered down through my sleep-fuzzed senses. Lifting my head slightly, I wiped a bit of drool from Ice's warm chest. Her low laugh sounded as she tousled my hair affectionately. "God, I am *so* sorry," I mumbled, struggling to pull away from her in my mortification of falling asleep on her. Literally. "I must be crushing you."

Her arms gave no quarter as she pulled me back down on top of her. "Relax. You didn't do anything wrong, Angel."

"I *fell asleep!*"

"So?"

"I…well …I…um…I've never done that before."

Her laugh sounded once again. "Then I'll take it as a compliment."

"Yeah, but it wasn't very fair to you."

Her hand slipped down and tilted my chin up to meet her gaze. "Angel, let *me* decide what is and isn't fair to me, alright?" She sealed her statement with a kiss that drove away embarrassment still lingering within me. Pulling away after a long, wonderful moment, she playfully tapped me on the end of my nose. "I love you, Angel. And if you wanna fall asleep on me, that's perfectly alright with me." Her grin turned rakish. "As long as you don't do it while we're otherwise engaged."

I snorted. "Morgan Steele, if I live to be a hundred, I will never, I repeat *never* fall asleep on you while we're otherwise engaged."

When the laugh I expected didn't materialize, I looked up into Ice's stormy eyes, my heart clenching at the look of desolation I saw there. Easing myself up her body, I reached out to gently cup her cheek and turn her head to face me. "Ice? What's wrong? Did I say something…?"

Ice tightened her embrace around me. I could hear her throat working as she tried to put whatever emotions were running through her head into words. I caressed her cheek again, offering whatever support I had to give and praying to any god who would listen to give her the strength to open up to me.

Finally, after what seemed like hours, she turned her head completely toward me and pressed a kiss to my forehead. Then she pulled away slightly, looking down into my eyes, her own completely open and unguarded. "It's nothing really. It's just that…" her throat worked again as she swallowed, "your talking about being old and gray makes me realize all over again how *this*, what we have, will only last for a short time."

"I don't understand, Ice. What do you mean?"

She smiled sadly. "Angel, there's gonna come a time in the near future when you're gonna be able to walk out of this dump. And don't think that I don't wish every day for that to happen. And when it does, you'll be free and I'll be…here," she finished with a whisper.

As I looked at her, many ways to answer this came to mind. My spirited heart overruled the others and made me speak the words closest to it. "Then why don't you fight it?"

"What?"

"You heard me, Ice. You're in here for a murder you didn't commit. You know that. I know that. The *warden* knows that. For God's sake, Josephina knew it and she *died* for it."

"I know all this, Angel. I'm living it, remember?"

"Yes, Ice, I do remember. What I wanna know is why you won't fight it. And don't give me the 'because I belong here' routine, either. I didn't buy it then and I'm not gonna buy it now."

She stiffened, as if about to push me away, but I grabbed her hard and held on. "No, Ice. You're not running away this time. I won't let you. I know you've killed, Ice. I've got that down pat already. I know you feel guilty about what you've done. That's patently obvious to anyone with half a brain. What I don't get, no matter how often I think about it, is how someone who is so strong and so courageous can just lie down and roll over without putting up any fight at all! You were *framed*, Ice! You were *betrayed* by someone you thought you could trust and cut off from people you considered your family! Certainly that has got to be worth *something* to you!"

Ice's eyes, so warm and tender during out lovemaking, became cold and stony as an arctic beach. Her face was set in grim lines and I could practically feel the anger radiating from her tense body.

"I don't want to talk about this right now, Angel." Her voice held a clear note of warning.

I refused to be cowed, though I well knew exactly how much danger I was in. I could feel her heart pound strongly beneath my breast but I continued to keep hold of her. It was like trying to harness a lightening bolt, but I was nothing if not determined. "I know you don't want to talk about it, Ice. You *never* want to talk about it. But I have news for you. It's not going away. This self flagellation kick you're on is not going to take care of the problem. You need to do something. If not for yourself, then do it for Josephina."

Her eyes narrowed, blue flame licking out and burning through me. "I intend to do something, Angel." Her voice was a deathly purr.

"How? Through murder?"

Her smile was death itself. "That's right. It's who I am. Remember?"

"It's *not* who you are, Ice. It's *not*. You can fight this through legal avenues. If Josephina knew, that means Salvatore did as well. And who knows who he told? And Morrison knows too! There's a whole slew of people who know the truth, Ice. Demand your case be reopened!"

"Like you did?"

I stiffened against her. "What?"

"You heard me, Angel. You're no more guilty of your crime than I am of mine. Yet you sit here while your own case gets moldy in some file drawer somewhere. Tell me, Angel, why are you so hot on me getting my case reopened when you left yours to die?"

Stunned, I could only look at her for a long span of moments. Logically, what she said in some ways made perfect sense. In my mind and heart, I knew I was no more guilty of murder than of jay-walking, yet I never once thought to appeal my case. And, if I were being totally honest with myself, it was because…. "Ice, my husband died because of me. I crushed his skull with a baseball bat."

"While he was *raping* you, Angel. It's not like he came home drunk one night and you clubbed him to keep him from waking up the neighbors. It was self defense! You don't belong in jail for that."

Releasing my grip on Ice, I slid from her body, lying between her and the cool concrete wall.

"Now who's running, Angel?"

"I'm not running, Ice. I'm right here. I just need to think."

"About what? The facts are plain to see. We're both in the same boat here."

"No we're not. Not really. I'm here because my husband is dead and I killed him. I pled self-defense, but a jury of my peers decided otherwise. You didn't kill that man, Ice. In fact, when you found out who he was, you *refused* to kill him. There's a big difference between our situations and you know it."

"Is there? We're both here for a crime we didn't commit. Your husband is dead, yes. You killed him, yes. But you didn't commit a crime."

After a long moment of silence between us, I looked back up at her. "I'll try if you will."

"Angel…."

"Ice…."

"Angel, listen. Please. You have a chance. I don't. Look at this logically. You have the word of a prison warden who's managed to get a bunch of powerful people elected in this state. And against him, you have the word of a convicted murderer, a psychotic inmate, a dead woman, and a Mafia don. They'll laugh the case right out of court. Can't you just accept my word that I'll handle this in my own way?"

"I want you to try to do it the right way, Ice. The legal way. Just sign a note to obtain your trial transcripts. I'll even write it for you if you want. It can't hurt anything for you to just look them over, can it?"

"You're really passionate about this, aren't you?" Her eyes held a slight hint of incredulity.

"Yes, I am. Will you do it?"

For a long time, I didn't think she was going to answer me. I contented myself with watching the fascinating interplay of emotions as they crossed through her almost colorless eyes. Finally, her white teeth flashed as she bit her lower lip. She sighed. "Fine. I'll do it. But if they're released, which I doubt, I look at them first, deal?"

I grinned so broadly that I though my face would split in two from the force of it. "Deal."

"And you try and get yours too. I'm not going through this alone."

After a moment, I nodded. "Alright. Though I don't think I'll find…."

She silenced me with a kiss. When it ended, I'd forgotten what I was going to say as my hormones played etch-a-sketch with my thoughts.

"Fight over?" she asked, a touch of amusement in her voice.

"Yes."

"Good. Cause I can think of a couple things I'd rather be doing right now."

The rest of the evening melted away in a haze of absolute bliss.

✒   ✒   ✒   ✒

"You're sure you don't have them."

"Positive Ma'am. I've checked and rechecked the files. Nothing with that name or docket number shows up here. As I've told you before, Ma'am, you need to call the Hall of Records. We don't usually keep court transcripts here unless there's an active appeal."

"I've *called* the Hall of Records. I've *written* the Hall of Records. They keep sending me to you!"

"I'm sorry for the inconvenience, Ma'am, but as I said, I really can't help you here. Perhaps you might think about putting in a call to the District Attorney's office?"

"I'll…think about it. Thanks for your help."

"Sorry I couldn't do more, Ma'am. Goodbye."

"Bye."

Stonewalled. Again. Frustrated beyond words, I slammed the phone back down on its hook so hard that the bell jangled back at me in outrage. Running my hand through my tangled hair, I spun away from the wall so quickly that I almost managed to knock Corinne, out in the prison square on a brief sojourn from her library, flat on her keister.

"Struck out again, huh?" she asked as she adroitly avoided our near-collision.

"Yeah," I replied, resisting the urge to rip my hair out of my skull just to relieve the pent up frustration. "The newest suggestion is to call the DA's office."

"That might be a possibility."

"Not one I'm ready to explore yet, Corinne. I'd rather keep that particular office out of the loop for the time being. No telling what would come up if they found out Ice has a sudden interest in her case, if you know what I mean."

"All too well, unfortunately." She slipped a hand through the crook of my arm, tugging slightly. "Come on back with me to the library. I think you've given our friends enough of the 'Angel blows her cool' show for one day, don't you?"

I looked around for the first time, noting the interested gazes of my fellow prisoners, and just managed to keep the blush from coloring my cheeks. "Alright. Not much more I can do today anyway."

When we arrived in the library, I threw myself down into my chair as Corinne busied herself at the hotplate. It had been two of the most frustrating months of my life. It began simply enough. I had typed up a letter requesting access to the transcripts in Ice's name and brought it up to her for her signature. To my surprise, she signed it with little fuss and even wished me luck, though with an expression that was a hair short of patronizing.

Ignoring the look, I happily went about my business, sending the letter away and waiting for a response. I received one, two weeks later. It appeared I had forgotten to put the docket number on the letter and the records could not be found using the case name. After several phone calls, I was able to track down the docket number and so sent another letter. That came back saying I was missing some *other* important piece of information. And so on and so on, world without end. Amen.

When I finally got a letter off that had all the required information in the required fields with the required names and the required numbers, I received a phone call from a very nice woman who kindly informed me that she had no record of either the case name or the docket number in her files. She then told me that perhaps it was better if I spoke to someone in the Hall of Justice and gave me the name and number of some clerk or other who might be able to help me find what I was looking for.

I would have done my mother proud with my utter politeness, disguising as it was the fits of apoplexy I was undergoing at the time. Back and forth I went, talking to one low-level clerk after another, all without success. Like the Dodo bird, Ice's court transcript seemed to have vanished from the face of the earth.

When a mug of steaming tea was slid in front of my face, I broke out of my frustrated musings, smiling as I breathed in the bracing aroma. Lifting the mug to my lips, I took a grateful swallow, then almost spit it right back up again when the hard burn of a strong liquor hit my stomach. I turned a hard-eyed look at Corinne, who grinned at me, totally unrepentant.

"Don't tell me you're a teetotaler, Angel."

"No. It's not that, really. I just wasn't expecting it." And that was the truth, as far as that went. As for the other, liquor and I usually didn't cross paths. On the few occasions I was allowed it at my parents' table, I hadn't liked the taste very much. Plus, you must remember that I lived with a man for whom liquor was a cruel mistress. Seeing its effect on Peter didn't make me want to run for the bottle any time soon.

"Yes, well I thought you could do with some unwinding." She saluted me with her own mug. "Cheers."

I returned the salute. "Thanks." Taking another, smaller, sip, I was pleased when the warmth of the tea and liquor settled in my stomach pleasantly, loosening some of the tension that had accumulated during a totally fruitless day.

"How goes your own hunt, Angel?" Corinne asked.

"That was the easy part," I responded, continuing to sip my tea. "I won't see the transcripts for at least another four months though."

"Four months?"

"Yeah. Apparently there's a real backlog in the Hall of Records. Something about state cutbacks and the lack of transcribers. She offered to put a 'rush' on it, but four months was the earliest she could offer me." I shrugged. "What choice did I have? I took it."

I looked up to find my friend looking speculatively at me. "What?" I asked.

"The fact that you're having trouble finding Ice's records wouldn't have anything to do with this laissez faire attitude you've adopted toward your own, would it?"

Setting my mug down, I narrowed my eyes at her. "One has nothing to do with the other, Corinne. If you remember, I haven't given a thought to my own case since I came here, and that was well before I met Ice."

Corinne must have found what she was searching for as we continued to lock gazes because she finally blinked and looked down, nodding slightly. I won't hesitate to say that I found more than a bit of pride in finally winning a stare-down with the woman. It may have taken almost two years to prove to her that I had some strength of will, but it finally happened, and for that, I congratulated myself with another swig of the potent tea. My limbs tingled pleasingly as my heart pumped the alcohol through my system. The tension started to dissolve away and I could fully understand, at least in part, why the bottle seemed a savior to so many.

The rest of the afternoon passed in pleasant conversation with Corinne and the other visitors to her library home. When I next looked at the clock, it was coming on dinnertime. Dragging myself out of my chair, I extended my good-byes and headed back toward the prison proper, hoping to catch Ice as she made her way back from her day at the auto shop.

I was just about to step into the brightly lit main square from the hallway when an arm wrapped itself around my waist and tugged, pulling me backwards into one of the utility closets that shared hallway space with the library. The liquor I'd drunk dulled my reaction time slightly, but I was able to thrust an elbow back toward my captor, though I managed to hit nothing but the handle of a mop sitting in an old bucket in the corner.

Rubbing my smarting crazybone (and really, is there anything that hurts worse, save for stubbing your toe or getting a paper cut?), I tried to use the rest of my body to struggle against the arm which held me trapped. The grip loosened somewhat and I whirled, teeth bared, ready, willing and able to show my abductor exactly what an Amazon named Angel could do in close quarters.

The skills I wound up using were quite different than the ones I'd intended.

Soft lips covered my own, their taste one with which I was intimately, wonderfully acquainted. Melting into the body of my captor-cum-lover, I returned the kiss with the fervor of new love too long apart. Our deepening breaths seemed to suck up all the air in the small room and all too soon we broke apart, though I continued to caress Ice's body in random patterns, happy again to feel her against me.

She squirmed away, slightly. "Hey! No fair!"

I looked up from my happy task toward her upraised palms. They were black with grease and dirt from her work in the shop. I'm afraid a quite evil grin mirrored my thoughts as I moved back in against her, pulling her zipper down just slightly and feasting on the flesh beneath.

"Angel…."

The moaning, breathless quality of the admonition rendered her attempted warning moot. "Mm?" I mumbled around a mouthful of succulent flesh.

"Unless you wanna walk through the prison to the tune of snickering inmates 'cause you have two big black handprints on your ass, I'd suggest you let me take a shower first."

Laughing, I pulled away only slightly, still remaining within striking distance. "I'm only practicing my counter-attack maneuvers, Ice," I said with a voice innocent as a newborn's. "Are they working?"

"Oh yeah."

"Good. I think I'll add them to my repertoire. What do you think?"

"You'd better not."

"Oh? Why is that?"

"Because then you'll have every woman in the prison wanting to 'fight' you."

I laughed again. "And that would be a bad thing…how?"

Mirroring my laugh, she leaned down and playfully nipped my nose. "Because they'll have to get through me first, and I have a very strict 'three broken arms a month' policy. You wouldn't want me to have to up my quota on your account, would you?" In the feeble light cast by the hallway, I could see her eyebrow arch as a grin played around her eyes.

Sighing in mock frustration, I pulled further away and obediently returned her zipper to its original position, primly patting her chest after I was done. "I suppose not."

"Good answer."

"I was on my way up to say hello before I was so wonderfully detained." Straightening, I executed a half bow, crooking my arm gallantly. "Would you do me the honor of dining with me at *Chez Dump* tonight? I've heard a rumor that the mystery meat might even be recognizable this evening."

"Sounds like a plan. Give me some time to grab a shower and I'll meet you outside the cafeteria, alright?"

"Will do." Standing on my toes, I kissed her quickly, then turned and left before that mischievous streak she always seemed to bring out wound up with me needing to change uniforms.

✍ ✍ ✍ ✍

The mystery meat remained a mystery as I finished off the last bite, wincing slightly as it stuck to the inside of my throat, dry as dust. We were sitting at a corner table with Critter who'd just come in, bearing a piece of paper and a big grin. "What's the smile for, Critter?" I asked, taking a big slug of lukewarm milk to wash the rest of the meat down.

"My first parole hearing's next week. Isn't that great?"

Standing up, I hugged my friend, then kissed her cheek. "That's wonderful news! You nervous?"

She shrugged, then nodded. "Yeah, a little," she admitted.

Grinning, I patted her shoulder affectionately. "You'll do great. Don't worry."

Critter had served five years for an 'assault with a deadly weapon' charge, coupled with 'breaking and entering'. The weapon in question was a brick that she'd used to break through the glass door of a local convenience store to grab some liquor. She'd made the mistake of retrieving the brick after she'd made entrance into the darkened store, and the sight of her, 'weapon' in hand, scared the elderly proprietor, who'd just finished closing up, into a massive heart attack. Emergency surgery saved her from a manslaughter rap and the proprietor from a date with a harp and white robe.

From the stories I'd heard, she'd grown up a lot in prison, from a street-smart young punk with a taste for booze into the beautiful and wise young woman that sat grinning across from me.

The rest of what passed for dinner went pleasantly, with Critter and I engaging in spirited conversation and Ice listening and contributing as she desired. Corinne's killer tea was still spreading its warm tendrils through my veins and I suspect I was a bit more animated than usual.

Finally, I wiped my mouth with a cheap paper napkin and looked to Ice, who nodded slightly, then rose and bore our dishes off to be washed by the kitchen help. Critter and I stood up as well and she tipped a wink at me, which in turn caused me to flush furiously. Grinning, she clapped my shoulder, waved, and left the cafeteria, humming off key to herself.

Ice returned, cocking an eyebrow at my slowly retreating color.

"It's…um…nothing."

She let it go. "Where to now?"

"How about a walk? Whatever we just ate has transformed itself into a ball in my stomach."

"A walk it is. Shall we?"

"Let's."

⚷　⚷　⚷　⚷

I rested my head on the flat plane of Ice's lower abdomen, savoring the taste of her on my lips as my fingers traced idle patterns on one muscled thigh. Her hand released its death grip on my hair as she relaxed, stretching slightly.

After a moment, her husky voice filtered down to my ears. "Well, you're certainly in a good mood this evening."

"Mm," I agreed, kissing the sweat-salty skin beneath my lips. "Just being near you, especially in my current position, does that to me." I grinned. "Of course, Corinne's magic elixir didn't hurt any."

Ice's hand returned to my hair, tugging to bend my reluctant neck up to meet her gaze. "'Magic elixir'?"

"Yup. Two-hundred proof and good to the last drop." I licked my lips. "Sorta like you."

Releasing my hair, Ice groaned and flopped back onto the pillow once again. "And why did Corinne feel the need to get you drunk?"

"She wasn't trying to get me drunk. Just…relaxed."

"And why did you need relaxing?"

I sighed. "Another fruitless round of 'find the transcript'."

"Well, I won't say I told you so," she replied drolly.

"How very big of you."

"I *do* try."

"Hmph."

A very comfortable, warm silence settled over us as my drowsy eyes idly scanned the room, not remembering quite how my jumpsuit managed to get tossed across the room to land, one sleeve draped over an outstretched limb of the Freedom of Power bonsai. I squinted as my eyes alit on something, like my uniform, that hadn't been there the last time I'd been in Ice's cell. Sitting against one of the other trees was the photograph I'd looked at when Ice had been in the hole.

This, most definitely, was an opportunity too big to pass up. Problem was how to introduce the topic without letting on that I'd already seen the picture in question. With the coming on of fall, I decided to go with the football analogy of an 'end around'. "Ice, what is that?"

Her body shifted slightly as she looked around the room. "What is what?"

"That," I pointed, "the picture near your bonsai. Is that your family?"

I could feel her body stiffen beneath me and I held my breath, hoping I hadn't again pushed things too far. After a long moment, she finally relaxed and I started breathing again in relief. "Yeah," she said, her voice barely above a whisper. "That's my mother, father, and Boomer."

I snorted against her belly. "Boomer?"

And received a light slap on the head for my sacrilege. "I was five at the time, if you must know."

"Oh I must. I must."

That earned me a hair ruffle, which I leaned into with pleasure. After a moment, I decided to push a little further. "Do you mind if I get a closer look?"

"You will anyway, so go ahead."

Grinning at her tone of melodramatic long-suffering, I slipped out of the bed, wrapping the sheet around my naked body and leaving Ice to lounge in nude splendor on the bottom sheet as I walked over to the table and picked up the photograph. As I turned back, the sight of her long, tan, gloriously naked body sprawled out on the white sheet, her dark hair fanned out on the pillow and her normally pale eyes darkened with residual eroticism, made my body hum again with need.

Unwrapping the sheet from around my body, I climbed on the bed to straddle her waist, then allowed the cloth to drape, tent-like, over my shoulders, shrouding us both in a field of white. "The interrogation can wait," I growled, leaning down to capture her lips in a fierce kiss which sparked the burning embers of my passion into a roaring bonfire once again.

🔑   🔑   🔑   🔑

Some time later, I sat, once again wrapped in the sheet, leaning against Ice's shoulder as I looked down at the black and white photograph now laying in my lap. "Tell me about them?"

Her breath tickled the hair at my ear as she turned her head to look down at the picture. "Nothing much to tell, really. Alexander, my father, was a chemical engineer at DuPont. My mother was a mezzo-soprano with the Baltimore Opera Company."

I turned wide eyes to her. "Your mother was an opera singer? I love opera!"

Ice shrugged. "Yeah. She was pretty good."

I snorted. "'Pretty good,' she says. Forgive me for saying so, but you're probably the type who looks at a Picasso and shudders, aren't you."

"What can I say? I'm not exactly the artistic type."

"Oh, you're not are you," I replied with a knowing grin as I looked over at the beauty of the bonsai sitting complacently on the table.

As I turned back, I swore I could see the faintest trace of a blush on her bronzed cheeks but wisely neglected to mention it as her face resumed its business-like mask. She shrugged again. "Anyway, I wouldn't know. She gave it up after she had me. Said she wanted to be a full-time mother and that was that." A small, almost shy, smile cracked the somber façade. "She could hum a mean lullaby, though."

"What about your dad?"

"My dad? He couldn't carry a tune in a bucket."

Groaning, I thumped my back against her shoulder. "That's not what I mean and you know it. What was he like? What kind of a man was he?"

"Uh…manly?"

"Ice…."

"Angel, listen. It's kinda hard to talk about this, alright? I only took the picture out yesterday. I was hoping you wouldn't spy it quite so fast."

Biting my bottom lip, I nodded, understanding her gentle rebuke for what it was. "I'm sorry, Ice. I didn't mean to push."

"You're not pushing. I just need to be able to tell this in my own way, at my own pace, alright?"

I smiled warmly at her. "No problem. We can continue this another time if you want."

"No, that's alright. Just give me a minute here." Shifting on the bed, she pulled me in close once again, nestling my head against her neck and laying her cheek atop my hair. Then she took the picture from me and laid it on her own lap, the very edge of her thumb brushing over the static figure of the tall, handsome man who was her father. "My father was a good man. Hyper-intelligent, but very easy going and friendly. I don't think there was a person in the world who didn't like him once they got to know him." I could feel her smile against my hair. "He probably should have gone into sales or politics, but instead he worked Research and Development at DuPont.

"He was also passionate about sports, especially the local teams. He had season tickets to watch the Colts play and even managed to score two Super Bowl tickets to watch Unitas get outfoxed by Namath. I was with him that day." Her voice grew slightly wistful. "It was one of the best days I can remember having, even though we lost."

"Sounds like a really special time," I remarked, more than a trace of wistfulness present in my own voice. I had spent most of my childhood aching for such a relationship with my own father. "How about your mother? Was she…jealous over your closeness to your father?"

She laughed. "Jealous? No, not exactly. She was an Orioles fan, with season tickets of her very own. She'd take me to some of the night games. I even got to hear her sing the National Anthem before a couple of 'em."

I straightened, gape jawed. "Your mother actually sang the Star Spangled Banner before baseball games?"

"Yeah. Her voice sounded really strange, echoing through the stadium. It was an…interesting experience, to say the least. I used to have a bunch of signed memorabilia from them. You know, jerseys, mitts, balls, bats," she shrugged, "stuff like that."

There was a moment of silence as she looked down at the photograph as if seeing into a past long buried. "She was a pretty soft touch as mothers went. Pretty much let me try my hand at anything I was interested in, as long as it wouldn't get me in trouble with the law." Her laugh this time was slightly bitter. "Bet she's rolling over in her grave about now. Her and my dad both."

I wanted so badly to tell her what she already knew. That if her parents were still alive, chances were excellent that Ice would never have done the things she did to wind up here. But I decided to keep my own counsel on the subject, hoping that by sharing more of this life with me, she'd eventually figure it out on her own.

"About the only thing she insisted on was voice lessons. Said that the human voice was God's instrument and you'd best keep it well tuned and not risk pissing Him off sometime down the road."

I shuddered with the memory of my mother forcing me to take deport-ment lessons for almost the exact same reason. "Did you hate them?"

"Nah. They weren't so bad. I suppose it could have been worse, if I'd been born with a voice like my father's. I was lucky, though. Singing came naturally to me, though I hated all things opera. Still do."

Tilting my chin up to meet her eyes, I smiled. "Maybe I can hear you sing sometime?"

She returned my smile with a little quirk of her lips. "Maybe."

Satisfied, I returned my head to its place burrowed against the warm skin of her neck. "How did your parents meet?" Not able to resist, I took a gentle bite of her sweet flesh, grinning as I felt a minute shudder pass down her body. Pressing a kiss into the mark I'd made, I felt her heart pick up its pace beneath my palm.

She shifted against me. "Keep this up, Angel, and you're never gonna hear the story."

If it had been any other story, the choice would have been an easy one. Ever since our first 'real' time together, my body had been in a constant state of sexual arousal. Just the smell of her would turn my insides into flaming gelatin and right now, I was surrounded by her heady, exotic scent.

The more logical part of my mind, however, reminded me that if I gave into my body's demands, I would more than likely have to wait months for the chance to question her on this topic again. If, indeed, that chance ever came. With Ice, nothing was ever a sure thing.

Lassoing my hormones, I pulled slightly back from temptation. "Alright, I'll be good. For now. More story, please?"

Leaning in, she gave me a kiss, then pulled away, resting her head against the wall. "Unlike me, my father loved the opera, as did his fiancée at the time. My mother's company was putting on their rendition of Massenet's 'Werther', and she was playing Charlotte. To hear him tell it, from the moment my mother walked on till the time she left the stage before the final curtain, he didn't have eyes for another living being."

"God, that is *so* romantic!"

"Yeah, well my father's fiancée didn't think so. After the show was over, he dragged her backstage to meet my mother. She might have been a piece of lint on the carpet for all the attention he paid to her after that point."

"Did your mother feel the same way when she met him? Smitten, I mean?"

"Oh yeah. She said that when she looked into my father's eyes, someone she knew was looking back, even though she'd never met him before." Ice laughed. It sounded almost frightened. "All my life, I never knew what that meant. Until now."

When this kiss connected, it was almost a carbon copy of the first we'd ever shared. Images flitted though my mind too quick for me to follow, but I knew, down deep in my soul, that we were connected on a level far deeper than mere surface attraction. There was something elemental and bedrock in what we shared, something both primitive and new and ageless at its very foundations.

It was not a kiss of passion, though it was indeed passionate. It was a kiss of healing and of home. If the ancient sages were right and we did spend our lives searching for the other half of our souls, I had found mine in almost as deep a pit of hell as it was possible to go and still be able to struggle to the surface intact and alive.

When it ended, I collapsed against her, weak and spent, yet filled with strength and energy, as if I had connected with some elemental force that nourishes the soul and relieves the heart of its heavy burdens.

My voice was very definitely plaintive as I asked my next question. "More?"

Ice chuckled. "Of what? The kiss or the story?"

"Mmm. How about both?"

"Nope," she teased, "one or the other."

"Oh alright. The story then. I'll always be able to get kisses out of you."

"Ya think so, huh?"

"I know so."

"Hmm. I'll remember that." She tightened her grip around my waist once again. "Let's see, where were we? Ah yes, the meeting. Well, after the girlfriend left in a huff, they sat and talked until the opera house closed for the evening. After that, they had what my mother called a 'scandalously short' courtship. Two months. The scandal came in because of the fact that the ex-fiancé's father was a noted patron of the arts and wasn't very happy to hear that his daughter had been dumped like yesterday's trash by the side of the road while someone whose career he funded made off with the goods."

"You have such a way with words, Ice," I snickered.

"Yeah, well in many ways, I'm my father's daughter. Anyway, after two months of dating, they got married, bought a new house, and a year afterwards, had me."

"It sounds like they loved one another very much."

"They did. Even though they'd have a fight every now and then, even as a kid I knew they'd always be together. I know most kids don't think their parents will ever split up, but there was just something about them that even I could notice, young as I was. It was almost like they were two halves of the same whole or something." She shrugged. "I can't explain it any better than that."

"I think you did a great job. That describes the feeling perfectly, don't you think?"

She smiled. "Yeah. It does."

I spent the next several silent moments trying to gather up the courage needed to take the next, obvious step. I was torn with indecision. Torn between needing to know and needing not to open up what was obviously a wound that still festered deep inside Ice's heart.

As if reading my thoughts, her body stiffened once again and she took in a deep breath before letting it out slowly. "They got hit by a bus."

"What?"

"My parents. You were wondering how to ask me how they died. They were hit by a bus. They had driven in to DC for their anniversary to see <u>Werther</u>. They never made it. My mother was killed instantly. My father managed to hang on for a few days, but he never woke up. They finally decided to pull the plug."

"Oh, Ice. I'm so sorry."

"Yeah," she said quietly, wiping the tears from her eyes. "So am I."

🔑 🔑 🔑 🔑

Later that night, in the solitary darkness of my own cell, I lay on my back as tears wended their slow course down my cheeks, dampening my pillow. As I replayed our conversation in my mind, part of me wondered whose life had the more tragedy. Ice's, whose family loved and doted on her and were taken away? Or mine, whose family had, at best, only tolerated me and now considered me, though still very much alive, dead in their eyes?

I cried for us both that night. For the young girls we had been and for the women we had become. For our families. For ourselves.

But within the tears of sadness there also mixed tears of joy. If new life can spring from the ashes of the old, then a new life had sprung up between us from the barren soil of our individual tragedies.

A snatch of an old lullaby I had heard in some movie or other sprung to my lips and I hummed it to myself as I fell asleep, tears slowly drying on my cheeks.

Chapter 9

As days turned into weeks, I felt my frustration level reaching new highs. Every new clue regarding the whereabouts of Ice's transcripts led to a blind alley with no answers and little hope of finding them.

When dead end after dead end spurred fantasies of homicide, I would take a walk outside into the crisp fall air and take out my frustrations on the ever-ready punching bag. I often found myself having to share it with a disappointed Critter who had failed her first parole hearing. She had found out during the hearing that while surgery had saved the store-owner's life, his health had never fully recovered. As months turned into years, he continued to become more and more frail. If he died as a direct result of the previous heart attack, Critter was afraid they'd add a manslaughter charge to the ones she was already serving time for. In any event, it looked as if she would have to wait yet another year for her next chance at freedom.

Pony and Sonny were on the outs over some failed love triangle and Ice was working long, enforced hours in the auto shop breaking down and fixing up a whole slew of stolen cars designed to line the pockets of our corrupt warden.

All in all, it was not a good season for any of us, and it was about to get worse.

Frustration is a dangerous emotion in that it often leads us to make stupid mistakes in trying to relieve it. I made one such mistake and it cost me dearly.

About at the point of tearing my hair out in frustration, I finally gave in to Corinne's oft-repeated suggestion of allowing an investigative reporter friend snoop around a little to see what he could find. All previous suggestions of this sort had been rebuffed by me with the knowledge that many reporters of this type are greedy bastards who will stop at nothing to blow the lid off a big story if they can find one. This was one story I didn't want to be taken public.

Corinne promised me that she had so much dirt on this man that he wouldn't dare act against her wishes or he'd find himself ruined both personally and professionally. After what seemed the hundredth time of hearing the same suggestions and the same arguments, I was finally at the point where I'd either tell her to stuff it or to go with it. I chose the second option.

The next two weeks crawled by with semi-regular reports from the man who called himself 'Slim Jim' for reasons I'm sure I don't want to know. And those reports didn't tell me anything I didn't know already; that there appeared to be a cover-up of some kind regarding Ice's court transcripts. His contacts within the justice system were rebuffing his overtures with uncharacteristic stoniness and he sensed something big was going on behind the scenes. Something he couldn't possibly be expected to uncover given the strict ground-rules I'd laid out for him. Though I understood the hint, I didn't rise to the bait and left the man grumbling but determined to crack what could well be the story of a lifetime.

I was beginning to become seriously concerned that this man's innate greed for a big story would outweigh whatever dirty little secrets Corinne had on him and had finally come to the decision to tell her to call off her dog.

I sat in the library, rehearsing my arguments in my mind, knowing Corinne would use all the verbal charm at her disposal to talk me out of this decision. Against my better judgement, I had bowed to her formidable will once already and didn't want to do so again. This was too important to me.

As I opened my mouth to speak, another voice interrupted before the first sound exited my lips. "Angel, may I speak with you for a moment?"

I turned to see Ice filling the doorway, her face an expressionless mask that usually denoted anger and her eyes cold as her prison name. I swallowed hard, my throat suddenly dry. I looked over to Corinne for support, but found her staring at Ice as well, her own face showing trepidation, an expression I'd never before seen on her. Turning back to my lover, I nodded. "Yeah, sure."

Taking a deep breath, I pushed myself away from the table and out of my chair, trying to control the shakiness in my muscles as I made my way across the library and out into the hallway. Ice led me halfway down the dimly lit hall before stopping and turning so that my back was against the wall, her presence looming over me. "This stops *now*."

"Um…excuse me?"

Her hand flung out, palm up. "This…investigation…of my missing files. You're in way over your head on this one and everything is about one step from tumbling down all around you. I must have been out of my mind for agreeing to this in the first place."

"But, Ice…."

"No, Angel. No, you listen to me. Call off whatever dogs you've got riding on this and close it down. Now."

"Ice—"

Her hands came down and clamped painfully on my shoulders. "Now, Angel. Do us both a favor and *back off.*" Releasing my shoulders, she glared at me for a moment more before turning on her heel and stalking off, leaving me to stand and stare after her retreating form, totally stunned.

A sound coming from the other direction caused me to whirl around. Corinne stood a few steps from the library door, looking down the long hallway. Her eyes slowly moved to meet mine. "I heard," she said in a soft voice. "And I'm sorry. I should have listened to you and not tried to bully you into something you didn't want in the first place."

"That's alright, Corinne. You were only trying to help."

"Regardless, this is more my fault than yours. I'll try to explain that to her."

I snagged her arm as she walked up to me. "No. I don't think that's a very good idea right now. I don't think she's in a listening mood."

My friend dragged a hand through her gray hair. "I suppose you're right. What should I do?"

"Get your friend on the phone and threaten him with every piece of dirt you've got. If that isn't enough, make something up, but shut him down now!" I stopped to study her worried eyes for a moment. "Please?"

Corinne nodded. "That I can do." She looked at me, her gaze both apologetic and compassionate. "Will you be alright?"

"I'll have to be, won't I?" That came out more harshly than I intended and I clasped her wrist. "I'm sorry, Corinne. That was uncalled for." I sighed. "I'll give her a while to calm down and then go up to her cell. Maybe by then she'll be willing to tell me what's going on, huh?"

"Good luck," she snorted, returning my clasp before disengaging and walking back into the library to carry out her instructions.

"Thanks," I whispered after she was gone. "I think I'll need it."

As it was almost time for my assigned exercise period, I headed down the hall, intent on taking in some fresh air to soothe my troubled emotions. As I stepped out into the prison proper, Digger spotted me and loped over, excitement broadly painted on her face. "Angel, I'm glad you're here. I need to talk to you."

"Not now, Digger. I need to get some fresh air for a bit. Maybe later, ok?"

"Please, Angel, it's really important. I'll even go outside with you. The guards won't know if we stick close to the building. Please."

The sense of urgency in her eyes made me acquiesce, though I really wasn't in the mood for company of any sort, let alone that of my shadow. "Alright, Digger," I said finally. "But just for a few minutes, ok? I've got a killer headache."

"Just a few minutes, I promise."

I followed her through the prison and out the door into the yard, feeling the sun on my face start to dissolve the incredible tension tying my body in knots. After taking several deep, cleansing breaths of the autumn air, I turned to Digger, eyebrows raised. "What was it you needed to talk to me about?"

"Alright. I was in the warden's office today, cleaning up like I usually do, right? I was only there for maybe an hour when the door opens and a guard comes in leading Ice."

I turned to her, my interest fully captured. "What?"

She nodded. "It's true! Ice looked like she was ready to tear the whole place apart, and twice as bad when she came back out! I almost peed my pants, I swear!"

"Did you hear what was said between them?"

"Some. I couldn't get it all. People were comin' in and out of the office and I had to be real careful 'bout listening in, you know?"

Resisting the urge to throttle the woman for not getting to the point, I simply nodded encouragingly for her to continue.

"Anyway, she goes in and the guard leaves. Which is really surprising, cause the guards usually go in with the prisoners when they're brought up to see the warden, ya know?"

Her plaintive look seemed to demand some response, so I forced a smile to my face. "I understand, Digger. Please continue."

"Alright. So anyway, being as I was alone for the moment, I picked up my polishing rag and went right up to the door, making like I was polishing the knob and nameplate, you know? And I heard the warden tellin' Ice that he was on to her about somethin'. And Ice told him that she didn't know what he was talking about. Then another guard came in, so I pretended to be working and didn't hear anything until the guard left. When I got back to listenin', Ice was telling the warden that she was gonna stop everything. I didn't know what she meant, but the warden sure did, cause he started yellin' at her."

"What was he saying?"

"He was yellin' something about how she wasn't gonna stop anything if she knew what was good for her. Said if she didn't shape up and fly right, things were gonna start getting real bad for her. He even said that he'd make it so that her little girlfriend would get transferred to Hell's Kitchen. I didn't even know she had a girlfriend. Did you?"

My throat became dry again as my heart skittered in my chest. The reason behind Ice's warning became frighteningly clear to me. Hell's Kitchen was the nickname of another women's state prison in Pennsylvania, and rumored to be one of the most dangerous of its kind in the country. Almost every woman released from the prison either made it out in a pine box, or immeasurably changed from the experience. And not for the better.

My emotions must have shown on my face because Digger grabbed my shoulder and shook me. "Angel? Angel, are you ok? You look like you seen a ghost."

"No. No, I'm fine. Did you hear anything else?"

"No. The warden musta called for his guards, cause one came in right after that and took Ice away. Man, she sure looked like she was ready to rip someone a new asshole. And since I'm kinda partial to mine, I played like a houseplant and kinda shrunk into a corner till she left."

"Did the warden say anything after she left? Make a phone call or anything?"

Digger shrugged. "I don't know. By that time, all I wanted to do was finish cleaning and come down and tell you what I heard. I figured with you and Ice being friends and all, maybe you'd know what was goin' on." She looked toward the fence, where the guards were looking down from the towers. "I'd better get goin'. Don't wanna get in trouble for being out here. Talk to ya later?"

"Yeah…sure, Digger. See you later."

She grinned and waved. "Bye, Angel."

"Bye, Digger."

Turning from the doorway, I slowly walked across the yard and up to the fence protecting the outside world from me. My thoughts were a clutter racing amok in my mind like a dog chasing its tail. It wasn't hard to fill in the missing spots in the conversation between Morrison and Ice. The warden had obviously found out about the investigation into Ice's missing transcript, which was something I had been desperately trying to avoid. He most likely called her out on it and she responded by threatening to pull her contributions from his little automobile laundering scheme, which in turn led to his threats toward her and her friends, myself included.

This was not what I had in mind when I begged Ice to at least look into the possibility of reopening her case. In hindsight, her warnings to me on this very topic were crystal clear. Why I hadn't heard them at the time I'll never know, but I didn't. My mind was on the injustice she'd suffered, sparked by her sadness that we wouldn't always be together.

I've always been somewhat of a crusader. It's been part of my nature since I was very young and making up plans to free the dogs from the local humane society. I'd thought, however, that I'd gotten over the 'leap before you look' philosophy while still a girl. Apparently, I needed to study up a bit more because I'd obviously blown it, big time.

Threading my fingers through the links, I rested my forehead against the cool metal, trying to come up with a way to make things better. Ice had every right to be angry, though she *had* agreed to my attempting to get her records. Still, I hadn't told her that I'd given in to Corinne's suggestion about using her reporter friend to help with the search. And I had no doubt that *that* was what brought the whole matter to a head.

I was deep in my thoughts when Sonny approached, laying a compassionate hand on my shoulder. "Are you alright, Angel? Was Digger bothering you?"

Swallowing back the tears in my throat, I pasted a semblance of a smile on my face and turned to her. "I'm ok. And no, Digger wasn't bothering me. She just had some news to share with me."

"Was it about Ice? I saw her coming in from the warden's office looking like she was ready to kill someone."

Not trusting myself to speak, I nodded in affirmation.

"Shit. Is there anything I can do to help? Maybe get together with the others?"

"No. Thank you though. This is something I need to work out with Ice."

"Are you sure?"

"Positive."

Sonny squeezed my shoulder, smiling slightly. "Alright then. You know where to look if you want to talk, right?"

Covering her hand with my own, I returned her smile. "I do. That means a lot to me, Sonny. Thanks."

"*You* mean a lot to *us*, Angel. Don't forget that, alright?"

"I won't."

Despite the gravity of the situation, or perhaps because of it, her words made me feel a little better. I hadn't been as close to Sonny as I had been to Pony and Critter. But after the stabbing, we became friends. Beneath her somewhat rough and tumble exterior, she was a sweet, kind and caring woman who was always available to help someone in need.

Of course, she was also an armed robber, the only female in a bank and armored car robbery ring who met their demise during a botched bank hold-up. Everyone in the band was killed by the SWAT team except for her. She said that the only reason she remained alive is that at first the police thought she was a hostage and not one of the robbers. She almost got away with it too, until one of the actual hostages pointed her out as she was leaving the building.

Giving me a final pat on the back, Sonny turned and walked back to the weight area where the rest of the Amazons were congregated. As I looked out onto the black parking lot, part of me damned my insatiable curiosity, for it was what led me out to this very spot those months ago to see what Ice was looking at. If I had not walked up to this very fence, I would not have seen the warden and Ice's betrayer, and perhaps none of this would have ever happened.

But another part of me jumped all over that maudlin thought. If I hadn't seen what had happened in the parking lot, Ice most likely would never have taken me down to the chop shop that fateful evening when she bared her soul to me. We might never have made love in that very room.

Had I destroyed the trust she had so painstakingly given me with my zealotry? In my quest to right an injustice, had I ruined everything between us that I had fought so hard to build? I took a deep breath and mustered my courage.

There was only one way to find out.

⚷ ⚷ ⚷ ⚷

Ice was sitting on her bed, back ramrod straight, her hands resting lightly on her thighs. Her feet were flat to the floor and her eyes were closed as if in meditation. The air was still around her. Even the always present hum of the fluorescents seemed subdued in her presence.

I stood there, watching her for long moments in silence, knowing somehow that she was aware of me, yet not wanting to shatter the seemingly peaceful scene. I worried at my lower lip with my teeth as I tried to stand against the signals my body was sending me to leave and not look back.

Just as I was about to give in to my panic, her eyes snapped open, bathing me in their pale blue fire. "Is there something you need?" she asked, her voice calm and uninflected.

I stayed outside the boundaries of her cell, not sure where I stood with her. The feeling was uncomfortable for me as I had considered this place a haven of sorts. What could I say to make her understand? What words could I use to make everything better? There seemed to be none adequate enough. The two secrets I held within burned me like a brand.

"Well?"

I decided to wait and hear what I was going to say with my own ears. The dam broke. "I just wanted to tell you that I heard…about what happened with the warden. And that…." I trailed off as Ice rose to her feet, her face a mask of rage.

"I'll kill that bastard!"

"No! Ice, wait!" Moving to block the door, I held my hands up. "It wasn't the warden. It was…it was Digger. She was in the office when he called you in. She overheard some of the conversation. She was worried and so she came to talk to me about it. Honestly!"

To her credit, and my utter relief, Ice didn't try to come through me. Instead, she narrowed her eyes. "What did she say." It wasn't a question.

Taking a deep breath, I replayed the conversation for her as best I could, trying not to put my own spin on things in case I was wrong. As I spoke, I could see the tension gather in the long lines of her body until she fairly radiated it as if from her pores. My heart picked up in response. When my voice finally trailed off to silence, she simply stared at me, though I knew it wasn't me she was seeing. Her hands were fisted so tightly that I could see the white of her bone pressed against the tan of her flesh.

"Ice?" I asked tentatively.

She blinked once, slowly coming back from wherever she'd gone in her rage. Her shoulders slumped slightly. "You weren't supposed to know," she half-whispered.

I smiled a little. "I'm glad I do."

"I'm not."

Chancing it, I took a half-step closer to her, reaching out and laying a hand on her muscle-knotted forearm. "I *am*. I think I have a right to know when I'm being used as a Sword of Damocles to hang over your head."

That got a small smile out of her. "Only one of many swords, Angel."

I grinned back. "Maybe, but I'm just egotistical enough to believe that I'm one of the bigger ones," I teased.

"The biggest." She tipped me a ghost of a wink as the tension began to release from her body, easily felt through my fingertips.

Becoming serious once again, I gripped her arm with more fervor. "Ice, I need you to know that I'll willingly go to Hell's Kitchen if it means you can continue your fight to get out of this the right way."

"Your right way, Angel. Not mine. And no, I will not let that happen. As I've told you before, I'll deal with Morrison in my own way and in my own time. You just concentrate on getting *yourself* out of this slag heap the 'right' way, alright?"

"Ice…."

She laid a finger over my lips. "No, Angel. No more. I asked you to stop and I meant it. This is my problem. Let me deal with it. Please." Removing her finger from my lips, she gently pried away from my tight grasp on her arm, then turned back toward her bed. "I just wish I knew how he learned about it."

I felt myself color. "Um…about that…."

She turned back to face me ever so slowly. "Yes?"

My blushed deepened, me ears burning hot with embarrassment. "Well, it was just that I was so frustrated and Corinne was so persistent and…."

"Corinne?" Her face was becoming dangerous once again.

"It wasn't her fault!" I interjected, raising my hand again. "It was mine. I take full responsibility here."

"Spit it out, Angel. What's going on?"

Scratching the back of my neck, I sighed, giving in to the inevitable. "Well, I was tired of getting the run around from those bureaucrats at the Hall of Records. Everywhere I looked, every letter I sent, every call I made, it was always the same thing. Nothing. I finally got so frustrated that I okayed Corinne's suggestion about her reporter friend…."

"Her *what?*"

"Her reporter friend?"

Her fists clenched again. "Damn it, Angel!"

"I know, Ice. I know. It was stupid. And I shouldn't have done it. But I was just about to tell her to call it off when you walked into the library today. It's all taken care of now. I promise."

Shaking her head in amazement, she snorted out a breath of air. "What am I gonna do with you?"

I winced. "Forgive me?"

"Do I have to?"

"It would be nice. I promise I won't do anything like this again without speaking to you first."

She smirked. "Don't make promises you're not sure you can keep, my little crusader. C'mere."

I gratefully walked into her open arms, grinning widely as she wrapped herself around me in a warm hug. "You're lucky I love you, Angel," she said against my hair.

"Yeah," I sighed. "I sure am."

✒   ✒   ✒   ✒

The winter rolled along and brought a flu epidemic with it. It raced through the Bog like a lightening-sparked wildfire, leaving almost no one standing in its wake. While all the hospitals in the area were full to over-crowding, the only place the inmates were allowed to be treated, the County hospital, had shut its doors tight to all but the most severely afflicted. And that didn't include any of us.

In the space of days, the entire prison became an infirmary. The guards had also been hit hard and were operating at half staff. If there was any time to have a replay of the riot of last year, this would have been it. Fortunately for everyone involved, any potential troublemakers were too busy puking their guts up to plan or take part in such a venture.

The infirmary overflowed by day two of the epidemic and most of the prisoners were left to fend for themselves as best they could, some even spending hours in pools of their own body fluids when fever made them too weak to make their way to the commode. The guards put in repeated requests for help, but all were ignored by a warden who believed that sickness was God's vengeful wrath upon sinners.

I was one of the lucky ones. I had myself a tall, dark and absolutely gorgeous nurse who attended to my every need. Granted, my needs at the time weren't as *stimulating* as they might have been normally, but I've never been one to look a gift horse in the mouth, and having Ice treat me with such loving tenderness in my so called hour of need wasn't going to make me start anytime soon.

Ice kept me clean, warm and dry when the drenching sweats of nighttime fevers alternated with the bone wracking chills that came with the rising of the sun. She sat with me and held me when the spasms of coughing stole the breath from my lungs and the will from my body. Her strong fingers were gentle on my skin as she massaged the wrenching gut cramps that hit with unpredictable and vengeful force.

Even within the terrifying depths of my feverish delirium, I knew she was there and took strength and comfort from her solid presence. I felt surrounded by a blanket of love and caring, no more so than when the sound of her humming an old lullaby would soothe me into a dreamless sleep.

It was a week later when my fever finally broke, leaving me weak and shaky as a newborn. I awoke to find my head pillowed in Ice's lap, her fingers brushing through my sweat-drenched hair in a hypnotic and pleasurable rhythm. My scalp tingled to her gentle touch.

I blinked my eyes open, wincing at the over-bright glare of the glowing lights. A second later, her hand left my hair and instead shaded my eyes. Her smile was crooked and sweet. "Hey, stranger. How ya feeling?"

"Like that heavy bag out in the yard must feel after going a few rounds with you," I managed to croak out through an aching throat and cracked lips.

"That good huh?"

I just groaned.

"Do you think you can sit up if I help you?"

"Do I have to?"

"You're pretty dehydrated. You need to drink some water at least."

"I don't think I could hold it down. My stomach feels like it's been dragged behind a horse or something."

Ice shifted behind me, gently pulling me up so that my head rested against her chest. When she had me settled, she reached over and grabbed a styrofoam cup filled with water and held it to my lips. "C'mon. Just a sip."

Wincing, I took a small sip into my mouth. It was cool against my parched lips and soothing to my scorched throat and I swallowed it eagerly. My stomach stayed quiet, so I took another sip, and then another until I'd finished half the cup.

Pulling the cup away and resting it on the communal nightstand, Ice dried my lips with a soft cloth, then smoothed my hair from my forehead before wrapping me in an embrace and resting her chin on the crown of my head. "Is it staying down alright?"

"No trouble yet," I replied, reveling in the feeling of her arms around me. Looking around, I noticed that the bed next to mine, usually occupied by my new roommate of one month, was empty. "Where's Edie?"

"She was a bad asthmatic. The flu hit her hard and they didn't get her to treatment fast enough. She didn't make it."

"What?" I stiffened in Ice's embrace. "She's dead?"

"I'm afraid so."

If I had any moisture in my body to spare, I would have cried. I hadn't know Edie all that well, but she seemed like a nice, quiet, well-spoken woman who, like many of the rest of us, simply wanted to do her time in peace. Because she roomed with me, she was spared some of the almost ritualistic hazing that befell all new inmates, and for that I was happy. And now she was dead. A young woman taken down in the prime of her life by the flu of all things. I sighed, then thought of my other friends, particularly the elderly librarian. "How's Corinne?" I asked, inwardly dreading the answer.

Ice snorted against my hair. "That old battle axe? She's fine. Down for two days and then right back up again. She's got the constitution of an ox."

I laughed, weakly elbowing her in the side. "Sounds like someone else I know. Were you sick?"

I could feel her shrug against my back. "Nah. Couple days. No big deal." I came to find out later that she had been horribly sick for almost four days, yet came down to care for me each and every day, despite her illness.

My eyelids grew heavy as I snuggled into her, though, like a sleepy child on Christmas Eve, I struggled to stay awake.

"Sleep," she whispered, pulling me in close against her. "Your body needs to heal."

"I've slept too much already," I complained. "I wanna try and stay awake for a little while. Please?"

My head warmed as she chuckled against it. "I'm not your mother."

"Wish you were sometimes," I mumbled before succumbing to the demands of my body and falling into sleep once again.

♪ ♪ ♪ ♪

When I next awoke, I found myself propped on my side, facing Ice who was sitting on the other bed, reading quietly. I tried to sit up, but quickly gave that effort up as futile as my body decided to shout out its protests quite loudly. Ice looked up quickly and put her book down, coming to kneel beside my bed. "Good morning."

"Morning."

"Sleep well?"

"Well, it wasn't bad. For a nap."

She laughed. "Awful long nap, Angel. You've been out since yesterday afternoon."

My eyes widened. "Yesterday *afternoon*?"

"Yup. Told you your body needed the rest."

"And you were right. Again," I grumped.

"How do you feel?"

I took stock of my body, realizing that Ice was, indeed, right. "A whole lot better than I did yesterday."

"Good. You look better too. Your cheeks have a little color to them," she replied, gently stroking the body parts in question, to my immense pleasure. "You have the softest skin."

Of course, I blushed in response to that, which no doubt increased the color to my face, a fact which Ice noted with an amused smirk and one raised eyebrow. Which, of course, only caused me to blush that much harder.

"Thirsty?"

"Yeah. My tongue feels like sandpaper."

Raising up to sit on the bed, she gently lifted me up beside her and we repeated the same process as the day before. This time I managed to drink the whole cup without my stomach rebelling in the slightest. It seemed I was well on my way to recovery.

Ice nodded in satisfaction. "Later we'll try some broth and tea, courtesy of Corinne."

"Alright." Much as I hated to admit it, I was weakened even by that weak attempt at sitting. But this time, I was determined to remain awake and enjoy Ice's tender companionship. "How about telling me a story?"

Her voice was doubtful. "I don't know any stories, Angel. At least not any nice ones."

Sick I might have been, but not too muddled not to recognize a perfect opportunity when it was resting in my lap, as it were. "Then tell me a not nice one. Maybe about some of the times when you were out on your own?"

She stiffened against me. "Those aren't nice at all, Angel."

"I know, Ice. But I'd like to know more about you. And how can I if you won't share them with me?"

"Some things are better left up to the imagination."

I kept quiet, acknowledging her position, determined not to push against her inflexible barriers this time. My headstrong nature had caused enough problems between us already.

"This really means something to you, huh?"

"Yes. It really does. But not enough to make you upset, Ice. Never enough for that."

When she started speaking again, her voice was so soft I thought I was hallucinating it at first. "When my parents died, the only one left to care for me was my grandmother. I was twelve at the time and she just didn't have the energy needed to raise a young girl. She was pretty frail. I overheard some of the lawyers talking to my grandmother during the funeral. They were going to make me a ward of the state and put me in an orphanage."

"Oh, Ice…."

"Yeah. I might not have known much at that age, but I *did* know that I wasn't about to let myself get stuffed into a home."

"What did you do?"

"I ran. I waited until everyone was caught up in other things and I took off. The funeral home wasn't too far from my house, and my parents had given me a key when I was five, so I bolted for home. I went inside, grabbed some clothes, stuffed 'em in a backpack, took my mother's 'fun' money from her hiding place, grabbed Boomer, and left."

"Where did you go?" I shifted a little to get more comfortable against her chest. My arms, neck and shoulders were aching from residual fever and days of enforced inactivity.

I felt a moment of weightlessness as I was borne up easily in Ice's arms, then settled down to sit between her legs, my back once again against her chest. The sheet was tucked around my breasts and warm hands lowered themselves onto my shoulders, beginning a truly wonderful massage.

My muscles turned to liquid beneath her skilled touches, the pain fading like a distant memory. My head lolled back to rest against her shoulder as her hands continued to probe, soothe and caress in an orgy of sensation. It was bliss.

"Oh God," I groaned as the massage softened and turned sensual. "Where did you learn to do that?"

"Assassins need to keep loose. We can't afford muscle cramps. It screws up our aim."

"Oh."

"Yeah. 'Oh'."

"I guess there really are some questions that I don't wanna know the answers to, huh?"

"Most likely."

I allowed my eyelids to drift closed so as to better appreciate her welcome touch. There was nothing overtly sexual about her movements, but I felt energized just the same, her hands waking dormant parts of my body in pleasing tingles. "You're not trying to divert my attention from the subject at hand, are you?" I mumbled.

"Would I do that?" Her voice was innocence personified.

"Mm hmm."

She laughed. "Well, actually, I was just enjoying touching you. But if you want me to stop...."

"Oh no. You can keep doing that till your hands fall off. You won't hear me complaining."

As her hands moved beneath the sheet to continue their dance across my skin, she cleared her throat and picked up her tale once again. "To answer your question, I headed west. There was a decent stand of woods at the back of the house that I knew from previous experience led to the highway. It hadn't really sunk in that my parents were gone yet. I tried to tell myself this was just an adventure and that worked for awhile."

"Kids are really good at pretending."

"Yeah. I was pretty lucky in that way. My parents encouraged my fantasy life." She shrugged. "I think it was an art thing."

I hid my smile. "Must have been."

"Anyway...." The timbre of her voice let me know that my ruse had been discovered. "I made it out to the highway pretty quick. After that, it was just a matter of waiting for the right ride to come along."

"You *hitchhiked*?"

"Well, I didn't exactly *walk* from Baltimore to Pittsburgh, Angel."

"Don't you realize how dangerous that was?"

"Of course I realized it, Angel. I was young. Not an idiot. But what choice did I have? My parents were dead and I wasn't about to sit around and wait to be shoved in some home somewhere against my will. I saw the opportunity to get out and I took it. I didn't really have much time to think about anything else, even if I had been thinking clearly, which I wasn't."

Hearing the defensiveness in her tone, I reached down and clasped both of Ice's hands in my own, briefly stopping their delicious motion. "I'm sorry, Ice. That was incredibly pretentious of me to say."

She sighed. "It's alright. It *was* a stupid thing to do. But I knew enough not to accept rides from certain people. Boomer was a pretty good judge of character as well." I could hear the smile in her voice. "I got pretty lucky. It was near the end of summer and a lot of kids were going back to college. I managed to hook three rides, the last one all the way to Pittsburgh. I had intended to go further west, but for some reason, just wound up staying here. I guess when you're a kid, even a few hundred miles seems like a world away."

"What did you do then?"

"Well, my options were kinda limited. I had about five hundred dollars from my mother's money and that could last a long time, especially considering I didn't need to pay for a roof over my head. Not too many people would rent to a twelve year-old, you know?"

"But where did you live?"

"Here and there. Pretty much any place that would keep the rain off would do. Abandoned buildings, highway underpasses. Places like that."

"Weren't there shelters?"

"Sure. But that would have been, to my mind anyway, just like being in the orphanage. I didn't want to be hemmed in. So I stayed away. I was able to live almost six months on the money I'd taken. It probably would have lasted longer, but I didn't know anything about living on my own. When you're twelve, five hundred dollars seems like a gold mine. You don't think it's ever gonna run out."

I nodded in agreement. On the rare instances I received cards with money in them, I felt wealthy beyond the dreams of kings. And invariably I'd wind up blowing the whole thing in an orgy of gumballs and cheap paperbacks.

"When the money ran out, there weren't a whole lot of options for me. I could have joined a gang, but I've never been much of a follower. Plus, girls weren't treated any better than non-paid whores, so that was out for me. I tried shoplifting food and stuff, but it isn't easy to be inconspicuous when you've got a hundred and fifty pound attack dog at your side."

Her hands, which had resumed their lazy caress of my body, abruptly stilled and I felt a small shiver of dread flow down my spine. Suddenly, I was sure I didn't want to hear her next words. Suddenly, I wanted to be anyplace but where I was.

I battled down my fear. After all, this is what I had asked for, right? Right. Whatever I was going to hear would give me insight into the woman with whom I'd fallen in love, and no matter what it was, that was something I wanted more than anything.

Behind me, Ice took several deep breaths. I could feel the strong beat of her racing heart against my back and knew that whatever this secret was, it frightened her worse to say it than it frightened me to hear it.

Minutes ticked by before she softly cleared her throat. "Anyway," she said in a horse voice, "word on the street was that there was this guy who'd pay decent money to take …pictures of kids. Boys, girls, it didn't matter." She cleared her throat again. "As long as they were young. The younger, the better, in fact."

I couldn't suppress the shiver of revulsion that ran through me at her words. "A pedophile." More things made sense to me now. Like why Cavallo would set Ice up using the lie of pedophilia, something obviously guaranteed to get her fire up.

"Yeah. Into selling kiddy porn. By that time, I'd started going through my growth spurt and looked older than I was, but I needed the money and figured what the hell. It seemed as good an option as any. After all, what harm could a few pictures do?"

"Jesus, Ice…."

"Yeah, well, I didn't think about those things then. I just needed money and it seemed an easy way to get it. So I got directions over to his place and took Boomer with me. Figured with Boomer there, he couldn't make me do anything I didn't want to do."

She pulled her hands from under the sheet and I sensed she was going to try and distance herself from me during the rest of this tale. I grabbed her wrists as I'd done before, demanding contact with my body to let her know that it was safe to tell me her story. "Please, Ice, go on. I need to hear this and I think you need to tell it. It's been festering inside you too long."

Relaxing slightly, she allowed me to pull her arms back around my body and laid her cheek against my hair. "He was an older man, maybe mid- or late fifties. Longish greasy gray hair and always a day's growth of beard. He lived in a really seedy apartment in a run-down building on the outskirts of the city. I tell you, if there were a quintessential pedophile, this guy would probably rate a picture in the dictionary."

When I didn't laugh, she sighed. "Yeah, I know. It isn't very funny."

"Not by a long shot."

"Are you sure you wanna hear this? It's not something about me you really need to know."

"Ice, I want to hear it. I think it's very important that I do. Please."

"Alright. Anyway, the guy didn't seem to have enough money to buy decent furniture or even a mop or vacuum cleaner, but he had this extremely expensive studio in one of the bedrooms. The photographic equipment alone must have set him back big time, let alone the lighting and other stuff. I went up to the door and knocked and when he opened it, I thought Boomer was gonna take his head off. The guy almost peed his pants, though by the look of them, I doubt anyone would have noticed. He asked me what I wanted and I told him. He said that the dog had to say outside. To which I replied, of course, no dog, no pictures. He thought about it a minute, then let us both in. The apartment was dark and smelled like a gas station bathroom."

"I bet you were pretty scared, huh?"

"Scared isn't the word. I was terrified. But I just kept telling myself that both Boomer and I needed the money. It got me into the studio. He didn't talk much. Just told me he'd give me twenty-five dollars if I'd get undressed and sit on the bed so he could take pictures of me."

"Twenty-five dollars?" I gasped.

"Yeah. Doesn't sound like much, does it. But it was a huge deal for me, considering I had about quarter to my name by that time."

"So you did it."

"Yeah. I had Boomer sit in the corner and I stripped down to nothing. He just kinda stared at me for awhile, then told me to sit down. He shot a few pictures. Then he began to put me in some pretty suggestive poses. I just kept reminding myself how much I needed the money."

I could feel the sting of tears as they leapt into my eyes. Ice rubbed her hands briskly up and down my arms, comforting us both.

"After he was done," and here she took another deep breath, "he offered me another twenty-five to have sex with me. I took him up on it. Fifty dollars could keep me alive for a week, if I played my cards right. My virginity didn't seem that high a price to pay, given what I'd already been through."

That did it. The sob broke out before I could even attempt to stop it. Ice immediately wrapped me in her strong arms, kissing the crown of my head and rocking me. "Don't cry, Angel. Please don't cry. It happened a long time ago."

It incongruity of it all hit me hard. That a young woman who'd given up her innocence for the price of a few meals would be holding and comforting me, a woman who'd never had to worry about food or shelter, made my tears of sorrow turn to tears of shame.

I tried to pull away, but she only held me closer, stroking my tangled hair in an almost desperate way as she continued to beg me not to cry.

My shame and sorrow quickly turned to burning anger. I raged at the man, and so many others like him, who had preyed on the innocence of my friend and untold hundreds, if not thousands, of other young children just like her, forced by tragedy to trade something so overwhelmingly important for a pittance.

I longed to lash out at the image in my mind. The image of Ice as she was in that photograph; young, pure, beautiful being posed and fondled and invaded by a slathering, unnatural beast masquerading in the guise of a man. My body followed through on what my mind so desperately wanted and before I knew it, my tightly clenched fists impacted sharply on warm skin.

My eyes flew open in stunned disbelief. Ice stared down at me, shock naked on her beautiful features. She released me quickly as if my body burned and stood up from my bed, the stoic mask quickly settling over her face.

"Oh God," I moaned.

"It's alright, Angel," she said in a totally calm tone of voice. "It isn't something I haven't imagined doing to myself a dozen times over since it happened." Her eyes were hooded. "I was right to have wanted that story kept where it belonged. I'm sorry you had to hear it."

"No, Ice! God no. Please, listen to me. It wasn't you I was lashing out at. It was *him*! That *monster* that took your innocence away from you."

"Angel, my innocence left the minute I found out my parents had been killed. He didn't take anything that I didn't give freely."

I sat up straight on the bed, bringing the sheet up with me. "Freely? As freely as a bear gives up its life when it walks into a hunter's trap?"

"A bear doesn't know it's walking into a trap, Angel. I knew what I was doing."

"Ice, bears and all kinds of other animals are lured into traps all the time. Just like young children are lured into cars by the offer of candy or some other treat. You weren't any different. You went because he offered you something you needed. Money to stay alive."

Though she didn't say anything, I knew my words were penetrating that thick shield of guilt that she wore, twisted around herself, like a shroud. Her body relaxed slowly and I thought I detected just the faintest glint of gratitude in her eyes. I held my arms out and, to my great surprise, she came into them, allowing my embrace.

I moved back on the bed, gently guiding her down with me and, for the first time since we'd met, she allowed me to hold and comfort her. I molded her against me, stroking her hair and murmuring nonsensical phrases, feeling oddly maternal, as if I were soothing the young girl Ice had once been. And, in a way, that's exactly what I was doing.

She didn't cry. I think all of her tears had been used up long ago. But I knew that there was some deeply hidden part of her that was taking comfort in my love just the same, and that knowledge filled me with an elemental joy. After all, I had asked for this. Striven for it for two years now. To know the woman behind the mask. And here she was, snuggled tight against me, her head on my chest, showing a naked vulnerability that I had never thought to see. It was a gift of such immense proportion that mere words will never do it justice.

When she began speaking again, I was surprised, but held her close and listened to her cathartic words, knowing that I was most likely the first person ever to hear them spoken aloud.

"When it was over," she began, her voice soft and faintly muffled as she spoke against my chest, "he gave me the money he promised and told me I was welcome to come back anytime. He also said that, if I wanted, he could give me the names of other people who would be able to 'give me a hand' in the same way he did." She sighed. "I didn't much care at that point. I had my money and the only thing on my mind was finding a place with a hot shower and plenty of soap. I was sore and dirty and just wanted to get as far away from him as I could."

Taking a deep breath, she pulled away from my embrace, sitting back to lean against the wall of my cell, though she kept us connected by laying a hand on my thigh. "The money ran out pretty quickly and I found myself going back to him. Pretty soon, I was going to his friends as well. Some paid better, some not as well. Some wanted sex, some didn't. It didn't seem to matter much anymore."

She ran a steady hand through her midnight hair. "It went on for three years, almost. By that time, I'd gotten too mature to be of much use to the pedophiles anymore, but there was this man in Chicago who had apparently purchased some pictures of me and wanted to see me very badly. He was offering five hundred dollars and free airfare if I would come and pose for him. I did some asking around and found out that this guy was pretty reputable in certain artistic circles. I saw it as a one-in-a-million chance and took it. The only problem is that I needed to leave Boomer behind."

"What did you do?"

"I'd developed, I suppose you could call it an acquaintance, with one of the corner store owners in the city and Boomer seemed to like him well enough. He promised me that he'd keep Boomer in the store to act as a guard dog until I came back, no charge. Seemed like a fair deal to me."

As her voice trailed off, a premonition stole through me, humping my skin into gooseflesh. "Ice...."

"Yes?"

"Corinne told me that you...well, you went crazy after your best friend was killed. She was talking about Boomer, wasn't she."

The tears I thought used up sprang into her eyes then, magnifying their luminescence. "Yes," she whispered in a choked voice. "It was Boomer. There'd been a break-in at the store where he was staying and the street gang that did the robbery somehow overpowered him and took him out. When I got back, I heard that they tortured him to death over three or four days, then threw what was left of his body in front of the store as a warning."

She blinked once, freeing the tears from her eyes. They rolled down her cheeks silently as her gaze became lit with the fire of rage. "I knew who did it. They weren't shy in their boasting." When she grinned, it was like a shark displaying a mouthful of deadly teeth to a baby seal. "I stalked them for a month. I learned every little detail of their day-to-day lives. When one of them even so much as took a piss against a brick wall, I knew about it. I was patient. Very patient."

Her fingers mindlessly plucked at the sheet trapped around my body. She didn't even seem to be aware that I was still in the room, and I made myself as still and quiet as possible. I didn't want that rage turned on me. "My patience paid off. I found out they were having a little get together of the whole gang in honor of the leader's birthday. It was gonna be in an abandoned warehouse on the outskirts of the city and everyone would be there." She laughed. "They just didn't plan on having an uninvited guest."

Her hand convulsed suddenly, trapping a corner of the sheet against her tightly clenched fingers. Her face was a grinning death's head mask. "I killed them all. Slowly. I wanted them to hurt just like the defenseless animal they had tortured to death. I wanted them to feel pain. Exquisite pain. I wanted to see the fear in their eyes and smell it coming out of their pores. I thrived off of their screams. I laughed when they begged for mercy. They were less than nothing in my eyes and that's what I made them. Stains on the floor."

When Ice started her tale of her killing spree, I felt my still-weak stomach knot up. By the time she had finished, I found myself hung over the bed, expelling water and bile into the basin she'd left there, my guts heaving and threatening to turn themselves inside out.

Ice's warm hands came down gently on my back, rubbing in circles as the last of the dry heaves left my system weak and reeling. When I was sure I was done, she handed me a rag and I wiped my mouth, then sat up slowly. "Sorry about that," I croaked around a raw and aching throat. "That hit me unexpectedly."

She nodded, cupping my cheek. "I told you it was a pretty ugly story."

"Yes, you did. But I needed to hear it as much as, I think, you needed to tell it."

Ice snorted. "I *never* need to tell that particular story, Angel. Believe me when I tell you that getting it out in the open hasn't made me feel any better about what I did. The courts were right. I did murder them. Intentionally. Calculatingly. In cold blood. I may have regretted it afterwards, but regret doesn't erase my actions."

"Do you?"

"Do I what?"

"Regret what you did?"

As she looked at me, her eyes were very serious. "Yes, Angel. I regret it very deeply. Though part of me revels in what I did to those kids, a bigger part feels very guilty. But regretting my actions won't bring them back any more than it will bring Boomer back. And regretting my actions won't stop me from doing it again. If you need proof, just look at what I almost did to Psycho when she killed Josephina. I'll never be able to control that part of myself. I'm not even sure that I *want* to." Smiling sadly, she tilted my chin up. "I am who I am, Angel. All the regret in the world won't change that."

Placing my hands over her larger ones, I gently drew them away from my face, kissing each before clenching them in my own. I looked deeply into her eyes and began to speak. "Ice, I know you believe that. That you're nothing but a murderer. But you're not, you know. You are so very much more than that."

Chafing her hands gently with my thumbs, I smiled. "You might think that what happened with Psycho proves your point, but it really proves mine quite nicely."

Ice tilted her head. "How do you figure that?"

"You could have killed her. I know you were ready to. But you didn't."

"I would have, if you hadn't been there."

"Maybe. But that's not the point. The point is, you didn't."

"Because you *stopped* me, Angel!"

"Exactly how did I stop you, Ice? Did I physically overpower you? Did I pull you off of her and fling you across the jail?"

"No."

"Right. I simply talked to you. I reminded you of things you already knew. I only appealed to the goodness already in you, Ice. Nothing more than that."

She opened her mouth, then closed it again. I could tell by the expression on her face that she very much wanted to argue the point. "But...." Her voice trailed off.

I smiled more broadly, doing my own impression of a shark moving in for the kill. "No 'buts', Ice. You're a good woman underneath all that bluff and bravado. You know it. I know it. There are things that you've done which are horrible, some might even say evil. But you've also done some wonderful things. Things that even people who are supposedly 'good' all the time would never think or try to do. Yes, there's a side of you that's fueled by an intense rage. And there's another side of you that's capable of great things. What you have to do is choose which side rules your actions."

"It's...not that easy, Angel."

"No, it isn't. And maybe that's part of the reason why I'm here. Why we've become such good friends. Because I can see that part of you that maybe not many others know is there. And maybe I can help you bring it out more often in situations where rage is the only thing you know to turn to."

Ice shook her head. "Those are noble sentiments, Angel, but...."

Releasing one of her hands, I placed my own hand on her chest, palm down over her strongly beating heart. "This...is a good heart, Ice. It's an honorable heart that's been beaten and bloodied. Let it heal. Let the rage and the guilt of the past go. You're right when you say that those emotions won't bring anyone back. Don't let them kill you too. You've been dying inside for too long already."

"I don't...."

"Ice, let me help. Let me try to help you see the person *I* see every time I look at you."

With a sad smile, Ice gripped my hand as she stepped away, lifting it up and brushing her lips against my knuckles. "I don't think that's possible, Angel. But thanks. It means a lot that you would want to do that for me."

Leaning in toward her, I placed my hands lightly on her hips. "Let me try, Ice. At least give me that. Please?"

I found myself falling into her eyes once again. "Alright," she said after a moment, her voice deep and warm. Leaning over, she sealed her words with a gentle kiss. Then, grinning, she stood, gripping my legs and swinging them fully onto the bed. "And that, my dear, concludes story hour. Off to bed with ya. I'll have some tea and broth ready for when you wake up."

She untwisted and smoothed out the sheet, then tucked it up under my chin. Brushing the hair from my eyes, she placed a kiss on my forehead, then straightened up, tipping me a wink. "Sleep. Now."

"Yes, Ma'am!" I grinned.

"You're learning." Smirking, she turned to leave.

"Ice?"

"Yeah?"

"Thanks."

With another wink and a casual wave, she left my cell. I fell asleep almost immediately, a smile on my face.

Spring's triumphant return brought with it a return to health for most residents of the Bog. The flu had hung on long and hard, eventually taking the lives of three more inmates by the time it decided to leave us.

As I child, I'd always been prone to head-colds that turned quickly into bronchitis, and as an adult, it appeared, that hadn't changed. Sickness had stuck with me like a secret lover through the rest of the long, dark winter, leaving me thin, pale and weak.

When the sun came out to play, warming our little corner of the world, I went out right along with it, running through the grass like a giddy schoolgirl and stopping only when my still weakened lungs saw fit to voice their displeasure through a spasm of coughing.

Every time I ventured outside, I fended off the pleas of my fellow inmates to again reprise my role as the Bog's 'star' short-stop. Breathing infield dust all day was something I had the feeling my lungs wouldn't be very thankful for. Instead, I spent my time slowly rebuilding my weakened muscles with the other Amazons at the free weight area.

Spring also brought with it some welcome news in the form of a plain white package stamped with the official State Seal. Inside was the printed copy of my official court transcript. Corinne and I spent many an afternoon laboriously going through each and every paragraph, word and punctuation mark looking for that elusive piece of evidence that could lead to an appeal for me.

Those afternoon searches were fruitless exercises, for the most part. No magic Rosetta Stone appeared to guide us through the hundreds of pages of legalese that twisted the mind and beguiled the eyes. Even Corinne's 'jailhouse lawyer' friends couldn't provide answers where there seemingly were none to be found.

During one such afternoon, Ice came to the library to visit on an infrequent break from her auto shop duties. Her hair was in wild disarray, her face lined with greasy smudges and, at that very moment, my welcoming eyes had never seen a more beautiful sight.

Grabbing a chair and turning it, she sat down, her forearms resting casually on the back as she looked down at the sheaf of paper decorating the table. "Any luck?"

I sighed, resisting the urge to just sweep the whole pile onto the floor. "I'll take that as a 'no'."

"A big one. I'm about ready to just chuck it all."

"Don't do that yet. I may have someone who can help."

"Oh? Who?"

"A friend. She's an excellent criminal defense attorney and I've heard she's recently narrowed her practice to handle cases just like yours."

A pang of hope lit my heart before I could stop it. "Really?"

Ice smiled crookedly, laying a hand atop my wrist. "Yeah, really. Her name is Donita Bonnsuer and if she's still talking to me, I'll try to hook you up with her. Maybe she can help."

"Still talking to you? What happened?"

She shrugged. "We had a little difference of opinion."

My curiosity gene kicked into high gear. "Over what?"

"She wanted to represent me at my trial. I refused. End of story."

"Oh, come on, Ice! You've gotta give me more than that!"

Rolling her eyes, Ice looked over at Corinne, who was sitting beside me, then back to me. "Angel, there really isn't any more to tell than that."

"Of course there is! Why wouldn't you let her represent you?"

"A couple of reasons. One was that this was a case involving some very bad individuals who, as you now know, will stop at nothing to get what they want. I didn't want her tangled up in the middle of all that."

I nodded. "That makes sense. The other reason?"

Her eyes twinkled as the corner of her lip smirked upward. "A bit of conflict of interest. She's an ex-lover."

My jaw dropped, but before I was able to investigate *that* interesting little bombshell, I was interrupted by the strident ringing of the fire alarm. Seconds later, Sonny, face and uniform smelling strongly of smoke, ran into the library, her breath coming out in heaving pants. "Quick! The laundry room's on fire! There's about twenty women trapped in there and Critter's one of them!"

Ice and I jumped up from the table at the same time, though her longer strides led her more quickly from the library and toward the site of the fire. The klaxon rang loudly in my ears and was soon joined by the screams of terror coming from within the laundry room. Smoke plumed out into the prison proper from the long hallway housing the laundry facilities and I choked as I ran closer to the conflagration, pushing the milling, panicking inmates and guards aside as I tried to keep Ice within my sights.

I skidded up to the doorway just in time to hear Ice demand to know what had happened. Pony was there, a panicked look on her face. The doorway itself was on fire, a beam of some sort having fallen diagonally across it preventing entry or exit from the room.

"I think it started with one of the dryers," Pony choked out, her voice hoarse from the thick smoke that bellowed from the room. "A whole table of sheets went up like a bomb. Critter and I tried to get out as many as we could, but then that beam fell down and trapped the rest inside. Please, Ice, you gotta do something!"

By this time, several guards had arrived carrying buckets of water and thick towels. Ice grabbed two towels, dunked them into the water and tied off one around her lower face and draped the other over her head, covering her hair and neck.

My stomach sinking through my feet, I grabbed her arm, whirling her to face me. "You can't be serious! Ice, don't go in there! That's suicide!"

Pulling my hand from her arm, Ice pushed me back into Pony, who clamped me tightly against her body.

"Ice! No!"

Taking a step back to stand against the opposite wall, Ice took in a deep breath, then launched herself at the door, diving through the small space above the burning beam. I saw her tuck and roll as she landed, then spring quickly to her feet and run almost directly into the fire.

Wrestling myself away from Pony's tight grip, I grabbed one of the buckets and threw the water on the fire blocking the doorway. Steam hissed out at me as the flames drew away for a moment, only to spring back to life quickly. Sandra pushed me aside to add her own water, then tossed down the pail and accepted another from the quickly forming bucket brigade made up of inmates and guards alike.

The fire in the doorway went out just as the first of the trapped women was propelled out into the hallway, gasping and choking, sooty tears making ghoulish tracks down her blackened face. I gently passed the woman down the human chain of onlookers just as another came stumbling out, followed quickly by another.

I looked up to see Ice carrying another woman in her arms. She ran up to the door and thrust the limp body into Pony's sure grasp before turning back for more. She'd made it just a step or two away from the door when a huge explosion sounded inside the room. A large tongue of fire belched out from the charred doorway, instantly turning one of the guards into a human torch.

Without thought, I stepped forward, tackling the woman onto the floor and smothering the flames with my own body. My hands were instantly burned, but I continued to beat the fire out with them until more people arrived with wet towels. Then I jumped away, patting out the smoldering areas on my own uniform.

"Angel!" Pony yelled.

I turned. "What?"

"Your hair! It's on fire!"

Reaching up, my hands burned again as I touched the flames that seeded themselves in my long hair. I almost lost consciousness as a towel, heavy with water, came flying down over my head, dousing the flames and obscuring my breathing and vision. Yanking the towel away, my first sight was of Pony's concerned face peering closely into my own.

"Are you alright?" she asked.

I took stock of my body. My hands were red and swollen and I'm sure I looked a mess with half my hair missing, but I was okay for the time being. "I'm alright," I confirmed. When I looked back into the laundry room, all I could see was an unbroken wall of fire just beyond the doorway. My guts twisted up inside of me as I realized the implications and I had to fight not to vomit on my feet. "Ice!" I screamed, fighting to be heard from beyond the blockade of flames.

Hearing nothing in return, I spun to glare at Sandra. "Where in the *hell* is the fire department?"

"They're getting here as quick as they can, Angel."

"Fuck that!" I screamed, grabbing a few towels from one of the guards and throwing one to Pony. "I'm not waiting for the fire department! People could still be alive in there!"

Running back toward the door, I used the towel to try and beat down the flames. After a second, Pony joined me. I felt a push against my other side, and when I looked, I saw Sandra stepping in, a determined look on her face as she tried to help douse the fire.

Buckets of water flew over and around us, dousing us and the fire in an attempt to beat it back. Another towel was handed to me and I tied it around my face. I was already choking from the smoke but wasn't about to stop what I was doing. I would help get this fire out or die trying. Stopping was not an option. *Hang on, Ice. God damn it, you'd just better hang on.*

It was soon very obvious that we were fighting a losing battle. For every small step we made, another explosion would chase us away and the wall of flames would rise up once again. I began to sob as I continued to beat at the flames as if they were a living thing. I could hear myself screaming incoherently as rage filled me, eclipsing everything else.

Several pairs of hands reached in to pull me away. I snarled like a wild beast, refusing to be turned from my task. My throat was raw from screaming and my eyes stung from smoke and heat and heartbroken tears.

Sandra and Pony worked together, one grabbing me high, the other, low, literally lifting me off of my feet and carrying me away from the fire. I thrashed and squirmed, my balled fists hitting any inch of flesh I could in an attempt to get free.

Their combined strength was too much for me and I screamed Ice's name as the wall of flames became smaller and smaller in my tear-trebled vision.

Big men in bulky suits and breathing units pushed past us in the narrow hallway, bearing axes and thick hoses with which to fight the fire. Thanking any and every god who would listen, I let myself go limp in the grip of my captors, and when they relaxed as well, I squirmed out and away from them both, running back down the hallway screaming Ice's name.

Pinning myself between a firefighter and the wall so I couldn't be re-captured, I watched as the men quickly and efficiently doused the flames with the high-powered spray from their hose. Within moments, the fire was out, leaving behind a thick, black, oily smoke that continued to stream out into the hallway, choking us all.

What was left of the laundry room was almost pitch black. The light from the hallway invaded scant inches into the room. One of the firemen lit a high-powered flashlight, illuminating the interior.

I moaned and retched as the charred remains of human beings became all too visible in the brilliant light. Water dripping from within the cavernous room was the only sound to be heard.

"*Noooo!*"

A voice I didn't even recognize as my own filled the silence as I rushed forward, deftly dodging the outstretched arm of the fireman.

Bodies littered the floor, many burned beyond recognition. I stumbled over them, running onward, searching, sobbing. The sound of running foot-steps grew loud in my ears and when a heavy hand came down on my shoul-der, I whirled and punched a very surprised fireman in the chest, sending him back several steps.

Turning again, I stumbled forward, my mind screaming as my heart pounded out my wild grief. Another ceiling beam laid out across the floor and I ran to it, slipping in the dirty water that pooled on the floor.

Pinned beneath the beam was Ice, the bottom of her uniform burned almost totally off her body. Beneath her, protected by her long frame and tight embrace, lay two more women, one of which I could easily identify as Critter. All three forms were totally motionless.

"Oh God," I sobbed, squatting down to my knees and reaching out a shaking hand. "Ice? Oh, God. Ice? Please wake up! Please!" I touched the skin of her upper face. It was still warm, but that could have been from the fire. Her neck was obscured by the beam crushing against her back and her arms were pinned beneath the two women she'd tried to save.

Standing up quickly, I grabbed the still smoking beam, not caring that my hands were being scalded. With an effort that came from somewhere outside of my natural ability, I moved the beam upward an inch or so, then pulled it toward me, grunting with the strain.

Within seconds, several pairs of hands came to my aid, pulling the beam completely away from the trapped women. I dropped to my knees again, reaching beneath the towel that still covered Ice's mouth and nose, searching blindly for a pulse.

"Oh, thank you, God," I sobbed, finding one. It was weak and thready and much too fast, but it was there. "Oh God...Oh God...Oh God...Ice, c'mon now. It's time to wake up. You can do it. Just open your eyes. Let's see those beautiful baby blues, alright?" I reached in, grabbing her shoulder and shaking it hard. Her head lolled with my motions but she remained deeply unconscious.

Rough cloth brushed against me as one of the firefighters squatted down next to me. I turned to him, grabbing the fabric of his coat and pulling his upper body toward mine so that we were face to face. "*Do* something!" I wailed, not caring in the least how desperate I sounded to him or anyone else.

He covered my hand with his own gloved one, making no attempt to pull away. His dark eyes were compassionate as they looked into mine. "We have to wait until the paramedics get in here, Ma'am. We don't want to move her yet."

"Why not? She could be dying for all you know!"

"That beam that fell across her back was very heavy, Ma'am. There's a good chance it may have damaged her spine. If we move her now, we could make things worse. Just wait a few more minutes. The paramedics should be here by now, alright?"

Releasing my grip on his heavy jacket, I reached down and eased the towel from around Ice's soot-blackened face, then brushed sweat-soaked bangs back from her high forehead with shaking fingers. As if my gentle touch was some sort of magic elixir, her eyes blinked open, a moan coming softly from her cracked lips. "Angel?" she croaked, her voice raw.

Yet another sob came up from my throat and I covered my mouth with my free hand. "Ice?"

"Angel?"

"Ice! Thank God! You're awake!"

She blinked her stinging eyes rapidly, then winced as she tried to move. "Is that what this is."

I put a restraining hand down on her shoulder. "Don't try to move, Ice. Part of the ceiling collapsed on your back. You could be really hurt."

The firefighter added his hands to mine. "Best to do as she says, Ma'am. The paramedics are on their way."

Getting her strength from I don't know where, Ice managed to shrug us both off as she rolled from atop the pile of bodies she had tried to protect. "I'm fine," she said hoarsely. "See if you can help these two."

"Ice...."

"I'm *alright*, Angel." Overcome by a sudden spasm of coughing, her body convulsed, drawing in against itself as she heaved and gasped for breath. I saw, with great relief, that her arms and legs appeared to be moving freely, though I guessed the pain of her injuries was intense.

As I stepped over to help her, the paramedics rushed in with their equipment and stretchers, quickly working over the bodies of Critter and the other woman. To my surprise, and happiness, both women were alive, though still unconscious. Critter's golden curls were caked with sweat, soot and water, but I could see her chest rise and fall in a regular, though shallow, rhythm that caused the first smile to break over my face since the fire started.

The other woman was older, more frail. I knew she worked in the laundry room, but didn't know her except to wave to in the hallways. She had some nasty burns on her face and arms and her leg was cocked at an impossible angle at the knee where it had been trapped beneath the heavy beam that had fallen across Ice's broad back.

As the two women were being cared for and made ready for transport, a third paramedic joined me at Ice's side, slipping an oxygen mask over her face. Her paroxysms of choking immediately eased with the fresh flow of air into her breathing passages.

After the paramedic was sure she was breathing freely, he grabbed her right arm and swabbed it with a pungent alcohol wipe, while his other hand held an IV needle, intent on piercing her skin with it. Seeing what he was about to do, Ice ripped the mask from her face and pushed him away, snatching her arm easily from his grip. "No."

Throwing down his contaminated equipment, the man grabbed another packet from his kit while simultaneously making another grab for his uncooperative patient's arm. "Look lady," he sighed, exasperated when Ice wouldn't willingly hand over her flesh to be pierced. "I need to start an IV so we can get you to the hospital, alright?"

"No hospital. Just take care of those two and the others. I'm fine." Her calm assurances were belied by another fit of coughing which passed through her body.

I grabbed the oxygen mask, but her hand lashed out and batted it away. "No hospital," she repeated in a raspy, wheezing voice. "I'll...go to the infirmary...but...no hospital. I mean it."

The paramedic looked helplessly back at his superior, who in turned looked over at Sandra, who'd moved in to join us just as Ice awoke. Sandra and Ice locked gazes, heating up the air between them with the intensity of their stares. A free woman had a choice to refuse treatment. A prisoner had none.

"I'm *alright*, Sandra," Ice rasped out in a tone that brokered no argument.

I could see the indecision in the head guard's eyes. When Ice was completely set in stone over something, she was a person you most definitely didn't want to cross paths with. Yet Sandra was a very strong, and head-strong, woman in her own right.

After a moment she nodded slightly, blinking to break eye contact with Ice. She turned to the waiting supervisor. "She'll go to the infirmary with me. Our doctor's coming in from home. If she even blinks the wrong way once she's there, I'll take her over to the hospital personally. Fair enough?"

"It's highly irregular, Mrs. Pierce," the paramedic supervisor stated doubtfully. "Sickness from smoke inhalation can show up hours after the event. There's a good chance someone could die before you could even get them to the hospital. I highly recommend against this course of action, Ma'am."

Sandra looked back at Ice, who shook her head once in a savage gesture. Though I wanted to convince Ice to go to the hospital, I knew that not even my persuasive skills could sway her decision. Instead, I kept quiet, watching the silent interplay between the parties. After another long moment, Sandra seemed to deflate, her shoulders uncharacteristically sagging. "I'll take full responsibility for the prisoner," she finally said. "Our infirmary is fully stocked and should be enough to see to her needs for now."

The supervisor looked as if he was going to argue the matter further, then simply sighed. "You'll need to sign this AMA form then, Mrs. Pierce. I'm going on record as stating that this is against my better judgement and that this woman's life may well be at stake."

"I'm aware of that, and I'll sign anything you like. Let's just get this over with so that the other women can be treated."

Rifling through his papers, the supervisor eventually came up with the correct one for the situation and handed it to Sandra on a clipboard. Grabbing the proffered pen, the guard scrawled her signature and handed pen and clipboard back to the waiting paramedic, nodding curtly.

Reading over the signature carefully, the man stuffed everything back into his kit, then gestured to the others to gather their things for the ride back to the hospital with their injured charges. I stood quickly and gently kissed Critter's soot-streaked forehead, silently wishing her a speedy return to health as she was wheeled from the carnage.

When I turned back, Sandra was gently helping Ice to her feet. My lover winced and gritted her teeth against the pain of her injuries. Though the bottoms of her uniform had been burned away, her legs didn't seem to be badly burned and for that I was grateful.

When she was fully upright, Ice tried to shake off Sandra's assistance, but the large woman would have none of that and eased one of Ice's long arms around her shoulders, slipping one of her own arms around my friend's narrow waist. Then she leveled a no-nonsense glare at me. "You too, Angel. And before you try that oh-so-innocent act with me, I can see your hands from here. You're just lucky I didn't sic the paramedics on ya."

Quickly, before Ice could see, I hid my burned hands behind my back and adopted my best contrite expression. "Yes, Ma'am," I said, trying hard not to smile. Truth be known, so much adrenaline was pumping through my body that I couldn't even feel my hands, let alone know if they hurt or not. I was sure that would come later and I wasn't looking forward to it.

🖋   🖋   🖋   🖋

That night in the infirmary was the first we had ever spent together. Unfortunately, we couldn't do much, not even talk. My hands were liberally slathered with burn ointment and heavily bandaged, while Ice was stuck lying flat on her stomach, her burned back likewise bandaged and an oxygen mask secure over her face. And believe me when I tell you that seeing the graceful curve of Ice's backside as it rose from the pristine sheets of the hospital bed made for one very frustrated Angel.

We'd both been stripped, scrubbed and tended to by the very kind, if a bit elderly and doddering, penitentiary physician, Dr. Soames and his trio of efficient nurses. He tsked and muttered and harrumphed his way through the examination, but despite his gruff mannerisms, his hands were very gentle and soothing to my burned palms and skittish spirit.

After he was finished treating the both of us, he had his nurses administer some pain-killing injections, then dim the lights and lock us in for the night. One of the nurses would keep an eye on us through the reinforced glass window of the adjacent office.

Alone at last, I turned my head to the side to see Ice looking at me, the mask obscuring her features. Her eyes, though, were filled with a curious combination of amusement and adoration as they almost twinkled in the muted lighting. My heart again filled to overflowing with the love I had for this sometimes violent, sometimes gentle, but always heroic woman who chose to share her own love with me.

Reaching out a bandaged hand through the rails of my stretcher, I beckoned contact with my eyes alone. Her face crinkled beneath the mask as one long arm snaked out from under the sheet, touching my wrist above the bandages lightly, her fingers warm and gentle on my sensitive skin. My body relaxed immediately.

So linked by the gentlest of touches, we continued to stare into one another's eyes until the stress of the day and the painkillers caught up to us and we both fell into a well-earned sleep.

Chapter 10

Several weeks later, I found myself sitting with Ice in one of the stuffing-impaired vinyl chairs that populated the visitor's room at the Bog. My bandages had finally come off the day before and the newly healing skin was driving me mad with its incessant itching.

Ice seemed to be fully healed, of course. Though, to be truthful, she could still be in agony and neither I nor anyone else would ever know it by her demeanor. The Queen of Stoicism, that was Ice.

Still, though my hands were driving me to absolute distraction, I counted myself truly blessed. I had survived the fire with minor injuries and a new haircut while seven other women had lost their lives to its consuming flames. Two more were critically burned and two others, of which Critter was one, were still in the hospital suffering the after-effects of smoke inhalation. To everyone's great relief, though, all the women were well on their way to full recoveries. Critter was due back by the end of the week, which made us all happy, particularly her Amazon friends.

If not for Ice, things would have been a great deal worse. She was touted as a hero throughout the prison by guard and inmate alike. Brushing it off with her typical style, she told us all to thank the firefighters and those of us who tried to put out the fire with buckets, towels and bare hands (the last was always directed at me, of course). We, she said, were the true heroes.

So now I was sitting in the sparsely decorated visiting room for the first time ever, nervously tapping my fingers on the mounds of paper sitting on my lap and waiting for a lawyer who just happened to be my lover's ex-lover. I didn't know whether to laugh or throw up.

The rattling of the key in the lock startled me out of my reverie and I sat up straighter, wanting very badly to make a good first impression on this woman, for a variety of reasons. The door squealed open on rusty hinges, and I was glad for the noise as it covered the sound of my jawbone rattling to the floor.

Donita Bonnsuer was, to be perfectly honest, absolutely, positively, drop-dead *gorgeous*. As Ice rose gracefully to greet her friend, I studied the woman with frank appraisal. She was tall and slender with flawless mocha skin, beau-tifully rounded cheekbones, full, soft lips and sparkling chocolate eyes. She was dressed in a devastatingly impeccable business suit, the bright red set-ting off her dark skin and jet hair perfectly. Her smile when she greeted Ice seemed to swallow up her entire face and displayed gleaming, perfect white teeth.

My sense of insecurity, so long dormant, waltzed right up to my guts and shouted "howdy!" as it tap danced on my stomach and decided to stay awhile. I looked at them both, greeting one another like good friends too long out of touch, and thought that they could be on the cover of some magazine featuring the world's most beautiful couples.

When Ice turned to me, though, the look in her eyes shriveled my inse-curity like a slug under salt, and I felt a smile break out over my face that grew even broader when she responded with a rare one of her own.

After placing my paper mountain on the chair beside me, I stood, care-fully wiping my suddenly sweaty palms on my uniform. Donita approached and clasped my hand warmly, smiling at me. "It's a pleasure to meet you, Angel," she said in a low, smooth and cultured voice. "I'm Donita, as you've probably guessed already, and Ice has talked to me about your case. I'd like to know more, if that would be alright with you?"

"Um…yeah! Sure! That'd be great!" Insecurity might have shriveled, but foot-in-mouth disease seemed to be making a comeback.

If she thought me odd, she didn't show it, but rather grasped her brief-case and led the way to a battered table set up, more or less, in the center of the rectangular room. Grabbing a chair, she hunkered right down, beckon-ing for the pile of papers I held in my hands. I slid them across the table to her, then sat down myself, crossing my hands in front of me like a good little schoolgirl as I looked on curiously.

Ice squeezed my shoulder in passing and I looked up, panic-stricken, as she made her way to the door. "Where…where are you going?"

"Back to work," she replied, smiling slightly. "You two can get along just fine without me."

"But…."

She held up a hand. "Relax, will ya? You'll be fine. Just answer her questions and take it from there." She smirked, looking over at Donita. "She doesn't bite, ya know."

The lawyer grinned. "Not hard, anyway."

I gulped. Ice tipped us both a wink, then waved and left the room. Donita give me a grin full of shining teeth.

🔑   🔑   🔑   🔑

Two hours later, the session was wrapping up. My jaw ached from hanging in awe as I watched her work. She was, simply put, amazing. She whipped through the thick transcript as if it were child's play and took the time to explain everything to me, never once making me feel ignorant or foolish with my questions. She was a true master of her craft and I was honored to be in her presence.

Calling an end to the session, Donita snapped her briefcase closed, then set it on the floor next to her own copy of the transcript which she would take with her. She stretched her long arms, then straightened the cuffs of her blouse and suit jacket, a pleased smile on her face. "I think you have an appealable case here, Angel. Mind you, I can't be sure until I've subpoenaed that hack you had for a lawyer, but I definitely think we've got some good stuff to work with."

"Subpoenaed?" I repeated blankly.

"Yeah. I need to get a hold of his worksheets, what witnesses, if any, he talked to, questions he asked, stuff like that. That way, we can see exactly where our starting point is."

"Starting point? But…."

Her eyebrow rose, reminding me strongly of Ice. "Yes?"

"I, um…" I sighed. "I thought that I was only talking to you for advice."

She grinned broadly. "Exactly. And you got some. We can win this case."

"We?"

"Is there an echo in here? Of course, we. Unless you've passed the bar in the last week or so and Ice neglected to mention it to me."

"No, it's not that." I sighed again, the need to explain warring heavily with my sense of pride. "You see, I don't…well, the fact is, I'm positive I can't afford what you're worth. I'll be happy to give you what money I have, but I'm afraid it isn't very much. And my parents…well…we're not on speaking terms anymore."

Donita's smile broadened. "Not to worry, Angel. As you might have guessed, I do pretty well for myself with my caseload. But I also do several appeals a year on a *pro bono* basis. Yours will be one of them."

"I…can't let you do that."

"Sure you can. All you have to do is say 'Donita, I'd be happy for you to take my case.'"

I looked at her, dumbfounded.

"Say it."

My dumbfounded look turned to a narrow-eyed stare as I contemplated refusing like a child who has been told to apologize. But the warmth in her eyes and the smile on her face stopped my petulance unspoken. "Donita, I'd be *very* happy if you'd consider taking my case," I replied, an eyebrow lifted in small triumph.

Grinning, she stood and sketched a mock bow in my direction. "I'd be honored, Angel."

Grabbing her briefcase and balancing the thick pile of papers precariously with the same hand, she reached out and shook my hand to seal the deal. "Remember that the wheels of justice turn slowly. There's a lot of work to be done before I can even think of bringing this up before a judge. Just sit tight and I'll be in contact as often as I can, alright?"

I smiled and nodded happily, excited over the chance for an eventual release for the first time since I'd entered the Bog three years ago. "Thank you so much," I gushed.

She beamed. "My pleasure, Angel. And tell Ice thanks for me, alright? This is gonna be fun." With a final wave and a beguiling, blinding grin, she knocked on the door and was soon gone from my sight.

⚭   ⚭   ⚭   ⚭

The next several months went by quickly for me. The continued positive news from the appeal front kept my mood up even if it did seem, at times, that the wheels of justice Donita had spoken of were mired in quicksand and sinking fast.

One early summer morning, I sat in the cool dimness of the library, excitedly turning a gaily wrapped package over in my hands while pointedly ignoring the demanding over-the-glasses look I was getting from Corinne. I had been waiting for this particular package for almost two months, almost fainting in excitement when I'd heard from a friend that it suddenly became available at an estate auction. My excitement doubled when I found out that it was, amazingly, within my budget.

"A Thousand and One String-Bead Art Patterns," Corinne muttered from her darkened desk.

"What?" I asked, inwardly grinning at finally having the chance to turn the tables on my oh-so-in-the-know friend.

"The name of the book you're holding like some kid who got into her parents' Penthouse collection."

"What makes you think it's a book?"

"Oh please, Angel. Give me some credit, at least. I'm a *librarian*, for Moses' sweet sea-parting sake. Or didja think all these square things with pages in between them were decorations." Her hand flicked out from it's shadowed corner, its gesture encompassing the entire library.

Oh, I'd definitely gotten her dander up, alright. And I was enjoying every moment of my innocent little torture session. "It could be a box, you know. A flat one, filled with all sorts of interesting little goodies."

"Those little goodies are called 'words', Angel." She leveled her best 'no-nonsense' glare at me. "They form sentences, which in turn form paragraphs. Unless, of course, it's a book of poetry, in which case, they form nothing at all."

"You're such a romantic, Corinne."

"I have better uses for this mouth of mine than spouting poetry, my dear Angel." Her tone was absolutely dripping with seduction and, considering her age, she did a good job at it. To my credit, though, I stopped the threatened blush cold. When she saw her ruse wasn't going to work, she frowned, eyeing me once again over the tops of her half-glasses.

Giving in just a little, I leveled my own parental expression right back at her. "You know, the word 'please' has been known to work on occasion."

"I don't know what you're talking about," came her prim reply.

"Then I suppose your curiosity is going to have to suffer." I turned the package around in my hands, making sure the indirect lighting caught the foil wrapping at just the right angle. I'd grown up in a house full of cats as a child and well knew how to entice them.

Minutes ticked by, measured by the under-her-breath grumbling Corinne was turning into an art form. Finally, she huffed out a sigh that would have done Paul Bunyan proud, almost toppling a stack of papers as it did. "Alright. Angel, dear, may I *please* know what's in that wrapped little package of yours?" Her voice was positively overflowing with sugared sweetness. "I'm afraid my poor old heart will simply *explode* out of my chest if you don't tell me right this very moment."

As heartfelt pleas went, that was about the poorest example I'd ever heard, but, knowing Corinne, it was probably the best I could hope for. I allowed myself a small victory smirk as I turned my attention her way. "This little ol' thing?" I asked, hefting my prize.

"Angel...."

I burst out laughing, unable to help myself. After a moment, she joined me and the quiet air was soon filled with boisterous laughter. After a long moment, I looked back at her, flipping the package in my hands. "You're right, of course. It *is* a book. A rare one, actually."

"And?"

"It's an original printing of <u>One Day in the Life of Ivan Denisovich</u>, signed by the author himself, and you know he didn't do autographs. It's in Russian."

Corinne's eyes widened in awe. "Amazing. How'd you manage to come on to such a prize?"

"An estate sale, if you can believe that one. One of my outside contacts dabbles in literature. He saw it and asked if I wanted to bid on it."

"And, of course, you said yes."

"But of course. It came in well under my budget too. Apparently, there just wasn't any interest."

"Philistines."

"Hey, I'm not gonna look a gift barbarian in the horns."

"Good analogy."

"Glad you liked it." I grinned, shifting on my chair. "Anyway, like I said, it's in Russian. Problem is, I don't know whether Ice reads Russian. And before you ask, yes, it's for her."

Her eyes twinkled. "Had that one figured out already. And don't worry, I think she reads it. In fact, I'm almost sure of it."

"I don't get it," I replied, shaking my head. "She became a street kid right out of elementary school. Yet I saw the Tao, written in Chinese, mind you, sitting on the floor of her cell. And it looked like she had read it quite a bit. How could she have learned so much living on the streets?"

"That part of her schooling took place before she went to live on the streets, Angel. Her mother, as an opera singer I think, was an absolute fanatic about other cultures. Ice told me that she was taught to read other languages at the same time she was taught to read English. It was just something that her parents believed in."

"That's interesting," I replied, hoping that my voice didn't sound as envious as my thoughts were.

Apparently, it did. Corinne took off her glasses and looked at me, smiling slightly. "Ice was quite young when she shared this with me. I suppose she looked upon me as somewhat of a grandmotherly figure." She moued her lips in self-deprecation.

I instantly felt the sting of embarrassment. "I'm sorry, Corinne. I'm just glad that you were there for her. It must have been hard, especially in the beginning. I'm glad she could turn to you when she needed to."

"She didn't do it all that often. But yes, there were times even the famed Ice needed comfort." She smiled knowingly at me. "I suspect that's true even to this day."

I made sure my answering smile gave away little and she nodded in acknowledgement.

"So, is there a special occasion for this lovely little gift?" she finally asked, tone rich with innocence.

I couldn't stop my blush from rising this time. This day was an anniversary of sorts for me, as well as for Ice, though she probably didn't think the date significant. It was a year ago to this very date that I had helped the inmate team beat the guards in softball, and a year ago this very date that Ice and I made love for the first time. It was something that was very important and special to me, but damned if I was going to give Corinne the satisfaction of knowing that. Instead, I simply looked at her and silently pleaded the Fifth.

She smirked at me, but decided against pursuing the issue. Instead, she went back to the work her curiosity over my package had interrupted. Silence descended over the library once again.

Several hours later, the time for dinner had finally arrived and, like a schoolchild on the last moment of the last day of school, I shot out of my seat the second the clock struck 5pm. Corinne laughed knowingly as, in my excitement, I almost batted my prize off the table, just managing with quick reflexes, to save it from falling to the floor.

I shot her a glare, but my heart wasn't really in it. It was with a certain tall, dark woman who, that very moment, should have been closing up shop and on her way to a rendezvous with me in the cafeteria.

After waving quickly to Corinne, I grabbed my package and slipped out of the library, striding as quickly as I could down the hallway while still trying to look like I wasn't striding quickly down the hallway. Not an easy task, let me tell you.

The prison square was filled with a sea of orange as inmates fresh from their daily labors bustled to and fro, some on their way, like I was, to the cafeteria, others congregating in small groups near the walls, and still others headed for points unknown. The incoherent babble of voices was loud to my ears as my eyes sought out a dark head that towered over the rest.

Not seeing her with the first visual sweep, I swallowed a pang of minor disappointment and headed toward the cafeteria, figuring to meet her there. As I was almost to the doors, a large hand clasped my elbow and I whirled. My pleased, welcoming grin faded as I looked up into Sandra's hazel eyes.

"Hi, Angel," she said, "I'm glad I caught up with you. Can you come with me for a second, please?"

I opened my mouth to protest, but then thought better of it. Regardless of our seeming friendship, she *was* a guard and I was a prisoner under her control. So instead I nodded as she released her grip on my arm.

"It'll just take a moment," she assured me.

I looked around vainly one last time before turning to follow her back the way I'd come, my bright hopes for the evening starting to dim just the slightest bit.

She led me through the crowded square, past the guard room, and down toward the visitors' room, which was closed for the evening. Turning left just before the visitors' room, she led me down a shorter hallway toward a guarded exit door. Though this was another area of the prison where I'd never been before, I knew where that particular door led and my steps slowed almost to stopping.

Not noticing my hesitancy, Sandra continued down the hallway and spoke in low tones to the guard stationed there before turning to me. Her look of expectancy turned to one of puzzlement when she saw me still standing at the end of the hall. She beckoned me closer.

"Um…if it's all the same to you, Sandra, I'd kinda like to know what it is you need from me out there?" All sorts of warnings were jangling through my head. Sandra might have been the head guard, but even she had to report to Morrison, who most likely wasn't too happy about my successes in the possible appeal department. If I were to be released some time down the road, a very large card the warden was holding against Ice would disappear right along with me.

As if she divined my thoughts, Sandra's look of impatience softened to one of compassion as she smiled and walked back over to where I was standing with what I'm sure was a 'deer in the headlights' look on my face. She laid a gentle hand on my shoulder. "Angel, there's nothing funny about this, I promise you. I just need your advice on something. It won't take more than a minute."

I looked in her eyes, not finding even a trace of deceit within their depths. Still, I'd learned my lessons the hard way and wasn't about to easily repeat past mistakes, especially if they could wind up getting me injured or worse. "Can you at least tell me what's going on?"

"I know this doesn't sound all that great, but it really is easier if I show you." Then she smiled. "Tell you what. All you have to do is stand next to Barbara right here at the door. I can show you what I need to outside and if it seems safe to you, you can join me, alright?"

I looked over at the other guard, who nodded reassuringly to me. After a long moment, and against my better judgement, I nodded back.

Sandra grinned and squeezed my shoulder before turning back to the guard and getting her to unlock the door. It opened inward slowly and I got a quick glimpse of the fenced in area before Sandra's body obscured my view as she stepped outside into the warm summer air.

The sunlight streamed back in as she walked further away from the door and up the short wooden steps to the door of what I knew was the conjugal visit trailer. I watched as she inserted a key into the lock and pulled the door slowly open, peeking her head inside as she did so. After a second, she pulled back and, to my great astonishment, Ice's head replaced hers in the doorway. Smiling almost sheepishly at me, Ice jerked her head back, beckoning me on.

A thousand scenarios rushed through my mind, none of them good. Keeping with my brutally honest tone here, I must admit that my first thought, given Ice's unexpected location, was that Donita was also in the trailer with her and that they'd chosen this relatively private place to finally tell me that they had rekindled their romance. A huge part of me denied this thought, but insecurity can be a harsh master and right now, it was controlling my emotions. I froze where I was, trying to decide whether to go forward and have my worst fears confirmed, or run as far and as fast as I could to hide from the truth that my fanciful mind had conjured from thin air.

Sandra turned, smiling and waving. *Damn them*, I thought. *Damn them all to hell. How can they be laughing when my heart's breaking?* When the second guard, Barbara, murmured "Go ahead, Angel," from right next to me, I almost ripped her eyes out.

Then, forcing the more adult side to my personality to the forefront, I squared my shoulders, swallowed painfully, raised my chin, and stepped outside. Walking those few yards from the prison to the trailer was one of the most difficult things I've ever had to do.

Consciously releasing my clenched fists as I walked up the rickety wooden steps, I brushed by Sandra without looking at her, and stepped, with a firm tread, into the small trailer. As I slipped into the cool interior, my eyes did a quick, accusatory scan, slowly adjusting to the dim lighting within. The trailer was otherwise empty, though I didn't rule out my erstwhile lawyer hiding out in the bathroom, such were the turbulence of my thoughts at that moment.

When I looked back to Ice, really *seeing* her for the first time since I'd entered the trailer, my mouth opened wide in shock. Gone was her customary prison jumpsuit. In its place was a deep blue robe that looked like it was made of silk on satin. It had bold golden embroidery on the cuffs and sash, and ended at mid calf. In the 'V' of the robe, I could see a lighter blue camisole in a sheer but not *quite* revealing material that stopped just at the swell of her magnificent breasts. Her hair was glossy clean and loose as it fell across her shoulders. Her legs and feet were bare and one hand cupped a single red rose, which she held out to me, smiling gently.

Taking a step closer, I tried to blink away my tears. "Ice? What...?"
"Happy Anniversary, Angel."

I took the rose and brought it to my nose while cupping my hand over my mouth to stifle the sob that was waiting to come out. As I inhaled the delicate, wonderful fragrance, I damned myself for seventeen kinds of fool for believing that Ice's feelings for me were somehow shallow and convenient until something better happened along.

Resolving not to ruin the moment with my histrionics, I pushed all negative emotions to the back of my mind and resolved to enjoy the precious gift I'd been given. My self-chastisement was further halted by an embarrassed clearing of the throat and when I turned to the door, I saw Sandra standing half in and half out of the trailer, her face darkened by a blush.

"I think I'll leave you guys alone now. Have fun." With a smile and a wink, she turned and left the trailer, locking the door carefully behind her.

I looked over Ice, who was still smiling at me, though her eyes were full of questions. "Is this…alright?" she asked, a rare note of hesitancy clear in her voice.

"It's *perfect*," I babbled, "just…god it's absolutely wonderful."

"Then why are you crying?" she asked softly, not moving from her place beside the small table set into one of the walls.

"God, I'm just…it's…I'm happy," I finally ground out. *And bewildered. And embarrassed. And so totally in love with you that I think my heart's about to burst.*

Cocking her head, she looked at me. "Are you sure?"

Placing the rose down on the table, I ran into her arms, wrapping myself around her and squeezing tight. "I'm sure. One hundred percent, absolutely, positively, heart swelling sure."

She engulfed me in her embrace, laying a gentle kiss to my hair. "Good. I'm glad." I could feel her sigh against my chest. "I remember once you mentioned that you'd give anything just to be able to spend one night together. I figured that you didn't really mean spending it in an infirmary with burns and smoke inhalation, so I thought this up."

Stunned, I pulled away. "You mean we have this *all night*?!"

Smiling, she nodded. "Yup. It's all ours, so to speak, till noon tomorrow."

"*God* I love you!" I exclaimed, pressing her to me once again. Her low, rumbling laugh vibrated through my ear and put an answering grin on my own lips. I inhaled again, smelling something beyond the scent of the rose and Ice's warm, intoxicating presence. Opening my eyes once again, I peered down on the table, which was covered with a variety of instantly recognizable white boxes. I pulled away, astonished. "You got Chinese?"

Ice laughed again. "Best I could do under the circumstances. Hope you don't mind Kung Pao chicken."

"Are you kidding? I *love* Chinese food!" Truth be known, after three years of barely recognizable prison fare, Ice could have served dog food on a stick and I probably would have been happy.

"Good." When she pulled away, I detected a slight blush of color on her cheeks as she looked to the bed. "I thought you might be comfortable in something other than your uniform for the evening, so…."

Following her gaze to the bed, I gasped out loud. There, colors bold against the clean white sheets of the bed, lay a shimmering forest green floor-length robe. Next to it lay a beautiful dressing gown with spaghetti straps and a demure neckline in a lighter shade of green that deepened to aquamarine near the hemline, which was also floor-length.

Walking over to the bed, I reached out a shaking hand to brush against the fabric, feeling the exquisite softness against my fingers. A tear dripped from my face to land, sparkling, on the silken fabric. I brushed it away, then picked up the dressing gown, holding it against my body and watching the highlights shimmer down its length. I turned wide eyes back to her. "This is so beautiful, Ice!"

She gave me a little cockeyed grin. "I'm glad you like it. If…you wanna try it on or anything, the bathroom's right off that little alcove over there."

I tracked her pointing finger, spotting a half-shadowed doorway sitting to the right of the main room. "Yeah, I'd like that a lot. Be back in a minute." Lifting the robe from its place on the bed, I made my way to the bathroom, closing the door behind me.

The bathroom was well appointed for being in such a relatively tiny trailer. It even had a small stand-up shower that looked much cleaner than the shower in the prison. "Oooh," I whispered to my reflection in the small mirror over the sink, "I think I'm gonna take advantage of *this* situation too!"

Quickly stripping out of my jumpsuit, I reached into the stall and turned on the shower. Surprise of surprises, there was actually hot (well, tepid might be a better adjective here) water coming from the showerhead! Stepping in quickly, I grabbed the new bar of soap and proceeded to take my first warm water shower in over three years. I was in heaven.

After loitering about for a bit, I finally shut off the water and stepped out into the cooler air of the bathroom, grabbing a large, fluffy bath towel and drying myself off with alacrity. One of the good things about having short hair is that drying is a comparative breeze, and so with a thorough toweling and a bit of finger-combing, I was set.

Taking in a deep breath, I held up the gown, pressing the soft, shimmering fabric against my face and inhaling the clean, fresh aroma while feeling the smoothness glide against my cheeks. I groaned in sensual pleasure before pulling it away and slipping it over my head to let it fall, in soft waves, down my body. It was a perfect fit, but I didn't stop to ponder how Ice could have known that.

Settling the straps over my shoulders, I chanced a look in the mirror, awed to stillness by the image looking back at me. Gone was the scared little girl that had come into the Bog three short years ago. In her place stood the woman I'd become with the experience. The color of the gown deepened the green of my eyes, making them somehow wiser and more knowing. The maturity came across in my short, tousled hair and the new lines of experience painting my face. The gown's straps sat smoothly on my newly muscled shoulders, which bore the weight of my world without complaint.

Yet still, I felt somehow a fairy tale princess all done up in silk and satin. As I pulled the robe on over me, letting the cool fabric slide sensually over my bare arms, I smiled, feeling pampered and cared for and very much loved.

Taking a deep breath, I smoothed the fabric over my body, then opened the door and stepped out into the main room of the small trailer.

Ice was sitting behind the table, her long fingers drawing what I was sure were abstract designs on the Formica. When she saw me, her eyes widened to my secret delight and she gracefully came to her feet, her own clothes shifting with her movement in a most pleasing way. A smile softened the angles of her face and lit her blue eyes from within. She was, at that moment as in many others past and future, the most beautiful thing I had ever seen.

She echoed my sentiments, holding an arm out toward me. "You're so beautiful, Angel," she almost-whispered. "Like your namesake, come to earth."

I stepped toward her, grasping her hand, which she lifted to her lips, brushing a soft kiss against my knuckles. Then she escorted me to the other side of the table, where she pulled out the chair and aided me into it with flawless grace and impeccable manners. I had never been treated with such care before and I must confess that I reveled in the attentions.

Walking over to the other side of the table, she bent down slightly and retrieved a tall bottle and a couple of glasses. "Champagne," she said, turning the label toward my sight. "Not the best vintage in the world, but beggars can't be choosers, and all that." Popping the cork, she filled both glasses with the bubbling, amber liquid, then handed one to me across the table. "Cheers," she said, raising her class to softly clink against mine.

I took a sip of the liquor, feeling it tingle as it washed down my throat. Not being a champagne connoisseur, I couldn't tell if it was supposed to taste that way or not, but it was good as far as I was concerned. I grinned over the rim of my glass as Ice set her own down and proceeded to open up the white cartons. Intoxicating aromas wafted up on the steam that escaped its confinement, making my mouth water and my stomach chime in its opinion.

Two chipped, but clean, stoneware plates received their bounty and Ice passed one over to me, together with a set of chopsticks and a cellophane-wrapped package of plastic utensils. I smiled and set the plastic-ware aside, having developed the skill of eating with chopsticks when I was still quite young.

Not much was said over dinner. The food was delicious and I appreciated it as only a prisoner or a college student can. My taste buds tingled their thanks as my mind busily recorded every nuance of the flavors hitting my palate for future remembrance.

When my stomach finally rebelled against having even another morsel packed inside, I pushed my plate away and leaned contentedly back in my chair, patting my belly and grinning at nothing. Surely royal feasts hadn't been as well appreciated as was this simple dinner.

Ice, who had finished long before me, picked up the plates and stacked them in the tiny sink that shared space on the wall with the table. When she turned back to me, she had something else in her hands that was neither food nor drink.

Stepping around the table, she presented it to me with a smile that was almost shy. I took it, open mouthed with awe. In my hands was a tiny bonsai tree carefully and wonderfully shaped into an angel. Tied around the miniature trunk was a tiny yellow ribbon of the type used when loved ones are far from home.

Tears, those ever-present distorters of my vision, sprung once again to my eyes as I looked on the gift she'd created for me. "My God, Ice," I blubbered through a throat choked with tears, "this is so beautiful! Thank you so much!"

"Do you like it?"

"God, I love it! It's wonderful!" I carefully turned the ceramic planter holding the tree, looking at the exquisite artistry from all angles. It was absolutely perfect. "You have such a wonderful talent, Ice."

I was *sure* I caught an embarrassed blush that time and I grinned, partly to put her at ease and, I'll confess, partly in happiness at having finally caught the normally unflappable Ice with her proverbial pants down. "You do, you know," I said, finally. "It's a gift. One you should treasure as much as I do." Carefully setting the tree down, I captured the hands that had created such beauty and urged her down, capturing her full lips with a kiss of thanks that quickly turned to something deeper and more primal.

After several moments, she pulled away and cupped my cheek, smiling down at me, her eyes sparkling and warmed from within. "I love you, Angel."

"I love you too, Ice. So very much." I reached under the chair where I'd stowed my own gift and handed it to her. "This is something for you, obviously." I felt my own shy smile spread my lips.

Taking the package, she carefully pried open the folds and slipped the book from its paper confinement. Her smile lit up her whole face as she looked at the object in her hands, opening it almost reverently. Her look became one of shock when she saw the author's signature on the front leaf. Her wide eyes met mine and I knew that I'd done alright.

"He's *never* signed his work," she breathed softly, disbelieving.

I shrugged modestly, though my pleased grin told the real story. "I got lucky."

"I'll say. This is fantastic!"

"I'm glad you like it." I scratched at the back of my neck. "Um…I'm not sure if you read Russian."

"Oh, I do." Flipping quickly through the pages and smiling like a child on Christmas morning, she carefully closed the book and set it down on the table, then reached down and clasped my hands, bearing me to my feet and into the circle of her arms.

She engulfed me in a hug, lowering her head so that her lips just brushed against my ear. A shivering tingle shot all the way down to my toes as she murmured a phrase I knew had to be in Russian. Though the language was guttural to my ears, her low, purring voice galvanized me.

"What . . .what did you just say?"

"'I want to make love to you, my sweet Angel. May I?'" she translated, capturing my earlobe between her lips and teasing her tongue along my flesh in slow, sensual strokes.

My knees turned to pudding.

She chuckled low in my ear as her strong arms easily bore my weight. "Is that a yes?" she teased.

"Oh, you betcha."

Somehow, I managed to regain the strength in my legs and stood up tall. Ice smiled down at me, her teeth flashing in the dim lighting. I felt a slight tug, and when I looked down, I found that Ice had untied the belt to my robe. Her hands were warm as they slid within the parted fabric to rest gently on my hips.

Her head slowly lowered until her lips met mine in an explosion of warmth and desire. Her hands roamed over my hips and downward, grabbing the mounds of my backside and pulling me into her body, melding us as we kissed.

Her fragrance was intoxicating as my starved senses pulled it in on uneven, panting breaths.

I pulled away just enough to untie her robe, then slid my hands inside the folds of the garment, needing to feel her body beneath my palms and fingers. My bold exploration revealed a waist-length camisole and French-cut briefs, both in the finest of silks. I nearly died of wanting her, my need was so intense.

We finally broke off the kiss by mutual consent and I looked up into eyes darkened and half-lidded with arousal. The tip of her tongue peeked out to taste her lips and I found myself tightening at the sight.

Her large, gentle hands with their tapering fingers reached up and slipped the thin straps from my shoulders, laying intimate caresses to my bared flesh as she stared deeply into my eyes.

My own hands joined the ballet, grasping the hem of her camisole and lifting upwards. I broke our gazes as my hungry eyes feasted on each inch of flesh revealed to me as the incredibly soft fabric slid away.

Her hands came away from me as she lifted her arms above her head, aiding me in my task. Her breasts became exposed to my ravenous gaze and I licked my lips at the sight of them. When I could go no higher, given the vast difference in our heights, she took over and pulled the top off, shaking her hair free in a totally unconscious gesture that threatened to take my legs out from under me once again.

I had to have her. That very minute. I could no more stop the raging in my blood than I could stop a flood with my bare hands.

Placing my hands on her hips, I guided her backwards until the edge of the bed bumped against her calves. I kept pushing, lowering her to the bed, and then onto her back. Releasing her, I took a step back, admiring the artistry before me. The white of the sheets and the white of her briefs stood out in a sort of stark purity against the deep tan of her skin and the raven black of her hair which fanned out across the pillow in turbulent waves. The dichotomy was intoxicating.

Taking a deep breath to restore a modicum of equilibrium, I slid my own gown off slowly, teasing her as she had always teased me. Her gaze was rapt upon me. I could see her nostrils flare in the semi-darkness. I grinned wildly.

Finally I stood naked before her, swearing that I could feel trails of fire where her scorching gaze lit upon my flesh. I started to tremble as I felt a dampness between my legs which had nothing to do with the sweat that suddenly broke out across my body.

Stepping up to the bed, I crawled aboard, straddling Ice briefly before coming to rest between her body and the cool wall behind me.

I managed to pull myself up to sit cross-legged on the narrow bed, my knees just brushing against the warm, soft flesh of Ice's side. I looked into her eyes again, catching the slightest hint of a vulnerability that hadn't been there before. It filled my heart to overflowing.

I tracked down her body one more time before meeting her eyes and locking in, smiling softly. "I love you, Morgan," I whispered, reaching out a finger and brushing it across her lips. She pursed them slightly, kissing my finger, before relaxing them into a smile that matched my own.

My finger traced across her lips once more, then outlined her sharp cheekbones before smoothing against her expressive brows and up to her high forehead, brushing the fringe of hair back from her brow. My touch was gentle and undemanding and filled with as much love and devotion as I could possibly give.

I traced around the delicate shell of one ear, my smile deepening as I saw a shiver make its way down her long body in the periphery of my vision.

I had fallen into the clear ocean of her eyes and could not break away if my life depended on it. I saw so many emotions running through those eyes. It was as if I were seeing into the soul her body held in its keeping.

My fingers continued their meandering journey as I mapped out her body by touch alone, my eyes only for her eyes, our breath coming together. I slid down the strong, elegant column of her neck, tracing over corded tendons and skimming over a pulsepoint, which bounded out a welcome.

Her shoulders were next, and then the warm, moist valley between her breasts. Her eyes darkened more as I brushed against the sensitive underside of first one, then the other, feeding me her emotions through the intensity of her stare.

I circled nipples that were hard and straining for my touch, brushing over them ever so lightly and watching her lips part as a single, almost silent, sigh escaped from between them.

I traced lower, over the soft down that covered her belly, rising and falling over the bands of muscle girding her torso.

My hand reached the lace band of her briefs and her chest expanded with the sudden breath she took. I dipped a finger teasingly beneath the fabric, running it along the seam from one hip to the other and then back again.

Removing my finger, I continued my journey downward, skimming over the silken material until my hand moved to cup over her. Her thighs spread involuntarily, and when my fingers slid over the smooth, hot, wet curve of her body, her hips jerked as she moaned, sharing her pleasure through her heated gaze.

I could feel her readiness through the silk of her briefs and I hummed in anticipation of what I was about to do.

My finger dipped in again, though this time it was beneath the band of her right leg. A sound almost like a whimper came from her lips as I came closer to the place we both needed me to be.

God, she was so wet and open that I almost passed out from the hunger of needing to possess this gift beyond price.

I painted my fingers in her desire, never once breaking the lock of our gazes, the look of her pleasure tearing through me like a wildfire. Her eyes glowed with an inner light, sucking me in deeper against my conscious will. With every stroke of my finger, I felt as if the touch were upon me as well and my body responded, helplessly pulled into the tide of her want.

I entered her quickly, helpless to do anything else, and she hissed out a breath as her hips responded to my thrust, bucking up against my hand, impaling herself further while capturing me and holding me close.

Together we worked into a rhythm, staring so deeply into one another's eyes that it was as if we were but one soul sharing two bodies, both of which were aflame with need.

"Yes," I breathed as I watched her climb the peak of our mutual creation.

Her eyes grew heavy lidded.

"Don't close your eyes. Don't shut me out. Share with me. Please." I used my voice in tandem with our shared movements, bringing her up and setting her free to soar.

She fed me her climax through open eyes which drilled into me and took me with her on her flight to the heavens. My whole world became the blue sky above and the sea below with nothing else from horizon to horizon. It was a soul-shattering experience; her vulnerability and total openness to me in that bright second the most precious gift I'd ever been given.

As our breathing began to steady, I noticed that the vast blue ocean had prismed with tears. My heart jumped up in my throat and I tucked down close to her, gathering her in my arms and sprinkling her face with tiny kisses. "Oh no, don't cry. Oh, god, please don't cry, Ice."

She didn't make a sound. Sobs didn't shudder through her body. Her tears were silent ones. But she responded to my fervent embrace, holding me almost convulsively as the tears scalded the skin of my neck.

After a long, silent moment, the world whirled around me and I felt myself pressed flat on my back, pinned in place by six feet of aroused and passionate prisoner. Her mouth met mine without gentleness and I tasted the salty tang of tears on her lips as her tongue deftly wove its way around mine.

There was an urgency to her movements as I felt her reach down and jerk the briefs from her hips. When she settled back down against me, straddling my leg, I groaned aloud at the heated moisture liberally coating my thigh.

Ice grunted in reply, her hand sliding quickly down my body, her weight shifting slightly so that my thighs parted wider beneath her. Her fingers worked their way between our sweat-glued bodies as she continued to kiss me with a feral, primal intensity that might have been frightening if it hadn't been so arousing.

She pulled her lips from mine at the same time she entered me, burying her face in my hair and groaning as she thrust deeply into me, using the weight and motion of her entire body to add power to her movements.

I gasped as I was suddenly filled, squeezing my eyes tight against the invasion, moaning deep in my throat with the pressure and feel of her long fingers stroking and thrusting against me.

Sweat liberally coated our bodies, making us slide against one another in an effortless, erotic dance. Ice kept tempo with her soft grunts in my ear. My moaning entreaties added a melody line. My heartbeat was loud in my ear. Her murmuring, first soft, now guttural, even louder.

Her strokes became long and hard as she bucked against me, rucking the sheet up under my shoulderblades and knocking the pillow to the floor of the tiny trailer.

I urged her on, wanting, *needing* more. Always more. I was so close. I could see the precipice painted on the inside of my eyelids.

She responded instantly, surging into me, her whole body in motion. Her soft grunts gave way to sharp pants and I knew she was nearing the edge. At what seemed the very last second, she slid another finger into me, stretching me wide, filling me completely.

I knew the second she went over. Her body shuddered down its sweating length and her hand convulsed, claw-like, within me as her sharp teeth sunk into the muscle of my shoulder. I cried out.

Her fingers pressed hard against the very spot I needed them to be and I took off like a rocket, my own wracking shudders all the more sweet for being subdued beneath the weight of her heavy, muscled body.

With a last, low, protracted growl, she slumped full on me, her breath gasping out against the sweat-soaked skin of my neck.

Pleasant spasms continued to spark through me as the motion of her breathing caused her now limp fingers to move deep within me, touching off tingles of sensation that rose to the crown of my head and fell to the tips of my toes.

I sighed out my bliss and she responded by nuzzling closer, kissing the mark she'd made on my shoulder before burrowing into the fall of my hair and cleaning the sweat from my neck with long, languid strokes of her tongue.

"Oh, sweet...*Jesus*," I whimpered as her fingers withdrew from me to move up and caress the slickness, stroking me gently, but with a surety that was intoxicating to my befuddled senses. I turned my head, needing desperately to connect with her.

She latched on to my lips, kissing me with a tenderness that was the antithesis of our previous coupling, yet no less arousing because of it.

Shifting again, she came up onto all fours, straddling my hips with her knees planted on either side, all without breaking the heart-stopping kiss or her tender, erotic stroking.

In a show of supreme control, she lifted her free hand from its place beside my head, and captured my hand, sliding it down her drenched torso to where she was all heated openness for me. Releasing my hand to continue on its own path, she collapsed down on her elbow again, moaning softly into my open mouth as I explored her softness.

I mirrored her movements against me as best I could. I must tell you, though, it was very hard. She seemed to have my entire body under her seductive control. I felt like a marionette in a puppet-show for adults.

I stopped trying so hard and gave my hand free rein. When she gasped and surged against me, I knew my instincts had been correct. I didn't have time to gloat, however, as her touches turned more insistent and coaxing.

My own sounds of pleasure filled the cool night air.

The end came quickly. We were both too ready for it. I climaxed first and she positioned herself over me so that she could get what she needed from me during that eternal minute of blinding passion.

When it was over, she came to lie between me and the wall. With ease, she turned my pliant, nerveless body so that my back was to her chest. Slipping one arm around my waist, she tugged slightly till we fit snugly together as two pieces of a human puzzle. "I love you, my Angel," she whispered, laying a kiss to the back of my neck.

"I love you too, Ice," I mumbled, shivering with warmth as she nuzzled against my neck.

Within seconds, we fell asleep, spooned against one another, spending the first night ever lying in one another's arms.

My dream had come true.

✿   ✿   ✿   ✿

I awoke the next morning to the sound of a heart beating steadily in my ear and the feel of gentle fingers tracing abstract patterns on my back. I blinked my eyes open to find gentle blues centered on my face. Ice smiled. "Morning."

I yawned, arching my back in a stretch. "Morning. What time is it?"

Her head tilted as she looked over to the clock hanging over the sink. "Almost eight. Sleep well?"

Yawning again, I dropped my head back down on Ice's warm chest with a thud. "Best three hours of sleep I ever had."

Her chuckle rumbled through my ear, vibrating against my whole body.

We had woken up twice more during the night to make love. The second time had been near dawn. If the trailer had had windows, I would have loved to watch the sun rise with her, but since there were no windows, we performed our own little ritual.

Ice's gentle touch against my back was making me sleepy again. "Mmm. I had the most wonderful dream."

"Oh yeah?"

"Yeah. You and I were sitting on the porch of my cabin by the lake, watching the sun set over the water. I could smell the pines in the breeze and we listened as the crickets and bullfrogs came out to play. It was wonderful."

I could feel Ice stiffen beneath me as her heart picked up its rhythm. I slumped, damning myself for fifteen kinds of fool. *Why did you have to say anything, Angel? You've just ruined the morning. Way to go, kid.*

But Ice relaxed again, her hand picking up where it had left off, tracing over the lines of muscle and bone in my back. "Sounds like a nice dream."

When I looked up, I caught that look of almost infinite sadness in her eyes once again and in that moment I would have given up anything, even my chance at freedom, even my chance at loving her, to take it away forever.

I blinked and the look was gone, pushed down to whatever hell the demons of her soul resided in. "I'm sorry," I whispered.

Her smile was as sad as her eyes had been moments ago. "Don't be. Dreams, sometimes, are the only thing that makes this place bearable."

And again, the next question came out of my mouth without my permission. "Do you dream?"

"Sometimes."

"About what?"

"Nothing as nice as yours. Mostly about those I've hurt or killed. Their families."

"Those aren't dreams, Ice. Those are nightmares."

I could feel her shrug beneath me. "Nothing more than what I deserve."

I sighed. "Ice, I told you this before. Guilt can be a good thing. It can stop you from repeating mistakes. But you can't let it rule your life. If you do, you'll never be able to live it."

"That's easy to say, Angel. It's a whole lot harder to do."

"I know."

"You *have* given me something, though."

"I have?"

"Yes. Hope. That one day I'll find another way of dealing with my anger. That I won't become that person I was before I met you." Her smile was brighter as she ruffled my sleep-tousled hair. "You really are my Angel, ya know."

She sealed her words with a kiss.

🔑   🔑   🔑   🔑

When the knock finally came to put an end to our wonderful day, we were ready, packages in hand, orange jumpsuits once again covering our bodies.

I felt tired, pleasantly sore, and deliriously happy. We'd made love again before slipping off to the shower. The tight quarters, and resulting close press of our bodies, sparked our passions once more until it was all I could do to breathe, let alone think about moving.

Finally, we prodded ourselves to get dried and dressed. The packing came next. The clothing would be kept with our other personal effects in the huge storage room next to the warden's office. My new piece of bonsai art, since I couldn't keep it in my cell, would reside in the library where I could look at it daily. Ice promised to teach me how to care for it myself.

Keys slipped in the lock and the knob turned. Bright sunlight filtered in, causing us both to wince at the change from the dimness of the trailer. Sandra greeted us both with a friendly smile. I smiled gratefully back, beyond happy with her part in this wonderful experience for me.

Taking our clothing and tucking it under her arm, Sandra led us back down the fenced walkway and into the prison proper. After stepping inside the musty building, the door guard patted us both down, then Sandra escorted us down the long hallway and into the main square.

The sounds of talking and the quick rush of bodies was almost overwhelming after our short interlude in the trailer. I blinked, trying to get my bearings once again.

A noise started off to my left, low, then gaining in volume and pitch until I wondered, blankly, who had let a bird into the prison. Then I saw a flash of orange and white and stepped back, almost dropping the bonsai tree as Cassandra came running toward me, her mouth opened wide in a hideous screech while her manacled arms and legs jangled from the weight of the chains.

I stood there, dumbly wondering how she move so quickly, bound as she was, before I was shunted hard to the right as Ice's long body smoothly interposed itself between me and the screaming banshee heading toward us.

Normally, I might, at some level, have resented the protective stance Ice took, knowing that I could now well take care of myself. But Cassandra was, as they say, a whole different kettle of fish and I accepted the protection of her strong back gratefully.

I was pushed further away as Sandra dumped the clothing in her arms into the grip of the door guard and moved to stand next to Ice, protecting me further from the impending explosion of blonde, insane fury that was headed our way.

Cassandra kept coming, her fisted hands held chest high as her screech continued unabated, it seemed. Startled prisoners automatically stepped aside to let her pass as her guards tore across the square after her, red faced and huffing.

Ice took a long step forward, neatly intercepting the enraged woman. Cassandra pounded my lover's chest with her manacled hands, screaming obscenities in an abnormally high voice.

From what I could gather, both my ancestry and what I might have done for a living prior to being incarcerated here were being called into question. Then, her head turned, insanely sparkling chocolate eyes meeting mine and I was left with no doubts. "You're *dead*, little Angel. You're nothing but a little *whore* who's tempted my precious Ice away from her path with *me*. I'll see you in Hell, Angel. Hell! Do you hear me?!"

Though I was well protected by both Sandra and Ice, I couldn't help the fear that ran through me at her screamed invectives. If there was anyone in the prison who could easily carry out her threats, Cassandra was that person. Still, I captured the fear deep within me, determined not to give her the satisfaction of knowing she had slipped past my defenses.

The other two guards caught up to Cassandra finally, grabbing her around her skinny waist and shoulders and yanking her hard away from Ice. She refused to relinquish her grip and there was a loud tearing sound as Ice's jumpsuit began to give up the ghost under the pressure of her insane strength.

Ice lifted her hands. grabbing Cassandra's manacled wrists. Jabbing her thumbs over the sensitive nerves just under the skin, she forced Psycho's grip loose and the screaming woman was pulled fully away, hissing and spitting like a feral cat in a hunter's net.

"Call the hospital," Sandra shouted to be heard over Cassandra's howling. "I think it's time for her shot." After the women dragged her away, the guard turned to me, concern in her eyes. "Are you alright?"

"Wha—? Oh, yeah. Fine." I let out a shaky little laugh. "I guess I should be flattered, huh? Looks like I've become Public Enemy Number One with her."

Sandra patted my shoulder. "God willing, she'll be in the hospital for more than twenty-four hours this time. When she gets back here, we'll keep an extra close eye on her." *Like you did just now?* I almost said aloud before thinking better of it. In a way, Cassandra was like a greased pig at the county fair. It seemed almost impossible to keep her from doing something once she had her mind set on it. I'd just have to keep an eye out and protect myself as best I could. "Thanks," I said finally.

Ice turned, not bothering to hold together the jumpsuit which had been totally rent at the chest. I found my eyes drawn to the swell of her bare breasts just visible in the 'V' of the parted fabric. "Sorry about that," she said in a low voice, totally unselfconscious.

"Hey, no problem. She didn't almost rip *my* clothes off, after all."

Ice looked down at her exposed cleavage, then back up at me, and shrugged. Her gaze was intent as it locked into mine.

I smiled. "I'm fine. Really. Between you, the Amazons, Corinne and the guards, I've got more eyes on me than a rotten potato."

Ice screwed her face up at my analogy, startling a laugh out of me. Sandra and the door guard joined the levity and soon the fright of Cassandra's murderous threats slipped to the back of my mind.

As soon as the coast was clear, Sandra led us onward to our cells.

Chapter 11

Summer turned to fall, which quickly gave way to winter. Things went on pretty much as usual in the Bog. The gangs remained quiet, leaving the Amazons free to pursue other interests, namely, one another. After their spat, Sonny, who I'd always thought had a thing for the male gender, and Pony began courting one another in an amusingly old fashioned way. And I, being the writer of our little group, was pressed into love-note writing service for them both. I felt like a modern day Cyrano de Bergerac, sans the large nose, but it made the time pass quickly and so I did it with pleasure.

On a Thursday afternoon in the middle of winter, Phyllis came to me in the library telling me I had a phone call. Donita, sounding cool and collected as always, told me she had some news, though wouldn't divulge the topic, and asked to meet with me the next morning. I, of course, agreed.

Needless to say, Thursday night's sleep was all but non-existent.

I spent Friday morning in the visitor's room, twisting the fabric of my jumpsuit into new and interesting abstract shapes while trying to calm my similarly twisting stomach. Finally, the door was unlocked and opened, and my lawyer, impeccably dressed and gorgeous as always, strode in, a sparkle in her eyes.

"Angel," she greeted, grasping my hand warmly, "good to see you again. Come, sit with me at the table. I've got some news."

Soon, we were both seated and sipping at the cool water the guards had so thoughtfully provided (at Donita's pointed request). Opening her briefcase, she pulled out a thick file with my name emblazoned on the cover. "We've got 'em," she said, her smile triumphant.

My heart picked up its pace. "What do you mean, exactly?"

"You're aware of baseball's 'three strikes and you're out' policy?" At my nod, she continued. "We've got three huge strikes here. And when I say huge, I *do* mean huge."

Opening up the folder, she pulled out several pieces of paper and placed the flat on the table, turning them so that I could easily read the text. The first was a simple hotel receipt. I looked at her questioningly.

"You remember your across-the-hall neighbors, the Gracesons? Two of the star witnesses for the prosecution at your trial?"

I nodded again, remembering indeed. Tom and Maggie Graceson had each testified that they had heard me arguing and threatening Peter on the night of his death. I remembered no such argument, but their testimony was compelling, and obviously was believed by the jury. "What about them?"

"Well, if your original attorney, whom I'm seriously considering putting up for disbarment proceedings, had bothered to do just the tiniest amount of research, he would have found out, as I did, that the Gracesons weren't even home on the night your husband died. They were in *this* hotel, participating in something that they probably didn't want to get spread around."

"What do you mean?"

"They're swingers."

"Swingers?" I asked, completely lost. The only swingers I knew were dancers. And even if they weren't very good at it, I didn't see how it would be something embarrassing to them. I said as much.

She grinned at my naïveté. "No, not *that* kind of swinger. The kind where groups of married folks gather around and swap partners. Sexually."

My eyes must have widened to the size of saucers because she covered her mouth over the laugh that came forth.

"Exactly. Apparently, from what I gathered from other members of this particular group, the Gracesons were quite upset because they had asked your husband and you to join them and Peter told them that you had turned him down flat. It seems Tom really liked you, in that special way," she winked, "and Maggie was quite attracted to your husband."

"You're *kidding*!"

"Nope. Do you ever remember a conversation of that nature between yourself and Peter?"

"Not at all! Of course, I would have turned him down if he had asked me, but he never asked."

"I didn't think so. Apparently, on the night of Peter's death, he had told both Tom and Maggie that you'd finally consented to give it a try and that, if they rented a room somewhere, he'd swing by the house and pick you up. Of course, that never happened."

"My God," I breathed. "I can't believe this." I shook my head, my anger building. "They made up testimony about me because they were pissed that Peter stood them up?!"

"That's what it sounds like."

"Unbelievable!"

She laid a calming hand on my wrist as I thought I was about to burst out of my skin with rage. "That's only strike one."

"There's *more?*"

"Oh yes." Moving the hotel receipt out of the way, Donita pushed a white sheet of paper closer to me. It was what looked to be an Emergency Room treatment sheet. "Do you remember this?"

I looked at the date and nodded, remembering the incident.

Peter had come home from work and had tried to get me to go out to the bar with him. When I refused, needing to get up early to get some shopping done before work the next morning, he beat me quite severely, bruising my ribs and giving me a hairline fracture of my eye socket. I had managed to hail a cab which took me to the Emergency Room, convinced I was bleeding internally. Thank God, that hadn't been the case, but I still felt as if I'd been hit by a truck. I remembered telling the ER staff that I had fallen down some stairs. The looks in their eyes told me they didn't believe me but they didn't press the issue. "I remember." I blushed, embarrassed.

"In one of his infrequent bouts of actual competency, your attorney tried to present this as evidence of Peter's abuse of you. The prosecution, for whatever reason, argued it as irrelevant and the judge agreed to have it suppressed."

I sighed. "I told them I fell down some stairs," I mumbled to the table.

"Yes, I know. It's in the report. But look at the last paragraph."

Pulling the sheet closer to me, I peered at the writing. Apparently, I had been right. The treating physician *did* believe that I was the victim of a beating and he further believed that it was done at the hands of my husband. I looked up at Donita. "Why didn't he ever say anything to me?"

"That I don't know. But it's a law that when a member of the medical staff believes there has been abuse involved, he or she *must* report it to the proper authorities, no matter what the victim says or doesn't say."

"Did he do that?"

"Yes, he did. He filled out the proper forms and sent them to the proper agency."

"But no one ever contacted me about it."

"No, they didn't. My investigator followed up this lead and found that it had never been researched. They had everything they needed to open an investigation. They just never did."

"But why not?"

"I'm afraid I don't know the answer to that either. But the thing here is, Angel, that, by rights, this piece of evidence should never have been suppressed. Even if no abuse could be proven, at the very least, the treating physician should have been called to the stand to state what he found. This document shows that there was at least a possibility that you were telling the truth when you said your husband abused you. It would have gone a long way in helping you prove your case."

I put my head in my hands, my sigh fogging up what little varnish was left on the elderly table. "This is just so bizarre."

"Ready for the kicker?"

I lifted up my head to meet her eyes. "Yeah. Might as well."

"A member of your jury, its foreman, in fact, was a man by the name of Robert Cort."

"I'm sorry, that name doesn't ring any bells."

"I didn't think it would. My investigator went to some of the bars your husband used to hang out in and found that this same man was one of Peter's drinking buddies."

"Please tell me you're joking, Donita."

"Nope. And that's a good thing. You see, when my investigator talked to some of the bar's other patrons, he was told that on the night after Peter's murder, Robert swore that he was going to find a way to get on your jury and, quote 'convict that bitch' unquote."

"He *what*?!"

"That's what the witnesses say. We've got sworn statements from four of them. We don't yet know how he managed to get into the pool of potential jurors, but when we pulled out his sheet, we found out he lied quite convincingly to get in."

"Jesus Christ."

"It gets worse. When we polled the jurors, the only two women on the panel had been convinced of your innocence when they went in for deliberations. They both stated to me, personally, that they were intimidated into changing their votes by the foreman, Robert Cort."

The sound of my hand slamming down on the table was loud in the small room. "Then why didn't they ever *tell* anybody?"

Donita's chocolate eyes were compassionate. "They said they were scared to come forward. So they didn't."

"Why are they talking now?" I couldn't help it. My voice was filled with the bitterness in my heart.

"They've both been eaten away with guilt over it, Angel. They've both given us sworn statements as to what happened and are both willing and ready to testify at a new trial. They know they've made a mistake, but they're willing to try and rectify it."

"Don't they *care* that their *mistake* cost me *four years* of my *life*?!" Tears, scalding and bitter as my words, flooded my eyes and streamed down my cheeks, wetting the table beneath me in a flood of anger.

Donita came around the table and put an arm around my shoulder. Her skin was soft and warm. The light scent of her perfume soothed me even as my mind was a whirling torrent of delayed grief. During the entire four-plus years I'd been a resident of the Bog, I'd never indulged in self-pity over the events that caused me to be here.

But the knowledge that my freedom had been taken away by a combination of an incompetent lawyer, a failed protection system, a bully and two timid women brought all home to me. I couldn't stop my sobs as I thought of what might have been.

A guard, who was keeping tabs on us through the reinforced glass window set into one wall, entered the visitor's room with a box of tissues, which she slid across the table. Donita thanked her pleasantly and the guard nodded, then left. I knew my crying spell would hit the grapevine in less time than it took to write out this sentence.

A dark arm threaded its way through our embrace, handing me a tissue. I swiped my eyes with it, then leaned back and emptied my sinuses, feeling the pressure in my head ease slightly. I felt exhausted. "Sorry about that," I mumbled.

Donita smiled at me. "No need to be sorry. If it had been me, I'd probably have torn this room to shambles." She looked around. "Though to tell you the truth, that might have improved things."

That surprised a laugh out of me and she grinned back, handing me another tissue and discarding the used one in an overflowing wastebasket near the table. I took in a long, shuddering breath, then let it out slowly. "So," I said, tracing my tears on the table, "where do we go from here?"

"Well, I've talked to the DA about dismissing the conviction altogether. But he's a hard-line butt-hole who wears his church pin on his lapel. He won't budge. Convinced they still have a case against you. So I've set up a date to talk to one of the appellate judges in the district. It's in two weeks. I'll present this new evidence and see what he says."

"What do you think he'll say?"

"He'd be crazy not to overturn the conviction, Angel. This evidence is damning. Especially the jury tampering. The DA won't let it go, though. So even if the judge does decide to do what's right and overturn your conviction and sentence, the State will demand a new trial." She laid a hand on my wrist. "What do you think about that? Do you think you can go through that again?"

I looked directly at her, knowing my eyes were intense. "Donita, to get my name cleared of this mess, I'd walk through Hell itself." I looked down at the table again. "It didn't much matter before. Peter was dead. I did it. I thought I deserved punishment. But this…this travesty has changed my whole way of thinking."

Donita smiled. "Ice was right about you." "She was?"

"Yup. She said you were a fighter with the heart of a lion."

I felt my eyes go wide. "Ice said that? About me?"

"Sure did. That's why I agreed to come in and talk to you in the first place. Ice doesn't give out compliments easily you know." Her warm hand squeezed my wrist. "She has a lot of faith in you, Angel. And, she loves you very deeply."

I could feel my blush burn my neck, cheeks and ears as it spread over my face. I ducked my head again. "I love her very much, too."

"I know."

I traced the moisture on the table again. "I'm…um…sorry,…Donita."

"Sorry? For what, Angel?"

My blush deepened. I damned myself for my fair skin. "Ice…um…told me about…um…."

"She told you we were lovers in the past?"

"Yeah. That'd be it."

"And it bothers you because the two of you are together now and I'm here to see it?"

"Yes." If I could have sunk my chair through the ground right then, I would have done it.

Her hand reached out and cupped my chin, bringing our gazes level. "Angel, never apologize for being happy. And never apologize for making Ice happy."

"But…."

"No buts, Angel. Ice is a very important person in my life. To see her as happy as she is makes me very happy. It wasn't meant to be for Ice and I. We both knew that while we were together." She smiled. "Still, in a way, we were a good match. She took great pains to keep her personal life a secret from everyone, including me. Though it shouldn't have been a surprise to find out what I did about her with her arrest, it did. Of course, we never lived together and were never in one another's presence for long stretches of time. Still, I felt a bit guilt-ridden that I missed some kind of sign I should have seen. And, of course, I was very angry."

"I can understand that. I would have been as well."

She spread her hands. "And when she wouldn't let me defend her, well…." She sighed. "It almost ended our friendship." Then she smiled. "I'm glad it didn't. And I'm also glad that it gave me a chance to meet you. You're a good soul, Angel. And there are damn few of those around anymore. So stop worrying and, for God's sake, stop blushing. Everything's fine from that angle, alright?"

Reading the absolute sincerity in her eyes, I nodded. "Thanks."

Donita tipped me a wink. "Not a problem, Angel. Not a problem at all."

Moving away from me, she went around to the other side of the table, stuffed my file into her expensive leather briefcase, and latched it shut before pulling it off the table by the handle. "I'll talk to you in a couple of weeks, if not before, alright? Just try to take it easy and relax. Let me do the worrying for the both of us."

I gave her a half smile, the best I could offer. "I'll try my best."

"You do that. Bye for now."

With a final smile and a wave, she was gone, leaving me alone in the visitors' room with only my tears and my thoughts for company.

🔑   🔑   🔑   🔑

I pulled what we all referred to as "an Ice" and hid out in my cell after finally dragging my exhausted butt from the visitors' room. For some reason, the tears, of frustration, of anger, of grief, just didn't seem to want to stop falling.

Critter came up to talk, but I remained sullen and uncommunicative, and she finally gave up in frustration, leaving me to my enforced solitude.

I must have fallen into a doze of mental exhaustion, because the next thing I knew, my eyes opened to see Ice standing just inside my cell, concern seemingly emanating from her every pore. "You okay?"

I managed a weak smile. "I've been better."

"Wanna talk about it?" she asked from her position by the door.

And suddenly, I did.

Seeing my expression, she closed the distance in a quick stride and lowered herself onto the bed, gathering me into a hug that went a long way toward taking a great deal of my pain away. I pressed my head against her chest and let the tears fall again. Only this time, they seemed to be tears of healing rather than pain.

Ice rocked me gently within her embrace, seeming to know what kind of tears these were. Normally, the sight of my crying distressed her greatly. Now, however, she silently waited out the minor storm, content only to be there for me. It was a quiet strength I relied on more than words could ever articulate.

After several moments, I finally pulled away, wiping my messy face with the back of my sleeve. Then, after a few, deep, hitching breaths, I blurted out the whole tale, leaving nothing out.

Ice's expression became thundery, but I didn't fear it, knowing her anger was directed against those who had harmed me and not at me, myself. She growled in frustration, her fists clenched uselessly against an enemy she knew I would have to handle myself.

"Of course, the good side to all this," I began, gently taking one of her fisted hands and relaxing it into my own, "is that this goes a long way toward assuring me a new trial. This kind of evidence is something that you can't just ignore."

She grunted in agreement.

As I sat there, contemplating my words, the one thought I'd heretofore successfully kept at the very back of my mind demanded to make its presence known. I willed the tears away, but when I turned to look up at Ice, my words were stilled by a finger to my lips.

"Don't," she said, her voice low.

"Don't what?" I murmured around her finger.

"Don't say it. Don't even think it."

"How do you know what I'm thinking?"

"Because I can tell by the expression on your face. You're wondering if you should fight for this opportunity, because if you're successful, and you will be, that means that you'll leave here. And you don't know if you want to do that because of what we have." Her eyes bit into mine, her eyebrow arched, daring me to contradict her.

I couldn't. I blinked, then looked away, flushing guiltily. "You're right," I whispered.

"I know I am. I know you and how you think. And I also know that I'm not going to let you give up this chance for me."

"Not even for us?"

Smiling, she cupped my chin. "Angel, there will always be 'us'. In here, out there, it doesn't matter. You're a part of me, and you always will be, no matter where you are."

I sighed, knowing she was right but still wanting to fight the issue. Trouble was, I didn't have any good ammunition to argue with.

"Angel, you've spent the last four years here trying to get me to see inside myself. You've tried to get me to see that guilt shouldn't rule my actions. That's a hard lesson to learn, and it won't be made any easier if you decide to give up your fight for freedom."

"I don't understand."

"Don't you? If you give up this fight for what's right, this fight for *freedom*, because of me…."

She didn't need to finish her sentence. The meaning was all too clear. Though it would be my own decision whether to stay or fight, if I decided to do the former, she would always feel the guilt of that action.

"So…I guess that means you want me to go for it, huh?"

"Damn right I want you to go for it, Angel. This is your ticket out of this shit-hole. Run with it and don't look back."

After a moment, I gave her a watery smile and thudded my head against her collar-bone. "Alright, coach."

We settled into a comfortable silence that the growling of my abused stomach chose to interrupt. I blushed again as Ice patted it. "Let's go down and feed this monster before the cafeteria closes and you keep all the inmates up tonight with those weird growling noises."

Lazily back handing her on the arm, I allowed her to pull me to my feet. In step, our hips brushing casually against one another, we walked down to the cafeteria to attempt to consume God only knew what.

🔑 🔑 🔑 🔑

The next few weeks went by in a blur that was full of disappointing news. Donita called twice to tell me, each time, that the judge she was scheduled to speak with had other cases that had priority over mine. It was difficult, this 'hurry up and wait' roller coaster ride of emotions I was going through. One minute I was up, ready to take on the world. The next, I was swimming in a sea of depression, shunning everyone. Everyone, even Ice, started to treat me with kid gloves.

As if feeding off my swirling emotions, the prison natives also began to get restless. There was a feeling of increasing tension within the Bog; a tension so thick that even I, who was deep in a morass of my very own, could feel it. It was almost like the time before the riots, when the stress was so thick, you could snip at it with dull scissors if you had a mind to.

Ice was putting in inordinately long hours at the auto shop, going down each day after morning head count and not returning to her cell until shortly before lights out. Apparently, Morrison had struck paydirt in his stolen car racket and was using Ice's special skills to the limit. What little spare time she had, she seemed to want to spend alone, or, almost grudgingly, it seemed, with me from time to time over those long weeks. There was something deeper going on with her. But, my mind tied up with my own troubles, I didn't take the time to dig deep enough.

Given the events that transpired only a short time later, everything in me wishes that I could just turn back the clock and do it all again, the right way.

One evening, after shutting down the library, I walked down the silent, dim hallway toward the main square, my thoughts awhirl with turbulent emotions. More than anything, though, I wanted to see Ice and resolved to head up to her cell before I did anything else.

As if by magic, an arm captured me and pulled me into yet another of the doorways that stood silently in the long hallway. My hormones surged and a smile split my lips before the chilling feel of metal pressed up against my neck froze my blood in its veins.

"Hello, little whore," a sing-song voice sounded very close to my ear, "didja miss me?"

Psycho!, my mind screamed as I tried desperately to control my breathing. *Keep calm, Angel. You can figure a way out of this. Just keep calm and don't react to anything she says until you can use it to your advantage.* The words of Montana and Critter and Ice played through my mind in a soothing mantra, calming my heart rate slightly. "What do you want, Cassandra."

A tinkling laugh sounded behind me. "And here I thought you had all the brains in the relationship, tramp. Isn't it obvious what I want?"

"Can you just…explain it to me? So I know for sure?" I tried to sound as vacant and pitiful as I could, knowing that sometimes that worked on people like Cassandra.

I could feel my plan working when her sigh brushed against the short hair framing my ear. Her grip twisted on the knife just the slightest bit and I readied myself for action. "Oh, alright," she said in a tone reserved for teaching the profoundly mentally disabled. "It's simple, really. You cuckolded Ice away from me, and so you must die. Is that easy enough for you to understand?"

"Yes, I think I've got it now."

"Do you? Good." I could feel her smile against the skin of my cheek as she brought her head down next to mine. "Any last requests?"

"Just one."

"Yes?"

Stamping down on her foot as hard as I could, I brought my hands up hard, fingers stiffened to thrust between her arm and my neck. Prying her away, I brought her arm down with all my strength. "Get your *damn* knife the *hell* away from *my neck*!!"

I could tell she was surprised, because the maneuver, never practiced against a real opponent intent on severing my head from my shoulders, worked perfectly. After a split-second, though, I could feel her start to respond, stabilizing her grip on the knife and turning its lethal edge inward.

There was the muted sound of cloth parting and then I felt a warm trickle run down my left thigh. Though I couldn't feel anything, I knew I'd been cut. Looking down, I saw the orange of my jumpsuit quickly darken to a rust as my blood seeped from the slice in my flesh.

Determined not to give her another chance, I brought my other hand down on her wrist, twisting for all I was worth. We both grunted. The knife came free, spinning through the small room where I had been taken.

Her reflexes cat-quick, Cassandra dove for the knife right as it skittered across the cement floor. I was just a half step behind her. As she grabbed the knife, my foot came down once again, this time trapping both weapon and flesh beneath my shoe.

During the rush for the knife, the door slammed close behind us, and so Cassandra's scream of frustration, and I hoped, pain, was unheard by the prison in general. Psycho struggled like a fish on a line, trying to pull both the knife and her hand free, but I was having none of it. "Let me go, you *bitch*!"

"Let go of the knife and I'll raise my foot, Cassandra."

"Like *hell* I will!" Turning her head, she opened her mouth wide and the next thing I felt was my wounded thigh, the same leg that was trapping Cassandra, being bitten into. Hard.

I opened my mouth wide, but panted through the pain, slapping her head as hard as I could to get her to disengage. She shook her head like a terrier, growling as her jaws spasmed shut. The pain was so intense I almost fainted.

My leg weakened, then jittered. Shouting in triumph, Cassandra pulled the knife free. Her shout freed her teeth from my thigh and, clamping my own teeth down so hard I nearly bit off my own tongue, I jammed my foot back down as hard as I could, the abused muscles literally screaming out their own agony. I could hear the sickening crunch of small bones breaking and my stomach did a lazy flip-flop, making me thank God that I'd been too busy to eat dinner. "Let it *go*, Cassandra!"

She literally howled this time, her voice raising in pitch so high that I was forced to slap my hands over my ears and wonder if any glass that happened to be in this little room would shatter from her voice alone.

"*Let...it...go*!" God help me, I actually *twisted* my foot, grinding her hand further beneath the hard sole of my prison shoe.

She turned to bite me once again and I knew I couldn't stand another one. So, putting all my weight on my injured leg, the one that had Cassandra's hand trapped against the rough cement floor, I brought up my free leg and kneed her in the head as hard as I could. My leg screamed out in agony at the same time Cassandra screamed in reality, slumping onto her back, trapped only by my foot still on her hand.

Quickly, I lifted my leg, then bent down and retrieved the knife, holding it almost as one would hold a gun, in a two-handed grip, the tip pointed at her head. "Alright now," I said, trying to keep the waver from my hands as well as my voice. "You're going to listen to me Cassandra."

Inhaling deeply, she pursed her lips and spat at me. Though I tried to dodge, it landed right on my midsection, causing my stomach to do another slow roll. "*That's* what I think of your talking, whore." She wiped her heavily bleeding nose with the back of her hand, her dark eyes glittering with hatred.

"Think whatever you want, Cassandra. But I'm the one with the knife here."

"Not for long," she muttered. "You don't even know how to hold it, let alone use it as a weapon."

"I didn't know how to use a baseball bat as a weapon either, but my husband's dead anyway. Check the obituaries. It's in there."

That silenced her for a short period as she thought about what I'd said. "So spit it out already," she finally said grudgingly.

"Fine." I knew I had to make this convincing. "I don't really care what you think happened between Ice and me. Fact is, I'm getting out soon, on appeal. After that, she's all yours again. So…how about we make a little deal?"

"And what kind of deal would *you* make, little girl," she said, sarcasm dripping from her words.

"Only this. You walk away like nothing ever happened and I don't rat you out to Ice. Because if she ever finds out what you did to me, you can pretty much rule out living long enough to ever make that dream of yours a reality."

She simply looked up at me from her place on the floor, her chocolate eyes wide. I could have sworn I saw just the tiniest shard of respect there. Still… "You wouldn't rat."

"Wouldn't I? What's to stop me, hmm?"

"The prison code."

"The prison code," I repeated. "As in, the prison I'm leaving soon? That prison code?"

I could tell I had unbalanced her. I decided to move in for the figurative kill. "Besides," I said, smiling, "it's not as if I can hide this from Ice, you know. The cut I might be able to explain away, but the bite mark? That'd be a little difficult, don't you think? And since I've never lied to her before…." My voice trailed off teasingly, letting her finish the thought herself.

Of course, I was lying through my proverbial teeth. There wasn't a chance in hell that I would ever let Ice get close enough to my naked thigh to see what Cassandra had done to it. I would never make good on my threat, but Cassandra didn't know that. It was my one and only card to play, aside from, of course, the knife I held in my hands. If Ice ever found out what happened, Cassandra would be so much blood on the wall. Of that I was sure.

The tiny room was bathed in silence as Cassandra stared at me, calculating. "You're a tough little bitch, I'll give you that."

Some type of perverse pleasure filled me at her words, though I struggled not to let it show. I was already enjoying this little dominance/submission act way too much and that was scaring me more than the thought of what Ice would do if she ever found out about this little adventure. "Well?" I asked, prodding her into making some type of decision. "Do we have a deal?"

"And if I refuse to go along with this little delusion of grandeur you're having here?"

"I parade you though the jail at knife point. Right up to Ice's cell."

She looked at me, then at the knife. The very tip of her tongue darted out to smooth her lips. She smiled. "Do you really think you could do that? To me?"

I hardened my gaze. "Try me."

I could see the muscles of her throat move as she swallowed, the flickering of light and shadow over the ivory column of her neck. "Alright," she said softly. "I'll go along with your little deal." Her lips curved upward in a faux smile. "For now." She held up a hand. "But when your injuries heal and it's your word against mine," her smile broadened, "well...don't think this is over."

"Believe me, I don't."

"Good. As long as we understand one another." Her white teeth flashing, Cassandra hopped nimbly to her feet, making a half-hearted grab for the knife, an attempt which I easily avoided, as she did so. Throwing back her head, and cradling her broken hand against her chest, she laughed, long and loud. Then, grasping the doorknob with her good hand, she opened the portal and stepped back out into the hallway, turning her head and giving me a malicious, knowing wink before she disappeared from my sight.

As she left, I stood there, frozen, well aware, suddenly, of the mistake I'd just made. It was a sure bet that the guards had discovered her escape by now. They were, no doubt, combing the prison for her. And when they found her, all she had to do was turn the tables on me, stating that I'd accosted her and threatened her with a knife, and I'd be in the hole for God knew how long. My chances at a new trial would go up like so much smoke from a forest fire. And she'd get away with it, too. I was the one with the knife. My fingerprints were all over it. So what if I was the one bleeding? I already had more than enough experience with how being injured defending oneself could lead to all sorts of nasty accusations. After all, I was an inmate, wasn't I?

The knife hanging limply in one hand, I listened carefully through the door, which I'd closed after Cassandra left, my ear pressed up against the rough, splintered wood.

After a few moments of silence, I heard the sounds of running feet and shouting that told me that the guards had found Cassandra. I held my breath, my palms sweating, my leg throbbing like a rotted tooth in some ghoulishly grinning death's head mask. Plainly put, I was scared. My bladder was sending out an urgent summons which I crossed my legs against receiving.

Cassandra's high-pitched cackle filled the air and I almost screamed. The knife dropped from my clenched fist, clattering against the cold floor. The rich iron-copper taste of blood filled my mouth as I bit my lips against the noise forming in the back of my throat.

"I was just taking a walk, ladies. Can't a girl have a little freedom around here?" Psycho's laugh filled the air once again, getting dimmer to my hearing as she was, no doubt, led back to her cell.

I waited in absolute, terror-filled silence for the footsteps I was sure were coming for me. Minutes went by during which entire worlds were born, thrived, and reduced to their component atoms. My throat clicked as I swallowed. I counted to one thousand in my head several times, slowly, like I used to do when we would play touch football during recess at school. "One Mississippi, two Mississippi, three Mississippi," I breathed against the door.

Then I counted once more, for good measure.

The expected footsteps never came. Then, my bladder shouted out a warning too harsh to be ignored. If I didn't leave my hiding spot right that second, blood on my uniform wouldn't be the only stain I'd have to explain away.

I gripped the knob with a trembling hand and turned it as slowly as it was possible to do so, wincing at the telltale 'click' that disengaged the lock. Opening it the tiniest sliver, I peered down the hallway. Empty silence greeted my gaze.

Taking in a deep breath, I slowly, silently pulled the door open wide enough to slip through, taking one last cautionary look around before exposing myself. The hallway was as empty as it had been a second ago. I slipped out, turning left and making my way, limping, back toward the safe confines of the library. Not surprisingly, the need to empty my bladder disappeared as soon as I was safely inside.

Slipping into and being instantly calmed by the familiar surroundings, I flipped the lights on and made my way to the far corner behind Corinne's always-messy desk. On the shelf behind her hotplate, teakettle, teabags and assorted mugs lay a fairly large box emblazoned with a red cross on its white plastic finish. She'd put it there after the last riot and it was fairly well stocked with the requisite bandages, tape, scissors, hydrogen peroxide, alcohol swabs and quite a few drugs more commonly seen in hospitals, pharmacies and, in some cases, on the mean streets than in a prison library. There were even syringes to inject some of the more potent, and highly illegal, drugs.

Secreting myself in the shadows, I quickly stripped down to my underwear, letting the jumpsuit puddle down around my ankles as I took my first good look at the wound Cassandra had given me. It was, to be blunt, ugly. The cut itself wasn't that deep. It had already stopped bleeding, for the most part. But the bite mark was a different story altogether. There, on my thigh, outlined in vivid, angry red, was the perfect imprint of Cassandra's front teeth, upper and lower. The puncture wounds looked like a dentist's mold in reverse.

"Jesus." I whispered the oath as I gingerly fingered the lividity, watching it blanch a sickly yellowed white before turning back to red when the pressure was removed. The punctures bled sluggishly and I supposed that was one of the few good things about this whole experience. I tried to think back to when I'd received my last tetanus shot, well knowing that human bites were more dangerous than dog bites could ever be. Then I remembered that I'd received one in the Emergency Room after I'd been beaten by Peter, which, of course, put it well within the ten-year limit of the vaccine's protection.

Reaching into the kit, I grabbed the bottle of peroxide, twisted it open, and upended it, allowing the liquid to flow unhindered onto my thigh. The peroxide hissed and bubbled as it seeped into the wounds and I hissed right along with it, wincing against the stinging in my leg.

Then I grabbed a rolled bandage and blotted off the excess liquid, careful not to touch the wound. "Ok, Angel, what next? You cleaned the wound. You probably should bandage it, right?" My whispered words sounded loud in the emptiness of the library.

Agreeing with myself, I opened a sterile gauze pad, placed it on top of the wound, and wrapped a rolled bandage around my thigh several times before grabbing a roll of tape and securing the wrapping.

Then I pulled my jumpsuit back over the whole deal, wincing at the bloodstain which liberally coated one thigh. I'd have to figure out a way to disguise that when I walked back to my cell for the night.

Knowing that infection would more than likely set in no matter how well I had cleaned the bite marks, I pawed through Corinne's little pill factory, looking for antibiotics. When I was a young girl, I'd stepped on a nail and the doctor had given me Keflex. I figured that would be good for bite punctures as well, and when I saw a bottle labeled with that name, I grabbed it, slipping it into the front of my jumpsuit with another roll of bandages and some sterile gauze pads and zipping back up.

As I was closing up the first-aid kit, the warning buzzer for lights out sounded. Looking around quickly, I picked up the largest book I could find and held it awkwardly against my leg, hoping to cover the blood stain just long enough to get back to my cell. It wasn't great, as disguises go, but it would have to do. Hopefully, I wouldn't pass too many people in the hallways.

I managed to make it back to my cell without passing anyone who thought to give me much more than a quick glance. Once there, I stripped out of my bloodied uniform, tossed it in the laundry bin, and slid in between the cool sheets with a sense of utter relief. Then, remembering, I hobbled over to the sink and swallowed two antibiotic pills before returning to bed.

✒   ✒   ✒   ✒

The next day was Saturday, and as soon as the in-cell headcount was completed, the sounds of guards opening the cell doors, keys rattling loudly in ancient locks, woke me from a sleep plagued by nightmares.

The sheets were sweat-soaked and tangled around me, and as I struggled to get them loose, a shadow crossed into the cell. I looked up to see Ice standing there, an almost apologetic half-smile gracing her flawless features.

As much as I wanted to see her last night, that's as much as I didn't want to see her this morning. There was no way I could let her know what had happened to me, and if she got close enough, that was exactly what was going to happen. With, I was quite sure, disastrous results.

Ice's piercing eyes narrowed as I reached up to wipe my stringy, damp hair away from my forehead. I could feel the heat gusting off my skin like a furnace and willed myself not to tremble. "Are you alright?" she asked, taking one step into my cell.

"Yes! Yes, I'm…."

Her eyes narrowed still further, till they were glittering blue slits, peeking from beneath lowered, elegant brows.

"No. I'm not alright. I don't feel too well."

And that was the absolute truth, as far as that went. My leg felt swollen and tight, like an overcooked sausage. Its continual throbbing matched the headache thumping sickly behind my eyes. I'd also managed to forget that when I was young, Keflex had made me violently ill, killing all the good bacteria in my digestive tract and giving me a form of colitis that made me beg God to just kill me and end my misery.

The night before, those same prayers winged their way Heavenward.

Ice took another step forward. "What's wrong?"

Oh boy. She would have to ask me the one question I didn't have the answer to. Well, not the false one I needed to give her. *Quick, Angel. Think. Something. Anything.* "Cramps," I said finally.

Her eyes widened in understanding, then narrowed again. "You're a little early, aren't you?"

Oh shit. "Um…yeah. I am. I think it's stress." I attempted a weak smile, which I knew fell flat. "You know, with my case and all."

"Are you sure that's all there is? You look pretty feverish to me."

"Sometimes that happens," I responded, trying to get my clouded mind to think quickly. "When they're really bad like this."

Another step and she was almost at my bedside. "I could give you a massage. Sometimes loosening those muscles helps."

I sat up quickly, stifling a groan and pulling the sheet up to my chin. "No! No, that's ok. See…when I'm in a lot of pain like this, I don't like to be touched." *C'mon, Ice. Get the hint already, please? Lying to you like this is killing me.*

Ice pulled back slowly, her face expressionless. "Alright." She crossed her arms over her chest, disbelief showing clearly on her face. "Is there anything I can do?"

"No. Wait...yes. There is. Um...sometimes milk makes me feel a little better. Is there any way you could go down to the cafeteria or the commissary and pick some up for me?" I was going on the most desperate hope that the milk would help coat my stomach so I could at least somewhat tolerate the antibiotic I needed to have.

She smiled slightly. "Yeah. I can do that."

I contained my sigh of relief. *Two birds with one stone. Temporarily at least.* "Great. Thank you."

She nodded, that calculating expression still in her eyes, then turned and left the cell. When she was gone, I slumped back against the wall. "Damn you, Psycho. Damn you and damn your crazy obsessions. Damn you for making me lie like this. Why can't you just leave us alone?"

Blinking my tears back, I lifted the sheet and quickly unwrapped the bandage covering my thigh. The area around the bite marks was reddish-purple, swollen, and hot to the touch. The wounds themselves were weeping a cloudy yellow fluid which I took to be infection. At least the knife wound seemed to be healing without problems. So far.

Ice returned just as I was putting the finishing touches on my bandage. Quickly dropping the sheet over my body, I managed a smile as she walked into the cell bearing three half-pint cartons of milk. She handed me one as she set the other two down on the nightstand. Opening the carton, I downed the entire contents in a couple of gulps. It was cold, smooth and refreshing, especially to my dehydrated body. "God, that's good," I said, wiping my mouth with the back of my hand.

Smiling, Ice leaned down slightly and wiped up a trace of milk from my upper lip with her thumb. "Ya look better without the moustache," she pronounced, joking.

I managed a weak laugh that was interrupted by a jaw-popping yawn. "God, I guess I'm more tired than I thought."

"You do look pretty wiped out," she agreed, reaching down and brushing the hair from my eyes. "You're still pretty warm, too. You aren't getting sick again, are you?"

Snuggling down under the sheet once again, I gave her my best convincing look, which probably wasn't all that convincing, to tell the truth. "No, I feel fine. Just in pain from these damn cramps. I should be good to go by tomorrow, or at the latest, Monday." Which was, of course, yet another lie in a speech full of them. While I had hopes that the infection would be gone by the new week's beginning, I would definitely *not* be good to go. Especially not the type of 'going' that Ice's close presence was conjuring visions of deep within the recesses of my muddled brain.

I tensed as she grabbed the sheet, but relaxed when she simply pulled it tighter under my chin before bending down to place a kiss on my forehead. "Alright then. I have to take care of some things with Critter and Pony. I'll try to come back this evening and send someone to check up on you periodically, alright?"

"No. That's ok. I'll be fine. Really. The way I feel, I'll probably just sleep straight through to tomorrow morning anyway." I yawned again to make my story convincing.

Crooking me a smile as she straightened, she fiddled with my sheet for a brief second more before backing away. "I'll be back here tonight to check in on you. And I'll be sending some of the Amazons up during the day just to make sure you don't need anything."

I gave her an overly-dramatic sigh. "Oh alright, Ms. Warden wannabe."

She threw back her own mock-hurt expression in return. "Fine. Just for that, I'll send Critter up here *every hour* with a thermometer and some lube to take your temperature…the *right* way." Her eyes were positively sparkling with glee.

I gulped. "I'll be good," I squeaked.

Winking, she gave me one of her full-on smiles, leaving me dazzled. "I know you will be. Sweet dreams, my Angel. Feel better soon."

Pain? What pain?

♏   ♏   ♏   ♏

Miraculously, I suppose, I managed to make it through the rest of Saturday and all of Sunday without any major incidents. The milk did its job, allowing me to keep down the antibiotics which, in turn, did *their* job in decreasing the swelling, redness and pain in my leg so that, by the time Monday morning rolled around, bite and knife wounds were healing nicely and I was able to once again dress in my uniform without an appreciable bulge showing.

Still, after the cell doors had been opened for the day, I waited an additional few minutes to be sure Ice was safely down at the auto shop before venturing forth to start my Monday. The woman had a sixth sense about things, and I knew this weekend had pushed my credibility to the limit, if she had even bought my act at all, and the jury was still out on that particular count, to use an apt analogy.

After a solitary breakfast, I made my way down to the library. The tension I'd missed by playing 'possum all weekend returned with a vengeance. I'm sure it had never really left, but the more or less peaceful island of my solitary cell kept me in calm waters over the weekend.

As I walked, I counted no less than fifteen separate incidents, mostly arguments between guards and inmates, inmates and guards. Thankfully, none of the ones I saw denigrated into out and out physical confrontations.

While I felt much better, I wasn't yet ready to test my body's healing by trying to get between two angry women with hurting on their mind.

As I slipped into the sanctuary of the library, I did so with a sigh of relief. Corinne greeted me with a smile. She bustled over to the table and sat down next to me, her hands folded on the scarred wood, her expression expectant. "So?"

I looked at her, confused. "So…what?"

"How do you feel?"

"Fine?"

She smiled. "Good. That's good."

I narrowed my eyes at her. "What's going on, Corinne?"

Her own eyes went wide. "Whatever do you mean, Angel?"

"Alright," I spat. "Out with it. Why is everyone in this damn prison acting like they're in need of some serious laxative therapy and why are you sitting there like you just ate the canary."

"Actually, I noticed that the natives were getting a little restless too, now that you mention it," Corinne commented, adjusting her glasses. "Not sure why, though."

"You?" I asked, shocked at the admission. "The woman who knows when someone's gonna sneeze before they do it? The great Corinne, Oracle of the Bog?"

She frowned at me. "I'm hardly perfection personified, Angel."

I laughed. "I'm going to have to write that one down."

Folding her meaty arms across her abundant chest, Corinne gave me her best affronted glare. "Fine. If you don't want to hear the *good* news, which, let me tell you, I kept safe from the ravaging hordes of inquisitive little noses just for you, then you can trot your little fanny right out of this little library of mine."

Having, by this time, known Corinne more than four years, I could usually tell when her hurt was real or feigned. By the look in her eye, I knew she was leading me on, as was usually the case with her. Still, I decided to do the honorable thing and give in. Besides, I really wanted to know what the good news was. "Please, Corinne," I began, with as much faux-docility in my voice and manner as I could manage without laughing, "I'm very sorry if I offended you with my attitude. Please say you forgive me?"

"Oooo. You're *good*, Angel."

I smirked. "Thank you. Now, what's the news? Or do you want me on my knees, begging."

"Don't tempt me, child. Just seeing you in that position would almost make getting torn into five equal pieces by Ice worth the pain." Her dark eyes were filled with mirth.

"Corinne? The news? Please?"

Grinning at me, she reached through her shawl and into the folds of her jumpsuit, returning with a piece of paper in her hand. "Early Saturday morning, Phyllis came looking for you about a phone call. Ice had been up to see you already and told us you were a bit under the weather, so I asked Phyllis if she could take a message. She agreed, and a short time later, came back with this." She held the paper tauntingly, the printed area for her eyes only.

Groaning in frustration, I threw my hands up in the air. "Come on, Corinne!"

She saw my groan and raised me an over-dramatic sigh. "Oh, fine. Be that way. Here." Slamming the note face down, she pushed it across the table to me.

"Thank you," I responded with forced politeness as I picked up the paper and turned it over. Printed across the blank tableau in Corinne's bold, distinctive hand, were three simple words. "We did it!"

Cocking my head in confusion, I looked back up at my friend who was trying unsuccessfully to hold back a grin. "Who did what?" I asked. "Corinne, who's this message from?"

Corinne let her smile show through. "Your lawyer, Angel. It was Donita on the phone. She didn't give out any more information than that, but Phyllis said that she told her to make sure you called her at her office when you were feeling up to it."

"And that would be right now!" Grinning like a madwoman, I jumped to my feet, the printed note crumpled in my hands. With a whooping yell that almost startled Corinne into a heart attack, I left the library, walking as quickly as my injured leg would allow.

❧   ❧   ❧   ❧

When I returned, my color was high, my chest was laboring, and my eyes were wet with happy tears. I nearly bowled Corinne over as I wrapped her portly form in a huge bear-hug, sending her glasses skittering off her nose to hang on the silver chain she kept around her neck. I planted a big kiss on her dry, weathered cheek, then released her, stepping away, laughing.

"Well, I can only hope to be the bearer of more good news in the future," she said, bemusedly touching her cheek and smiling dazedly at me.

"I feel *great*!" Throwing my arms out, I twirled around the library, missing the assembled furniture and patrons only by luck. "She did it!"

My friend gave me an infinitely patient smile usually reserved for two-year-olds who have hidden mommy's wallet and don't possess the requisite verbal skills to tell her where it might be. "I think we've all gotten that bit by now, Angel. The question here is, what is 'it'?"

"Donita talked to the judge on Friday evening. After seeing the evidence, he's agreed to overturn the verdict!"

"Heaven bless the persistent," Corinne breathed, clasping her hands over her breast. "Angel, that's *wonderful* news!"

I was grinning so hard, I thought my face would shatter. " God, I'm so excited!"

"So, when ya bein' sprung?" one of the inmates asked from her place near the stacks.

"Well, my lawyer and the judge talked to the DA, but he refuses to drop the charges. He thinks that despite everything, he still has a case against me."

"What about bond?" asked a second prisoner.

"Donita and the DA couldn't agree on a figure. I told her it was alright, though. I don't mind being here till a new trial." I shrugged. "I don't have anywhere else to go anyway."

"Have they set a trial date?" Corinne asked.

"Donita says it'll probably be in a month or two. They've got a pretty heavy caseload over there, but she's throwing around words like 'deliberate jury tampering', 'perjurious eye-witnesses', 'unjust incarceration' and 'lawsuit'. She's pretty sure my turn will come soon."

This time it was Corinne who enveloped me in a full-body hug. Totally giddy, I willingly sunk into the soft roundness of her frame, taking in her scent of ink and paper and tea. "I must be dreaming," I whispered.

"No, you're not, sweet Angel." Releasing me, Corinne gently cupped my cheeks, then turned my head, planting on kiss to either side of my face and one full on my lips. Then she smiled and stepped away. "This is real. Enjoy the feeling. God knows, you deserve it."

"I just can't believe it's happening. I don't think it's really set in yet. God." I looked wildly around. "I need to see Ice. I need to tell her the news."

Corinne stepped forward once again, putting a restraining hand on my arm. "That's not the best of ideas right now."

A thrill of fear skittered down my spine. "Why not?"

"Digger came looking for you when you were off talking to Donita just now. Apparently, Ice got into another row with the Warden."

"Oh no. What was it about?"

"Digger didn't know. All she said was that there was a whole lot of shouting. She thought it might have had something to do with a job of some sort, but she wasn't sure."

"Did she get sent to the hole?" Even my heart stopped as I waited for the answer.

"No. Back down to the auto-shop, I'd expect. Digger said she'd never seen Ice as angry as she was when she came out of the office. Said she almost pushed another inmate through the wall on her way out."

"I'd better go talk to her."

"It's probably best if you wait, Angel. Give her a chance to cool down."

Before I could argue any further, a scream sounded from outside the library.

Jumping to my feet once again, I dashed out of the library, following the sound of the scream into the prison square. Halfway to the center of the square, I stopped and followed the crowd's gaze upwards. "Oh shit," I half-whispered, shouldering my way through the crowd.

There, on the second floor, poised equidistant between Pony to the left and Phyllis on the right, was an inmate I'd never seen before straddling the iron railing. Almost directly behind the young woman, her face pressed hard up against the bars of door enclosing the segregation unit, was Psycho, grinning maliciously.

The crowd parted suddenly and I skid to a stop next to Critter, who was standing almost directly beneath the catwalk, her neck craned at a tendon-stretching angle as she looked almost straight up. I took a step back so as to more easily appraise the situation.

The woman looked to be my age or maybe a little younger, with a plump, well-rounded figure, lank blonde hair and thick glasses. Her round face was doughy-white and shiny with sweat. Her gray eyes were magnified behind the lenses of her glasses, giving her an absolutely terrified expression.

I watched as Pony took a careful step forward. The woman flung out an arm, almost toppling over the rail. "Don't move! I'll jump! I swear it! Not one step closer!"

Psycho's cackling laugh sounded. "Oh *please* jump, little fish. You'd absolutely make my day. Why, if you tried hard enough, I bet you could even manage to break an ankle or two on your way down…from the *second floor*."

"Shut up!" the woman screamed, releasing her grip and slamming her hands over her ears. Her body wobbled once again and she skittered quickly for a handhold, still straddling the iron bars. "Just *shut up*!!"

Cassandra just continued to laugh, rattling the bars of her cage just to frighten the girl some more, which she did.

"What's her name?" I shouted to Critter to be heard over Psycho's howling laughter.

My friend turned to me. "I don't know. I've never seen her before."

"Shit." I looked up at Pony, who shrugged. Phyllis also looked down at me, her expression fixed, intent. After what seemed like an hour, at least, Cassandra's laughter wound down and I saw my opportunity. "What's your name?" I shouted up to the girl on the rail.

Startled, she looked down at me, and the crowd gathered in the square, as if seeing us all for the first time. She tightened her grip on the railing, her lips clamped into a small line on her face.

I gave her my warmest smile. "C'mon. You can tell me. What's your name? Mine's Angel."

"I…my…my name's Iris," she half-whispered.

"Speak up, dear!" Psycho's jeering, insanely gleeful voice echoed through the silent square. "If you're going to put on a show, you need to let *all* of your audience hear your lines."

"It's alright, Iris," I said, warmly. "I heard you. Can you tell me why you're up there?"

"Yes, tell us *all*, fishie! Tell us *all* what your little problem is. We'd *so* much like to hear it."

Iris turned her head back toward Psycho. "Shut up!" she screamed. "Shut up! Shut up! Shut up! *Shutupshutupshutupshutup*! SHUT! UP!"

As Cassandra howled in laughter once again, Pony made a move toward her cell. Iris caught the motion and shifted, overcompensating and sliding from the top rail.

The entire crowd sucked in a breath.

The girl managed to catch herself at the last moment and quickly yanked her body back onto the railing, still straddling it with one foot on the lowest rung. "Stay back!" she yelled to Pony.

Pony came to an abrupt stop as Cassandra opened her mouth once again. "Keep it shut, Psycho!"

"You're gonna meet your maker for that one, Horsey-Girl," Cassandra snarled, rattling her cage once again.

"Remind me to piss my panties later, Psycho. For now, just shut the fuck up why don't you."

"Make me, bitch."

Pony's intent lunge was interrupted by yet another scream from Iris. She froze once again, mere feet from both Cassandra and the girl. Letting out a breath, she backed away slowly, her empty hands raised. "Alright," she murmured soothingly. "Alright. I'm not gonna hurt you. See?"

"Iris," I said, directing the terrified woman's attention back to me. "Please, why do you want to do this? There must be something we can do."

"She's the reason!" Iris screamed, pointing a shaking hand toward Psycho. "It's all her fault!"

Cassandra howled again.

"Two weeks trapped inside with that...that...that *monster*! She wouldn't let me sleep! She wouldn't let me eat! Threatening me every minute of every day!" Tears streamed down her full face, magnifying her eyes even more. "And every night...*every night* she'd send that damned awful disgusting rat of hers into my cell!"

As I listened to the hysterical woman, I could see, from the corner of my eye, the truly evil grin that spread across Psycho's face. When I saw her duck away from the door, I reached out and grabbed Critter, yanking her backward against me. "Go get Ice," I hissed into her ear.

"Wha—?"

"Go get Ice. Now. She should be down in the auto shop. Hurry."

Critter nodded once, then pulled away, sprinting through the square and down the hallway leading to the shops. I turned my head away from her just as another piercing scream rent the air.

I didn't have to be at ground zero to know that Heracles had just put in an appearance.

Iris jumped so that her feet were balanced, almost like a surfer's, on the top bar of the railing. Her body swayed violently to the left and right as she tried to keep her balance, all the while staring at the floor to her left and screaming without pause. "Get it away from me! Oh dear *God*, get it away from me!"

Cassandra's vibrant voice could easily be heart through the panicked screaming. "Oh yes, little Heracles. Bite her. That's it. *Bite* her legs off, Heracles. *Suck* her eyes out! Attack! Attack!" The woman was positively braying with insane laughter as Heracles skittered back and forth at the very edge of the catwalk, his long whiskers twitching with animal excitement.

Screaming, Iris lost her balance, her feet slipping off the railing and plunging over the outside. She managed to catch the top rail under her elbows and locked on tight, kicking her how free legs as the inquisitive rat came closer to explore this new prize.

From my vantage point down below, I knew that, in that very instant, was the time to strike. But I could also see that both Pony and Phyllis were frozen to their spots, watching instead of acting. I wanted to scream at them to break their paralysis, but just as I opened my mouth, Iris managed to hook one flailing leg over the lowest rung and pull herself back onto the rail, still screaming in terror.

Phyllis removed her baton and raised it high over her head, her eyes fixed on Heracles. "Call him back, Cassandra!" she shouted. "I'll kill him if you don't!"

That threat cut Psycho's laugh off immediately. "You wouldn't dare, piggy," she sneered.

"Just try me, Cassandra. Call him back *now*!"

There was several moments of a tense standoff before Psycho finally sighed. "Oh alright. This prison is such a bore." She whistled. "Come here, little Heracles. Come back to mommy, won't you?"

Apparently, however, Heracles was too fond of his newfound freedom because he studiously ignored the pleas of his mistress, preferring instead to continue pacing beneath the screaming woman above him, his brown, beady eyes seeming to check her out from every angle.

"Heracles! You naughty boy! Come back in here this instant!"

A flash of orange sparked across the periphery of my vision and, when I turned my head, I saw Ice as she bounded up the stairs four at a time, her hair streaming behind her in an inky cloud.

Everyone's focus turned to her. Even Iris stopped her screaming.

Cassandra smiled with what looked to be relief. "Oh, Ice, there you are. Would you be a dear and get my little Heracles back for me? He doesn't seem to want to listen to his mommy today."

Arriving on the catwalk, Ice casually crossed her arms and smirked, eyebrow lifted, in the direction of Cassandra. "Seems like your little 'pet' has developed an attitude problem."

Psycho's smile grew larger. "Oh, we have one *more* thing in common, then, don't we."

Ice simply stared at her. My muscles tightened as a sense of foreboding washed over me.

"It seems that *your* little pet has developed an attitude problem of her very own. Isn't that right, Angel." Her words echoed, like a death knell, through the square.

Ice looked down at me, her gaze inquisitive. I stood frozen to my spot on the floor.

Cassandra laughed. "You mean you didn't tell her, Angel? You actually kept your word? Oh, isn't *that* rich!"

"Spit it out, Cassandra," Ice ordered. "What are you talking about."

I wanted to scream, shout, fall down on my knees in a grand mal seizure…anything to stop this topic in its embryonic stage. For a brief second, I even found myself praying that Iris, the person who started this whole thing, would just jump so nothing else could be said.

My prayer went unanswered. Iris seemed as riveted to these new turn of events as everyone else was.

"I can't believe she didn't tell you of our little adventure, Ice!"

"Cassandra…."

"Oh, alright. If it'll get my sweet little Heracles back, I'll tell you." She stuck her skinny arms through the bars, linking her hands together casually. "Let's see. Friday, I think it was, I was just sick of this new fish and her incessant whining. So, I decided to take a stroll. Nothing much, really. Just a chance to stretch my legs, see what was happening, that kind of thing."

"I assume there's a point in here somewhere?"

"Oh there is. There is. Never fear. You see, I just *happened*, for some strange reason, to find myself outside the library very close to lights out. Now, locked in my miserable cell all day like I am, I've been deprived of the great pleasure of seeing this remarkable bastion of lower learning in the flesh, so to speak. And I did *so* want the opportunity to meet the great Corinne." She sighed dramatically. "But, alas, it was near closing time and our dear librarian had already made her tottering way back to her cell, I'm afraid."

Then she clapped her hands together as an expression of almost beatific joy overspread her fair features. "But I wasn't disappointed. Oh no. Because instead of the great Corinne, I got her *wonderful* assistant, Angel."

Ice's expression became stony. Cassandra laughed. The inmates and guards, Iris included, all turned to stare at me. I wanted to run. I wanted to hide. But I couldn't. My body was refusing my mind's commands. I remained frozen, landlocked in a sea of misery.

"So I invited her into one of the paint closets. You know, just to chat." She shrugged.

"What happened." Ice's voice was completely devoid of all emotion. I knew right then just how angry she was.

Cassandra scowled. "The little bitch disarmed me!"

Some of the inmates started to laugh. There was a smattering of applause as well. Cassandra snarled, loudly.

"And?"

Her insane good humor restored, Psycho smiled once again. "Well, I didn't give up without a fight. Managed to slice her leg open before she could take my knife away. But it wasn't over there. Oh goodness, no. I went after my pretty little blade and she actually *stepped on my hand!*" Scowling, she held up the appendage in question. I noticed with equal parts satisfaction and guilt that her hand was swollen and bruised. "You really should spank her for her impertinence, Ice," she said in a sly undertone which, nevertheless, carried to all ears.

There was some snickering over that particular comment. Ice, however, remained unmoved.

"Anyway, like any good psychotic, I went with my best option."

"Meaning?"

"I bit her."

"You did *what*?!"

"I bit her. Right on one of those luscious thighs of hers." She trailed off, opening her eyes wide in a show of mock surprise. "You mean she didn't show you? You didn't see it when the two of you were rutting like a couple of crazed weasels? I *know* I left a mark. I could even taste the hot tang of her blood through the material of her uniform." Rolling her eyes, she ran a tongue across her front teeth, body writhing as if in ecstasy.

Ice's hands clenched slowly. I could easily see the corded muscles and tendons of her neck protrude. I thought for sure she would rush the bars holding Cassandra inside the segregation unit. But she didn't. She just stood there, staring. "What happened next." Her voice was so soft, I had to strain to hear it.

"We made a deal."

"And that was?"

"I wouldn't fight her for the knife she now held at my neck, and in return, she wouldn't tell you about what happened between us." *Oh, please look at me, Ice. Please. Look down here and see how sorry I am. Please.*

But she didn't hear me. And even if, by some miracle, she had, I knew right then that she would never have listened. I had never seen her as angry as she was right then. I felt as if I had lost my entire world.

"Why would she make that kind of deal?" Ice asked, almost rhetorically.

But Cassandra, as always, was ready with an answer. "Isn't it obvious, dear Ice? It's because she knows that you and I are two of a kind. The unredeemable. She knew that if she told you what had happened, you'd come over here and try to kill me without a second thought! And that's how it should be! It's who we are!"

She cocked her head, a look that frighteningly resembled compassion shining from her eyes. "Oh come now, Ice. You don't think she really believes all that goody-goody tripe she spouts at you every day, do you? About your soul having worth? Of course not! She knows you'll never be anything more than you are right now. A cold blooded murderer." She grinned. "Like me! That's why we belong together, you and I. Because I'll never lie to you, Ice. I *know* who you are."

I could see Ice shaking her head slowly, though tears had blurred my vision. I wanted to scream out. To negate Cassandra's words. But my throat wouldn't open enough to let the words come out.

"That she hid her injuries from you proves my point, Ice. Her words are just lip service. After all, you're a good bodyguard." She leered. "And a wonderful lover." She shrugged. "And if she has to lie to get you to feel good about yourself, well, it's not a bad return on her investment."

Through my wavery vision, I could see Ice's whole body as it started to shake, as if in the grip of some palsy. It broke me from my terror-induced paralysis. Gathering up my strength, I sprinted for the stairs. Two bodies closed ranks to prohibit my passage. Looking up, I saw Critter and Sonny standing before me, their arms crossed over their chests, their expressions as stony as Ice's had been.

"It's not that way!" I screamed. "That's not why I did it!"

All heads turned to me, but in that moment, I didn't care. In some way, my actions had betrayed the woman I loved more than my own life. I needed to talk to her; needed to explain what was going through my mind when I made the decisions I did to keep what had happened from her. I *did* believe in the goodness in her heart. It wasn't lip service. None of it was. I spoke from a belief in her that was as deep as the bedrock of the earth.

Or did I? Were Psycho's words in some way true? No. No, they couldn't be.

"Ice! Please! Listen to me! Please!"

In the split second that my scream diverted all attention, Ice moved quickly, grabbing Iris and tossing her into the arms of a surprised Phyllis. Then I watched as she bent down and retrieved Heracles, likewise tossing him through the bars to an ecstatic Psycho.

Then she bounded across the catwalk and down the stairs, jumping over the railing before she got down to the first riser and running back down the hallway to the auto shop. I turned to run after her, only to be stopped yet again by twin arms to my elbows.

"Let me go!" I shouted, struggling to break free.

"Go back to the library, Angel," Sonny said.

"No! I have to go after her! Psycho's lying! Can't you see? I need to explain it to her! Please! Please, I'm begging you!"

Critter's face softened infinitesimally. "Go back to the library, Angel. Ice is too angry to hear anything you'd try to tell her right now. Let her calm down a little."

I looked over at Sonny, who nodded, reluctantly, it seemed.

"Are you sure?" I asked, sniffing back my sobs.

My friend smiled slightly. "Yeah. I'm sure. Just let her calm down. I think she'll realize who it was who told her these things pretty quick. After all, it's obvious Psycho has her own agenda, especially when it comes to Ice. Just give her a little time and I'm sure she'll be ready to listen to whatever you have to tell her." The expression on Critter's face let me know that I had better have a damn good excuse, too.

I looked over their shoulders and down the long, empty hallway, willing with all my being for Ice to appear. When that didn't happen, I finally nodded. "Alright. I'll wait. Though if it's all the same to you, I'd rather go to my cell. I don't think I can face Corinne right now."

Both women nodded and released their grips on me, parting to allow me to walk up the stairs and into my cell.

I never did see Ice again that day. Nor did anyone else I asked, or even begged. It was as if she had disappeared.

I spent the evening before lock-down in a total panic, half-expecting the alarms indicating an escape to sound.

But they didn't.

I spent the evening pacing the tiny confines of my cell, wearing down the path from my cell to Ice's, scaring the guards as I popped into their spaces to beg for information on Ice's whereabouts, and vomiting in the toilet.

I went to my knees, praying to God to let me find her and explain my side of the story.

He didn't listen.

It was well into the darkest part of the morning when my grief-induced exhaustion finally caught up to me. I fell asleep on a pillow drenched with tears of sorrow and shame.

Chapter 12

I was dreaming.

I knew it. But that knowledge didn't help. The guilt I felt came with me into my subconscious, where it settled in to roost.

My dreams were filled with courtroom scenes. In them, I was always in this enormous witness box, sitting in an impossibly huge chair, looking up at a judge's bench that seemed to be as tall as a skyscraper. Corinne, for some reason, was always the judge and sported a fancy white wig that I once read English judges still wear. She said only one word, and that oft-repeated.

Guilty!

Guilty!

Guilty!

And in a line that stretched from just in front of my chair to as far as I could see, were my accusers, each clad in fancy dress costumes.

The first to confront me were my parents who were, for whatever convoluted psychological reasons, dressed as King Louis XIV and Marie Antoinette. They carried large gavels, which they banged repeatedly on the humongous arms of my chair, doling out my crimes of being a horrible daughter and a heart-wrenching disappointment to the family.

Guilty!

Next came my grade-school classmates, bearing accusations ranging from being the teacher's pet (which I was) to being a milk-money thief (which I wasn't).

Guilty!

Then came friends from high school, with their own accusations, which ran together like wet paint in the rain.

Guilty!

Peter followed next. Unlike the others, however, he wore no fancy dress. My husband, removed by death, was completely naked. His skin held death's pallor and lividity. His head was oddly shaped and blood ran from both ears in a sort of beard of gore. He stank of formaldehyde and grain alcohol. He leaned over toward me, his fetid, putrid breath buffeting my face and hair.

When he started to speak, he used the same words he had used on the night he tried to rape me. His voice and body language were overwhelmingly aggressive, and for a moment, I was actually in that position again. I could feel my dream hand reaching down, searching for the weapon that wasn't there anymore.

"This isn't happening!" my dream self screamed.

Guilty!

"You're not real! You can't hurt me anymore!"

Guilty!

"You're dead! Don't you understand? You're dead! I killed you!"

Guilty! Guilty!

"Please, Peter! Stop this! I don't want to hurt you! Please, stop! I don't want to hurt you anymore! Please! Just…stay…dead!"

Silence.

The kind that makes you want to scream just to fill it up with something.

The kind that makes you know exactly how it feels to be buried under six feet of heavy earth.

I closed my eyes tight, rubbing at them and trying to wake myself up. When I opened them back up again, Peter was gone. The line was gone. Corinne was gone. The entire room was an empty morass of white except for myself, my overlarge chair, and….

Ice. Clad as she was on our anniversary, in blue silks, a rose in her hand.

Unlike the others, however, she didn't accuse. She didn't demean. She didn't demand an accounting of me. She merely looked at me, holding out that one perfect, blood-red bloom.

But her eyes. God, they were so empty. Like a doll's eyes, almost. Worse even than when she had come back from her time in isolation.

For the first time during this dream, I cried. I reached out to accept the rose, but it was too far away. "Forgive me, Ice," I sobbed, my fingers straining. "Oh God, please forgive me. I didn't do it to hurt you. Please believe me. I love you, Ice! I love you!"

Finally, stretching as far as I could, the very tips of my fingers brushed against hers as I retrieved the rose from her grasp. The moment our fingers touched, she crumpled to the floor, as silent as the world around me.

I woke up screaming.

When I opened my eyes, the difference between my dream world and my living reality was so great that I felt a brief moment of intense claustrophobia. The chipped and peeling walls seemed to me living things, closing in on me, wanting to crush the life and breath from my body.

I wondered, for a brief moment, if I was still dreaming.

I pinched myself, then winced at the resulting pain. When I looked up again, the walls had regained their normally placid nature. I breathed out a long sigh of relief, wiping the tears mixed with sweat from my face.

Twisting in my bed, I looked at the ever-humming clock. It read nearly eleven in the morning. I was struck with an almost overwhelming urge to get out of bed *right now!* Listening to my body's instincts, I jumped from the bed and threw on my uniform, pausing only long enough to run a quick brush through my hair. My nerves were tied in tight knots but I couldn't tell if it was just the aftermath of my nightmare or something more urgent.

I let my feet carry me at their own will as I left my cell behind and descended, once again, into the depths of this Hell called the Bog. At first, I headed in my customary direction, toward the library, when I was overcome with the need to get out into the fresh air.

Running down the hallway now, I slammed open the door to the outside, almost knocking an inmate to the ground in my haste. The sky was the deep gray of an approaching storm and I wrapped my arms around myself as the gusting breeze pricked gooseflesh up on my arms.

The inmates moved sluggishly and without purpose, like a colony of ants benumbed by winter's biting chill. Even the Amazons seemed listless at their appointed place. I looked around quickly, then once again, my heart not ceasing in its frenetic pacing.

Something was wrong. I didn't know what, but I knew that the tension in my body continued to build in incremental segments.

Out of the corner of my eye, I saw, suddenly, Ice standing by the fence overlooking the parking lot. A strong sense of deja-vu washed over me, edging out the tension. As if still dreaming, I felt myself cross the yard in slow, measured steps, watching as more of the outside world became revealed to my sight.

I walked as quietly as I could, not wanting to alert her to my presence just yet.

A gust of wind whipped past again, musically rattling the chain-link fence and blowing Ice's hair wildly around her shoulders and back.

I stopped several feet away from her, peering past the corner of the prison and into the lot beyond. Like last time, the warden stood conversing with Cavallo, the latter all spit-shined and polished and greasy, cap-toothed smiles. The warden returned the grin, smirking in the way of evil men pulling something over on unknowing innocents. They reached out to shake hands.

Only this time, when the gesture was done, Cavallo didn't slip into his car. As if knowing he had an observer, he turned his head slowly, looking directly at Ice, his eyes shining chips of obsidian. The dark smile grew fixed on his boyishly handsome face.

Another squall flattened the grass in the yard, almost pushing me into the fence. Grabbing the billowing edges of his jacket, Cavallo turned his body in the direction of his head and began to walk toward Ice and the fence. After a moment, Morrison followed suit, striding quickly to catch up to his guest.

I shifted my gaze back and forth between the duo and Ice. The long lines of her body fairly radiated a lethal energy and spring-coiled tension. I resisted taking a step closer, instead contenting myself with controlling my breathing so that I might have a chance to hear the words sure to be spoken.

Cavallo came to a stop right in front of the fence. Leaning forward casually, he hooked a hand through the chain links, just inches away from Ice's own grip. His oily smile broadened, a look of false camaraderie on his face. "If it isn't the infamous Morgan Steele. How you doin', Morgan? Get fucked by any big bull-dykes lately?" His twinkling eyes fairly radiated good humor.

"Cavallo," she greeted quietly, her voice overly controlled.

"I must say, though, you're looking good. Orange agrees with you." Leering, he raked his eyes over her body, from head to toe and back up again. Then he cocked his head toward the sky. "Kinda sad though. You being all cooped up in this tiny little box while the world just continues to spin out here." A smirk curled his full lips as his eyes met hers once again. "Sorry to hear about Josephina's little 'accident'."

From my position to the side, I could see Ice's profile and the way her lips pulled back from her teeth in a feral snarl.

Cavallo laughed. "Don't have to worry about her getting lonely or anything, though. Her dear husband's gonna be joining her in the next couple of days." His chest puffed out like a proud rooster's. "Yes, indeed. The old man's gonna be taking a long ride and I…well, let's just say I'll be left to pick up the pieces." His smirk became more pronounced. "It's too bad you screwed up, Morgan." He leered at her again. "I just might have had a…position…for you in my new family."

The mobster pumped his hips twice against the fence, laughing at his obscene parody.

Ice's control broke. Quick as a viper, she released her grip on the fence, only to clamp it down over Cavallo's own fingers which were threaded through the links. His laugh turned into a screech, which turned into a howl of pain as Ice's enormous strength literally cut his fingers into the thin metal bands. His blood began to paint the metal in ribbons of red.

"Release that man, Ms. Steele!" Morrison commanded, stepping up to the fence and trying, fruitlessly, to pry Ice's fingers from Cavallo.

"You've got a big mouth, Joey," Ice snarled. "Somebody's gonna shut it for ya one day. Permanently."

I could see that Cavallo badly wanted to respond. Unfortunately for him, he was too busy screaming.

Morrison took over that particular task. "It's the hole for you, Ms. Steele. Ninety days, this time, for threatening civilians. I suggest you let him go right now before you spend the rest of your miserable life down there."

Ice ignored him. "You made a real big mistake, Joey-boy. Letting Warden Pious over there do your dirty work for ya." She shook her head in condescension. "You know that if you want something done right, you've got to do it yourself, don't ya."

By the look in his eyes, I could tell that Cavallo knew exactly what Ice was referring to. If he didn't before, he knew beyond a doubt that Ice was well aware who had set her up. There was fright in his eyes, shining through the pain like a beacon.

"Step away from the fence, inmate!" came the bullhorn-amplified voice of one of the tower guards.

I looked up and saw four of them, their high-powered rifles aimed directly at Ice's head.

As if she hadn't heard, Ice increased the pressure of her fingers. "Just remember, Joey. Paybacks are a real bitch."

"Step away from the fence, inmate, or you'll be shot! Release the civilian and step away. Now!"

With one last squeeze, and a scream from Cavallo, Ice released her grip and held up her empty hands, grinning. Taking two careful, deliberate steps back from the fence, she winked at the mobster, then turned.

Our gazes locked as she completed her turn and the world began to spin in slow motion. From the corner of my eye, I could see Cavallo reach beneath his coat with his good, right hand.

"*Ice!*" I launched myself at her, aiming for her legs. "Nooo!"

Her eyes widened in question.

The sound of a gun firing, oddly flat in the turbulent air.

The question turned to shock as a bloom of red stained the small, burned hole that suddenly appeared in the upper left chest of her jumpsuit. She looked down, then back at me.

Then her eyes went as empty as they were in my dream and she crumpled to the ground silently.

I landed on top of her, screaming.

I pulled myself away quickly, slapping at my tears as I turned her over onto her back. "Oh God, no. Ice, no. Please. Oh God."

Blood pumped out of the exit wound in slow, sluggish bursts. But that meant that she was still alive. Pressing one hand over the hole in her chest, I used my free one to stroke the hair back from her face. "Oh God, please wake up, Ice. Please don't die on me. Please. Don't do this to me. Please. Oh God. Oh God."

I was panicking, and I knew it. But I couldn't seem to stop. Blood welled up in the spaces between my fingers, painting me with its heated vibrancy. "Don't you die on me, Morgan Steele. Don't you *dare* die on me!"

The sound of running footsteps caused me to look up. The pale, scared faces of Sonny, Pony and Critter stared down at me.

"Oh *fuck!*" Pony grunted, squatting beside me and pushing her own hand down on top of mine in an attempt to stem the bleeding.

"Get an ambulance!" I screamed, not even feeling the pressure of Pony's hand against my own. "Now!!"

Nodding abruptly, Sonny turned and sped away, running back toward the prison in a furious burst. The shocked crowd parted easily to allow her passage.

"Are they gone?" I asked Pony, my rearward view blocked by her muscled body.

"Who?" Pony asked distractedly, her face grim as she increased the pressure on my hand.

"The warden and . . .the shooter."

My friend looked over her shoulder, still blocking my view of the fence and the area beyond it. "A car's peelin' rubber outta the parking lot," she grunted, returning her full attention to her task of slowing the bleeding pumping out of my lover with every beat of her heart.

"Thank God."

"What are you thankin' God for? That might be Ice's killer getting away!"

"She won't die. I know it. She can't."

"I wish I had your faith, Angel."

"You don't need it. I have faith enough for all of us."

More prisoners came up do join us, crowding around and blocking what little light there was. Critter jumped to her feet and pushed the women back as several other Amazons wove their way through the massing women, surrounding us in a protective circle.

Some of the other inmates began to grumble. A clattering sound was heard and I looked up just in time to see a fist-sized rock bounce off the guard tower and land against the fence. Two more rocks flew past me, crashing against the metal frame of the tower.

"What's happening?"

Grunting, Pony pulled Critter down and slapped her hand against mine. "These idiots were just looking for a reason to riot. Looks like they found one."

"But the guards didn't shoot her!"

"That doesn't matter. Just keep that pressure on. I'll see what I can do."

That wasn't a hard order to follow. If the atom bomb was getting ready to land on me, I wouldn't have moved. Critter looked down at Ice's marble-white face. "Is she...."

"For now," I said, trailing my trembling fingers over my lover's still lips. "Please hang on, Ice," I whispered. "I'm so sorry. Please hang on. Just a little longer, alright?"

Pony took some of the Amazons guarding us with her and I was now able to see more of the yard. The inmates reminded me of angry wasps, clad in orange. Their faces were angry, their postures tense, ready to explode with the least provocation. Isolated knots of violence flared up, only to die quickly. The crowd's mood and actions mirrored the fitful breeze surrounding us perfectly.

The only thing keeping me in once piece was the feel of Ice's broad chest moving rhythmically beneath my hand. She looked so peaceful, lying there. If I didn't look down at my gore-coated hands, I could almost believe that she'd just fallen asleep in the yard. "Please wake up, Ice," I whispered, brushing back the windblown tendrils of her hair. "Please don't leave me like this, alright? I love you. And I know you love me. So...just wake up. Please."

The sound of the door slamming open echoed through the yard, and I watched as very nearly the entire contingent of guards marched into the yard, batons in hand, grim expressions on their faces. Sandra broke from the ranks when she saw Critter, Ice and me, running toward us at a sprint.

"Who did this," she demanded, coming to a full stop and crouching next to me.

I looked at Critter, who looked back at me and shrugged.

"Come on, Angel. Who did this? Was it one of my guards?"

"No. No, it wasn't one of the guards."

"It wasn't an inmate...."

"No, not an inmate either."

Her chest caved with her relieved sigh. "Then who? Who was it, Angel?"

It may have been the dire situation, but this time, I didn't hesitate. Ice had asked to be given the chance to handle Cavallo on her own, and as long as she was alive, I was going to keep my word and give her that chance. I returned Sandra's stare directly. "I don't know, Sandra. I wasn't standing close enough to be properly introduced."

Her expression showed her shock at my words. "But…."

I used my free hand to clamp down on her wrist. "It's not important now, Sandra. None of this is important. What *is* important is keeping her alive. So…quit with the questions and find out where the hell that damned ambulance is, alright?"

Her eyes the size of saucers, the head guard jumped to her feet, and turned back toward the building just as the door slammed open once again. Three paramedics ran out into the yard, pushing a stretcher over the broken ground.

Within seconds, they were upon us, with their dented orange boxes and airs of polite, detached, professionalism. Pony and I were pushed out of the way and Ice was quickly loaded aboard the stretcher and buckled in.

When they raised the stretcher to its full height, I jumped to my feet, grabbing one of the rails. "Take me with you."

Sandra grabbed me from behind. "You know they can't do that, Angel."

Pulling away from her grip, I turned on her, holding my wrists up. "Sure they can. Handcuff me. Shackle my legs. Send a couple guards with me to make sure I don't try to jump out of the back of the ambulance. Just please, Sandra, let me go with her. She has no one else."

The head guard turned to one of the paramedics and my heart blazed with hope. "You taking her to County?"

"Yeah. It's got a good trauma team. They should be able to fix her up just fine."

Sandra nodded. "We'll be in touch by phone then." Reaching down, she gently released my grip on the stretcher, then tapped the medic on the shoulder to send him on his way.

"Wait!" I yelled, struggling to free myself from Sandra's confining grip. "You can't do this! Sandra, please! Let me go with her!"

Pulling me into a strong embrace, Sandra lowered her head to whisper in my ear. "You can't go with her, Angel. You know that. You need to be strong, both for Ice and for the rest of us. These women are about one bad second away from exploding into a full-bore riot. If they see you collapse out here…."

I knew she was right, and in that moment, I felt a red flare of hatred for her because of it. How could she expect me to give one care about the inmates or the guards or the potential for a riot? How dare she expect me to pretend like nothing was wrong while my heart was slowly dismembering itself?

But her embrace was warm and full and tender. And from within it, I was able to find the strength to pull myself back together, if only temporarily, if only to show the false face of confidence to the outside world.

Finally, I nodded and pulled away, wiping the tears from my face with relatively steady hands. "I'm alright. I'll be alright."

Sandra smiled. "I know you will be. Ice is a strong woman. She'll pull through fine. You'll see. And when she does," cocking her head, she captured my eyes with her own, "the three of us are going to sit down and have a little talk."

✐   ✐   ✐   ✐

The rest of the day became an eternal sea of wait and worry. I spent most of it near the guards' room, jumping in anticipation and terror every time the phone rang. The Amazons came by regularly for updates, but aside from the fact that Ice had been taken in for emergency surgery, there wasn't anything else to tell during those long, frightening, empty hours.

Then came the phone call I'd been waiting for. I knew it before Sandra even picked up the receiver. The certainty stole through my guts like a hurricane. I could tell she sensed the same thing because her eyes were deeply concerned, and her hand a little shaky as she picked up the receiver and cradled it against her head, clearing her throat. "Rainwater, Pierce here."

Her face remained carefully neutral as she listened to whatever was being said to her over the phone. This, of course, drove me almost to the breaking point and I actively resisted the urge to tug on her shirtsleeve like some preschooler trying to get her mother's attention.

After several, non-informative minutes, Sandra finally gave her thanks to whomever was on the other end of the line, then hung up the phone.

"Well?" My heart was thundering so quickly in my chest that I could hear it in my ears. I didn't want to hear what she had to say almost as much as I *did*.

Putting her hand on my shoulder, the head guard smiled. "She's in recovery."

I almost slid down the wall in relief. "How is she?"

"Resting comfortably at the moment, the doctor said. The surgery went well. The wound wasn't as bad as they had first thought. They had to do a little vascular repair, and she has some muscle damage to her chest which, the surgeon said, might give her some problems with her left arm, but otherwise, she came through it just fine."

"Oh, thank you *God*." I felt dizzy with relief. "Did she wake up at all?"

"Yeah. She was pretty groggy, but he said that she knew her name and all that stuff. They're pretty positive about her full recovery."

"God, this is *such* great news!" Without thinking, I caught up a very surprised Sandra in an embrace and pressed a kiss to her cheek. "I've got to go tell the others. Thanks!"

As I darted out of the room, I turned to look over my shoulder, smiling inwardly when I saw the intimidating head of the guards standing there dumbstruck, a finger resting on her cheek where I'd placed the kiss.

Chapter 13

Ice escaped today.

No, not from the Bog, though, from what I've learned in the past eighteen hours, I think that might have been her plan all along. Rather, she escaped from the hospital where she'd been taken after the shooting almost a week ago.

I sit here, alone in my cell, writing, as my friends cluster around an illegal black and white portable television down in the library, watching the live local coverage of the manhunt that's gone on since word of the escape became known. The prison is ringed by uniformed police officers, all waiting for Ice to come back and murder the warden.

I know I'll never see her again. I know that as certainly as I know my own name. The police aren't looking to recapture her. They're looking to kill her. And, wounded and hunted as she is, there isn't much in me that has faith that she'll foil them.

I started writing this entire story on the day she was shot as a way, I suppose, of keeping her close to me during the time we were apart. I've always enjoyed writing, and it seemed a good way to pass the time. I never knew it would be all I'd ever have; these words, these memories. They seem so inadequate somehow, given what I've lost today.

But, if words on a page are all the universe deems me worthy of, then I'll continue through to the end, wherever that may lead me. I'm crying as I write this, as I'm sure you've already guessed. The words before me are blurred with tears, but if I can somehow write through them, these tears, perhaps I'll be able to forget, just for a little while, that empty place where my heart used to be.

Know this, however, before continuing any further. Morgan Steele was (*is*, I have to believe she's still alive out there, somewhere) a good person. If you have learned nothing else in the reading of these pages, know that she well earned her redemption.

Around one a.m. this morning, I had been awakened from a sound sleep by two guards, males who I hadn't seen before, grabbing me and pulling me from my bed. Cuffing my wrists together, they led me through the mostly silent prison and into the warden's office. Morrison looked worse than I felt. His eyes were puffy and bloodshot, his normally perfect hair was a mass of cowlicks and tangles, and his suit, normally impeccable, was wrinkled and ill-fitting.

"Where is she," he growled as soon as the guards had closed the door behind me.

He might as well have been asking me for the secret of life. "Where is who?"

"You know damn well who. Where is she!?" Spittle flew in an unattractive spray from his snarling lips to land on the otherwise pristine surface of his mahogany desk.

Groggy and frightened though I was, I struggled to keep what little composure I had. "Sir, respectfully, it's one o'clock in the morning. I've been asleep for a few hours. I have no idea who or what you're talking about."

His fist slammed down on the desk, rattling the frame of a portrait showing him shaking hands with a well known Right-Wing religious political figure whose name I won't mention. I stiffened as the guards' hands clamped even harder over my aching biceps. "That bitch, Steele! For the last time, *where is she!?*"

"In the hospital!" I shouted out when it looked like he was going to come over the desk at me.

"She's *not* in the hospital! If she was in the fucking *hospital*, do you think I would have pulled you into my office in the fucking middle of the night to ask you where the fuck she is?"

As I stared at the man, his eyes fairly bugging out of his head, I was struck with the sudden certainty that he was insane. Totally, completely, and without reservation. As insane as Cassandra, if not moreso.

And then it hit me. Ice was *gone*. She'd escaped. Part of me screamed out in joy while another sobbed in grief.

One of the guards shook me, and I realized that Morrison was waiting for an answer. "I'm...sorry. I can't help you. I don't know where she is if she's not in the hospital."

This time, he *did* come across the desk at me, grabbing the front of my jumpsuit in his fist. "You're *lying*, bitch! She fucking planned this escape and I know you helped her!"

Stunned, I shook my head, trying to make sense of my whirling thoughts. "Sir," I said finally, trying hard not to show him how truly frightened I was, "she was shot in the back. I really don't know how that could have been planned. But if it was, Sir, I assure you that I knew nothing about it. I thought she was dead when she hit the ground. If all that was just a setup for an escape, it's news to me."

I could tell by the look in his eyes that he suddenly knew I knew more than he thought, at least as far as the shooting went. Suddenly, I was faced with the overwhelming temptation to tell him exactly what I knew, just to see him squirm. And, perhaps, if the men holding me had been police officers instead of jailers who might, or might not, be in his back pocket, I might just have done so. Instead, I contented myself with letting the knowledge shine in my eyes.

After a moment, he backed off, releasing me and sliding back across the desk and into his chair. "Get her the fuck outta here," he said, slumping down in his seat.

And suddenly, I could see it. The man was enraged, yes. But more than that, he was absolutely terrified. I could see it easily, now that I knew what to look for. The area around his bulging eyes was white and a line of sweat beaded at his upper lip and hairline. I smirked slightly as the burly guards pulled me out of the office, watching as Morrison reached into his suit pocket for a handkerchief.

There are no windows in my cell, but when I was finally uncuffed and left alone, I sat on my cot, looking at the blank ceiling and imagining a canopy of stars overhead. "Ice," I whispered, "I know you're out there. I just don't know where. Please, be safe. I love you. And as much as I want to see you, please, *please*, just...stay away. Please."

Tears came, then, and I let them fall, knowing deep in my heart that the last picture I'd have of her would be the one of her wounded and unconscious, lying on the cold ground of the yard.

The next several hours were spent in a fruitless search for sleep. Finally giving that particular activity up as a lost cause, I got up and put on a fresh uniform, determined to start the day and face, head-on, whatever news it would bring me.

I waited patiently by my cell door, waiting to be sprung for the day. But when the time for release came and went without a sign of the guards, I began to get worried. Full lock down during daylight hours was a very rare thing in the Bog. So rare, in fact, that the only other time I could remember it happening was for the first few hours after the riot which had resulted in Derby's death.

Pressing my head against the bars of my cell, I looked down the catwalk, seeing nothing but the arms of my fellow inmates as they awaited release. Muttered conversations, invective, and questions began to fill the prison in sporadic bursts. I was obviously not the only one who wondered what was going on, though I had a feeling that I might just know a bit more than most. I didn't think it mere coincidence that this aberration of normal prison procedure came the morning after Ice had supposedly escaped from the hospital (and, at that point, despite the warden's behavior, I still wasn't sure what happened, if anything).

The sound of a voice whose owner could only be Morrison suddenly echoed through the prison, silencing all other talk. Though individual words couldn't be heard, I could tell the man was in an insane rage. The sounds of a cell being turned out filled the air with destruction. I didn't have to think very hard to know which cell was being 'examined'.

Scant moments later, running feet resolved into the form of Sandra as she hastily shoved her key into the lock in my cell door, opened it, and grabbed my arm. "Come with me," she ordered, pulling me out of my cell and down the catwalk.

"Wait! But…." Hard as I tried, I couldn't break free of her grip. "Where are…?"

"The warden is about to blow his top. I'm getting you somewhere safe, for the moment. We need to talk."

Deciding that in this case, discretion was the better part of valor, I kept my mouth shut and allowed her to lead me down the steps and through the hallways to the empty visitors' room. She sat me down in one of the chairs, then pulled out another and straddled it, fixing me with a 'no-nonsense' look.

I stared back, determined not to give an inch until I had to.

The silence between us grew oppressive.

"What's going on here, Angel?" she asked, finally.

"Could you be a little more specific?" I knew very well what she was trying to get at, of course, but I wasn't about to be bullied into anything.

She sighed, rubbing her forehead. "You know Ice escaped last night." It wasn't a question.

"So the warden tells me, yes."

Her eyebrows rose into her hairline. "The warden?"

"Yeah. His goon squad dragged me out of bed at one this morning to give me that little bulletin. He didn't seem very happy about it."

"So…you didn't know about this beforehand."

I slammed my hand down on the table, startling her. "Of *course* I didn't! I haven't had any contact with her since she was shot. You *know* that, Sandra!"

She looked at me for a long moment, and then nodded, apparently convinced of my sincerity. She took in another breath, then let it out slowly. "Angel," she asked softly, "who shot Ice?"

At that moment, I wanted, almost more than anything, to tell her. Wanted to share this terrible burden of knowing with her. But I couldn't. For a thousand different reasons, not the least of which was that if something ever happened to Cavallo, whether Ice was involved or not, she would be the prime suspect if I told Sandra. As far as I knew, only four people—myself, Ice, Morrison and Cavallo himself—knew who shot Ice. And it was a sure bet that the latter three wouldn't tell anyone. Sandra, however, would be duty-bound to notify the police. And I couldn't allow that to happen.

"Who, Angel?"

I looked her dead in the eye. "I can't tell you that, Sandra."

"Can't? Or won't."

I said nothing.

"I could put you in the hole for not answering me," she warned.

"Yes," I agreed, not breaking eye contact. "You could."

"And you're willing to risk that?"

"I am."

We stared at one another for a long time in that small, silent room. I could almost see the arguments running behind Sandra's dark eyes, each one pondered carefully before being discarded as useless against me. "She would have done it sooner or later, you know." Her voice was very quiet, and somewhat sad.

"Excuse me?"

"Escaped. If it hadn't been from the hospital, it would have been from here. Do you know anything about that?"

"No." And again, I was telling the truth. In all the time I'd known Ice, the topic of escape had never come up in conversation. "Why do you think so?"

She smiled a little. "It's what the warden was screaming about. They turned out her cell."

"And?"

"She was apparently working on a tunnel before she was shot. I can only imagine that was why she was so adamant against going to the hospital that night after the fire."

"A tunnel?" I asked, confused. "From the *eighth floor?*" The thought was ludicrous.

"Well, I can't get into the details, obviously, but let's just say that there was a rather large hole around the commode in her cell. One that had been carefully carved out."

I shook my head in disbelief. "Sandra, I've been in Ice's cell more times than I can count, and I've never seen a hole, there or anywhere else. Are you sure it didn't just conveniently…appear?"

"Positive. I was there when the warden 'discovered' it."

"But…how?"

"That I can't say. Trust me, though, it was quite damning."

I managed a weak smile. "That's ok. I think I'd rather not know." I honestly didn't know what to think. If you had asked me yesterday if I thought Ice would be a person who would try to escape, I would have laughed in your face. Now? I just didn't know what to think anymore.

My reverie was interrupted by a hand on my arm. "This line of questioning isn't over, Angel," Sandra said, her voice and expression set in stone. "I'll give you a little bit of time to think about why you feel the need to protect Ice's shooter, but when we talk again, I'm gonna want some answers. Do you understand me?"

"I understand."

"Good. Let's go then."

By the time she escorted me from the visitors' room, lock-down had been lifted and the inmates were swarming through the prison. I could tell that the grapevine was in good working order by the looks almost all of the inmates gave me as they passed.

Sandra released her hold on my arm. "Remember what I said, Angel," she murmured close to my ear. "I will."

With a nod, she was gone; swallowed up by an orange tide.

♪   ♪   ♪   ♪

And so here I sit in my cell, with a caged bulb and a stack of cheap paper for company. It's almost time for lights out, and since no one has come to give me any updates in the past several hours, I can only guess that Ice is still out there, somewhere.

They now know, though, Corinne and the Amazons. I told them some of my secrets. I think Ice would forgive me that, wherever she is. They deserved to know why she was shot and what kind of pressure she was under just trying to exist in this rat warren day after day. But more than that, I told them because I couldn't stand to see the faint sheen of disappointment in their eyes. And a kind of hurt. That Ice had left them without even saying goodbye.

They expect me to lose it, I think. To just fracture into a million pieces. And though there have been times today when I felt about one step away from doing just that, I seem to have developed this inner core of strength that I never knew I had. I think it's the only thing that's keeping me going. That and the hope that Ice is still out there, alive if not safe.

I want to hate her, you know. For putting me through this. For putting us all through this. I want to. But I can't. That same strength that won't let me just fall to pieces won't let me hate her either.

I keep waiting for the anger to come, but it seems content to bide its time. Maybe one day, when I'm far away from this place and the memories it invokes in me, maybe then I'll be able to just scream at her to a barren wall. Maybe someday.

The lights have just flickered. It's time to put this away in my little safe space and settle down for the night and wait and wonder if sleep will decide to take me with him when he leaves.

And then, maybe, I can see her again in my dreams.

⚿   ⚿   ⚿   ⚿

When the cells were opened in the morning, I was greeted by a grim-faced Pony. "You need to come and see this, Angel."

My guts instantly tightened as my heart sped up. "What is it?" *God, no. Please don't let it be Ice. Please.*

"It's better if you see it. C'mon."

I followed at Pony's heels as she led me down the stairs and through the prison to the library. It was a Saturday, a day where, with the warden's absence, the rules were relaxed, slightly. The television, which had been hidden in the deepest corners of the library yesterday, sat out in plain view in the middle of one of the tables, Corinne and the Amazons gathered around it as if by a campfire.

They all turned grim faces to me as Corinne and Critter parted to admit a chair, which they directed me to.

"What's going on?"

Corinne gestured to the flickering screen. "Watch."

The picture dissolved from a commercial to a newsroom, where an attractive woman was seated, staring earnestly into the cameras. "Recapping our top story of the morning, Joseph Cavallo, linked to the Briacci Mafioso family, was found gunned down early this morning outside of this restaurant in what the police are calling a gangland-style shooting."

The view then switched to the outside of a popular Italian restaurant which was adorned with yellow police tape and literally crawling with officers of the law. The anchor continued in voiceover. "Details of the shooting are sketchy at the moment, but a police spokesman states that two witnesses inside the restaurant have said that they saw three figures step out from the shadows to the west and advance on Mr. Cavallo as he was exiting his car, which was parked at the curb in front of the restaurant. Mr. Cavallo was observed to be reaching into his pocket for what police are guardedly saying was his gun when he was shot down in front of his car. The three figures then left the scene and were observed driving westbound in a dark-colored sedan. No further information on the shooting is available at this time."

"Jesus," I hissed. "Do you think Ice— "

"Shh," Corinne interrupted me. "There's more. Listen."

The scene switched back to the anchor desk. "In related news, when Mr. Cavallo's car was searched in the aftermath of the shooting, paperwork was discovered that linked him to a stolen-car ring that was headed up by this man," and here, a picture was inset into the upper left hand corner of the screen. I gasped, "Reverend William Morrison, warden of the Rainwater Women's Correctional Facility and a well-known supporter of State Senator Robert Gaelan, among other noted political figures. Reverend Morrison was arrested at his home early this morning and taken into police custody for questioning. More information on this developing story as it becomes available. And now, here's our own Ken D'Julio with this morning's weather."

As the screen switched over to the weather map, I sunk back into my chair, letting go a long-held breath. "Holy shit."

"You can say that again," Corinne said, her tone a touch smug. "Looks like Ice bagged herself two birds with one stone, so to speak."

I turned to her. "Do you really think she did it?"

Corinne snorted. "Does an ursine mammal defecate in the buckwheat? Of course she did it."

"I'm not so sure," I replied, though without much conviction.

"What do you mean, Angel?" Sonny asked from her position across the table. "After everything you told us yesterday, you don't think she did it? After what Cavallo did to her?"

"She did it alright," Critter chimed in, nodding her head sagely.

I could feel my anger rise, and my body rose right along with it, sending my chair clattering against another table as I stood. "You think so, huh? You all think she just went out there with a couple of partners and blew him away, is that right?"

Pony shrugged. "Sure. She owed him."

The rest nodded their agreement.

I barked out a laugh, shaking my head in disgust. "You know, you guys sound just like what I imagine her jurors must have sounded like when they were deliberating. Only I have more respect for them. Because at least they waited until her *trial* to convict her."

Fixing each and every one of them with a stern glare, I turned and left the library at a quick walk, not needing to look back to see the shocked faces I'd left behind.

✒   ✒   ✒   ✒

It's been almost three months since I've last looked at these words I've written. So much has changed, yet so much more remains the same.

Ice is still among the missing. The latest jailhouse poll is betting that she's dead. I'm betting against those odds, as are most of the women who knew her well, or at least as well as anyone *could* know her.

But I must confess that there are times, mostly deep in the night, when I wonder. Because if she is, by some small miracle, still out there, somewhere, she's made no attempt to contact me whatsoever. And believe me when I tell you that it *is* possible to get word like that through to me with none being the wiser. It's been done before.

And so sometimes, when the pain in my heart is flaring up like the supernova of some distant sun, I wonder. Because at those times, it's easier to imagine her dead then uncaring. And it's at those times when the tears I hold inside come bursting forth, an unstoppable force.

The anger hit, much sooner that I though it would. When I made it back to my cell that long-ago morning, it hit with a vengeance. I tore my cell up in an orgy of anger. I ranted. I raved. I punched. I kicked. I threw. I screamed.

I was angry at the Amazons for believing that Ice, when it came right down to it, was an unchangeable, and therefore unredeemable, person. I was angry at myself for harboring, deep in my heart, those same beliefs. But mostly, I was angry with Ice—for giving up, for giving in, for taking what seemed to me to be the easy road.

I think I might have hated her a little too, in those dark moments of rage. If I only knew why she had chosen the path she did, perhaps it would have been easier for me to deal with her loss. But I didn't. And it was killing me inside.

One of the images that helps me through those times of rage and desolation is of her last day here with us.

She turned away from the fence, you see.

She didn't have to. When she had Cassandra up against the bars, even the threat of a horrid beating from the warden and guards didn't make her back down.

This time, when the circumstances were equally bad, she turned away. Not because the guards had their guns aimed at her. Ice wasn't afraid to die. In fact, I think she craved it, sometimes. No, she turned away for her own reasons. And I pin all of my remaining hope on the thought that she turned away because she finally had a dream of her own to hold onto.

Even her escape and the death of Cavallo can't tear that image from my mind, nor the hope from my heart. Because, you see, I think that that dream had something to do with me.

The prison has changed as well. The warden, and I say this with no small amount of glee, went down in flames. With Cavallo's death and his arrest, there was no longer a reason to keep my secret, and so I told Sandra everything that I knew. And, of course, she did what I'd known she would. She went to the police with my information.

The police, in turn, came to me and asked me many pointed questions, all of which I answered truthfully and to the best of my ability. They've added the charge of attempted murder to the rest of Morrison's long list of misdeeds. I hope he gets put away for a long, long time.

The riot that seemed so imminent fizzled out with word of Ice's escape. I don't know why, really. Maybe she took some of this place's spirit, such as it is, with her when she left. It's an uneasy sort of truce, but a truce nonetheless.

Which is good, in a way, because the Amazons are, for all intents and purposes, leaderless. No one wants the job, least of all me, who everyone looked to to pick up the pieces. Though it shames me to admit this, I just can't drag up the strength to do it.

My life has once again been reduced to a simple day-to-day existence. It's all I have the will for anymore.

Yes, I still fight when the cause is right, either by word or deed. But it lacks that sense of…I suppose *magic* is the best word I can use to describe how it felt when Ice was still here. The sense of being part of a team that fought the good fight seems to have vanished with her. We're still the Amazons and we're all still friends, but it's as if our ship has suddenly become unanchored and we're drifting at the mercy of the sea.

That's not a good place to be in, especially given what this gang represents. I can only hope that we can all hang in there until someone steps forward to claim the mantle of leadership once again.

As for me, well, if the gods are kind, it may be the last day I sit in this cell that is no longer a home for me. Donita kept her promise, and tomorrow, I'm scheduled to be transferred to the county jail to await the beginning of my trial, which starts the day after.

She's brought some beautiful clothes for me to wear. She says I'm innocent and should look the part, instead of coming to court in the guise of a convicted killer. It's amazing how much the styles have changed in the five years I've been here. I wonder what else has changed?

I suppose it's best to keep that question tucked away for now. I'm nervous enough having to go up in front of the public to rehash the events leading to the death of my husband five years ago. I haven't been able to eat anything substantial (even if the cafeteria served something that could be called that) in the past couple of days, and sleep seems more like a distant memory than a living reality.

Donita has already informed me that I'm going up on the stand. What if they don't believe me? It's been five years. My emotions, when I think about the killing, aren't the same as they were then. What if they think I'm lying and that I have no remorse for what I've done?

Donita's coached me well, playing the DA's role and, frankly, scaring the living crap out of me several times with her lines of questioning. But she assures me that I'm ready. That I can take on the world.

I just wish I believed her.

✒ ✒ ✒ ✒

Well, Donita kept her word. Here I am, in a tiny, cramped cell in the county jail, scribbling on a bright yellow legal pad that she was nice enough to give me. The court was recessed today after opening arguments, as she said it would be.

I wasn't surprised by the prosecution's angle, having heard it, almost verbatim, five years ago. In the DA's eyes, I'm still a jealous, possessive harpy who couldn't stand the fact that my husband wanted a little time with the boys after work.

Donita was simply brilliant. Her opening arguments were clear, concise and to the point without a wasted word or over-dramatization. She was the consummate professional and appeared magnificently prepared. The jury, which this time was a nice mix of women and men (my previous jury had only the two women sitting on it), seemed to me to eat up her words, and a few times, I thought I caught them looking at me with compassion in their eyes. At least, I hope that's what it was.

Nothing to do now but stare at the walls and wait to see if I can sleep tonight.

Fear and time make strange bedfellows.

It's been five long years since I last graced this place, and the fear is still here. Only it seems to have changed direction. Five years ago, I was afraid that I was going to go to jail. Now I'm afraid I'm not going to get out. And, conversely, I'm *also* afraid that I *am* going to get out.

Was it just such a short time ago that I asked Ice why she didn't just up and move away after she was released from prison the first time? Could I actually have been that naïve, that condescending? Just the possibility of that happening with me causes my stomach to jump rope inside me.

My family has disowned me. All of my friends are prison inmates. The degrees I've earned are about as useless as the paper they're printed on. I have no home, no job and no money.

And yet…and yet, I still have that sometimes damning sense of optimism about everything. The same sense that sat here next to me five long years ago when I was battling for what I thought was my life. The same sense that tells me, despite everything, that Ice is still alive out there.

What I've discovered, you see, is that, no matter how much we might not want it to sometimes, life does go on. The world keeps on spinning. And if we're really lucky, we learn something along the way.

I've learned that love, and companionship, and a simple sense of belonging can be found even in the deepest pits of one woman's hell. I've learned that sometimes good things happen when you least expect them. I've learned that freedom isn't something that can be taken away, only given up. And I've learned that no matter what happens to me in this life, I have the strength to overcome, adapt, and even to thrive, despite, or perhaps because of, the adversity thrown in my path.

Would I be the same woman I am now, with the same strength of purpose, if those events five years ago had concluded differently? Perhaps. Perhaps, one day, I would have been able to find this strength on my own: the strength to leave a loveless marriage and a husband who saw me more as chattel than partner. Perhaps.

But without the love and guidance of Pony, Montana, Critter, Sonny, Corinne and, most of all, Ice, I might never have truly realized what I was capable of. I love them all, very much, and will always carry them in my heart, no matter what the outcome of this latest trial.

Enough philosophizing for one evening. Time to lie down and see if my insomnia has become a permanent condition.

🐎   🐎   🐎   🐎

I had a dream.

It started out like the one just months before, with the huge courtroom and all my accusers (the embodiment of my guilt, I told myself rationally) dressed, literally, to kill.

But this time, when each person stepped forward, preparing to place the yoke of guilt around my neck like some blackened albatross, I found myself responding differently. I accepted responsibility for those things I might have done wrong, but refused the weight of their anger for things that could not be changed.

Perhaps I *could* have been a better daughter, a better friend, a better wife. Looking back on my life from this new perspective of maturity and experience, perhaps I would have made different choices back then.

But the words I had spoken with such conviction to Ice on those long ago days finally bore fruit in my own mind. The actions I'd taken, the choices I'd made, came from within the soul of a good woman. I accepted responsibility for them. I owned them. And I long past paid my debts for them.

Finally, after a lifetime of living under my own soul's oppression, I put paid to my guilt and let it go. And when I did that, all of the figures who had come to accuse simply vanished in a clean-scented mist.

It was an incredibly freeing feeling.

The mist coalesced into a shape of shifting colors. The outline became more distinct, finally resolving itself into Ice. Her face and form were covered in a shimmering radiance and her hair was blown back from her brow by a non-existent breeze. She smiled, and it lit up the room.

"Ice!" I screamed in my dream, almost delirious with joy. I ran toward her, only to be stopped by her upraised hands. "What?" I asked. "What is it?"

"I need to ask your forgiveness, Angel," she replied, her voice rivaling the best Beethoven concerto in its utter beauty to me.

"Forgiveness? For what?"

"For leaving you. For not saying goodbye. For not giving an explanation."

I knew that there were a lot of questions I needed answered. But some part of me also knew that this was just a dream and I wasn't about to ruin it with conversation. "Yes," I said, knowing that even without explanation, without words, I *had* forgiven her, just as I knew, by the love in her eyes, that, in this dreamspace at least, she had forgiven me.

She opened her radiant arms and I flew into them, feeling all the burdens of my heart tumble out of me as she enclosed me within her warm and loving embrace. It might only have been a dream, but the body in my arms was warm and solid, every curve and line remembered, every scent the same as the last time we'd embraced.

I started crying, begging whomever would listen to just grant that I would never wake up.

A hand clasped onto my shoulder from the back, as if trying to pull me away from Ice. I tried to hold on tighter, but as I did, Ice's form became insubstantial again. I felt my arms go right through her. "No! Come back! Don't leave me again!"

"Angel," a voice sounded in my head.

"Please, Ice! Come back!"

"Angel," the voice repeated.

"What!?" I snarled, turning my head.

Donita, very much in the land of reality, stepped back, her dark eyes blinking in surprise. "Sorry to wake you," she said, softly. "You need to get ready. The jury's just come back. The verdict is in."

"The ver…" I sat straight up on the meager jailhouse cot, raking a hand through my hair and attempting to blink the sleep out of my eyes. "Already? What time is it?"

My lawyer looked down at her gold wristwatch. "A little after eleven."

"The case just went to the jury at ten. This isn't good, is it?"

Smiling, she gave my shoulder a little squeeze. "Not all quick decisions favor the prosecution, Angel. Let's just go in there like we own the place." Her smile broadened. "I have a feeling you're gonna like what you hear."

Chapter 14

I'm free.

As I sit on a wooden bench outside of the courtroom, waiting for Donita to finish up her discussions with the judge (she is filing a civil suit on my behalf for wrongful imprisonment) I look down at that phrase I've just written as if reading it over and over and over again will cause it to sink in.

It's such a small word, a minor word, and yet what it represents ….God, it represents the *world*!

As I sit here, I'm looking at a young gentleman with what looks to be his girlfriend. They just came out of traffic court (the nice security guard told me that much—it's amazing how much differently you're treated when you're sitting on *this* side of the bars. I'd almost forgotten that.), and they're heading for the door.

And it just hit me. I can do that too. I can just get up off this rickety, scarred bench, walk those few feet down that highly polished floor, open the glass door, and step into the sunshine beyond. I could just pick a direction and start walking and not stop until my legs gave out. No bars or fence to hold me in, to keep me back, to keep me from people and people from me.

I'm free.

I can't seem to write or think or say it enough. Free to do what I want, where I want, when I want and with whom I want.

What, where, when and with whom I'm going to do these nebulous things is a question I've neither asked, nor answered myself yet. It's back there, simmering, but I'm gonna leave it there for awhile. I don't want to spend my first few minutes of freedom frozen in terror like a deer in the headlights of an onrushing semi.

Donita, bless her huge heart, has offered to put me up until I can get back on my feet again. I didn't answer her right away. I couldn't. I need to exist in the moment right now. The possibility of a future is suddenly too overwhelming for me to consider.

She smiled in understanding and slipped a business card into the breast pocket of my woolen blazer. She knows I'll call her once I come down off this cloud I find myself on. I know I will too.

After all, where else can I go?

🔑　🔑　🔑　🔑

Donita gave me a lift back to the Bog so that I could collect my personal belongings and say goodbye to my friends, who were really my family.

How do you say goodbye to people you've shared every waking moment with for the past five years? How do you thank them for giving you their love, their support, their friendship? How to you express your undying gratitude for the many times they've saved your life and even your soul? What words can you possibly use to cover the enormity of your feelings for them?

I found myself in the strangest position. It was almost surreal. I was allowed to stay in the visitors' room while my belongings were gathered from the prison to be brought to me. The door into the prison itself was locked against me and a guard stood at my side, for my protection, no less.

Whereas before I was barred from getting out of the Bog, now I was barred from stepping into it.

The door to the prison side opened and Sandra stepped through, her face wreathed in a smile, and her hands filled with a cloth sack bearing my worldly possessions. Placing the bag on the table, she opened her arms, and I ran into them, hugging her hard and starting to cry.

"Angel," she whispered, her own voice heavy with tears, "I'm so proud of you. I knew you'd beat this. We all did."

"Thank you Sandra," I blubbered, holding her strong body close. "For everything you've done for me. You helped make this place livable and I'll never forget that. You're a wonderful person."

Squeezing me one last time, she stepped away, drying her tears on the sleeve of her uniform. "You made this place better for everyone just by being here, Angel. Thank *you*. It won't be the same without you. I wish you only the best of luck in your life. I know you'll do yourself proud. With a heart like yours, how could not?"

Clearing her throat, she gave me a watery smile. "We seem to have quite a lot of inmates who've requested a visitor's pass for today. Coincidentally, they've all requested to see the same visitor. Mind if I show them in?"

Wiping my own tears away, I managed a smile. "Of course not. I'd like to see them."

"Alright then." Grinning, she opened the door.

The sound of cheering, shouts and clapping filled the central square as women streamed through the doorway and into the visitors' room. I could hear the sounds of my name being chanted with a tenor and an excitement almost rivaled Ice's entrance into the prison five years ago.

A giddy smile broke over my face as my friends came inside, hugging and kissing me. There were a lot of tears and a lot of laughter, just how I imagined a real goodbye to family and friends might feel. It warmed me right down to my toes.

Pony, Sonny and Critter gathered around me in a tight circle, our heads bowed inward, tears streaming down our faces. Pony and Critter were both due for parole hearings within the next several months, and I had good feelings about each of them and told them so.

When we finally broke apart, I looked at each one individually.

"Pony, if you hadn't been there when Mouse was trying to rearrange my face, I don't know what I would have done. Thanks for being there for me and introducing me to the Amazons. Thanks for teaching me how to fight and how to stand up for myself. I won't ever forget you." Leaning in, I gave her a light kiss on the lips.

Everyone in the room burst out into laughter as Pony's face turned a fiery red. "Awww, damn," was all she could say.

I turned slightly. "And Sonny, thanks for everything you've done for me. Especially helping me build back my strength after my little flu problems. You've been a good friend." Grinning, I hugged and kissed her as well.

Returning my smile, she punched me lightly on the arm. "You've taught us a lot too, Angel. Good luck out there, alright?"

Nodding, I turned to Critter, my closest friend among the Amazons. We both started crying again, and embraced one another tightly. "You're the best, Critter," I whispered in her ear.

"So are you, Angel," she whispered back. "I won't ever forget you. You made this an okay place to be."

Holding the hug a moment longer, we then pulled away and kissed. Reaching up, I brushed the tears from her eyes. "Knock 'em dead at your parole hearing."

She laughed through her tears. "If I do that, I'll *never* get outta here."

From her place in one corner, Sandra cleared her throat, looking faintly chagrined. "Alright, guys, it's time to get back out there."

There were a few grumbles of good-natured protesting, but then my friends began to file back into the prison, each one touching me and wishing me goodbye and good luck as they passed.

Soon, the door closed with a muted click, leaving the guard and one other person left behind.

Corinne.

Seeing her standing there, her face a curious tableau of loss and pride, I, for the first time, broke down completely, running into her arms and hugging her soft body tightly to me.

It was only with this woman, who was more of a mother to me than my own would ever be, that I could feel safe enough to let the fears of my future out of their tightly locked closet. Like a small, lost child, I sobbed on her shoulder. Even the sweet fragrance of her sachet, which will forever signal 'home' to me, failed to comfort me. "Oh, Corinne," I sobbed, "what am I gonna do? I feel so lost. This is my home. You are my family. I don't know if I can make it out there."

"Nonsense," she murmured back, sniffing away her own tears. "You'll thrive out there, Angel. You're one of the strongest people it's ever been my privilege to know. You'll do just fine. All you have to do is believe in yourself."

"But how do I do that? I don't know if I have the strength...."

Pushing me away, she gripped my shoulders in an almost painful grip. "You listen to me, Angel. You have the strength of twenty people. You brought a hope and a joy to a place which, before you came, had none. We might have taught you how to survive here in the Bog. But you...you taught us how to *live*."

"But...."

"No 'buts', Angel. You did what you did to a bunch of hardened criminals with little hope for a future. You taught me how to feel again, something I thought could never happen. For the first time in a long time, I look forward to getting up in the morning. *You* did that. No one else. You." She touched my chest with her finger. "That heart of yours is as big as the whole world out there. It's been caged long enough. It's time to go out there and show everyone else what you've shown us. What you've shown me."

Taking off her glasses, she wiped at her eyes. "I think I'll unlearn this crying thing, though, if you don't mind," she grumbled, polishing her glasses before balancing them on her nose once again.

Reaching down, she picked something hidden on the chair behind her, and held it out to me. It was the tiny bonsai that Ice had made for me for our anniversary. A fresh yellow ribbon adorned its trunk. "Here."

As I took it, fresh sobs starting again, she handed me something else. It was the book I'd given to Ice, also on our anniversary.

"But how?" I managed to choke out, setting the tree down and opening up the cover. Inside was the photograph of Ice and her family. "Oh god," I sobbed. "Oh god. Corinne, I miss her so much. How am I going to do this without her?" I pressed both the book and the photo close to my body, hugging it to me and rocking.

Stepping up to me, she placed gentle hands on my cheeks. "My sweet little Angel, if there's one thing above all that you've taught me, it's to always have hope. Carry it with you now. It'll give you the strength you need."

Looking deep into her eyes, I swore I could detect the faintest shimmer of some hidden knowledge deep within her gaze. My heart leapt into my throat, but when I opened my mouth to give voice to my question, she placed a finger over my lips. "Always have hope, Angel," she whispered.

Taking her finger away, she leaned forward and kissed me warmly, lingering a bit. Then she pulled away. "I love you, Angel."

Turing away quickly, she stepped to the door and opened it.

"Corinne! Wait!"

She turned back, tears liberally streaming down her cheeks.

Walking back over to her, I kissed her soundly. "I love you too. Never forget that. Ever."

Smiling, she touched her lips, then cupped my cheek. "I won't, sweet Angel. Ever."

With a small, sad little wave, she turned once again and stepped through the door and out of my life.

The door closed and I stood there for a long moment, touching the cool metal with my palm as if I could imprint everything that had happened to me somewhere deep inside where I'd never forget it. I leaned my forehead against the door. "Goodbye," I whispered.

Behind me, the guard cleared her throat softly. "Should I call a cab for you?" she asked.

After a moment, I turned to her, a brightly false smile affixed to my face. "Thanks for the offer, but I think I'm gonna walk."

"Alright then. Just be careful, alright? Lotta crazies out there."

That statement broke my somber mood and I brayed out my laughter. Just yesterday, I *was* one of those crazies. And now, I was being cautioned against them.

As someone I'm sure much wiser than me has been known to say, what a difference a day makes, huh?

Epilogue

I'm writing this beneath the flickering lamp of a hotel room that saw 'new' two decades ago and 'clean' only shortly after that. But the door has a lock that I can open any time I want and the bed is the most comfortable I've slept on in years.

That bed is calling to me longingly, and I'll go, willingly and joyously, just as soon as I get this pressure of words out of my head and on to this paper.

Walking out that door and into the fresh air was the hardest, and conversely, the easiest thing I've ever had to do. As I began to take my first steps into freedom, the Bog seemed intent on pulling me back, as if it had sunk invisible talons into my spine. My legs became almost leaden with the strain I was under. The prison seemed to whisper to me on a current of wind; promising to hold me and keep me safe if only I would look back.

But I didn't look back. It was a promise I'd made to myself and one I was determined to keep. Looking back would only make things harder and I knew that. So I didn't.

And because I didn't, my next steps, and the ones following that, became easier as the weight I didn't know I carried was lifted off my shoulders to be tossed into the drifting spring breeze.

The first sound I truly remember hearing as a free woman was the tether of the American flag slapping forlornly against its metal pole. It was a lonely, desolate sound, and seemed like a bad omen until I recognized the sound of birdsong playing a melodic counterpoint to the 'ting ting' of the rope against metal.

The noise of passing cars, fairly uncommon this far out, drew my attention to the road. How the styles had changed in just five years. I hadn't really noticed it on the drive to and from court, being so wrapped up in my own emotional struggle.

I looked at that road, pitted and pot-holed by winter's icy reign, curving gently over the breast of a small hill, and wondered where it led. My future was on that road, somewhere, unfettered by the constant metal specter of chains and cuffs and bars and fences. It was as broad as my imagination and as narrow as my fears.

Freedom's siren call was infinitely sweeter than the Bog's brutal cacophony, and so, with a lightness to my step, I walked into that future, alone, afraid, but carrying with me the hope that things would turn out well for me in this new life I was being urged to make for myself.

When my legs began to tire, I headed to a small park, interspersed with walkways and drive-paths, and settled on a wooden bench to watch the sun set over the small pond dug there. A flock of ducks had obviously chosen to make this quiet, out of the way place their spring nesting grounds, and I watched as, tame and winter lean, they were fed by giggling children holding out crusts of stale bread.

Innocent, joyful laughter filled the air around me and I felt a bubble of happiness well up from inside me. The bench's warmth seeped into my body through my clothes and I leaned back to watch the activity going on around me, just another woman taking a brief interlude from an otherwise stressful day.

Young couples passed by, their hands intertwined, their faces wreathed with the smiles of young love, a smile which had seemed permanently etched into the lines of my own face such a short time ago. I was hit with a pang of jealous longing so strong that my breath seemed to have taken leave of my lungs as I sat there, watching them pass slowly by, their interest only in one another.

When I could breathe again, I noticed that a young mother had come to sit beside me, watching her two youngsters chase the ducks and each other while she worked at her knitting, her hands moving quickly with casual skill. We conversed briefly about nothing of importance and I felt myself gradually begin to relax once again.

When she left, carefully grasping her children by their grubby hands and leading them back to their no-doubt safe and comfortable little lives, I contented myself with watching the play of light on the gently rippling water. I allowed my mind to go mercifully blank for a long stretch of moments, existing only in this moment of perfect peace and solitude, unencumbered with thoughts of future or past.

Gradually, with some subliminal sense that had been honed to a razor's edge in the Bog, I became aware that I was being observed. Looking casually, first to the left, then to the right, I saw nothing out of the ordinary. Still, the hairs at the back of my neck stood at stiff attention and a warning tingle caressed the nerves of my spine.

As nonchalantly as I could, I turned to look over my right shoulder. There, beneath a grand oak cloaked in the first vibrant green of spring, a man stood straddling a motorcycle. He was clad, from head to foot, in black leather with red and white piping running down the sides of his jacket and leather pants. His black helmet had a mirrored visor that reflected the fiery orange blaze of the setting sun back at me. It was impossible to tell if he was my observer, but his head seemed to be inclined in my direction and my heart sped up in an autonomic reaction.

Just as casually, I returned my gaze back to the pond before me, considering my options. When you've been in prison for awhile, you begin to listen to your body's signals. And my body was warning me that something bad was going to happen if I didn't either prepare to run or prepare to fight.

Was it just jailhouse paranoia, the kind that presupposes a killer behind every locked door? Was this something I was going to have to deal with every day of this new life I was going to forge for myself? Would every stranger's glance spark this adrenaline rush within me?

My peaceful solitude broken, I concentrated on my breathing, determined to wait this particular test out. After all, people *were* allowed to look at the sunset in a park without having sinister motivations. I was living in the real world now, and jumping at every shadow just wasn't going to be an option for long. Not if I wanted to retain some tattered shred of sanity.

Hearing the motorcycle come to life behind me, I let out a relieved breath, congratulating myself for not bolting from something that obviously was turning out to be nothing.

But then, instead of moving away, the motorcycle appeared to be getting closer, its tires crunching over the remains of last autumn's bounty strewn over the newly luxuriant grass. My heart leapt into my throat again, and my hands, of their own volition, curled into tight fists, ready to defend me if need be. I could feel my spine stiffening as my muscles clenched in an instinctive 'fight or flight' response.

The cycle purred closer and I blinked rapidly, my eyes suddenly dry. "Alright, Angel," I whispered to myself. "Don't panic. Whatever you do, don't panic. If he's after you, and you don't know that he is, he won't dare do anything in broad daylight with all these people around, alright? Just keep calm. He probably just wants a closer look at the pond or something. He has as much right to be here as you do."

The motorcycle braked to a smooth stop right beside my bench and it took everything I had in me not to just jump up and start to run. Visions of Morrison calmly ordering my execution from the comfort of his prison cell ran through my head tauntingly.

The engine was turned off and I could hear the kickstand as it was lowered to the ground. I prevented my head from turning only with the greatest strength of will, keeping my gaze focused on the play of light over the rippling water. *Stay calm. Stay calm. Stay calm.*

I could hear the light crunch of gravel as the man got off his motorcycle. Then nothing but the quietly ticking engine and the seemingly far off sounds of children at play.

Why doesn't he do something? Why is he just standing there?

Because, the darkly paranoid part of my mind supplied, *he's just waiting for the opportunity to kill you without all these witnesses seeing it.*

That's nonsense, my more rational thoughts proclaimed. *He's looking at the water, same as you are.*

He could see the water just fine from where he was. Run now, Angel, while you still might have a chance.

Stay calm. Nothing's happened yet. Start running now, and you'll never stop. You'll be looking over your shoulder forever and screaming every time a dog tips over a trash can.

I was so wrapped up in my internal argument that I didn't even notice when the stranger walked closer to where I sat, stopping less than two feet to my right, just beyond where the bench ended. Knowing that I was betraying my terror more by *not* looking, I turned my head fully in his direction, summoning up a smile from somewhere.

My image was reflected back at me from the mirrored visor, showing my smile for the false thing that it was. My eyes were wide with barely controlled panic. My heart sped up even more as a sweat broke out over my forehead, stinging my eyes.

He stared at me for so long that I finally just wanted to scream at him to just kill me and get it over with so that I could have some peace.

His gloved hand came up then, and in my panic, I swore I saw a gun. My own hands raised, palm out, in pure reflex, before I noticed that his hand was empty and he was merely reaching for the visor of his helmet.

He moved the faceplate up slowly and I can remember thanking God that at least I would see the face of my killer before I died. Not great, as prayers of thanks go, but it was something to focus my panicked thoughts on.

I couldn't see much of his face. It appeared to be covered with a black hood of some sort, covering all features but the eyes.

I blinked.

The eyes.

I blinked again, bringing my hand up to shade against the nearly horizontal rays of sunlight shining in my face.

One step, and the sun was effectively blocked by a long body, leaving me free to stare into those beautiful, mesmerizing, magnificent, *blue* eyes.

Blue as the hottest part of a candle's flame. Blue as the center of a perfect block of....

"Ice?" I whispered, the tears already starting to fall.

Their shape changed to a smile's almond as they warmed, their color deepening.

"Ice?" I repeated in a voice thick with tears. "Is that you?"

A black-gloved hand reached down, and without thinking, I grasped it. I was pulled up with an ease I well remembered and my shout was suddenly muffled against her chest as the feel and scent of sun-warmed leather encompassed me as much as her arms did, folding themselves around my body in a tight embrace.

My words came out like a flood of water over a shattered dam. "Oh my God. I thought you were dead! I thought they'd killed you! How did you get here? What happened to you?"

Further questions were lost in my sobs and she tightened her embrace, rocking me gently. Beneath the heavy leather, I could hear her own heart racing and I could feel the tightness in her chest that told me she was trying to control tears of her own.

Gradually, she released her tight hold of me, urging me out to arm's length and gazing intently at me, as if needing to memorize my features again. Her stare was so loving, so intense, that I felt a blush rise to my cheeks.

Laughing weakly in embarrassment, I brushed the tears from my eyes, standing as a soldier might during a parade review. From the corner of my eye, I noticed some curious stares we were getting from passers-by. I looked back at Ice, nervous once again. "You shouldn't be here," I said in a low-pitched whisper that I hoped would carry through her hood and helmet. "The police are still looking for you. It's not safe for you here. They…they could have sent someone to tail me." I knew I was sounding like a paranoid idiot, but my fears were real.

Her eyes warmed in a smile once again as she slowly shook her head. Then, for the first time, she spoke, her voice slightly muffled, but exactly as I'd remembered it. "I've been following you all afternoon."

My eyebrow creased in puzzlement. "You have? But, I didn't…."

Shaking her head again, her eyes still smiling, she gently took my hand and led me over to her motorcycle, which was of a style I'd never seen before outside of the motorcycle races my father sometimes watched on television. It wasn't a touring bike, like some of the Harleys and Hondas that I'd seen outside the bars near my apartment in Pittsburgh. This motorcycle seemed to be built for speed and not so much for comfort.

Releasing my hand, she went over to the other side of the bike and picked up a second helmet which had been attached to the back of the molded seat, holding it out to me, her eyes full of questions.

Questions of my own, a million of them, flitted through my mind, but I could no more refuse that helmet than I could refuse to breathe.

Accepting the helmet, I pulled it over my head. It was a snug fit, the foam inserts dragging harshly over my ears. I kept the visor up, watching as she rounded the bike again and grabbed my sack of personal articles. The bag wasn't that big, containing as it did only a couple articles of clothing and Ice's book. It had two loops, which I slipped over my arms as Ice handed it to me, settling it comfortably on my back.

Picking up the bonsai, she walked back to the bike and lifted the seat, exposing a tiny carry space. She placed the tree almost reverently within, then closed the seat back up and swung her leg over the bike, straddling it once again.

Breathing deeply, I climbed in back of her, never having ridden a motorcycle before. The bike was built for the driver to lean forward, almost resting on the gas tank.

Once I was more or less settled, she took my hands and clasped them across her abdomen. "Hang on," was all she said before she kick started the engine.

And hang on I did.

We rode north, and north, and north, mainly through back country roads, but sometimes on lightly, and not-so-lightly, traveled highways. I spent most of the evening laying almost directly on top of Ice as she leaned over the cycle's gas tank, the handlebars at her chin, racing to beat the devil.

The miles flew by, my surroundings almost mystical, bathed in the diminishing glow of twilight spring. My terror with this new mode of travel almost caused me to dump the bike as my body rebelled against the gravity of the tight turns Ice was making at incredible speeds. Only her unparalleled strength kept us upright and moving.

Finally, I just gave up and gave in, laying my heavy head against her back and closing my eyes against the onrushing wind which buffeted my helmet. I felt my body relax and meld itself to hers, almost becoming one with it as we continued down the road and into the future.

After hours and hours of riding, my body stiff and sore and aching, my hands blocks of ice chapped by the early spring wind, we finally pulled to a quiet stop in a graveled lot outside of a rundown motel.

It took almost all that I had just to release my death grip on Ice's waist and straighten my cramped and aching back. She slipped off the bike with her usual seamless grace and then turned and helped me from my perch, releasing me as she dug into her pocket for a single key.

After retrieving the bonsai from beneath the seat, she led me over to a battered door and slipped her key in the lock. The handle turned easily and she ushered me inside.

The room was warm, small, and lit by a single lamp hanging over a battle-scarred table off to one side. A double bed took up most of the remaining space. A knapsack sat atop the tattered, threadbare quilt and I lowered my own sack of belongings to lay beside it. Then I unsnapped my chinstrap with cold-numbed fingers, sliding the confining helmet from my head and shaking my hair free.

From beside me, Ice copied my actions, pulling off helmet and hood and releasing her hair in tumbling midnight waves, running a negligent hand through it to settle the strands into some type of order. My heart doubled its pace at the simple beauty of the unconscious act.

She turned to me then, and smiled, and I fell in love all over again, tumbling headlong into a precipice I thought denied to me forever. Tears sprang to my eyes, and though I wanted nothing more than to be engulfed by her tender strength and powerful love, I needed one question answered. One above all others.

"Why?" That one simple word covered a hundred emotions, a hundred further questions. Why then? Why now? Why this?

Her smile grew tender as she stripped off her gloves and led me to the bed to sit beside her. My body groaned out its thanks for the soft padding beneath it.

"It was something I had to do," she said softly, looking at the table in front of us.

"I don't understand."

"I know."

"Then explain. Please. I thought I'd lost you."

"I know that, too." Her voice was faintly choked as she turned back to me, reaching out and grasping my hand, and pulling it into her lap. She kept her gaze focused on it, her thumb playing lightly over my knuckles, warming my chilled flesh with her touch. She cleared her throat. "When…I was in the hospital recovering, the warden…paid me a little visit. He told me that if anyone ever found out who was behind the shooting, or why Cavallo was even there in the first place, he'd make sure that you'd never see your appeal."

Her words, so softly spoken, froze me completely. "My God," I breathed.

"I knew right then that I could never go back. I needed to…take care of things so that his threat would never become a reality." She looked up at me, briefly, before looking down at our joined hands once again. "I was chained to the bed by a cuff around my ankle. But they put the cuff around a weak strut." She shrugged. "It wasn't that difficult to take care of that problem. Then, it was just a matter of waiting for the right opportunity." She took in a deep breath, then let it out slowly. "When it came, I ran."

"Where did you go?"

That quirky little half smile lifted the corner of her mouth. "I got a gun from an old…friend. Then I went to Cavallo's house." Her smile widened, went almost savage. "It was payback time."

I moaned softly and her eyes darted up to mine again, before looking down once more, her long lashes lowered. "Yeah. Well, I made my way over to his house and took out a couple of his 'bodyguards'."

"Did you kill them?"

"Nah. They never even knew I was there. Just put 'em to sleep for awhile. He was upstairs in his bed. Alone." She laughed dryly. "Could never even pay for a woman. Anyway, I walked in there, right up to his bed. I put the gun to his temple, thinking about what he did to Josephine, to Salvatore, to me. About what he, through Morrison, was gonna do to you."

Her hand left mine and curled into a tight fist. "I wanted to kill him so badly I could taste it. My finger was on the trigger—just a hair's worth of pressure and it would have gone off, ending everything."

She tilted her head up toward the ceiling, her jaw working as she dragged her hands through her hair. "I couldn't do it," she whispered, harshly. "I wanted to, *God*, so badly. I wanted to end his miserable, stinking little life." She sighed, shaking her head. "But I couldn't."

"Why?"

"As I was standing there, watching him sleep, I thought about you." And here, her eyes came to rest, for the first time, on my face. She smiled slightly. "About that time when I had Cassandra's life in my hands. I remembered you telling me not to give up on my dreams, how she wasn't worth it. And I realized that if I went back to that person I used to be, the one who killed to get rid of my problems, that's exactly what I would have done." Tears sparkled in her eyes. "My dreams might not be much, but they were all I had. And I couldn't give them up. Not for him."

"Oh, Ice…."

I reached out, and she took my hand in an almost desperate grip, holding it up to her chest. I could feel her heart thundering through the thin fabric of her simple cotton T-shirt.

"So, I walked away. I left him there, never knowing how close he came to never waking up at all. As I was leaving his house, I saw a notepad by the downstairs phone. The name of one of Salvatore's favorite meeting spots, an Italian restaurant in Pittsburgh, was written on the pad, together with a time and Sal's name written beneath. I knew it was a set-up, and I almost went back upstairs to finish the job."

"But you didn't."

"No. I decided to give Sal a warning. I went over to his place; didn't even know if he'd be in." She smiled crookedly again. "His guards weren't surprised to see me, for some reason. I guess wind of my escape had gotten out by then. But they let me by without much trouble."

"Was he glad to see you?"

"Not really. I was heat he couldn't afford. So I gave him my information, extended my condolences over Josephina's death, and left. I can't say he was sorry to see me go. And I wasn't sorry to leave. I realized, right then, that that wasn't a life I wanted to live anymore."

"What did you do?"

"Got on my bike and came out here. A couple of friends of mine own it." Her gaze encompassed the tiny room. "It's not exactly the Ritz, but it's safe enough, especially for someone like me."

"They had roadblocks set up all over looking for you. How in the world did you get past them?"

She smiled. "I think, at the time, they were more worried about who was coming in to town than who was going out. I knew Morrison would panic once he got word of my disappearance. I imagine a sizable chunk of the police force was guarding the Bog."

"They were. It looked like a policemen's convention."

Ice laughed softly. "I also figured that Morrison wouldn't dare to do anything to you with that much official business loitering around. He was hung by his own fears. I knew, too, that Salvatore would most likely take care of Cavallo if Cavallo tried to follow through on his planned hit. And if Cavallo fell, Morrison would fall with him."

"How did you know that?"

Her grin turned smug. "Who do you think planted those papers in his car?"

I gasped. "You didn't."

Both eyebrows raised. "Oh, I did."

Shaking my head, I let out a short laugh. "I don't know why I'm surprised."

"Anyway," she continued, "I hung out here and kept an eye on everything. I'm sure Cavallo knew I'd escaped before he went to try and take out Briacci. I have no idea what, other than ego, made him do it. But he got what he deserved, and so did Morrison."

Her smile became sad. "So, all I had left was to watch over you. I'll admit I went out and got pretty drunk when I heard you were granted the re-trial."

"But how? Donita?" My temper flared. "Damn her! I...."

"No. It wasn't Donita. I'd never get her involved in something like this."

"Then who?"

Her silence gave me its own answer.

"Corinne," I said with growing certainty. "It was Corinne, wasn't it."

Ice nodded, slowly.

I bolted from the bed, my hands fisted in anger. "God *damn* it! I can't believe she would hide something like that from me!"

She held up her own hands. "Don't blame her, Angel. I asked her to keep things quiet."

I turned on her. "But why? Ice, I thought you were *dead!* Do you *know* what I *went* through? Do you have any idea at all?!"

Her gaze dropped back to the bed. "Yes," she said softly. "But it was the only thing I could do."

"But why?" I asked again. "Why couldn't you just let me know that you were, at least, alive? What would that have done except ease my pain?" I was so angry, I was shaking.

"I wanted to, Angel. More than anything. But I couldn't. This was your chance to get what you deserved: your freedom. And if you knew that I was out there, somewhere, and that came out somehow, they could charge you with aiding and abetting a fugitive, and that chance would have been lost."

She met my eyes again, her own searing with the intensity of her convictions. "Your freedom is worth more than anything in the world, Angel. I did what I did because I had to do it. I don't expect you to understand, or forgive, my actions."

As I stared at her, my anger began to dissipate. Her actions were borne out of a deep love for me. That much I knew. And if I couldn't forgive the pain she'd caused, at least I could understand it and accept it as her truth. Loosening my fists, I returned to sit next to her on the bed, clasping her hand as she used the other to tenderly stroke my hair.

I smiled up at her. "So, ya spied on me, huh?" I asked, butting her shoulder with my head.

She crooked a grin back at me. "Somethin' like that, yeah. And when Corinne called me with the verdict, I hopped on my bike and drove down there as fast as I could. I got there about a half hour before you stepped out of the Bog for the last time."

Her eyes closed. "Seeing you again, it made my heart crawl up in my throat. I love you so much." Pausing, she wiped the lone tear which had escaped from beneath her lashes. "I wasn't going to talk to you, you know. I just wanted to see you one more time, make sure you got away safely. I would have made sure you had somewhere to stay until you were on your feet again. I suspect Donita offered."

I nodded. "Why wouldn't you have said anything?" I couldn't quite hide the hurt in my voice, and felt her stiffen beside me.

"Angel, you're a free woman now. An innocent woman. You can go anywhere; do anything in this life that you want to. I couldn't pull you back into my life, living on the run, always looking over your shoulder to wait for some police officer or simple citizen to recognize me."

She sighed. "But then, when I saw you in the park, when I saw the sunlight play across your hair, I couldn't ….I couldn't leave without telling you I loved you, without saying goodbye to you. You deserved that, at least. And then, when I had you in my arms, I just couldn't do it. I couldn't let you go. No matter how much I wanted to, I just couldn't. I know it isn't fair to you, and I'm not asking you to be with me. I just know that I needed to say more than goodbye. I needed to explain things. I needed…I needed you not to hate me."

The look in her eyes, so lost, so infinitely sad, broke my heart into shattered fragments.

"Oh, Ice. I could never hate you. Don't you know that by now?"

Her eyes were suddenly shy, and I caught a glimpse of the girl in that long ago photo. "I haven't been loved unconditionally for a long time," she said, her voice barely above a whisper. "I think I forgot what that was like. But your freedom…."

Reaching up, I clasped her face between my hands, directing her to meet my eyes. "Ice, freedom means having the choice to decide what to do with your life. And that choice was made a long time ago. Being with you is where I want to be."

"But…."

"No buts. My freedom has given me this choice, and I'm not backing down from it. You don't have to understand it. You just have to accept it. Or not. And that is *your* freedom."

"I can't let you give up your chance at a new life because of me, Angel. It's not that I don't appreciate the sentiment, because believe me, I do."

I could feel my eyes narrow. "So, what you're telling me is that I'm only as free as you'll allow me to be, is that it?"

"Damn it, Angel! If you stay with me, you'll only be putting yourself into yet another prison! Can't you see that?"

Yes, she was angry. But this time…this time, I wasn't afraid.

"Ice, the only prison I'd be going back to is the one you'd put me in by refusing to let me make my own decisions over what I want my life to be. There wouldn't be any bars except for the ones around my heart. That's a place I don't ever want to go to. It would be a thousand times worse than the Bog could ever be." I grasped her hand and held it tightly, bringing our joined hands upward so she could plainly see them. "My life is with you, Morgan Steele. It has been since the first day I saw you. That won't ever change, whether you let me stay with you or not."

For the first time since I'd known her, Ice looked frightened. It wasn't a panic fright, to be sure, but she was scared. "I…can't…."

I put my fingers over her lips. "Maybe not," I whispered. "But I can."

Leaning forward, I replaced my fingers with my lips, claiming her with all the love in my soul. After a moment, she responded, sinking her fingers into my hair and drawing me closer against her, to be engulfed by the scent of spices and leather. I was intoxicated.

Reaching behind me, I tossed my sack and Ice's duffel from the bed, then, wrapping my arms around her shoulders, pulled her down to lay beside me, never breaking contact with her lips, which had opened under my tender probing, allowing me to explore to my heart's content.

My hands worked with a sure dexterity on the unfamiliar zippers and buttons and buckles of her leather protection, needing beyond anything to feel the solid, living warmth of her.

She moaned at the first touch of my fingers on her skin and I let the full strength of my love and passion for this remarkable woman take me over. I went willingly into the light of my newfound freedom.

🗝   🗝   🗝   🗝

And so here I sit, writing while my lover sleeps bare feet away, her hair shining in the feeble light of the lamp above me. Her head is turned away from me, but I know without seeing that there is a smile on her lips. A smile I put there. That thought fills me with joy.

And in a moment, I'll go back to lay beside her, and nestle up against the long length of her strong body and fall asleep to the music of her heart beneath my ear.

In just a moment.

We've decided to head out for Canada in the morning. To attempt to make a life on the land that gave me so much joy as a child. Getting over the border might prove difficult, but Ice is confident that we'll make it.

The chance to share this dream place with her is all I could want in this world.

Some of you may be asking yourself why I would risk everything to live my life with a fugitive, always wondering when the other shoe is going to drop.

And to those questions, I can only give the answer my heart tells me is true. That if, by chance, that other shoe does drop, tomorrow or fifty years from now, I'll know that I lived my life the way I wanted to. I made my own choices in this world and was happy with them. I loved, and was loved by, the other half of my soul. I wanted for nothing.

And truly, what else can you ask of the hand life deals you?

THE DEAL

by Maggie Ryan

I'm gonna lose my job.
I'm probably not going to work in TV ever again.
And I'm gonna be sued.
She sat in her office with the door closed and the lights off.
Four TV monitors were on across the room, lighting her face with
their flickering. Her long, dark hair gleamed with blue highlights
from the various network late shows as she stared dully into space.
The monitors were always on; *god forbid some other station across
town would cut in and we not know about it*, she thought.
Sighing, she thumped her forehead down on the desk. She
could still hear some activity going on in the newsroom, though
most everyone had left after the 10 o'clock newscast. The over-
night crew didn't really get cranking until after midnight. *Well*, she
thought, *if I'm going to make a clean getaway, now's the time to
do it.*
Shit.
With that, Laura Kasdan gathered up her briefcase and her
box of belongings and left her office. You never brought more into
a TV station than you c
carry out in one box, running. Someone had told her that years
ago, and after today she understood the sentiment.
Deep breath, open the door and just walk, she told herself. Laura
strode purposefully across the newsroom, turned and looked back,
noticing the fresh bloodstain on the carpet. *Cleaning that will prob-*

ably coming out of my successor's budget, she thought. *Noses do bleed profusely, don't they?*

And with that, she walked down the hall and out of the building.

📺 📺 📺 📺

The General Manager of KDAL had two problems. One was his News Director and the other was his news anchor, Roger MacNamara. Roger was the number one on-air personality in Dallas. He spoke with authority, and his journalistic integrity was unimpeachable. He was Walter Cronkite and Edward R. Murrow all rolled into one.

At least that's what market research told the suits at Corporate. Dark hair with just a bit of silver on the temples, carefully colored every two weeks, and chiseled features, he oozed sincerity...*well, when you can fake that, you've got it made*, the GM thought. Roger was also a prima donna who hit the sauce pretty hard and was a lawsuit waiting to happen.

Laura Kasdan was the best News Director he'd ever worked with, and he'd worked with some good ones. She didn't take any crap or any excuses, and she'd gotten them back to number one on all the prime time newscasts. He pinched the bridge of his nose and grimaced. Two years ago when Laura Kasdan had been named as the News Director, everyone in the building had been shocked. She had the rep though, the GM thought as he drummed his fingers on the open personnel file in front of him. KDAL needed some fresh blood, and boy, did they get it.

There was opposition in the newsroom, of course. Just how did Corporate justify handing over the news operation of their flagship station in a top five market to a twenty-eight year old whiz kid?

But Kaz had done everything they'd asked of her. She'd trimmed the fat, streamlined the organization, and delivered the numbers. The ratings were everything they'd hoped for and a little bit more. The reporters and photogs, always an unruly bunch even in the best circumstances, were brought in line. And they'd finally gotten the right teams of on-air talent together.

Everything was going so smoothly, something was bound to screw up.

Then Roger had to go and grab her ass, the GM fumed. According to witnesses, Laura asked him to remove it.

He didn't...and all hell broke loose.

Laura spun around and punched him in the nose. *Punched is*

really too mild a word for what she did to his nose, the GM mused. *Socked, slugged, splattered, flattened…whatever, 'ol Rog is gonna be off the air for a while. Thank God it wasn't sweeps, but it's still a public relations nightmare.*

So there it is…I want to keep 'em both, but that's not gonna happen, the General Manager thought, as he picked up the receiver and punched in a phone number. *I bet Corporate already knows*, he smiled wryly.

They did.

📺 📺 📺 📺

It was a forty-five minute commute from the station to Grapevine where she lived, and even though it was March it was warm enough to have the windows open as she drove her Jeep down I-635. Laura had the music up really loud, partly because of the wind noise and partly so she wouldn't have to think about Roger and her job.

She'd been spoiling for a fight after a day of a million and one frustrations. Stories had fallen apart and the reporters couldn't seem to get a firm hold on the stories that were working. The newscasts had seemed incomplete. Not a good news day, she mused, running her hand through her hair as it blew in the wind.

There was still a lot of traffic on the interstate, especially for a Thursday night. Laura changed lanes to get ready for her exit. *Well*, she thought, *you can put it out of your mind for only so long. There's going to be hell to pay, on so many levels.* Her thoughts rambled on. *You could go to work for a news consulting firm. You could teach the part on what not to do when dealing with talent.*

The guard at the gate waved the Jeep through and Laura continued around the tree-lined street until she got to her house, opened the garage door with the remote, and pulled the Jeep inside next to the gleaming chrome of a Triumph motorcycle. She picked up her briefcase, shoved it into the box, and then carried it all inside, dropping the load just inside the door. Laura spared a glance toward her answering machine, noting that there were twenty-eight messages waiting. She unclipped her pager from her waistband and tossed it on the counter by the phone, making her way from the living room to the master bedroom and into the bathroom where she started the shower.

She stripped efficiently, tossed her clothes in the hamper, and stepped into the shower stall. After wetting her hair, she leaned back against the wall, then slowly slid down until she was sitting with her chin on her knees with the water pounding the top of her head. *Oh God, what have I done?*

She stayed like that until there was no hot water left. When it ran cold, she figured there was no point in it anymore and she stepped out of the stall and grabbed a towel, dripping water all over the bathroom floor. After slipping on an oversized t-shirt and boxer shorts, she began combing out her hair, looking into the mirror at tired blue eyes, ignoring the phone as it began to ring, figuring the machine would pick it up.

"Laura, this is Don Farmer at Corporate. We need to talk. Uh, you've put us in a hell of a position, and we need to talk about how this is gonna shake down. Give me a call in the morning…probably not a good idea to go to the station tomorrow…"

No shit, Laura thought as she listened to the machine echo eerily through the house.

"Anyway, I wanted to let you know that you still have some options…We're not ready to cut you loose, so just hang tight…call me."

Laura walked back to the kitchen where the answering machine was. There were twenty-nine messages now, and she deleted them all. She'd call Don in the morning, but there wasn't anyone else she wanted to talk to, or explain to.

Options. Laura snorted. All her choicest options disappeared when she plowed her fist into Roger's face. She crawled into bed, switched off the light and rolled onto her side, hugging a pillow to her chest. *Oh, come on, you have options…You can take some time off and play some golf.* She yawned, the fifteen-hour day catching up with her. *Brood about it in the morning*, she told herself.

And Laura Kasdan closed her eyes on the worst day of her thirty year old life.

📺 📺 📺 📺

The alarm didn't go off and for a minute, just a minute, Laura thought she'd overslept. The clock read seven-fifteen, and Laura rolled over with a concerted effort to prolong her sleep. *I know that Don's not going to have his butt into his office until nine Atlanta time*, she thought, *so go back to sleep.*

Except that her mind was off and running, making her stomach churn.

No point, Laura sighed after a few minutes, so she sat up and threw the covers off and ambled into the kitchen, rubbing her neck absently. *Staring into the refrigerator is not going to make food appear*, she told herself, *you have to buy it once in a while.* She grabbed a Coke and closed the door, popped it open and took a big gulp, feeling it burn all the way down. *Ah, the breakfast of champions*, Laura thought as the phone rang.

"Kaz, it's Brian," the General Manager, "Pick up the phone, I know you're there. I called the pro shop and they said you hadn't called for a tee time yet and I know it's too early for you to get a hold of your lawyer."

Laura picked up, "All right, what's going on."

"Jesus, Kaz, I left about 20 messages on your machine last night, could you have at least given me a sign that you made it home okay?"

"I made it home okay. How's Roger's nose?"

"Roger needs a plastic surgeon and he's gonna be off the air for a bit. God knows how we'll file the insurance claim. Couldn't you have just kicked him in the nuts?"

"I'm not sure he had any to kick."

"Very funny," Brian said. "Both of you are in a shitload of trouble, I called Don Farmer last night, he already knew everything."

"I know, I had a message to call him this morning," Laura told him.

"Well, forget that, my friend, he's on his way here. He called last night when you weren't answering your phone or your beeper…"

"I turned it off."

"…and said he'd be on the 10am Delta from Atlanta. So get dressed and get to DFW, pick him up, and do what you have to do to save your career."

"Roger grabbed me, and I have to save *my* career?"

"You know you can't fuck with the talent, Kaz, they're like racehorses: when they're running good they're money in the bank. News Directors pale next to a thirty share."

"I got you that thirty share!"

"I guess it comes down to this: You're young, you can still make it to the network if you want, but if you make waves, if you sue, you commit career suicide. Roger wins anyway. You are three years away from your vested stock plan. Can you swallow your pride and stay in this corporation for three years for half a million dollars?" Brian took a breath, "If you can walk away from that, then walk. But otherwise, get to DFW and pick up the head of News Operations at the largest employee-owned media conglomerate in the country and do what you have to do to save your career!"

"Brian, you know I'm out already...I'll miss you."

"Yeah, me too. I hope you end up someplace nice. If you never punch anyone ever again, you might even get your own station." He paused. "I'm sorry...maybe the deal won't be too bad."

"You're right, I'd better get going."

"One thing, Kaz...be careful what you agree to. Don't let them back you into a corner—or hang you out to dry."

"Later, Brian." She hung up and padded back to the bedroom to get dressed.

📺　📺　📺　📺

There wasn't much that frightened Laura Kasdan; she worked in an environment that was hostile at best and outright confrontational at worst. But driving to DFW was right up there with taking your life in your hands and it always made her nervous. Traffic around the airport was miserable on this Friday morning, and she resigned herself to a good long walk from the parking area to the Delta terminal. She stepped out of the Jeep and felt the wind gust around her, blowing her khaki pants against her legs. She shrugged into a jacket over her red polo shirt and started walking, not looking forward to the encounter with Don. As she entered the terminal, she moved her sunglasses to the top of her head and inhaled, smelling that strange airport smell that brought with it the promise of journeys ending and beginning.

She checked the monitors on the way down the concourse, noting that the flight was on time, and made her way through security, dumping her keys into the dish that the agent held out for her and reaching for her pager. Then she remembered that she'd left it on the counter, turned off, her one last unbreakable contact with the newsroom that had been her life for the past two years.

She stepped through the metal detector, picked up her keys, and continued on to the gate, getting there just as the passengers were arriving through the long plastic hallway connected to the plane. She waited with her arms crossed until she spotted the tall, stocky blond man carrying an oversized briefcase and then she moved toward him.

Don spotted her immediately and smiled, "Kaz," he said, "Good to see you, wish it was under better circumstances."

"Likewise, Don." She answered. "Did you check anything?"

"No, I'm just here to see you and then I'm gone. I've gotten us a meeting room; let's see if we can find out where it is." He stepped up to the check in booth, inquired after the location, then they both started back down the concourse.

They followed the signs and turned down a narrow hallway, past a small office where a woman at a desk looked up and smiled at them. "I reserved a conference room, William-Simon Communications," Don informed the woman.

"Yes, Mr. Farmer," she answered, "Room three, just down the hall; your lunch is ready as you requested." Laura and Don made their way to the room, Don opened the door and Laura stepped inside. Don followed, closing the door behind him.

"Well, Kaz," Don said as he pulled up a chair, "This is a supreme cluster fuck. What the hell were you thinking?"

"Wasn't thinking anything. He grabbed my butt and I slugged him." She reached up and plucked the Ray Bans off the top of her head and tossed them on the table. "I have grounds for a lawsuit, so does he. You want him back on the air, and that's sort of impossible if I'm running the newsroom. So unless you've become the hiring and firing fairy, I can only assume that you've come to cut a deal." She paused and leaned forward, "So, what's the deal?"

Icy blue eyes narrowed at him across the table and Don took stock of the woman seated there. Well, you couldn't fault Roger's taste; she was beautiful. That dark hair and those incredible eyes set in that perfectly proportioned face. She'd never be anchor material; no one would buy the news from looks like those. But in a business where everyone wanted to be on the air, she'd been an exception. Just a little while as a reporter, and then she'd turned into one hell of a producer. Now, regardless of her age, she was the best news director in the company and he'd be damned if someone else was going to snatch her up.

"Brief and to the point as always, Kaz," Don answered. "All right, you get to be News Director at another station, your salary and benefits stay the same. Roger is reprimanded and retires in three years, you come back to Dallas and run the show. How's that?"

"Which station?" Laura asked in a low, dangerous voice.

"WBFC in Burkett Falls," Don inwardly winced, waiting for the reaction.

"Burkett! Jesus, what is that, a number sixty something market?" She stood up shouting. "From top ten to Bum Fuck Egypt. I should have killed Roger—at least I could've stayed in Texas!"

"Look—it's just three years, Kaz, and when you get back, you run the show in Dallas…not just the News Department, the station. You'll be the GM." Don waited for the implications to sink in.

"What about Brian?" she asked quietly.

"Brian's going to be a Regional Manager in three years, he'll be over 15 stations, probably including Dallas." Don waited a moment, "You're on the same track, you know, if you don't hit anyone else." She was considering it, and he knew he was close.

Be careful, Laura, she told herself, and tipped her head back as she weighed her options. It was incredibly tempting to just tell Don, no how, no way, take your medium market pissant station and shove it where the sun don't shine. But no…*remember the plan, Laura,* she told herself. Three years was all she needed in the company, even if was in exile from Texas.

"You need an answer today, right?" Don nodded. "One thing…I have Cowboy season tickets and I'm not giving them up…get me to Dallas for the games and you have a deal." Laura smiled.

"Awww, they're not even a good team anymore." Don said.

Laura actually snarled, "Otherwise I go shopping—I start here in town, and I will make it my goddamned mission in life to see that KDAL never sees a thirty share again."

"You don't have to be nasty, we've got airline trade," Don smiled.

"You were pretty sure of yourself there, Don," Laura returned with a lopsided smirk.

"I won't fight if I can't win, Kaz. Learn from that." He pulled a file out of his briefcase, passed it to her and checked his watch. "Did you park in the short term lot?"

"No, long term." She smiled at him and lifted one eyebrow. "I always plan for most situations. Learn from that." Don gave a little snort and tossed two airline tickets out on the table. "We have tickets for the 12:15 flight to Burkett Falls. Art Dement, the GM, is expecting us. You'll arrive back around eight, and unless you just can't imagine going through with this, you'll have the weekend to start planning your move."

"What, no golf?" Laura said, half joking, then sobered. "What if Mr. Dement doesn't want me for a News Director?"

"It's not his choice anymore," Don said, standing. "He needs help and I'm gonna drop six feet of blue-eyed help on his station and watch what happens." Both of them looked back at the plate of sandwiches in the middle of the table that neither one of them had touched. They looked at each other, shrugged, sat back down and started on the sandwiches. It sure beat airline peanuts.

Other books by
Justice House
Publishing

Accidental Love, BL Miller

Accidental Love is a captivating story between Rose Grayson, a destitute, lonely, young woman, and Veronica Cartwright, head of a vast family empire and extraordinally rich. What happens when love is based on deception? Can it survive discovering the truth?

The Deal, Maggie Ryan

Laura Kasdan is cruising along as the News Director at the number one television station in Dallas. When a momentary lapse of control almost costs her a stellar career, she makes a deal to save her job and keep a promise and moves to a smaller station, where she meets a charismatic reporter who promises to turn her well-ordered world upside down.

Of Drag Kings and the Wheel of Fate, Susan Smith

Elvis isn't dead, he's just in Buffalo—and he's a she. When Shakespearean scholar Rosalind meets Taryn, a young drag king, they invoke a karmic cycle that began with recorded history. Is their love strong enough to outwit fate and revise their destiny? *Of Drag Kings and the Wheel of Fate* is passion, mystery, and magic, just as you like it.

Josie & Rebecca: The Western Chronicles,
BL Miller & Vada Foster

At the center of this story are two women; one a deadly gunslinger bitter from the injustices of her past, the other a gentle dreamer trying to escape the horrors of the present. Their destinies come together one fateful afternoon when the feared outlaw makes the choice to rescue a young woman in trouble. For her part, Josie Hunter considers the brief encounter at an end once the girl is safe, but Rebecca Cameron has other ideas....

Lucifer Rising, Sharon Bowers

Lucifer Rising is a novel about love and fear. It is the story of fallen DEA angel Jude Lucien and the Miami Herald reporter determined to unearth Jude's secrets. When an apparently happenstance meeting introduces Jude to reporter Liz Gardener, the dark ex-agent is both intrigued and aroused by the young woman. A sniper shot intended for Jude strikes Liz, and the two women are thrown together in a race to discover who is intent on killing her. As their lives become more and more intertwined, Jude finds herself unexpected falling for the reporter, and Liz discovers that the agent-turned-drug-dealer is both more and less than she seems.

In eloquent and spare language, author Sharon Bowers paints a dazzling portrait of a woman driven to the darkest extremes of the human condition-and the journey she makes to cross to the other side.

Redemption, Susanne Beck

Redemption is the story of a young woman who finds out that the best things in life are often found in the last place you'd look for them.

Angel is a small-town girl who finds herself trapped within her worst nightmare, a state penitentiary. She finds inner strength, maturity, friendship and love while at the same time giving to others something she thought she'd lost within herself: Hope. It is the story of how Angel rediscovers hope blazing within the piercing blue eyes of another inmate, Ice.

Tropical Storm, Melissa Good

Tropical Storm... Enter the lives of two captivating characters and their world that hundreds of fans of Melissa Good's writing already know and love. Your heart will be touched by the realism of the story. Your senses will be affected by the electricity, your emotions caught up by the intensity. You will care about these characters before you are far into the story... and you will demand justice be done.

And don't forget the exciting sequel to Tropical Storm

Hurricane Watch, Melissa Good

Now available!

Dar and Kerry are back and making their relationship permanent. But an ambitious new colleague threatens to divide them—and out them. He wants Dar's head and her job, and is willing to use Kerry to get it. Can their home life survive the office power play?